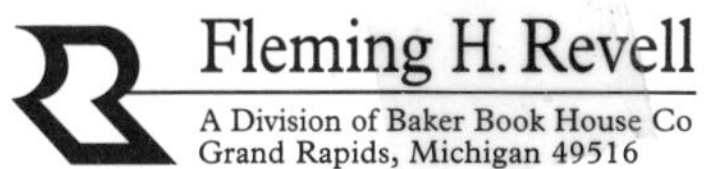

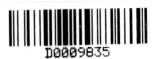

Fleming H. Revell
A Division of Baker Book House Co
Grand Rapids, Michigan 49516

Published by Fleming H. Revell
a division of Baker Book House Company
P.O. Box 6287, Grand Rapids, MI 49516-6287

Printed in the United States of America

Library of Congress Cataloging-in-Publication Data

McCourtney, Lorena.
Riptide / Lorena McCourtney.
p. cm. — (The Julesburg mysteries ; bk. 2)
ISBN 0-8007-5777-7
1. Pacific Coast (Or.)—Fiction. 2. Twins—Fiction. I. Title.
PS3563.C3449 R46 2002
813′.54—dc21 2002006204

For current information about all releases from Baker Book House, visit our web site:

http://www.bakerbooks.com

He reached down from on high and took hold of me;
he drew me out of deep waters.

Psalm 18:16

1

Would it be tonight?

He cruised the main street in third gear and braked at the light. Helen Maxwell sat behind the counter of the Calico Pantry. The inevitable pink jacket thickened her scrawny body, and her permed hair frizzed in a gray halo around her head.

Anger with an undercurrent of fear cranked up his nerves as he watched her ring up a sale on the cash register. *Grouchy old busybody, going all pious and self-righteous, threatening to spill her guts and rip everything wide open!* He flexed his fingers, hands hot with the urge to exterminate her on the spot.

He slammed a lid on the dangerous urge. *Back off. Don't mess with the plan.* He'd fine-tuned it for the past week, and now it was down to blueprint precision. The disguise was in a plastic bag next to the gun under the seat. At the right moment he'd walk in, empty the cash register, and blow her away. And a witness, the crowning touch in his plan, would swear it was just a robbery gone bad. No one would look for another motive.

All he needed was an absence of traffic and a little cooperation from the weather. Plus one car in the parking lot.

None of which was happening tonight. A half moon rode high in a star-speckled sky, and the temperature was unseasonably balmy for a November evening on the Oregon coast. Four cars loitered in the Calico Pantry's parking lot, two of them macho, four-wheel-drive pickups. A half-dozen high school kids clustered on the corner under the streetlight. One shaved head gleamed like a bowling ball.

He U-turned in the beach overlook area at the south end of town and cruised past the Calico Pantry once more. *No, not tonight.*

But he pointed a forefinger over his other wrist and clicked an imaginary trigger.

"Bang," he said softly.

He couldn't wait much longer.

"Hi, Julie!"

Sarah MacIntosh closed the car door as the woman in a leotard waved and dashed along the rock walkway from the health club at the far end of the building. A shaggy, tan dog loped at her heels.

Sarah had become accustomed to the wrong-name greeting in the week she'd been in Julesburg. She rather enjoyed the game that she and Julie had missed out on in their growing-up years. She smiled and returned the wave.

The woman, whom Sarah knew must be Stefanie Harrison, waited at the door beneath the discreetly lettered "Harrison Investigative Services" sign.

"Did you bring the painting? I'm dying for Ryan to see it."

"It's already inside. I just came out to get some touch-up oil for a scratch on the frame." Sarah held up the dark colored bottle and a stained rag.

"You got your hair cut, didn't you?" The slim woman gave an approving glance to the short cut that fringed Sarah's face with spiky wisps.

Actually, no, no haircut. But Sarah just smiled.

"Looks great! Which reminds me, I'd better get Lisa to trim mine before Ryan and I leave on our trip."

The woman stepped aside to let Sarah enter the door first, but stopped short when she spotted the ponytailed figure standing on a chair below the newly hung painting.

"Hey, whoa now, what . . . ?"

"Seeing double? Join the party. But first, my thanks for adding some class to my office. I love the painting." Ryan Harrison gave his wife an affectionate thank-you kiss on the cheek. To Sarah, he added, "In case you didn't know, the painting is my birthday gift."

Julie's painting of a girl poised by an old house on a windswept bluff indeed dressed up the utilitarian office. The girl wore a flowered hat and old-fashioned skirt that swirled around her ankles, and she gazed out to sea with an expression both wistful and dreamy. She looked a little like Julie . . . and Sarah too.

"I'm glad you like the painting." Stefanie patted Ryan's thigh with the easy intimacy of married couples. "Now, the next thing I want is an explanation about this double-vision problem I seem to have developed. I don't really think Julie's been cloned, but—"

"Oh, better than cloned!" Julie jumped down from the chair, her paisley skirt billowing and her copper bracelets clattering. She pointed a ringed forefinger at Sarah. "I'm scatterbrained, she's organized. I microwave, she cooks. And vacuums! The dust bunnies under my bed are living in terror. She balances her checkbook, I trust in the checkbook fairy. I look at the big picture, she reads the fine print. We make a great team!"

Julie interrupted her flamboyant tribute to their complementary natures to offer a formal introduction. "Stefanie,

I'd like you to meet my twin sister, Sarah MacIntosh. Sarah, this is Stefanie Harrison, owner of the Fit 'n' Fun health club next door. And you've already met her husband, Ryan, our local private eye, who sees all, hears all, knows all."

Ryan tucked his hand around his wife's. "My knows-all capabilities appear to have fallen short, since I didn't know anything about this until today." He gestured between Sarah and Julie.

Stefanie tilted her head. "The dark hair and smile and blue eyes are the same, but the clothes should have given me a clue, shouldn't they?"

Sarah and Julie exchanged glances and laughed. Their clothing did indeed set them apart. Julie didn't own anything as conservative as Sarah's narrow-legged black pants and oversized white shirt. And Sarah would never venture out in public in Julie's reckless combination of ankle-length paisley skirt, pink T-shirt sporting a print of an endangered pelican, toe-strap sandals, and chunky crystal necklace.

"It's all very simple," Julie said. "When we were born twenty-five years ago, Sarah and I were adopted by different families. Neither of us knew the other existed. But our great-grandmother did know, and a few months ago she brought us together. Voilà! Here we are, living happily ever after."

"Julie spent a couple of weeks with me in California so we could get acquainted—"

"Which was like getting to know the soul-sister I always thought I must have somewhere." Julie touched her heart with her fingertips. "Okay, I know that sounds melodramatic, but it's true. I always did feel something essential was missing from my life, and now I know what it was." She reached over and squeezed Sarah's hand.

What Julie said was true for Sarah too. She'd been raised by wonderful adoptive parents, but there'd always been an inexplicable hollow somewhere deep inside her, an incompleteness. Now, even though she and her twin sister were different in everything but physical appearance, the hollow was so warmly, wonderfully, filled to overflowing.

Yet Sarah wasn't as open and impulsive as Julie about sharing intimate feelings, so all she said was, "So we got acquainted, and now I'm here in Julesburg."

"Will you be staying long?" Stefanie asked.

"Shall we tell?" The excitement of a little girl with a secret sparkled in Julie's blue eyes. "Sarah is moving here, and we're buying the old Nevermore Theater! We're going to turn it into a mini mall for antique dealers and craftspeople and artisans. With hopes of selling a ton of our own stuff, of course. Sarah does incredible work with stained glass."

"It isn't a done deal yet," Sarah said, tacking a dose of reality onto Julie's bubbly announcement of their plans. "We're discussing remodeling costs with a construction company tomorrow. A lot depends on that."

"I suspect the owners of the Nevermore will be happy to work with you on a sale. After their deal fell through last year—"

Stefanie stopped abruptly, and Sarah glanced at her twin. Julie hadn't mentioned any former deal that had fallen through.

But Julie bubbled on. "I was going to try to do it even before Sarah came, but now that she's here, I know it will work. We'll remodel the upstairs office and projection area into a double studio for my artwork and Sarah's stained glass."

"Again, depending on the budget," Sarah amended.

"You should see her stained glass creations." Julie rolled her eyes. "They're absolutely gorgeous. Like jewels. She also does these whimsical little animal figures that are just awesome. You'll have to hang one by the nursery window for your baby."

"Baby?" Ryan raised his eyebrows at his wife. "Is there something you haven't told me?"

Stefanie laughed and patted his thigh again. "No, dear. When the time comes, you'll be the first to know. But I am delighted to hear about these plans for the old Nevermore. It's been sitting there empty and unused for so long."

Sarah tapped her twin on the shoulder. "Do you know why the deal fell through last year? Is there some awful secret about the old theater you haven't told me?"

"Oh, some people think it's jinxed, or cursed, or who knows what." Julie dismissed the local tales with a wave of her ringed fingers. She hiked up her skirt, climbed on the chair, and reached for the bottle of oil stain in Sarah's hand.

"Actually, it's just a series of unfortunate coincidences connected with the Nevermore," Stefanie explained. "No mysterious chains rattling or ghosts sitting in the front row."

Sarah wanted to know more, but Julie gave the frame a final flick with the rag and climbed down from the chair, and Ryan glanced at his computer screen.

"I have a couple of reports to wrap up—"

"And I should get back to work. Tina will be running Fit 'n' Fun while we're gone, and I'd better have the bookkeeping up to date." Stefanie wrinkled her nose in a wordless comment on bookkeeping.

"Did I tell you Ryan and Stefanie are leaving to spend several weeks in Japan?" Julie asked Sarah. "Ryan is going to teach a course in arson-detection techniques to law-enforcement officials there."

"And then Ryan's sister, Angie, is meeting us for a tour of Japan and Hong Kong. She's a model in New York, and I haven't seen her since she was a little girl," Stefanie added. "Sherlock will be staying with Tina."

"Well, have a great trip," Julie said as she gave the painting a final adjustment on the wall, like a loving mother straightening a child's collar before saying good-bye. "Maybe our mini mall will be in business by the time you get home."

"And then maybe I can get you to do a painting of our house," Stefanie said. "How about we all get together for a barbecue at our place when we get back so we can talk about it, okay?"

"Great! Sarah can make her 'Sweet Dreams of Chocolate' dessert, and I . . ." Julie paused as if running through a list of her own culinary gifts before she grinned and added, "and I will bring my specialty: a bag of potato chips."

The girls laughed as they exited Ryan's office. There was no reason to doubt the future, no shadow of impending disaster, no reason for apprehension or fear.

Sarah was not generally given to dark premonitions. Yet the fear and apprehension were suddenly there, clutching at her heart.

No mini mall. No painting of the house. No homecoming barbecue.

None of this is ever going to happen.

2

Outside Sarah shook off the odd feeling of apprehension as she took a deep breath of fresh air. The November day glittered in a heady blend of sunlight and blue sky and tang of sea. Maples tucked among the evergreens on the forested hills blazed gold and russet and bronze.

Stefanie waved to Sarah and Julie from the entrance door to Fit 'n' Fun. "Hey, Julie, why don't you take Sarah to church on Sunday? We'll be gone, but I know everyone would love to see you again and meet Sarah."

"Yeah, maybe I'll do that," Julie called back. "Have a wonderful trip! Eat some sushi for me, and don't let some geisha grab Ryan."

Sarah doubted a geisha or any other female could tempt Ryan Harrison, not with the loving relationship he shared with his wife. *Am I envious? No, of course not.* Sarah smiled to herself. *Well, maybe just a little.*

"You go to church here?" she asked after sliding into the passenger's seat of Julie's rusty-edged Honda.

"I've been a few times." Julie turned the key in the ignition. "Stefanie invited me. Both she and Ryan are really gung-ho Christians."

Sarah held her breath through the engine's usual rattle and growl of awakening. Would it run this time? The clunks smoothed to a less-threatening chatter, and Julie wheeled the car into the street.

"The church is okay," she continued. "I mean, I believe in God and all that, and the people are really friendly. And I love the music. But Sunday is when I get my best painting done, like it's God's special gift to me. Besides, I don't think you have to be in church to commune with God. I figure there are lots of connections to God, not just their Jesus way."

Sarah somehow doubted God was inspiring her twin to stay away from church to paint. But then, what did she know about God or how to commune with him? She'd gone to Sunday school a few times as a girl, and Christmas and Easter had always been important events in her family. Her dad was the jolliest Santa Claus ever, and she had fond memories of the Easter egg hunt her mother always organized for the neighborhood kids. But she'd never really given God much thought until she met the wise and caring great-grandmother who had kept an eye on her and Julie from afar over the years.

Sarah felt uncomfortable talking about God, though, so she changed the subject. "Okay, before we plunk down our money, tell me what's with these old stories about the Nevermore."

"Oh, it's all so silly. Like there's some evil force lurking there, just waiting to grab another victim." Julie braked at Julesburg's wide main street, which was also part of Highway 101. The only vehicle in sight was a black-and-white car with a police insignia on the door. Julie waved to the driver. "There goes the Julesburg police force."

"One officer? One car?"

"There were two officers, but Ben Mosely retired, so Randy Wilson got promoted to police chief." Julie turned onto the main street.

"What if two crimes happen at the same time?"

"Oh, that isn't allowed in Julesburg. Here the criminals politely wait their turn," Julie said with enough seriousness that Sarah could almost believe she meant it. "Although I think the county sheriff's department is available after hours. Actually, Randy takes care of the town quite nicely on his own. When some teen gang tried to get started here a few months ago, he clamped down on them like a big ol' pit bull."

"Fine. If I ever need a polite criminal bitten, I'll call your Officer Wilson. Now, to get back to the Nevermore . . . ?"

"Well, a long time ago, back in the sixties or early seventies, some guy was murdered there."

"Really? Murdered how?"

Julie braked as an enormous motorhome pulled away from the curb and lumbered down the street ahead of them. "Stabbed, I think. They never found out who did it. Then the woman who owned the theater committed suicide."

"Immediately after the murder?"

"No, she kept the theater open for years after that. Although she got really eccentric in her old age. She'd dress up in a fancy ball gown and walk up and down the aisles, emoting lines from *Gone with the Wind*."

"As Scarlett or Melanie?"

"Oh, Scarlett, I'm sure. Wouldn't you be Scarlett if you were headed off the deep end? Melanie was such a wimp."

Sarah thought for a moment. "I'm not the off-the-deep-end type. And I don't believe in curses or jinxes."

Julie eased the Honda into the Nevermore's asphalt-and-weed parking lot and turned off the engine. The customary gurgling sound followed. Julie, unconcerned about a noise that would have sent Sarah scurrying to the nearest mechanic, leaned her forearms against the steering wheel and looked up at the wood-shingle wall of the old theater. Bits of moss clung to the weathered shingles.

"I guess I'm open to believing a lot of things," Julie said, sounding thoughtful. Then she gave a sideways glance to Sarah, tease suddenly frisking in her blue eyes. "Which for you, of course, translates into being much too gullible."

"Not necessarily *gullible,*" Sarah protested, thinking of Julie's interest in crystals and auras and past lives. "But some of that New Age stuff just seems so . . . far out."

"Yeah, maybe it is," Julie agreed cheerfully. "Who knows? I guess I don't really believe in curses. Although I don't necessarily disbelieve in them either. But there's more in the Nevermore's past."

"Oh?"

Julie waved to a couple of teenage boys and a girl walking by on the sidewalk. The boys wore baseball caps turned backward, sloppy T-shirts, and pants baggy enough to conceal a small artillery. The girl exposed a belly button above skimpy denim shorts and lots of leg below. They all waved back.

"You know them?" Sarah asked, surprised.

"Haven't you noticed? I'm your stereotypical starving artist scraping up odd jobs to survive."

"You have money now."

"Yeah, I know." Julie wrinkled her nose, as if a hidden work ethic in her character made her feel guilty about spending any of that money. "But I'm used to filling in the financial gaps with whatever I can pick up. Sometimes I work at a teenage hangout called Website X up at the north end of town, so I know a lot of the kids." Julie waved her hand. "Anyway, somebody, a nephew, I think, inherited the theater and the old lady's other assets. He kept it open for a while, but he had a bit of a gambling problem and wound up losing everything. He also committed suicide."

"And it's been closed since then?"

"Oh, various owners tried to make a go of it as a movie theater, but they always had bad luck of some kind. One woman intended to remodel it into a supper club, but she had a heart attack. The weird thing was, she had no previous history of heart trouble at all." Julie paused for a moment. "And we saw the remains of the fire in the projection room. That discouraged someone else."

"The fire should prove there's no jinx. If the place was cursed, it would've burned down."

"Maybe the evil-jinx spirit didn't *want* it to burn down."

Sarah shook her head and laughed. "Where in the world did you pick up all these crazy stories?"

"Sometimes I run errands for little old ladies around town, and they love to talk. A couple of them even knew the original Gone-with-the-Wind lady."

"More of your odd-job financial fill-ins?"

"No. Just helping out. I like little old ladies." Julie smiled and gave the plastic, big-eyed frog hanging from the windshield a flick that sent it into a spin. "I plan to be one someday. Probably an old maid with seventeen cats."

Julie didn't have any cats of her own; pets weren't allowed in the apartment building. But she regularly fed the homeless cats that lived among the rocks down on the jetty.

"You're never going to be an old maid," Sarah assured her. "What about this guy . . . what did you say his name was? Donovan?"

"Donovan Moran. Donovan was his grandfather's name. He says his folks are sorry they gave it to him now, because he's kind of the black sheep of the family."

"When do I get to meet him?"

"He lives down in Gold Beach, so we don't see each other all that often. He's a great guy, but there are . . . problems."

Julie was a chatterbox on most subjects, but she tended to be close-mouthed when it came to Donovan Moran. A certain tightness around her mouth suggested she didn't want to talk about him now.

"Has anyone ever said why the theater has such an odd name?" Sarah asked.

"I think the theater had a different name at first. One of those usual old theater names. The Biloxi or Roxy or something like that. Then, after the murder, the old lady named it the Nevermore. Maybe she was into Poe and ravens as well as Civil War movie heroines."

"In any case, it's all in the past." Sarah peered at the sagging marquee on the front of the building. A couple of faded letters still clung to it.

"Well, that isn't quite true," Julie admitted reluctantly. "Last year a married couple had the same idea that we have for the place, making it into a mini mall for antique dealers and craftspeople. They moved down from Seattle and brought their boat along. But when they took the boat on the ocean, something went wrong and the boat exploded."

"Exploded? How can a boat just explode?"

"Something about gas fumes leaking from the engine. They were both killed. So the sale never went through." Julie tucked a stray strand of dark hair behind her ear. "So it does seem as if bad things happen to anyone connected with the Nevermore."

To someone superstitious there might be a meaningful connection between all these tragedies. It sure would make for great tabloid stuff: "Evil entity lurks within faded glory of crumbling old movie palace." But Sarah was not superstitious.

"I feel sorry for all those people who had such bad luck with the place, but none of that has anything to do with us and our plans," she said firmly. "It's just what Stefanie Harrison said, a string of unfortunate coincidences."

"Right. But if there *is* some weird jinx or curse or evil force lurking here . . ." Julie paused, and Sarah could feel another one of Julie's "great ideas" coming on.

Julie frequently had "great ideas." One had involved a flaming dessert, a project that had singed Julie's eyebrows, scorched the tablecloth, and set off the smoke alarm.

Another one had involved going down to the beach at midnight to see "if the creatures of the sea come out to dance under the light of the moon." They hadn't found dancing sea creatures, but they did find a slimy blob of jellyfish goo underfoot.

Now Julie tossed her a mischievous glance that confirmed Sarah's suspicions. "C'mon, let's go inside. I have a great idea."

3

Sarah fished the key to the door of the theater out of her purse. She had become keeper-of-the-key when Julie admitted to losing her keys every other day.

Sarah felt a flash of uneasiness as they rounded the corner of the building. Someone, in a misguided attempt to freshen the old building, had painted the double doors a garish red. The paint was thick, ridged by weathered wood underneath, and looked as sticky as drying blood.

"Isn't this great? Doesn't it give you goose bumps, our doing this together?"

Julie hugged her, and the simple, spontaneous gesture, so typical of Julie, set Sarah's mind at ease. And when they opened the door of the lobby, Sarah was as entranced as she'd been the first moment she'd stepped into this theater from the past.

Rich, red carpet, threadbare spots lost in the dusky shadows. Gold-flecked wallpaper. Grand expanse of mirror behind the curved candy counter. Big popcorn machine that lit up when you flicked the switch. Clock over the center-aisle curtain of red velvet dramatically stopped at midnight. Concealed lights in the gilded sconces high on the walls above the seats in the main part of the theater. A gold satin curtain hung across the stage, gateway to the world of silver-screen magic.

"It almost seems a shame to destroy all this," Sarah murmured, more to herself than Julie.

In a reversal of their usual roles, Julie became the practical one and gave an unladylike snort. "It's just a spooky old theater, not a shrine or something. And we're not destroying it, we're improving it. Right now, what we're going to do . . ."

Sarah turned back to the lobby and found that while she was reveling in the beauty of the old theater, Julie had been busy. A curious assortment of items formed a pile in the center of the lobby. Stray bits of yellow popcorn from the old machine. A shard of porcelain from the rest room. A section of torn hem from the velvet curtain, a swatch of peeling wallpaper, and a scrap of burned wood left by the fire upstairs. With a flourish, Julie added a letter J that had once graced the marquee outside.

"What is all this junk?" Sarah said with a sniff, suddenly aware that the air in the theater was unpleasantly musty. She crossed the lobby to brace one of the double doors open with a rubber stopper so fresh air could circulate.

"Not junk. Bits of the theater's soul!"

"Theaters do not have souls."

"Then it's like gathering bits of hair and fingernails so you can put a curse on someone. Except this will be a reverse curse, a jinx-and-evil-spirits removal ceremony."

So this was Julie's great idea. Sarah eyed the pile doubtfully. "I hope you're not planning something with matches and fire?"

"Of course not. We'll just say some magic words and wave my crystal and chase the evil spirits away." Julie tugged on the chain around her neck, and light bounced off the crystal and made a brilliant flash in the mirror. "By the way, did I mention that the old lady committed suicide here in the theater? She hung herself right there in front of the mirror. So she was looking at herself as she died."

No, you didn't mention that minor detail. In the car, the old theater's dark past had struck Sarah as quirky, even amusing, but she again felt a flicker of apprehension. She avoided looking at the mirror, half afraid she might see a ghostly image of the dead woman hanging there. In a purposely lighthearted tone, she asked, "And just what magic words do you know, twin of my heart?"

Julie lifted her arms over her head and entwined them with a snaky grace. She danced around the small pile, her body swaying to a silent rhythm, her crystal sparkling as she held it over her head. "Abba-dabba-doo . . . gigabytes and cyberspace . . . Los Angeles Lakers . . . lasagna and enchiladas . . . acupuncture . . . liposuction . . . evil spirits depart now . . . 'Amazing Grace' . . ."

Sarah couldn't help but laugh at Julie's nonsensical assortment of "magic words," but the mention of "Amazing Grace" suddenly broke her laughter. Even she, with her limited church experience, recognized it as one of the sacred old hymns, and invoking it somehow put a different spin on this quirky little ceremony. A peculiar chill prickled her spine.

"Okay, I'm convinced." She held up her hand. "If there ever was a jinx or curse here, it's definitely gone now. So let's—"

She jumped when a shadow fell across the open doorway. Julie stopped mid-dance.

"Hey, anybody in here?"

Sarah suddenly felt ridiculous for being so jittery. The shadow blocking the doorway, though large enough to be intimidating, was neither monster nor ghost. And the voice, though deep and male, was merely inquiring, not threatening.

"Only friendly ghosts and neighborly spooks in here now," Julie said cheerfully. "We just exorcised all the evil forces. Come on in."

The guy had started to step inside, but he stopped short. Sarah didn't blame him. *Exorcism. Evil forces. He must wonder what he's stumbled into.* She stepped forward.

"Are you looking for someone?" A different and much more realistic danger suddenly occurred to her. They hadn't finalized the deal on the Nevermore yet. What if someone jumped in and bought it out from under them?

"I happened to see the open door . . ."

He was tall and lanky, with sunglasses pushed back into a windblown tangle of reddish-blond hair. His cheekbones and strong nose were too rugged to be handsome, but the angular crags were interesting. Rays slanted from the corners of his blue eyes, and his tanned jaw was as clean cut as a piece of Sarah's stained glass. A plaid shirt with sleeves ripped off at the shoulders exposed competent-looking muscles, and the heavy black work boots were not on familiar terms with polish. The look bordered on disreputable, but it didn't detract from an air of easy self-confidence.

Then Sarah noticed the front end of a blue pickup parked at the curb. A metal rack extended over the cab. Enough printing was visible on the door that a connection clicked into place.

"Oh, you're from the construction company."

"Right. Nick Nordahl, Nordahl and Sons Construction. And you're the people buying the Nevermore?"

"Prospective buyers," Sarah corrected. "Although the sellers have given us free run of the place while we check into remodeling possibilities." She extended her hand. "I'm Sarah MacIntosh, and this is my sister, Julie Armstrong."

They shook hands all around.

"I know our appointment isn't until tomorrow, but I happened to be in town," Nick said. "We're building a couple of houses over in Dutton Bay, and our supplier there ran short of insulation, so I made a quick trip over here to pick up a few rolls. Then I saw the door of the theater open . . ." He eyed Julie. "But if I'm interrupting something . . . ?"

"Oh, you're not," Sarah assured him. "We were just indulging in a . . . bit of make-believe. Would you like to collect the information today that you'll need to make a bid on the remodeling?"

"I don't have time enough to do it all today." He glanced around the lobby and stamped his feet lightly, testing the solidity of the floor. "But you might tell me more about what you have in mind."

"Actually, I didn't realize you were in the house construction business. I was under the impression your company specialized in remodeling. We got your name from . . ." Sarah turned to Julie.

"Joe Argo. He's a commercial fisherman. You remodeled a big house into apartments for his cousin over in Eugene, and he was really impressed with the quality of the work."

"So this might be too small a project to interest you?" Sarah suggested.

"We do a little of everything, big or small." Nick Nordahl grinned, hands in the back pockets of his jeans. "No skyscrapers yet, but give us time."

Sarah started to give him a rundown of what they wanted to do with the old theater, but Julie interrupted. "Are you one of the sons in Nordahl and Sons, or do you have sons?"

Sarah thought the question unacceptably nosy, but Nick didn't seem to object. He leaned against the interior wall of the cashier's booth, legs crossed at the ankles.

"The company name is actually something of a misnomer now. My father started Nordahl and Sons years ago and named it when my brother, Jason, and I were still too young to be part of it. My brother turned out to be more interested in computers than construction when he grew up, and he's with a big computer company down in Texas now. And then my dad passed away a couple years ago. Maybe it will be 'and Sons' again someday, but right now it's just me. One Nordahl. No, actually there are two Nordahls. Maybe what the company ought to be called is Nordahl and Mom."

"And Mom?" Julie repeated. With her usual blunt curiosity, she asked, "Are you a mama's boy?"

"Well, I guess if saying I love my mother makes me a mama's boy, then that's what I am," Nick Nordahl said. His softspoken voice belied the cragginess of his face, and his mouth had a good-humored quirk. "She worked right alongside Dad in the early years. Now she manages our office over in Eugene."

Sarah suddenly felt uneasy. Julie was quite capable of rushing in to quiz him about marital or girlfriend status, home life, education, income, or anything else that struck her fancy. Hastily, she said, "Why don't you take a quick look around? And Julie," she suggested pointedly, "can clean up here."

Sarah pulled the red velvet curtain aside to let Nick enter the seating area. She continued with her explanation of what they wanted to do with the old theater as she and Nick toured behind the screen and circled the enormous, old-fashioned, oil-burning heater. A back door opened on the narrow space between the building and the old board fence. A smattering of trash, everything from soft-drink cans to plastic bags to an old shoe, covered the space. Only the roofs of the nearby houses were visible over the weathered boards.

"Cleanup job number one," Sarah suggested. "And probably a new fence."

"I'd suggest a concrete block wall rather than another wooden fence, and the parking lot definitely needs a new layer of asphalt," Nick said as he closed the door on the unattractive space.

He moved on, pounding and prodding. He opened an electrical box on a snake pit of wires, stepped off measurements, and dug his pocketknife into a rough timber. "Solid," he murmured approvingly. Now and then he jotted numbers in a battered notebook he kept in a shirt pocket.

"We've checked with the county building department, and what we have in mind is a permissible use of the property."

"Good."

"I'm concerned about how big a problem the concrete floor may be," Sarah said. Like in all theaters, the floor sloped down to the screen to give each tier of seats a good view.

"The high ceiling provides adequate space, so I don't think there will be a problem simply building a new, level floor over this one," Nick said. "More complicated will be bringing the wiring up to code and modernizing the heating system. That big oil guzzler looks like it might need its own oil well to supply enough fuel to keep it warm in here. I may as well warn you right up front that all this won't come cheap."

"We didn't think it would."

They continued on, Nick asking an occasional question. Although nothing personal passed between them, Sarah found herself aware of his physical presence. She'd noted his athletic jump to the stage and now almost wished she'd had the nerve to play the helpless female so he'd give her a hand up, instead of taking the steps as she'd done.

He voiced no further comments until they were back on the narrow area of stage in front of the satin curtain, gazing down on the rows of empty seats. The seats always looked expectant rather than abandoned to Sarah, as if they were just waiting for a herd of children to race in and fill the front row.

"It was quite grand in its day, wasn't it?" Nick said thoughtfully. "It's still rather grand. I think it would be nice to keep as much of the old-theater ambiance as possible. Maybe put a couple of rows of these old theater seats back-to-back out there in the center to give people a chance to sit down and relax." Nick smiled. "And then get up to shop again, of course."

"That's a wonderful idea! We do want to keep as much of the old-theater feel as possible. I've thought about hanging old movie posters on the walls, and maybe even getting that old popcorn machine working again."

He looked at her then, and the look suggested that he was not unaware of her either. "Have you lived in Julesburg long?"

"Julie has been here a couple of years, but I'm just in the process of moving here."

"From?"

"California." She smiled. "Isn't everyone from California?" She knew Julesburg had quite a few California transplants, although probably a smaller percentage than in some of the more prosperous areas of the state.

"I'm an Oregon native myself, although I've never lived here on the coast. But it's a great area. I've always been intrigued by the stories about sunken ships around here."

"I just hope it's a great area for what we have in mind."

"You said you work with stained glass, and your sister is an artist?"

"Yes. Which reminds me, we haven't even gotten upstairs yet. We want to make that into our work area."

He glanced at his watch. "I have to get this insulation back to the crew, so I'll have to let that go until tomorrow."

They returned to the lobby. Julie had cleaned up the small trash pile, although Sarah suspected she'd merely stashed the items behind the candy counter. Julie was standing there, now frowning at her crystal.

"I think I must need a new crystal. Or maybe a bigger crystal. Do they wear out? This one just doesn't seem to be working." She gave it a vigorous shake.

"What's it supposed to do?" Nick asked.

"Oh, lots of things. It's for healing and protection, focusing your vibes, telling you about the past and future, helping you make decisions. I was asking it a question about the Nevermore."

Nick laughed. "You've got to be kidding."

"No, really. But I think maybe this one has lost its power or something."

"What you need isn't a bigger rock," Nick said. "What you need is The Rock."

Julie looked up, interested. "There's a special kind of crystal called 'The Rock'?"

"I mean the true Rock. Jesus."

"Oh. You're another one of those."

"If by 'those,' you mean Christians, that's me, all right." Nick smiled, obviously at ease with the subject.

Julie planted her hands on her hips. "Are you going to give us a sermon or start tossing Bible verses at us?"

"Sure, why not? First Corinthians: 'They drank from the spiritual rock, and that rock was Christ.' And here's a psalm I like: 'My salvation and my honor depend on God; he is my mighty rock, my refuge.' I'm not much at giving sermons, but here's a short one: Everyone needs that Rock, and anyone who doesn't have it is lost for eternity."

"Scare tactics," Julie scoffed. "I think there are lots of paths to God and eternity."

"Okay, I'll toss you another Bible verse, one that quotes Jesus: 'I am the way and the truth and the life. No one comes to the Father except through me.' "

Julie eyed him thoughtfully as the dangling crystal swayed in slow circles at the end of the silver chain draped over her forefinger. "That's what Stefanie Harrison believes. And I think it's the same verse Gran quoted to Sarah and me. I suppose it could be true."

"It is true. And whoever doesn't believe it is truly lost."

"Okay, maybe I'll believe it. Someday." Julie airily flipped the chain over her head. With sunny self-assurance she added, "I have eons of time yet to make up my mind about all these deep, dark questions about God and the universe and everything."

"Do you?"

Julie rolled her eyes, but Sarah didn't know what to think. Except that it seemed strange that all the people who had really impressed her lately—her great-grandmother, the Harrisons, and Nick Nordahl—had turned out to be Christians.

"You look like a hunk, but you talk like a preacher," Julie grumbled.

"Thank you, ma'am. I'll take both as compliments." Nick bent at the waist in a courtly bow. Turning to Sarah, he added, "Look, I just thought of something. You're doubtful about my company's remodeling capabilities, since we're mostly into new homes at the moment, right?"

"Something like that."

"We did something similar to this up in Corvallis, where we remodeled a bowling alley into a food court to house a number of small ethnic cafés. It's very popular with the college kids from Oregon State. How about the two of you taking a look at it before I figure a bid on this job?"

Julie didn't hesitate. "Sounds good to me!"

"Maybe this will put Nordahl and Sons a jump ahead on getting the job," Nick said. "I assume you are taking bids from some other construction outfits?"

"You bet we are! Not that I'd have thought of it," Julie added. "Sarah did. She's one sharp cookie."

"So how about it?" Nick said, addressing the question to Sarah. "Tomorrow's Friday, and I'm heading back to

Eugene around midday. If you want to drive over, we could all run up to Corvallis together."

"C'mon, let's do it," Julie coaxed. "I *could* point out that even if he is kind of preachy, he's cute and single. He might even buy us dinner." Then she adopted a virtuous tone. "But I won't do that. I'll just remind you that we really should see an example of his company's work before we decide."

"She's right, you know," Nick said, although he didn't specify what Julie was right about.

Sarah felt embarrassed by Julie's frivolity, but the trip *would* be a business arrangement, after all. She nodded briskly. "Yes, I think seeing the building in Corvallis is an excellent idea."

4

Sarah opened one eye. "Go away," she murmured. But the hand continued to shake her shoulder, like a puppy worrying a toy.

"C'mon, sleepyhead. Time to rise and shine!"

"I can shine just fine right here, thank you," Sarah muttered. She burrowed deeper under the covers.

"I was planning to serve you this cup of coffee in bed, but if you're going to be a grump, I may just pour it over your head."

Sarah peered out from under the covers and saw that the cup was indeed poised over her head. But it was the fragrant scent of steaming coffee more than the threat of a hot deluge that stirred her into a sitting position. Julie handed her the cup, disappeared for a moment, then returned with a cinnamon roll on a paper plate. She presented it with an elaborate flourish.

Even with this bribe, Sarah still felt grumpy about the rude awakening. "And to what do I owe this royal treatment?" she inquired. Then she bit into the roll and realized no grudge could survive the seduction of warm cinnamon and drippy icing and plump raisins. She scooped a dribble off her chin and licked the sweet drops from her finger. "Ummm, this is sooo good."

As she took a sip of coffee, Sarah remembered that there had been no cinnamon rolls in the apartment when they went to bed last night. And, come to think of it, Julie was acting incongruously upbeat considering what a down mood she'd been in at the time. "Hey, where'd you get the rolls?"

"From the Pink Grinch."

The Pink Grinch was their name for Mrs. Maxwell, the elderly proprietor of the Calico Pantry. Sarah and Julie had speculated about whether the sour woman always wore the same bulky pink jacket around her narrow shoulders or if she owned a whole wardrobe of pink jackets. Of course, Julie claimed that the woman had her sunny side, but Sarah wasn't convinced. Mrs. Maxwell had once lectured Sarah when she'd presented a fifty dollar bill in payment for a $3.19 gallon of milk. And a minute later, Mrs. Maxwell had run to the door and yelled at a couple of teenagers that they couldn't tinker with their old motorcycle in *her* parking lot. But Sarah was willing to concede that maybe Mrs. Maxwell's crankiness was caused by illness. The woman always looked so haggard.

"You've already been to the Pantry? How long have you been up?"

"Oh, hours. I've been down to the jetty to feed the cats and to the post office to pick up the mail."

Sarah, her mind slowly gathering coffee-fueled speed, peered toward the window. Yesterday's gorgeous fall weather had vanished into a heavy layer of clouds spewing raindrops. A wind-whipped leaf from the maple in the parking lot below slapped the window and clung to it like a misshapen hand. *If I believed in omens . . .*

She shook off the odd moment of uneasiness. *What's with me lately?* She turned to look at Julie. "You went out in the rain?"

"Don't sound so flabbergasted," Julie chided. "Cats don't stop getting hungry just because it's raining. Besides, we Oregonians like rain. Hey, want another cinnamon roll?"

"Sure."

Sarah licked her fingers again, thinking about her twin as the sound of the microwave whirred in the kitchen.

Donovan Moran had called at around 9:00 last evening, and Julie had gone out to meet him somewhere. The hour had seemed late for a date, especially in Julesburg, but Julie had murmured something about Donovan not being a day person. She hadn't gotten home until almost midnight, and she'd been in a real downer of a mood when she stomped in.

Sarah had ventured a tentative question as Julie banged around the kitchen, making a peanut butter and jelly sandwich. She could tell all the slamming was a cover-up for the tears rolling down Julie's cheeks.

"Is something wrong?"

"Sometimes I think Donovan is the world's all-time biggest jerk. Sometimes I think *I'm* the jerk."

"Are you in love with him?"

"Most of the time. Except when I'm mad at him."

"Is he in love with you?"

"He says he is. But . . . debatable."

"What does he do?"

"This and that. He has a boat and dives commercially for sea urchins when the season is open. He also has a shop where he does motorcycle repair work and customized painting. He's very good at it, very artistic, and he could do great if he'd just . . . settle down. He had a small charter flying business, taking tourists up in his helicopter and stuff, but that went belly-up when—" Julie broke off and slapped the sandwich together. "Oh, I get so mad at him!"

Julie had then planted herself on the floor in front of the sofa and started scribbling furiously in the journal she kept more or less regularly. Sarah stayed up with her, and they watched an old Steve Martin/Goldie Hawn movie until after 1:00. The movie had some funny parts, but Julie never cracked a smile. Every now and then she'd grab the journal and scrawl more lines in it.

Now here she was this morning, happy and cheerful.

"How come last night you were ready to spit nails and this morning you're as perky and sunny as some cooking-show hostess?" Sarah inquired.

"What happened is that I've made up my mind. It's time for Project Dump Donovan. I'll do it as soon as we get back from Eugene this evening. I don't know what made me think it would work with him. He's never going to change his ways."

Sarah resisted an urge to applaud. After all, she didn't know much about Donovan or Julie's relationship with him. But she certainly had not liked the way he'd brought Julie to tears last night. She'd wanted to chase him down and yell, "Don't you dare make my sister cry!"

Sarah got up from bed and gave Julie a hug. With a fierce rush of affection, she said, "I love you, twin of my heart."

Julie smiled. "Sometimes you almost gotta believe in God, don't you?"

Sarah blinked at this unexpected detour.

"I mean, it looks as if he had his eye on us all those years, all the time planning for our great-grandmother to bring us back together eventually."

"I suppose you could look at it that way."

"And I'm so glad God did it. You being here helped me make up my mind about Donovan. Among all the other reasons I'm glad you're here." Julie kissed Sarah on the forehead, then glanced at her watch. "And now, before this gets any more maudlin, I have to run over to the Ocean Crest Motel. They called while you were snoring away.

One of my masterpieces has suffered a debilitating injury, and they want me to come over and do a repair job."

Last winter the motel had commissioned Julie to paint a whale and seascape mural in each of their more expensive suites. She deprecatingly referred to this as her "paint-by-the-yard art," but Sarah had seen photos of two of the murals, and they were spectacular.

"Somehow I can't believe Picasso and Monet had to start out like this," Julie grumbled as she grabbed a plastic raincoat from the closet. "I'll bet no one ever planted a heel print on one of their masterpieces."

While Julie was gone, Sarah showered and dressed, wiped up peanut butter smears on the kitchen counter, made the beds, and vacuumed. She carefully moved the painting Julie was now working on so she could vacuum the area near the window. She smiled as she glanced at the painting, a scene of cats peeking out from the rocks down at the jetty. Even though the painting was unfinished, it caught both the playfulness and poignancy of the homeless animals.

She and Julie had intended to leave for Eugene at around noon, but the mural repairs had taken longer than Julie expected, and it was past 2:00 by the time they dashed from the apartment to the parking lot. Clouds hung swollen and sullen overhead, and the air felt heavy, like it could rain at any moment.

"My car!" Sarah yelled as they ran. They hadn't discussed which vehicle to take, but the heater in Julie's old Honda put out less heat than a wet match.

Raindrops battered the windows of the big Ford Expedition as Sarah gave the engine a few minutes to warm up. By the time she pulled onto the main street, the heater blasted a reassuring flow of warm air.

Julie patted the dashboard Sarah kept carefully protected with Armor All. "This always makes me feel like I'm rid-ing in an upholstered tank. I know it burns way too much gas to be environmentally proper . . . but I like it!"

Sarah would never have bought the wine-red sport utility vehicle for herself. Too massive, too powerful, too expensive. It had been what her father, with a grin of embarrassment, called his "midlife-crisis toy." Now the car gave her a warm feeling of having a part of him to hold on to, and it also offered a sense of security. She hadn't encountered a foot-deep mudhole yet, but if she ever did, she figured she could blast right through it in the Expedition.

Julie dozed as they drove through the rain. Sarah wasn't surprised, given how little sleep Julie had gotten the night before. As she glanced over at her twin, Sarah again felt a powerful surge of protective love. *Did God really bring us together? If you did, Lord, I appreciate it. Thanks.*

At the junction where the highway separated from 101 and turned inland to snake along the river and pass through the mountains to Eugene, Julie woke up and immediately started chattering.

"Hey, do you think we should look for a larger apartment? By the time we get all your things moved up here, we're going to have wall-to-wall *stuff*."

Julie's small apartment had only one bedroom. They'd scrounged up an extra twin bed from a secondhand store when Sarah arrived.

"I'll rent an apartment of my own as soon as things get settled down. I never intended to move in on you permanently. Unless you're tired of my snoring and would rather I did it right away?"

"Oh, no!" Julie sat up straighter in the SUV's big bucket seat. "I was just kidding about the snoring. Hey, maybe we should buy a house!"

"Two old maids in a house with seventeen cats?" Sarah teased.

Julie ignored the loving jab. "Wouldn't something like the Harrisons' old Victorian house be cool?"

"We'll think about it," Sarah promised.

"Do you think he's married?"

Sarah didn't have to ask who she was talking about. "No, I don't think so."

"Why not?"

"He just didn't strike me as being married."

"Married men don't always act married."

In a quick sideways glance, Sarah saw that Julie was frowning. *Is she speaking from experience?* Close as they had become, there was still a lot they didn't know about each other. "Are *you* interested in the hunky Mr. Nordahl?"

"Me? No way." Julie's ponytail bounced as she shook her head. "I've had it with men for the foreseeable future. He's all yours."

The weather improved the farther east they went, the raindrops drying to spotmarks on the SUV's broad hood and the clouds giving way to blue sky. Julie chattered about touring some old mansion near Coos Bay, gave an excited command to pull over so they could watch two elk grazing in a roadside meadow, and then rushed on to speculate about the Harrisons' trip to Japan. Had Sarah seen the Golden Angel Shampoo ads in all the big magazines? That was Ryan's New York model sister in them.

By the time they reached the Nordahl and Sons office on the outskirts of Eugene, they were lustily harmonizing with Bruce Springsteen on "Born in the USA," and the coastal storm was just a bank of dark clouds caught on the mountains to the west.

The unpretentious office building was a woodsy brown, small but solid looking. Out back was a larger, warehouse-type metal building, with a chain-link fence surrounding a graveled yard of vehicles, equipment, and various building supplies.

When they entered the building, Nick came out of an inner office and introduced his mother, a tall woman with silver hair and a friendly smile who exuded a feminine version of Nick's air of competence. She acknowledged the introductions with a warm handshake and a lively curiosity in blue eyes that matched Nick's. Julie's clothes weren't quite as unconventional as they usually were, although Sarah would have felt like a walking rainbow in her brightly striped pants. The earrings were vintage Julie, though, huge, flamboyant parrots dangling from enameled palm fronds.

Sarah offered to drive her SUV to Corvallis, but Nick said he needed to drop off some roofing at another work site, so they could take a company pickup. Sarah and Julie jostled for position at the door of the pickup, each pushing the other to make her climb in the cab first. Julie won by whispering, "You have to sit in the middle by him, or I'm going to tell him you have the hots for him."

"You wouldn't . . . I don't!"

Julie just smiled, and Sarah, knowing Julie might well make good on her threat, reluctantly climbed into the center position of the wide seat. She could feel her face flush; she felt much too close to Nick, much too aware of the movement of his arm and hand every time he shifted gears, much too conscious of his leg when he pressed on the gas pedal or brake.

They dropped off the roofing at a little town east of Eugene, so it was 6:00 by the time they reached the "Variety of Life" food court in Corvallis. By then, Julie and Nick were on a lighthearted bantering basis. He teased her about the wild earrings, and she gave him a hard time about his preference for country and western music.

Students from nearby Oregon State University and several families crowded the food court. Nick pointed out what his company had done to turn a bowling alley into an attractive mini mall of food. The noise level was surprisingly low, considering the crowd, and Nick explained how they had designed and built for noise abatement.

Then they started eating, sampling here and there "like wandering vultures," as Julie put it. Greek salad, Japanese sushi, Indian curry, Thai noodles, Chinese egg roll. Sarah had tried to pay for some of the food, but Nick had waved off her money.

"I think he's trying to bribe us," Julie whispered to Sarah.

Nick didn't miss the unsubtle whisper. He grinned. "I'm trying," he agreed, although Sarah had her doubts. She suspected it was more an old-fashioned attitude that when a man was with a woman, or a pair of them, he paid. "Is it working?" he added.

"It's the size of the bid Nordahl and Sons offers that really matters," Sarah replied.

Nick groaned. "The hard-nosed businesswoman. Unbribeable."

"But a very pert and lovely nose, don't you think?" Julie asked.

"Of course, the fact that this lovely nose is exactly like yours is irrelevant," Nick teased Julie. "You've never mentioned it, but you two have to be identical twins."

"Of course! We even have the same little mole on our—"

"Julie!" Sarah gasped. "Don't listen to her," she added to Nick. "We do not have identical moles anywhere."

Julie smiled mischievously, and Nick laughed again. They'd laughed a lot today, and it felt good to Sarah. She'd had a lot of heavy stuff in her life lately.

"But your last names are different," Nick pointed out. "Which means one of you was . . . is . . . married?"

Julie waved her fork airily. "No marriages, just a long, complicated story."

"I'm waiting."

"Someday," Sarah interjected. "We better get going for tonight."

It was 8:15 by the time they got back to the parking lot at the Nordahl and Sons office in Eugene.

"I'm stuck with paperwork here tomorrow," Nick said as he walked them from the pickup to Sarah's SUV. "But I'll be back over in Dutton Bay on Monday. How about if I come by the Nevermore late in the afternoon to finish gathering the information I need to make a bid on the remodeling?"

They settled on 4:00, but he paused at the door of the Expedition as if something were troubling him. He glanced up at the sky. Rain wasn't falling but storm clouds had moved in from the coast, and neither moon nor stars penetrated the dark cover.

"I shouldn't have kept you so late. I don't like to see you driving back through the mountains alone at night."

"We're not alone. There's two of us," Sarah pointed out, but she could see that didn't carry much weight with Nick.

"Look, my mother has a big house with plenty of room. I know she'd be delighted to have the two of you stay there tonight. I'll call her—"

"That's very nice of you, but we'll be fine," Sarah said before Julie could jump in and accept the invitation. "And we'll see you at the Nevermore on Monday."

As they pulled out of the parking lot, Julie said, "Let's invite him to dinner afterward."

"You're planning to whip up pot roast and apple pie?" Sarah inquired. "Or perhaps one of your flaming specialties?"

"Not me, you. It'll be a great chance to impress him with your cooking skills."

"And just why would I want to impress Nick Nordahl with anything, especially cooking skills?"

"Oh, Sarah, he's interested in you. Anyone could see that. Go for it!"

"He talked to you more than he did to me."

"Probably because I talked to him more. But he thinks I'm . . ." Julie paused. "Flaky. A fluffhead. A ding-a-ling.

He's a guy who prefers someone organized. Levelheaded and sensible. Like you."

"Levelheaded and sensible," Sarah scoffed. "Somehow this doesn't sound like girl-of-my-dreams stuff."

Sleepiness soon overrode Julie's interest in matchmaking, however. Within minutes, her chin drooped to her chest. She roused enough to try to tilt the seat back, but the mechanism was jammed. Sarah pulled over to the side of the road.

"You crawl in back where you can get some real sleep."

Julie sleepily agreed, and Sarah helped her into the backseat. She tucked a plaid blanket around Julie's slender body and folded an old jacket under her head. Julie was sound asleep even before Sarah climbed back into the driver's seat.

When they were midway through the mountains, the rain started again, as if it had been lying in wait, gathering strength for a full nighttime assault. By 10:00, when Sarah drove past the Julesburg city limits sign, windswept rain was hammering the windows and blurring the streetlights. An old "Welcome to Julesburg" banner across the street had blown down and now flapped around an electric pole.

Julesburg, rarely lively at this hour on any night, appeared deserted under the savage onslaught of the storm. Oregonians might like rain, but they obviously were sensible enough not to be out in it on a night such as this. Sarah started to drive directly home, but the lights in the Calico Pantry reminded her they needed milk for breakfast cereal.

She flicked on the turn signal and pulled into the empty parking lot.

5

Sarah peered into the backseat. Within the dim shadows, Julie's curled figure was lost in the tangles of blanket and jacket. She was so deep in sleep that the stop hadn't even wakened her. Sarah felt a rush of affection that was momentarily more motherly than sisterly. *Sleep tight, twin of my heart.*

Sarah left the engine running, grabbed her purse, and opened the SUV's door as quietly as possible so she wouldn't disturb Julie. Slanting rain battered her hunched shoulders as she dashed from her vehicle to the entrance.

A bell tinkled as she pushed through the glass door. "What a night!" She shook her hair, spattering drops like a wet dog.

"Glad I live right upstairs so I don't have to go out in it. 'Course, with my age and arthritis, just getting up those stairs is bad enough," the elderly proprietress muttered.

The woman sat within a square of cluttered counter that formed an island in the center of the small convenience store. Cold air blasted the island every time the door opened, and the woman had the inevitable bulky pink jacket zipped tightly around her body. Her scalp shone with baby pinkness through her overpermed gray hair.

A large, old-fashioned cash register sat catty-corner at the front part of the island. Small bags of potato and tortilla chips, fried pork rinds and beef jerky, hung from a canopy above. A glass cabinet on the counter held cartons of cigarettes, under a sign warning that no tobacco products would be sold to anyone under age eighteen. A telephone with oversized numbers sat beside the cabinet. The blurry image of a horse and cowboy galloped across a small-screen TV perched on a side counter.

The woman jiggled one of the metal rods of the antenna protruding from the TV. "One of these days I'm gonna get on that cable thing," she declared. "With these rabbit ears, sometimes I can't hardly tell if the cowboy's ridin' the horse or the horse is ridin' the cowboy."

The mild display of humor surprised Sarah; perhaps the Pink Grinch really did have a sunny side. Sarah smiled and headed for the refrigerated unit at the back of the store. The carton of milk was close to the expiration date, but she and Julie could use it up right away. She thought they might need cold cereal too. Of course, if she waited until tomorrow, she could buy it cheaper down at the grocery store, but she picked up a box of Total anyway. The half-empty shelves and shabby condition of the store suggested the Pink Grinch didn't do a roaring business here and could probably use the sale.

Sarah was headed toward the cash register when the door opened, letting in another blast of cold wind and rain and a customer wearing a long yellow slicker and matching floppy-brimmed hat. *Now that's what I need. Not much for flattery and style, but eminently practical.*

Then she stopped short, blinking in a moment of shock. It was not a face under the floppy rainhat, but . . .

A psychedelic swirl of colors, a skinless caricature of a human face, a demon's grin.

The box of Total slipped from Sarah's suddenly nerveless hands. She started to bend over to pick it up, but a quick flash of metal stopped her.

A gun in a gloved hand, muzzle aimed at her.

"Leave it!" a male voice snarled. "Over there." He motioned with a jerk of the gun. "Hands on the counter."

Sarah did as she was told, pressing her hands flat on the scarred surface of the counter. A nervous perspiration poured out of her palms. The elderly woman had risen from her stool within the island, but her body was still bent, as if she'd frozen into position, eyes huge in her wrinkled face.

"The cash register." Another jerk of the gun, this time at Mrs. Maxwell. "Open it."

The elderly proprietress moved as fast as she could. She pressed a worn key, and the drawer slid open.

"C'mon, old woman, move it!"

Keep calm. He's here for the money. He won't use the gun if we don't panic him.

With trembling hands, the terrified woman scratched bills out of the compartments of the cash register, but her gnarled fingers were clumsy, and half a dozen tens fluttered to the floor. She stooped to retrieve them.

"Oh no you don't, you old—"

The gun blasted, like an explosion of dynamite in the small store.

Sarah stared in horrified disbelief as the elderly woman collapsed. She leaned over the counter and saw the twisted figure crumpled on the floor.

Sarah reeled, dizziness spiraling through her.

Not real. None of this is real. No impossible face of a demon, no gun, no death . . .

The dizziness reached her eyes, and strange zigzags of lightning and stars distorted the counter and cash register. The roar of the gun echoed inside her head.

"But she was just going to pick up the money she dropped!" Sarah protested. *This will make him take it all back. Then everything will go back to normal.* "She's just an old woman. She wasn't going after a gun or anything—"

The gun silently rose and swiveled to her. The killer gripped it with two gloved hands and targeted it between her eyes. His slicker gleamed wet and shiny under the fluorescent lights, so bright that she had to squint against the glare. The gun enlarged to fill her vision, like a close-up on a movie screen. The hideous face-that-was-not-a-face, the mask of yellow and blue, green and bloodred, blurred behind the gun. Sarah dug her fingernails into the counter to keep consciousness from slipping away.

He let go of the gun with one hand so he could reach around the cash register and scoop money out of the drawer. He stuffed the bills in a pocket of the slicker, paying no more attention to the bloody body on the floor than to the package of tortilla chips that had fallen and spilled around it.

The gun never strayed from Sarah's direction, but it was only when the money was in the killer's pocket that the hideous face targeted Sarah again. And the eyes . . . Sarah stared at them, transfixed. Not human eyes of blue or green or brown; these eyes were yellow, cracked and splintered like broken glass, pointed irises with the gleam of a cat's eye . . .

Was it three seconds or three minutes that they stared at each other, fluorescent bulb flickering and humming overhead? One part of Sarah's brain froze, unable to move beyond the deadly magnet of the gun and the strange, inhuman eyes. Another part raced, as if frantically trying to gather memories and dreams before all were gone. *Mom and Dad, Gran, Julie, all our plans . . .*

He took a step backward toward the door, arm and gun still stretched toward her. *He's going to shoot! Drop to the floor! Duck! Throw something!*

Her body didn't respond. Even her eyelids felt frozen.

But primal fear jerked her body when he jumped forward, grabbed the phone, and yanked it so savagely that the cord snapped. He slammed the phone down an aisle, and the bell rang in a tinny rattle when it hit the wooden floor. He whipped the gun sideways and smashed the glass front of the cabinet. He reached inside with a gloved hand to snatch a carton of cigarettes.

Then he was gone, out the door in another rush of cold air, yellow slicker flaring like a cape. His rainhat fell off, but all it revealed was a hairless, earless head. He swept up the yellow rainhat without breaking his stride, his shapeless figure blending into Sarah's own reflection in the glass door.

Her frozen mind flared. *Help . . . phone . . . doctor . . . police . . .* She managed to move one foot on the worn wooden floor.

She stopped, again paralyzed with shock as she saw him fling the door of the Expedition open and jump inside. *You can't do that!*

The engine roared, and the SUV swung backward across the parking lot. The beam of headlights momentarily blazed in Sarah's eyes, then the tires screeched as red taillights raced toward the street.

Sarah shoved the glass door open and stared after the SUV. *Not real, not real . . .*

But reality overrode her frantic protest.

A dead body lay behind the counter. And Julie—Julie was out there now, hurtling through the night with a killer.

6

Like clockwork, exactly as planned!

He resisted a gleeful urge to gun the powerful engine and instead drove at a sedate pace down Julesburg's main street. *This is no time to draw unwanted attention. Not that how I drive matters much on a night like this.* He peered in the rearview mirror. The rain-battered street was as deserted as a graveyard.

A miserable night. A perfect night that made him glad he'd waited for it.

Except for the small detail of the girl in the Calico Pantry.

He frowned beneath the psychedelic ski mask. He'd waited a long time in the dark there behind the hedge, the yellow slicker concealed under a drape of black plastic, until the unfamiliar, out-of-state SUV pulled into the parking lot. He'd praised the powers that be that the driver had not only left the keys in the ignition, she'd graciously left the engine running.

He'd watched the driver hurry into the store. That was the jewel in his plan—a terrified witness verifying that this was a simple robbery gone bad. But what he hadn't expected, given his careful selection of vehicle, was that the customer would be someone he knew. That wasn't supposed to happen. Could she possibly have recognized him?

The thought made a cold sweat break out on his palms inside the leather gloves. Then he looked at his own reflection in the rearview mirror and relaxed.

No way. In this disguise I could have been in bed with her last night, and she wouldn't have recognized me. Not an unappealing thought, actually . . .

He snapped his mind away from that line of distraction.

But should I have killed her anyway, to rule out any chance of recognition?

It would have made for a plausible scenario. Innocent bystander gunned down in robbery. It happened all the time. But recognizing her had jolted him. Shooting the old lady was one thing, but putting a bullet in Julie wasn't part of the plan.

Would that split-second decision not to pull the trigger a second time turn out to be a disastrous mistake?

No. No mistake. She was terrified. She'd be practically incoherent when the cops arrived—a perfect witness, unable to report anything except that the gunman had panicked and killed the old lady while he was robbing the store.

He turned on to a side street and ripped off the mask, glad to be rid of it. He tossed it on the seat beside the rainhat and the gun. He'd pop out the alien-from-outer-space contacts later. He didn't remove the gloves, of course. No fingerprints.

Now all he needed to do was joyride the rig back into the hills and run it off a ravine where it wouldn't be found until next spring, maybe not till the next decade. Then a fast hike back to town before daybreak. A roaring blaze in his fireplace would take care of the mask and the slicker, and he'd get rid of the gun out at Riptide tomorrow night.

He stroked the leather-covered steering wheel. *Too bad to junk a classy rig like this.* But it couldn't be helped. Actually, he could buy a dozen of these, if he wanted. The past year had been profitable.

Suddenly he heard something rustle behind him. His gloved fingers locked on the steering wheel. There was nothing back there to rustle. He'd checked before he went in the store. There'd been nothing in the backseat but a tangle of old blankets and jackets.

But now he could see movement in the dim shadows of the rearview mirror. A dog, maybe? Then a figure reared out of the tangle of blankets.

"Hey, what's going on?" She leaned forward between the bucket seats, eyes bright and interested as she peered at his unmasked face. Frivolous parrot earrings danced at her ears. "What're you doing here? Where's Sarah?"

And his grand, perfect plan exploded like a burst of fireworks.

7

Nick found his mother in the nursery after church. She supervised there one Sunday each month. She was handing a baby back to a young couple who'd started coming to church a few weeks ago.

"She's a real sweetie," Mrs. Nordahl assured the couple. "Do bring her back again."

"We will."

Another baby started squalling, and Nick's mother picked him up and cuddled him against her shoulder. The wails instantly quieted to a gurgle.

"See what a fantastic grandmother I'd make?"

"If I hear of any grandma openings, I'll be sure to let you know," Nick replied.

"I won't hold my breath." Mrs. Nordahl's tone was tart but her smile affectionate.

It was probably a good idea that his mother wasn't holding her breath. His brother, Jason, in Texas seemed in no hurry to marry and produce grandchildren, although he had recently acquired a fiancée. Which was a further step than Nick had ever taken.

Nick grinned and changed the subject. "How about going somewhere for dinner? Maybe that new Japanese place?"

Suggesting the Japanese restaurant reminded him of sharing sushi with Sarah and Julie at the food mini mall in Corvallis. Not that it was the first time he'd thought of them since that night. A full-blown image of Sarah skewered him now. Observant blue eyes, dark hair, fresh-scrubbed skin. Her smile came less readily than her twin sister's infectious grins, which somehow made it all the more meaningful when it did come. He'd sensed a big-sister protectiveness toward Julie, even though Julie had blithely informed him they were only three minutes apart in age. And Sarah's questions about the remodeling of the bowling alley had been both observant and intelligent. Not a Christian, but not closed to the possibility either, he was reasonably certain.

"Yoo-hoo." Mrs. Nordahl waved a hand in front of her son's face. "I just told you Marc and I are eloping and moving to a thatched hut in the South Pacific."

He smiled. "Sorry. My mind wandered for a minute. This calls for . . . what? A truckload of coconuts for a wedding present?"

Mrs. Nordahl tilted her head, her blue eyes curious about his wandering thoughts. She didn't question him, though. They often shared confidences, but neither one pried. "Okay, we're not eloping," she conceded, "but I am having dinner with Marc this evening. And I told Lili and Sue that I'll do antique stores with them this afternoon."

"What does it take to get on your social calendar, two weeks' notice?" Nick teasingly grumbled. Pulling a long face, he added mournfully, "I guess I'll just go stick a TV dinner in the microwave then and eat all by myself."

She gave him an unsympathetic rap on the shoulder with her knuckles. "Get a life, kid. Although you're welcome to tour antique stores with us, if you'd like."

They both knew how he felt about edging around shelves of trinkets and fragile glassware. He grinned again, planted a kiss on her cheek, and made his way through the crowd leaving church. In the parking lot, he tapped the steering wheel of his Mustang reflectively. *What now? Go back to the condo and watch football on TV? Try the Japanese restaurant alone? Call Sherm and see if he was up for a bike ride along the river?*

He suddenly had a much better idea.

The pickup was already loaded with more rolls of insulation, and it took him only a few minutes to pack his duffel bag for several days at Dutton Bay. He tossed it and his briefcase onto the seat of the company pickup. Driving over today made good sense, he assured himself. It would eliminate an early morning drive tomorrow.

Yet as he drove through the narrow valley of lush pasturelands by the river that wound through the mountains, he had to laugh at himself for coming up with that rationalization. Because what he really had in mind was driving down to Julesburg, hunting up a certain pair of twins, and persuading them to have dinner with him.

He turned the radio to a Eugene station and tapped his hand on his thigh to the rhythm of Shania Twain bouncing through a country song. The music cut to the news, and he only half listened to the stories about trouble in the Mid East and the president's latest trip. Then the announcer switched to local news.

"Residents of the small coastal town of Julesburg are still in shock after the Friday night robbery and shooting of the elderly proprietor of a local convenience store, the Calico Pantry. The victim is seventy-four-year-old Helen Maxwell, longtime resident who lived in an apartment above the store."

The Calico Pantry? Wasn't that just a few blocks from the old Nevermore theater? And Friday night. That was the night Sarah and Julie drove back to Julesburg.

With a flicker of apprehension, Nick turned up the volume.

"The gunman is described as being of medium height and, at the time of the robbery, was wearing a yellow slicker and rainhat over a brightly colored ski mask."

A larger wave of apprehension hit, because the description of the gunman meant someone had witnessed the crime. No reason to believe Sarah and Julie were involved, but . . .

"Still missing at this point is the woman asleep in the backseat of the vehicle stolen by the gunman from outside the convenience store. The woman, whose name has not yet been released, is described as being twenty-five years old, five-foot-five, approximately 120 pounds and having dark brown hair, blue eyes. The vehicle is a dark red Ford Expedition sport utility vehicle, California plate number . . ."

Red Ford Expedition with California plates? Dark-haired, twenty-five-year-old woman? The apprehension tightened in a clamp around his chest. *Sarah or Julie? No, surely not.*

He turned up the volume still higher, but all he heard was the request that anyone with information should call the Julesburg police or the county sheriff's office. He punched the scanner button, searching for another station with more news, frustrated when all the roving dial found was useless music . . . ball game . . . talk show.

Nick tried to be calm and rational. Why would Sarah or Julie have been asleep in the backseat of the SUV while it was parked at a convenience store? More likely it was someone else entirely, a tourist passing through. The matching car and personal descriptions were merely coincidental.

No. Too many coincidences. The timing. The vehicle. The description.

One of the twins was missing.

Lord, please keep her safe! Whichever twin it is—help and protect her! And show me what I can do to help.

He drove through Dutton Bay without stopping, and when he pulled into Julesburg he found he didn't need to search for the Calico Pantry. It couldn't be missed. Three police cars . . . no, four, were wagon-trained around it. Yellow crime-scene tape stretched from outside the high hedge that ran along one side of the parking lot, across the sidewalk, and back around the building. Even though the crime was more than a day and a half old now, people were clustered in small groups around the tape. Nick had to park at the next block and run back.

An officer with a German Shepherd on a harness and leash patrolled just inside the tape.

"Have they found the girl or the car yet? Has she been identified?"

The officer stopped politely, though his swift gaze assessed Nick with a hint of professional suspicion. "No information has been released yet. Investigators are still working the crime scene inside the store." Nick noted that the officer was not Julesburg police; his badge identified him as a deputy from the county sheriff's office.

"Look, I just heard about this on the radio. I'm from Eugene. I think the girl who is missing may be a friend of mine, Sarah MacIntosh. Or maybe her sister, Julie Armstrong—"

"If you have information, I'll get another officer to take your statement."

"No, I don't have information!" Nick snapped. "That's what I'm trying to get. *Information.*"

"An announcement concerning the woman's identity should be forthcoming later today." The officer moved on to warn a woman not to push against the crime-scene tape.

Nick watched for a few minutes, his frustration expanding. He could see several shadowy figures moving around inside the store. Once an officer came out and spoke over a police-car radio. It squawked something unintelligible back to him.

He looked around the milling crowd. Surely, even if official information wasn't being released, the locals knew something. He picked out a middle-aged woman wearing a crocheted lavender hat.

"What's going on? I heard someone was shot in a robbery here Friday night."

"Helen Maxwell. Sweetest old soul you'd ever want to meet. Lost her husband years ago, wouldn't harm a fly. Can you believe it? Punk kids these days'll shoot you for a quarter or a pack of cigarettes. Playin' those crazy video games, gettin' all hopped up on drugs—"

"What about the girl?" Nick interrupted. "The girl who was in the car the killer stole?"

"Wouldn't you think they'd be out looking for her instead of messing around in there?" The woman shook her head in disgust. "Look at 'em, milling around like a bunch of sheep. They'd better get ol' Ben Mosely back if they want to find out who done this."

Nick turned away impatiently. *I should have been in Julesburg hours ago. Yesterday!*

The truth rammed him like a fist to the midsection. He should never have let Sarah and Julie leave Eugene alone on Friday night.

8

"I've already told you everything I know!"

Told them once when the county sheriff's department deputies responded to her 911 call from the phone in the apartment over the Calico Pantry. Told them again yesterday when she'd sat in this same chair in the Julesburg police department's office and desperately scoured her memory for any scrap of information. Told them again today, until the words felt as if they had seared a brand inside her brain.

Sarah stared at the detective, angry words on the tip of her tongue. *Why aren't you out there searching for Julie instead of chasing around in circles with these questions? Why are you here, wasting time, risking precious minutes of Julie's life!*

The momentary flare of anger and frustration wilted, and Sarah's weary body sagged in the straight-backed chair. They were doing their best with what little information she could provide. None of this was their fault.

No. It's mine. My fault Julie is missing, my fault Julie is in the hands of a ruthless murderer. My fault, my fault, my fault.

Sarah put her hands over her ears, trying to shut out the words. But there was no stopping them, because they were inside her head and they were true.

If only she hadn't left the keys in the ignition, hadn't dashed into the store with the engine running. Everyone knew you should never do that. Never, no matter what the circumstances. It was an open invitation to any opportunistic criminal, a tempting enticement to any kid looking for an easy joyride.

Sarah's head throbbed, and she closed her eyes as fear and guilt and sleeplessness circled her like a vulture waiting to rip away her few remaining shreds of control. The questions and her useless answers shrieked in her head.

No, I don't know what the gunman weighed! She couldn't even guess. He was completely covered by that yellow slicker.

No, I have no idea how old he was. She could see nothing beyond his disguise, and his voice had told her nothing, except that he was ready to kill. Seventeen or seventy, she had no idea.

No, I don't know if he was white or black . . . or purple or green! All she'd seen was that psychedelic face and those eyes like shattered golden glass. It had taken her several moments just to realize the thing behind the yellow slicker and rainhat *was* a man, a man in a ski mask, not the alien demon her eyes and terrified mind told her it was.

She desperately wanted to give the police answers, but she couldn't. All she could think of was that chilling condemnation. *My fault this happened. If only I hadn't let the disguise distract me, if only I'd concentrated on observing some helpful detail . . .*

"C'mon, let's give her a break. She's had enough."

Sarah opened her eyes gratefully. The voice did not belong to the one questioning her. Julesburg's police chief, Randy Wilson, handed her a glass of water.

"Thank you," she whispered. She desperately wanted to gulp the water and wash away the bitter taste in her mouth, but her throat was too thick and tight to allow more than one small swallow.

Randy touched her shoulder lightly. "I know it's rough, but sometimes only by going over and over a situation will a detail surface that can be helpful."

Julesburg's police chief gave the detective from the county sheriff's department a meaningful glance, and the man crossed to a coffeemaker in the corner of the room. The detective did not appreciate the interruption, Sarah suspected. He'd have preferred to keep hammering at her.

"I don't really know Julie," Randy Wilson said, "but I joke around with her over at Website X once in a while when I'm checking it out. We have a few young trouble-makers around town that I keep an eye on. Julie always seems so cheerful and friendly, the kind of person who lights up a day."

Sarah's throat closed again, and it was a moment before she could speak. "I want to help in any way I can. My sister means so . . . so much to me." The words seemed weak and ineffectual, a universe short of the love she felt for Julie. She swallowed. "But I don't know anymore. Just find Julie, please?" She lifted her gaze, begging him with her eyes.

"A description of your SUV is spread all over the state by now, all over the country, for that matter. We'll get this guy." Randy patted her shoulder.

But will they get him in time, before—

Sarah shivered and wouldn't let herself finish the thought.

"How much gas was in the tank?" Randy asked.

It was a question the detective hadn't asked, an eminently sensible question. Sarah felt an uptick of excitement. So far the county sheriff's office had crowded Julesburg's one police officer out of the investigation, and he was perhaps sharper than any of them. And this was one question to which she knew the answer.

"The tank was about half full, and it holds thirty gallons. I usually get about fifteen miles to the gallon, seventeen on the highway if I'm really lucky." She felt irrelevantly apologetic about the low gas mileage. "It's kind of a gas guzzler, but it's so big and tough, and I always felt safe in it—"

She broke off. Julie hadn't been safe in the big SUV.

But Randy Wilson nodded approvingly at Sarah's information about the Expedition's gas mileage. He did a quick mental calculation based on her figures. "He'd have to stop for gas within no more than 250 miles then, or he'd be stranded by the side of the road with an empty gas tank."

The detective returned, Styrofoam cup of coffee in hand. "There's no way we can contact every gas station within 250 miles of Julesburg in any direction." His superior manner belittled Randy Wilson's question about the gas. "But if he's out there, the police somewhere will spot him."

"He could be headed out of the country by now," Randy argued. "Where he won't be spotted."

Sarah remembered Julie mentioning how Randy Wilson had singlehandedly cleaned out a teen gang that had tried to get a foothold in Julesburg. Something popped into her head. "About the gunman's age . . ." She addressed Randy, ignoring the detective. "I can't be specific, but now that I think about it, I'd say he was definitely younger rather than older. There was a certain quickness and agility about his movements and in the way he bent over to pick up the rainhat when it fell off."

"A kid? Teenager?" the detective asked.

What do you want, a birth date? "I don't know. Just younger rather than older."

Randy patted her shoulder again. "Good. That may be very helpful."

"Look, may I please go now? If I think of anything, anything at all, I'll get in touch with you."

She addressed the question to Randy, but it was the detective who grudgingly nodded agreement. "But don't leave town," he warned.

She found the order insulting and didn't bother to conceal her scorn. She lifted her chin and looked him in the eye. "With my sister missing—and apparently no one out looking for her—I have no intention of leaving town."

Randy Wilson handed her her jacket from a hook by the door. "I'll take you home."

"No, thanks anyway. I'll be fine."

"You're sure?"

"Maybe the air will help clear my head."

Outside, a brisk wind rattled a soft-drink can across the gravel parking lot. She was surprised to see the sun shining so brilliantly, as if the wind had polished it to a hard glitter. She felt as if she had been trapped in that hard chair for so long that darkness should surely have fallen.

Nick spotted Sarah just before he reached the door to the police department. She was standing at the far end of the building, wind whipping her hair to a dark froth. She looked lost and bewildered.

"Sarah!" he yelled.

He didn't wait for an answer; he ran to her and wrapped his arms around her. She sagged against him and her arms fell limp against her sides.

I'm so glad you're safe, Sarah, that you weren't—

A tide of guilt broke the thought. Because even if Sarah was safe, it meant Julie was missing.

He held Sarah's head against his chest, his chin tucked protectively against the top. Her shoulders shook with sudden sobs, as if she'd been holding them back and now let them burst through the dam of control. He let her cry, knowing there was nothing he could say that would make anything better. He smoothed her hair with one hand and turned to let his body shield her from the cutting wind.

Oh, Lord, bring Julie back safely, please! "Do they know anything more about Julie?"

"No. Nothing." His heavy jacket muffled her voice. "I—I guess someone must be out looking for her. But they just keep questioning me, going round and round, asking the same questions in different ways, like sticking knives in me from ten different directions."

Nick frowned over the top of her head. Weren't the police acting rather harshly to someone who was just a witness, someone desperately worried about her sister and close to breaking under the strain?

"Where is she, Nick?" Sarah asked in a whisper. "What is he doing with her?"

Nick didn't answer, but instead prayed silently again. *Lord, please, please, bring Julie back. Bring her back safely!*

Finally Sarah leaned back in his arms and looked up at him, her eyes still filled with tears, her face streaked and blotchy. "What are you doing here?"

"I heard about it on the radio. Sarah, I'd have been here earlier, but I didn't know! I'm so sorry. I went to the Calico Pantry, and I couldn't find out anything there, and I thought maybe someone here at the police department would tell me something—"

"They don't tell *me* anything! And I keep seeing that poor old woman crumpling and then lying dead on the floor. And Julie—" Her words broke on another sob. "She was just . . . lying there asleep in the backseat the last time I saw her. All tangled up in a blanket, like an innocent baby. And I went off and left her there with the engine running! How could I? Oh, Nick, how could I?"

Once more, Nick could only hold her, her terrible pain cutting deep into his own heart and soul. *Comfort her, Lord. Guide me in how to help her.*

She suddenly reared back in his arms and pounded his chest with her fist, anger now breaking through the fear and grief and guilt. "Why doesn't he just let her go? He can have the SUV! Who cares? He doesn't have to hold her prisoner!"

Her head touched his chest again, burrowing now more than sagging, as if she were desperately trying to hide from a truth that loomed larger with every passing minute. Maybe the killer wasn't holding Julie prisoner anymore.

"C'mon," Nick said roughly. "I'll take you home."

Sarah let him guide her a few steps toward his pickup, then stopped abruptly. "Oh no! I haven't fed the cats."

"Cats?"

"The homeless cats down on the jetty. Julie always feeds them. And I've forgotten to!"

"Sure," he soothed. "We'll feed the cats later—"

"No. We have to do it now. Julie went every day, even when it was storming. And they haven't been fed since she did it Friday morning."

Nick didn't argue with her, maybe because he thought doing something constructive would slow the path of destruction that the guilt and fear were ripping through her.

"The sack of cat food is in Julie's car." Sarah hesitated a moment. "And the car's back at the apartment. I . . . forgot for a minute, but they brought me here in a police car."

In the apartment parking lot, Nick transferred the oversized sack of cat food from Julie's old Honda to his pickup. He knew the way down the steep hill to the dock and jetty, but Sarah had to point out to him where the cats lived among the holes and crevices in the jumbled rocks that stuck out into the sea to protect Julesburg's small bay.

The tide was in, and a brisk wind spewed a salty sea-spray over the rock jetty. A rough, knee-high shelter of wood and tin protected a food trough from the weather and spray, and small bowls were tucked into various crevices in the rocks. All were empty, and he shook cat food into them from the bag while Sarah called softly, "Here, kitty, kitty. C'mon, cats, food's here."

A calico female came immediately, and others followed, tails high, meows eager. Others, more cautious, peeked heads out only when Sarah and Nick retreated to the cab of the pickup. Seagulls came too, squawking and swooping, arguing with the cats, stealing bites and retreating. It made for a noisy free-for-all that under different circumstances Nick might have found comical.

"So people just dump them here? Can't someone find homes for them?" He'd always preferred dogs to cats, but it dismayed him to see all the homeless creatures living among the cold, inhospitable rocks. He counted at least eighteen cats.

"Julie finds homes for them whenever she can, mostly the ones recently dumped and desperately looking for affection. But some, she says, are truly wild now, feral, and won't make house pets. She pets and snuggles them if they'll let her, just feeds them if they won't."

"We'll make sure they're fed until . . . she's back."

"Julie doesn't deserve any of this! And that poor old woman. . . . She was a cranky old grouch, but no one deserves being shot in cold blood like she was." Sarah leaned her head back against the seat and closed her eyes, her knuckles turning bloodless as she clenched her hands in her lap. "All she was going to do was pick up some of the bills she dropped out of the cash register . . . and he killed her!"

"Sarah, you don't have to tell me." *I want to know what happened, yes. But not at the expense of causing you more pain.* "I know how hard the questioning has been for you."

She was silent for a long moment, her eyes open again, staring out over the jetty. A wave broke over the far tip, sending a cascade of ragged whitewater down the rocky sides.

"It's different talking to you. I want to tell you. Maybe you can help me make sense of it."

She told him about driving home, about Julie sleeping in back. The storm, deciding to stop at the Calico Pantry for milk. Seeing the person in the slicker come in, not being alarmed until she saw the mask beneath the rainhat. The instructions for her to put her hands on the counter, a command to the old woman to open the cash register, the explosion of the gun.

Sarah covered her ears, as if the blast still echoed in her head. Nick reached across the seat and sheltered her in his arms again.

"And then he smashed the glass cabinet on the counter and grabbed a carton of cigarettes. Can you believe it? He's just murdered a woman . . . she's lying there dead on the floor. And he's thinking about cigarettes!" The incredulity in her voice teetered on the edge of hysteria. She swallowed convulsively. "And then he backed out the door and jumped in my SUV and roared off. With Julie."

And no one had seen him or the vehicle or Julie since. Did that mean Sarah's SUV was far away by now, maybe even in Canada or Mexico? With Julie still in it? Or was it wrecked in some wild joyride closer to home? Or perhaps already stripped and cut up in some professional chop shop? And Julie . . .

"If only I hadn't left the engine running! How could I have been so stupid?" She pounded her fist, unaware she was hammering his wrist. "If only—"

"Sarah, Sarah!" Nick shook her lightly, then put his finger under her jaw and forced her to look at him. "It isn't your fault the killer took the car. Even if you'd locked it up tight, if he wanted it, he'd simply have demanded the keys from you."

"Maybe he'd never even have thought about stealing the car until he saw that the engine was running, just waiting for him to jump in and take off! Maybe if he'd had to demand the keys, I could have bargained to get Julie out before he took it!"

"No one knows what's in a killer's mind but the killer himself. Don't do this to yourself, Sarah." Grimly, he added, "If you want to talk about guilt, there's plenty to go around. I should never have let you and Julie drive home Friday night. I should have insisted you stay there in Eugene."

A trace of a smile glimmered through the tears. "Do you really think two stubborn, independent women would have done something just because you insisted?"

Maybe not. But the weight of failed responsibility still throbbed like a raw wound. *All I'm doing now is sitting here by a jetty, feeding cats. Helpless . . .*

No. Never truly helpless.

"Will you pray with me, Sarah?"

"Will it help?"

He could hear both hope and doubt in her voice, and he hesitated. He wished he could guarantee success. *Yes, you put in your prayer, like a coin in a coffee machine, and out comes a hot answer. We'll pray, and Julie will be back at the apartment when we get there.* But God and prayer didn't work that way. Sometimes there seemed to be no answer at all, nothing but agonizing silence. Yet he could give her one powerful guarantee.

"God is always there to lean on, Sarah. He always listens and hears our prayers."

She hesitated but finally nodded, and he offered a prayer that the Lord would keep Julie safe, give her strength and courage, guide the authorities looking for her, and bring her home soon. Sarah didn't stir until he leaned over and kissed her gently on the temple.

"C'mon. We'll fill the cat dishes again, and then we'll go get some food in you."

He poured more cat food into the dishes, and Sarah cuddled the purring calico. Neither one of them noticed anyone approaching until a voice said, "You must be Julie's twin sister."

9

Sarah turned as the wiry, gray-haired woman approached. The woman reached out a hand that matched her lined face and scratched the cat in Sarah's arms.

"That's Clarissa. Isn't she a sweetie? She's always the first to run out to meet you."

"You're a friend of Julie's?" Sarah asked.

"Twila Mosely. Julie and I run into each other now and then when we're feeding the cats. I keep a bag of dry cat food in our boat so I don't have to haul it around." Twila gestured in the direction of the double lineup of boats and trailers on the wooden dock, everything from forty-foot commercial fishing boats to small pleasure craft. In Julesburg, because of the openness of the bay, boats were not moored to a floating dock at water level; a huge crane lifted them in and out of the water from this dock set on high wooden pilings. "But I don't get down here as regularly as Julie does," Twila added.

"I thought she'd want me to be sure they were fed."

"I'm sure she would. She's a wonderful girl. Myrna is always telling me about something Julie's done for her."

"Myrna?"

"Myrna Bettenworth. Myrna can't see much now, and Julie reads her letters and books from the library. Sometimes the Bible too, but only when Myrna wheedles." Twila smiled and picked up a longhaired black cat to cuddle. The smile lines around her mouth were well used, but there was an air of worry or sadness about the small woman. "Myrna says Julie complains that she likes books with happy endings and the Bible doesn't have any."

Julie had mentioned running errands for "little old ladies" around Julesburg, so it wasn't surprising for Sarah to hear that she read to them too.

"It came as a surprise to everyone that Julie has a twin. It's good that you're here."

But if I weren't here, if I hadn't rejected Nick's suggestion to stay at his mother's, if I hadn't left the engine running . . .

Sarah struggled with the fresh tide of guilt that threatened to suck her under but managed to slip a hand out from under the calico cat. "I'm Sarah MacIntosh." They shook hands, and Sarah tipped her head toward Nick. "This is a friend, Nick Nordahl."

"I can't begin to tell you how shaken we all are by this." Twila hunched her back to the wind to protect her cat. "It just doesn't seem possible it could happen here. Helen Maxwell, and Julie too."

Sarah resisted an urge to yell at Twila. *Don't lump Julie with Helen Maxwell! Julie isn't dead! Julie is coming home, and we're going to buy the Nevermore and—*

The Nevermore. She hadn't even thought about the old theater since Friday night.

The calico cat suddenly hissed. She leaped from Sarah's arms and scatted for the nearest hole in the rocks. Sarah peered down at the scratch left across the back of her hand.

Nick grabbed her fingers and looked at the drops of blood oozing to the surface. Sarah remembered the bloody body of Helen Maxwell and felt a storm of protest in her stomach.

"We'd better get something on that right away. Cat scratches infect easily," Nick said.

"It was my fault." Sarah tried to control the tremor in her voice. She knew what must have happened. She'd thought about Julie, and evil reaching out from the Nevermore, and her hands had clamped like pincers around the poor cat. "I—I held her too tight and frightened her."

"Yes, these cats can be quite skittish," Twila said. "By the way, Sarah, I tried to call you at the apartment earlier, but there wasn't any answer."

"Oh?" Sarah murmured without any curiosity as to why Twila had tried to call her. The woman was sweet and friendly, but Sarah wished she would leave.

"We're having a special prayer meeting for Julie at church tonight. I called to invite you to come. About seven, if you can make it."

Sarah glanced at Nick. Prayer meeting? She had a vision of people speaking in garbled tongues, fanatics beseeching mercy from a God with whom she was not even on conversational terms.

Nick put a steadying arm around Sarah's shoulders. "We'll see how things go this evening," he said to Twila. "We appreciate your concern for Julie. We've been praying too."

They drove to the apartment, and Nick insisted on disinfecting the scratch and doctoring it with antibiotic cream and a Band-Aid. But he didn't push Sarah about going to the prayer meeting, and she was grateful. At the moment, gathering with a flock of strangers in some mysterious ceremony was the last thing she wanted. She only wanted Julie, home safe again.

Nick kept up a running commentary about his own childhood wounds as he worked on her hand. He even managed to make her smile once when he told her about his and his brother's first building project, a well-below-code treehouse, and its subsequent collapse. He then made tea, toast, and scrambled eggs, rightly guessing that she hadn't eaten all day.

A gold-star guy, Sarah thought as she watched him refill her cup. One who warmed her heart even if, under the circumstances, it wasn't up to a flutter of feminine excitement. She checked the TV guide to see when the local news came on, hoping there might be something encouraging, but the news wasn't scheduled for another half hour. She suddenly realized how long Nick had been with her, how much time he had given to prop up her shattered emotions.

She stuck out her hand. "Thanks, Nick, for everything you've done. I really appreciate it. I know you need to get back to Dutton Bay, and I think I'll just catch a quick shower before the news comes on."

He raised an eyebrow at the outstretched hand. "You're telling me I'm dismissed?"

She let the hand drop, embarrassed that she'd made it sound as if she were rushing him out. "No, I didn't mean that. I'm so very grateful you came. But I know you have things to do. Your pickup is loaded with materials for your building site—"

"That can wait."

"I can't do anything more about plans for remodeling on the Nevermore now," she added. "But I can contact you later—"

"You think the reason I'm staying around is to keep my foot in the door for a business deal?"

"No— I just mean I don't want you to feel obligated. You barely know either of us."

"Actually, I've been thinking I'd run over to the church for the prayer meeting for Julie."

"That's very nice of you, but—"

"Prayer is powerful, Sarah. God tells us that where two or three come together in his name, he will be there among them."

Sarah hesitated. She hadn't much faith in prayer, solo or en masse, but she did appreciate the concern Twila Mosely, the church people, and Nick were showing for Julie. Finally she nodded. "I'll go along, then. I suppose it can't hurt."

They sat on the sofa to wait for the news, but it was not a restful half hour. Two reporters called. "No," Sarah told both of them, "I have no statement, except I hope everyone keeps looking for Julie." The elderly woman Twila had mentioned, Myrna Bettenworth, plus two other people with unfamiliar names, called to express concern and hope for Julie. Briefly Sarah wondered why she hadn't heard from Donovan Moran yet. It was possible, though, that he didn't know about Julie, since he lived in Gold Beach. Gossip had spread Julie's identity in Julesburg, but her name hadn't been officially released.

A fresh-faced blond anchorwoman from the Eugene TV station came on, but there was a frustrating five minutes of other local news before she got to the Julesburg crime. The anchorwoman identified Julie by name now, and a copy of the photo Sarah had given the police flashed on the screen. The anchorwoman repeated the details of the crime, along with the description of the gunman and Sarah's Ford Expedition.

"Not that the description of the gunman does any good. It could have been anyone under that ski mask. Sometimes, when they were questioning me, it almost felt as if . . ." Sarah hesitated, not quite able to identify the peculiar uneasiness she'd felt as they hammered her with questions.

"Yes?"

"They kept going over and over the same things. Almost as if they were trying to . . . trip me up or something."

"It's probably just a standard questioning technique."

"That's what the local police chief, Randy Wilson, said. They might still be questioning me," she added, "if he hadn't told them I needed a break."

Can there be something to Sarah's uneasy feelings about the questioning? Nick wondered as they drove to the church a few minutes later. The thought apparently hadn't occurred to Sarah yet, but he was almost certain the authorities were suspicious of her.

Reluctantly, Nick studied the situation through suspicious police eyes. Two young women, unlikely as it seems, decide to pull an easy convenience store robbery. Something goes wrong. The proprietor is shot. The sister with the gun runs to the car in panic. The other sister, left behind, makes up a wild story about a man in a demon mask with strange alien eyes.

Surely the authorities aren't concentrating on something as preposterous as that wild scenario rather than putting every ounce of effort into chasing down the real killer! I think I'll have to talk to the police myself.

Twila Mosely greeted them at the door of the small church. Perhaps two dozen people already filled the pews up front. Two candles burned on a wooden table below the pulpit.

"We'll be offering prayer for my granddaughter as well as for Julie." Twila's voice wasn't apologetic, but it did end on a questioning uptilt. She touched Sarah's arm lightly. "I hope you don't mind?"

"No, of course not."

Nick could feel the cold prickle of nerves on Sarah's skin. He was already holding her hand—it had seemed the natural thing to do when they entered the church—and he gave it a reassuring squeeze.

"Everything will be fine," he whispered. "You don't have to do anything."

By the time the pastor, who came over and introduced himself as Mike Gordon, offered the first prayer, over forty people had gathered to join in this plea for Julie's safe return. If they had been at the large church over in Eugene, the number wouldn't have surprised Nick, but here in tiny Julesburg it was an impressive demonstration of how deeply people cared about one of their own.

A short silence followed the pastor's prayer, and then people scattered throughout the pews began offering their own appeals for Julie. Some apparently knew her; some didn't. Nick offered his own prayer, while Sarah's hand clutched his like a vise.

Yet as the evening continued, he felt her slowly relax. The tremor left her hand, and her skin warmed to a normal temperature. He didn't know if she offered her own prayers or not, but her eyes were closed, and he thought perhaps she was trying.

From some other prayers, Nick gathered that Twila Mosely's granddaughter was seriously ill with cystic fibrosis and was currently awaiting a liver and lung transplant that could save her life. He offered a prayer for her too.

Afterward as they were making their way toward the door, Twila approached them again. "Julie is already on our prayer chain, of course. And will be until she's safely home."

Sarah shot Nick a quick glance. *Prayer chain?* her eyes seemed to ask. He gave her hand a squeeze, and she murmured, "Thank you," to Twila.

"And I also wanted to tell you— you know my husband, Ben, was the police chief here, before he retired and Randy took over last year?"

Sarah hesitated. "I'm sorry, no . . ."

"Ben was police chief here for years. And a top-notch one too." Twila nodded vigorously to emphasize her words. "Now Randy has asked him to come back to work temporarily, until all this is taken care of."

"I'm pleased to hear that," Sarah said. "Although it looks as if the county sheriff's office is running the investigation."

Twila frowned. "Well, as you know, with Julesburg having only a one-man police department, any after-hours calls to 911 or the police get routed to the county sheriff's office. But they're shorthanded because of budget cuts, and with Ben on the job here, they'll probably be glad to let him handle things. I don't mean to suggest the deputies from the sheriff's office aren't competent or dedicated, but they don't have the heart for something that happens right here in Julesburg like Randy and my Ben do."

Nick felt something awaken in Sarah, a quickening, as if perhaps hope was stirring to life.

"And they make a wonderful team," Twila went on. "Randy has big ambitions. He's not going to let something like Helen Maxwell's murder and Julie's disappearance go unsolved in his town and mar his record. No way! Ben's more dogged, nothing showy, the kind who just keeps plugging along. But with Randy's ambition and Ben's persistence, they'll handle this."

Nick glanced around the slowly thinning crowd. "Is Ben here tonight? I'd like to talk to him."

"Ben's down at the office with Randy. I get him to come to church with me once in a while. But it's been like trying to get a little boy out of playing in a mudhole to pull him away from those Sunday football games lately." Twila smiled ruefully. To Sarah she added, "But he'd have been here tonight, if it weren't that he's busy down at the office."

Again Nick felt that hope, almost like an electric current, pumping through Sarah. It crossed to his hand in a hot rush of energy.

"I'm so glad your husband is involved. And I appreciate all the prayers. I don't really know how to thank everyone—"

"You just keep praying. We're all in this together. And you might remember my granddaughter too, if you would."

Sarah hesitated, as if she didn't quite know what to do with the request, then nodded. "Her name is Sharilyn?"

"Yes. She's twenty-two. Our only granddaughter."

"We'll remember her," Nick assured Twila.

Outside, as he let the cold pickup warm for a minute, Nick glanced across at Sarah. "So, what do you think?"

"I was afraid it would be strange or weird, and it wasn't," she admitted. "It was a nice feeling, actually, being with so many people who really seem to care about Julie."

"They do care. That's what a prayer chain is also about." He explained how it worked, the name of a person in need being shared among all those on the chain, so all could target that person in prayer.

"It also makes me feel, with all those people believing and talking to him, that maybe God really is up there somewhere, listening." She didn't sound convinced. But hopeful.

"He is there, Sarah. He's right here, in fact. Open your heart to him. He can see us through the worst storms of life."

She gave him a smile in the dimness of the pickup cab. "I think maybe I have more faith in Ben Mosely and Randy Wilson than in a God I can't see."

"As the old saying goes, 'God works in mysterious ways.'" Nick smiled. "Maybe Ben Mosely rejoining the local police force is God's first move in his answer to our prayers."

Sarah lifted her surprised gaze to his, and Nick knew that had given her something unexpected to think about.

10

As they drove back to the apartment, Sarah intended to thank Nick again and send him on his way. It was almost 9:00, on a blustery night, with the threat of another storm closing in. Yet dreading the empty apartment, she found herself saying, "Would you like to come up for coffee?"

"I was hoping you'd ask."

They were barely inside the door when the phone rang. Sarah looked at it with dread. *Do I have to answer that?* She appreciated all the expressions of concern, but she wasn't certain she could handle another well-wisher. Or nosy reporter.

Nick touched her elbow lightly. "Want me to get it? What if—"

"Julie!" Jacket half on, half off, Sarah stumbled across the room. *The gunman might have dumped Julie somewhere, and the first thing she'd do was call home! Why didn't I think of this before? I should have been here . . .*

She snatched up the jangling phone, her arm still tangled in the jacket. "Yes?"

Nothing. In the moment of suspended silence, she had the eerie feeling the killer was there on the other end of the line. She fought a surge of panic. "Hello? Is someone there?"

Then fear and hope turned her voice uncharacteristically shrill. "Julie, is that you? Are you there? Can you talk?"

"No, I'm sorry—this is Donovan Moran. You're Julie's sister?"

Sarah's emotions teetered between relief that it wasn't a call from the gunman and savage disappointment that it wasn't Julie. "Yes, this is Sarah."

"I guess you know who I am?"

"Julie has mentioned you."

"You sound so much like her that it shook me there for a minute. I saw the news on TV yesterday about the shooting at the Calico Pantry, but it wasn't Julie's car they were talking about being stolen, so it never occurred to me she could be involved. Until they gave her name a couple hours ago—"

"It was my car."

"And this guy just drove off with Julie in it?"

"Yes. She was asleep in the backseat."

"Did he take her deliberately? A kidnapping?"

"I don't know." She hesitated. "No, I don't think he knew she was there."

"And no one's heard anything from the killer or Julie? No one's reported seeing the SUV?"

"No. Nothing."

"So you don't know anything?"

The words were not an open accusation, but an edge in the question insinuated she was at fault for not knowing *something.* Guilt, like a sneaker wave hitting her from behind, rolled over her again. *Yes, I should know something!*

"I'm sorry," Donovan muttered. "I didn't mean to jump at you. I'm just . . . shook up, I guess."

"We all are. But at this point, apparently only the killer knows what's going on. Actually, when the phone rang, I was hoping it was Julie calling. That he'd released her."

A silence suggested he saw that as a frail hope, but he finally muttered, "I suppose that's a possibility."

She didn't know why, but an unplanned question popped out. "Do you know anyone who could do something like this?"

Another silence, this one more taut.

"These little towns like Julesburg aren't as Norman Rockwellish as they look on the surface," he finally said. "Look, I'll let you go. I don't want to tie up the phone if Julie should try to call. But I want you to let me know if you hear anything, any time of the day or night, okay?" He gave her a couple of phone numbers.

"And if you hear anything, you call me," Sarah said. There was no reason why he should hear anything before she did, and her demand came out fierce with distrust. But she offered no apology. Even if he was "shook up" about Julie, she did not trust him. He hadn't given a straightforward answer to her question about a possible suspect.

Nick was watching her as she put down the phone. Briefly, she explained Donovan Moran and the phone call. "Let's see, we were going to have coffee, weren't we?" she added vaguely.

"I think it would be better if you just went to bed. You look beat."

"Actually, I think I'll camp out here on the sofa for the night. There isn't a phone in the bedroom, and if Julie should try to call . . ."

Julie isn't going to call.

Nick didn't let the thought that flared like a banner across his mind turn into spoken words. He didn't even let himself acknowledge the thought after its first crash through his mind. Forty-some people had concentrated their prayers on Julie tonight. Maybe she would call.

They decided to skip the coffee, but Nick made an offer he knew would be rejected. "I could stay and listen for the phone while you get some real sleep in the bedroom."

"Thanks, but I doubt I'll be getting much sleep anyway."

Sarah got a blanket and spread it on the sofa by the phone. He wanted to tuck it around her shoulders before he left, but he settled for fluffing the pillow and giving her shoulder a squeeze.

After Nick left Sarah's apartment, he headed for the police department. He doubted he'd find anyone there at this hour, but fluorescent lights lit the windows with an impersonal glare when he pulled into the parking lot.

Inside the cluttered office a wiry-built officer in a brown uniform with a gunbelt hanging around his hips was talking on the phone. The officer was around Nick's age, his angular face smooth shaven, his gestures quick and impatient as he talked. "Then let's get on it," he said into the phone.

A white-haired man in khaki pants and shirt, beefy but not belly-heavy, leaned over a fax machine. A frosting of gray whiskers covered his jaw.

Nick dredged up their names from his conversation with Twila Mosely. Randy Wilson and Ben Mosely. The Julesburg police force.

He introduced himself as a friend of Sarah and Julie's. "Any news?"

Randy put down the phone and answered the question. "A few sightings of dark-red Ford Expeditions around the country, wrong license numbers. But vehicles that match the description can't be stopped and searched simply because they do match, even though the license plates could have been changed." He looked at the fax sheet Ben handed him and snapped the page with a forefinger. "Sometimes makes a cop wish his hands weren't so tied with rules and regulations."

"Is the FBI in on this?" asked Nick.

"We've been in touch with the FBI office in Eugene," Ben Mosely said.

"But they're not involved at this point?"

"No."

Nick studied Ben for a moment. *Coming back to work on this case was a heroic thing for him to do.* He did not look in good health. Pouches hung below his eyes, and haggard lines around his mouth sagged into loose jowls. No gunbelt draped his hips, but there was an air of experience about him that Nick found encouraging. Randy Wilson struck him as determined and energetic, but also brash and impulsive. Perhaps, as Twila Mosely had said, they made a good team. But Nick still wanted to get one point straight.

"Is the FBI holding off because the local authorities suspect Sarah and Julie might be participants rather than victims in this crime?"

Randy and Ben exchanged glances.

"The county sheriff's office has kept that option open," Randy answered, sounding determinedly neutral, as if he felt obliged to defend the county law enforcement officers. "I believe they're taking into consideration the fact that these two women were involved in some expensive negotiations buying and renovating the Nevermore Theater."

Nick clenched his fists. "There wasn't enough money in that little convenience store to fix the popcorn machine at the Nevermore!"

Randy held up a hand, palm open. "Ben and I know that. And believe me, we aren't suspicious of them. Neither of us knows Sarah MacIntosh, but we're both acquainted with Julie and what a good, decent person she is."

"Then let's get the FBI and some heavy manpower on it! Isn't this some sort of kidnapping? And if Julie's been taken across state lines—"

"At this point no one has any idea where either the vehicle or Julie may be. The FBI isn't quick to jump into local crimes, but they'll come in if the situation warrants it."

It sounded to Nick as if Randy Wilson was trying to soothe him. Nick grabbed hold of his emotions; acting like a hothead was not the way to get action. He took a breath and forced reasonableness into his voice.

"I know you guys are doing your best, but if Sarah's SUV and Julie are already half a dozen states away—look, would it do any good if Sarah and I contacted the FBI?"

Ben tilted his head. Nick couldn't tell if he was considering the question or assessing Nick's hotheadedness. "Hard to say."

With a hint of resentment in his voice, Randy added, "The FBI sometimes tends to look on small town law enforcement officials as clowns in cop suits."

"Could you give me a name and phone number? I can call them. Or better yet, I can go to the office in person. My home is over in Eugene." Nick fished a business card out of his wallet and handed it to Ben.

Ben fingered the card with thick fingers. "You're an old friend of Julie and her sister?"

"No. We met just a few days ago. I was planning to make a bid on remodeling the old theater. But I . . ." Nick hesitated with the explanation of his involvement, momentarily distracted by the depth of his feelings. What he felt for Sarah seemed out of proportion with the brief length of time he had known her, and he was not a man to jump into relationships impulsively. Yet the feelings were there, deep and primal. They also were none of the police department's business. "I simply want to help any way I can."

"It may look like we're just sitting around, twiddling our thumbs, but we're not," Randy assured him. "Paperwork may not look exciting, but it's often more effective than chasing around the countryside like some Wild West posse."

Nick managed a smile. "I'm sorry if it sounded as if I were implying that you weren't doing anything." To Ben he added, "Sarah and I just came from the prayer meeting at church. We heard about your granddaughter. She'll be in my prayers."

Ben jerked his head up, looking startled. "Thank you."

Back in the apartment, Sarah sat by the phone, willing it to ring.

God, help her escape. Bring her to a phone so she can call me. Please. Make the killer let her go.

In surprise, she realized she'd just offered a prayer of sorts. She hadn't prayed at the church. She'd kept her head bowed, but she'd felt too much like an outsider, an onlooker more than a participant. Cautiously, she now considered the words she had impulsively directed to what some part of her mind thought of as "Nick's God." Did God listen to someone who had never made any profession of faith or commitment to him? Was it true, as Nick had suggested, that Ben Mosely's entry into the situation was already God's first step in answer to the prayers of many?

Awkwardly, she added a few more words. *Thank you for bringing Ben into this. I hope you'll guide Ben and Randy in finding Julie. Finding her alive and safe, God, please! And thank you for Nick too.*

She didn't feel serene or at peace after the clumsy prayer, but she did feel . . . less frantic. And not as if she were simply flinging words into empty space.

Even more awkwardly, she added a few words about Twila's granddaughter. *And I hope you'll make Sharilyn well. That she'll get the transplant she needs, and it will heal her.*

Sarah settled back on the sofa, drawing her feet up under the blanket. Outside, the wind had risen to a howl. She shivered. *Oh, Julie, are you out there somewhere? I hope you're praying too.*

Then another thought struck her as she stared at the silent phone.

A ransom.

The thought caught fire in her imagination. *Yes, that's why the killer hasn't released Julie.*

Sarah clenched her fists and closed her eyes, not in prayer but in a fierce plea to the gunman. *Do it. Demand a ransom! I have money! I can pay. I won't tell anyone. Call me!*

11

Nick forced himself to wait until 8:00 the next morning to call Sarah on his cell phone. He'd already called his mother and told her about Julie.

Sarah answered on the first ring. Her "Hello?" balanced on the jittery edge of hopeful.

"Hi, Sarah, it's me, Nick."

"Oh. Nick." He could tell she'd hoped this call was from Julie.

"Any news?"

"No." Wryly, she added, "Well, a call from someone trying to get me to change my long-distance telephone carrier."

That figured. The small annoyances of life went on, no matter what. "Have you had breakfast?"

"No, not yet." The vagueness of the response told him breakfast was not even on her morning agenda.

"I can bring something over—"

"You're here in Julesburg?"

"No, but it's only a half-hour drive."

She managed a laugh. "At what speed? No, Nick, you do not need to drive all the way over here to open a packet of instant oatmeal for me. But I appreciate the offer."

"Well, all right. But don't forget to eat that oatmeal," he said, then proceeded to tell her about his conversation with Randy Wilson and Ben Mosely the previous evening. "So I'll contact the Eugene office of the FBI later today."

"I appreciate that."

"And then I'll be at your place this evening. I know you want to stay by the phone, so I'll bring something for dinner." Then, wondering if he'd presumed too much, he retreated a step. "That is, unless . . ."

"Yes, please come. But don't bother to bring anything. The teen hangout, Website X, delivers pizza."

"Okay, I'll see you then. About 6:30."

Sarah wanted to get her mail, but she didn't want to leave the phone, and she couldn't do both; Julesburg had no home delivery service. All mail was sorted into rented boxes at the post office. She'd ask Nick to go to the post office when he arrived.

Nick's mother called a few minutes later, and her concern for Julie touched Sarah's heart. "Julie's already on our prayer chain here. And so are you," Mrs. Nordahl added.

After Sarah hung up the phone, she let her thoughts settle on Nick Nordahl. Under different circumstances she might have been quite smitten with him. Physically attractive, intelligent, responsible, dependable, caring, fun. And a Christian. Was that a credit or a debit in a man? She wasn't certain. It was not a point she'd considered before. Yet with Julie missing, all that seemed inconsequential.

The ringing phone broke into her thoughts. This time it was a glass company wanting to know if her windshield needed repair. She banged the phone down without responding. Next came a call from another reporter. She declined an interview. Then came a call from a teenage boy who said he knew Julie from Website X and expressed his awkward concern.

Sarah found a couple of packaged cake mixes in Julie's cupboard and opened the chocolate fudge. *Nick likes chocolate,* she thought, remembering the bag of Hershey's Kisses he'd shared with her and Julie. Baking a cake was a temporary diversion, and the scent filled the apartment with a homey fragrance that brought pleasant reminders of her mother's kitchen.

After she finished the cake, she called Twila Mosely about feeding the cats, then contacted the other construction companies with whom she'd discussed the Nevermore and told them the remodeling plans were temporarily on hold. She uneasily realized that she'd never told Julie's mother and father that Julie was missing. She dreaded talking to them. She'd overheard Julie try to call her father one time; Julie had been put on hold so long that she'd finally just given up. There was nothing the parents could do to help, so was there really any point in calling them?

I'll discuss it with Nick.

It was then that she realized, with a small sense of shock, just how closely her thoughts were wrapping around Nick. Wondering about his opinion on ransom possibilities. Needing him to go to the post office. Wanting to discuss Julie's parents with him. Making a chocolate cake because he liked chocolate.

And she couldn't deny feeling a sense of comfort and gladness when he arrived that evening and stood there filling the doorway of the apartment. She didn't even notice what he was wearing until he made a gesture of apology toward his work clothes and heavy boots.

"We were late finishing up today, and I was in a hurry to get here."

Sarah smiled. "I don't think there's a dress code for home-delivered pizza." She gestured to her own scruffy Reeboks, ancient leggings, and sweatshirt.

"I really think you should have a solid dinner. I can run down to the Julesburg Café—"

"I want pizza," she said, taking his hand and pulling him inside. "Smothered with cheese and pepperoni and other greasy stuff. Maybe it will make things seem more . . . normal."

Sarah looked up the number and dialed Website X. A candy-voiced girl said the pizza would be there in a half hour. When Sarah hung up the phone, she found Nick eyeing the cake on the kitchen counter.

"I'm starved," he announced.

"You can't eat dessert before dinner!"

"That's a Mother's Law that applies only to small boys. Besides, I missed lunch."

Sarah cut a generous slice and poured coffee. She was right. He definitely liked chocolate. Standing at the counter, he demolished the slice in a few bites.

"Great!"

"It's just a store-bought mix."

He grinned. "You mixed it well."

For just a few moments, the world seemed almost normal. Man, woman, a hint of flirty tease. Then they carried their coffee cups to the far end of the living room, and normal vanished. Sarah, sitting at one end of the sofa with a foot tucked under her, asked him about contacting the FBI. He shook his head in frustration.

"The woman I talked to assured me they were 'familiar with the case,' but I didn't get to talk directly to an agent. If I'd had information to give, I'd probably have gotten further. But since what I was doing was trying to prod them into entering the investigation, all I got was a runaround. I'm going to try again, in person."

"Thank you."

"I'd do a lot more, if I could just figure out what to do."

Sarah felt his frustration. It burned in her too. "I'm wondering if the gunman will ask for a ransom. I'm hoping he will."

"That possibility hadn't occurred to me." Nick set his cup on one of Julie's hand-painted wooden coasters on the coffee table. "But it would have to be an after-the-fact decision. He couldn't have planned a ransom scheme ahead of time, because he couldn't have known before he robbed the store that she was in the car . . . could he?"

"I don't think so. It was dark, and she was covered with a jacket and blanket. But it would be a wonderful opportunity for him! Grab the ransom money, ditch the SUV, flee the country."

He held up a hand. "You don't have to sell me on the idea that demanding ransom would be a great idea."

She acknowledged the truth of that with a rueful smile. "How about making a direct appeal to him? Money in exchange for Julie? Governments and big companies have done it with hostages."

Nick frowned, as if he doubted Sarah could scrounge up enough money to tempt the killer.

"I could come up with an amount large enough to interest him, I think. My parents left me fairly well off financially. My mother died of ovarian cancer about two and a half years ago. Dad had a heart attack a few months later." Sarah swallowed hard, the pain no longer fresh but still deep. "There was insurance. They weren't rich—Dad was an electrician—but they lived conservatively and invested well. There's the house. I can borrow on it—"

"Sarah, you don't have to explain your money situation to me."

"I just wanted you to know I can pay. We intend to use some of the money to buy and remodel the Nevermore, but it isn't solely my money we'll be using. Julie has money too. Didn't you wonder if we had the means to pay for the remodeling?"

"The thought did occur to me," he admitted.

"But without Julie, the Nevermore is . . ." She waved a hand in dismissal. "I'll gladly give the gunman every cent if it will bring her back safely."

"I doubt the authorities would approve of making a public financial appeal to the gunman. It's also possible an offer of money would simply bring every nut and con man in the country crawling out of the woodwork, which could simply confuse the investigation." He hesitated. "And sometimes a ransom is paid and . . . bad things happen anyway."

Sarah felt a flash of anger at Nick for bringing up such a possibility. She slumped back against the sofa cushion and ran a hand across her forehead, stress and frustration and worry settling into the beginnings of a headache. "I didn't have a chance to go to the post office today to pick up our mail. Could you do it?"

"Sure."

She gave him Julie's key ring and directions to the post office. Before he left, he made a suggestion.

"While I doubt offering the gunman money is the right thing to do, offering a reward for information leading to his capture might help. Silence may be golden, but someone close to the gunman might decide a nice bundle of money is more golden. It could offer a chance to get Julie back and capture the killer as well."

Sarah flung her arms around him, her headache forgotten. "Yes! Of course! I should have thought of that. It's a great idea."

He held the hug for a long moment, and when he released her, she felt a little embarrassed by her impulsive gesture.

"I'm sorry—"

"I'm not. First cake, and then a hug like that!" He smiled and swiped a hand across his forehead, pretending to wipe sweat away. "It's almost too much for one ol' country boy." He leaned forward, and for a moment she thought he was going to kiss her. It was in his eyes and in the tenderness on his face. But he just rubbed a rough finger across her jaw and tucked a curl behind her ear. "We'll check into how to offer a reward first thing tomorrow, okay?"

Sarah watched his pickup pull out of the parking lot, and a knock on the door came only a couple of minutes later.

"Pizza guy," a voice called. The detective's persistent questions about the gunman's age suddenly jumped into Sarah's mind. *Can I tell anything about age from this unseen voice? Young. Upper teens.*

Wrong. When she opened the door, the man who stood there with a flat, square box poised at shoulder level looked close to thirty. A leather thong gathered his blondish hair into a ponytail, and white embroidery scrolled the name "Steve" across the pocket of his red shirt. His face was narrow, with a straggly mustache that matched the thin-soup color of his hair.

"I thought you were younger," Sarah said, realizing even as she spoke how odd the comment must sound.

The man didn't seem to notice, however. "I'm Steve Lomax. I own Website X. Sometimes I make deliveries myself." He stared at her, and Sarah remembered that Julie occasionally worked at Website X.

"I'm Julie's twin sister, Sarah."

"Yeah, I heard she had a twin. I guess I just didn't expect you to look so much like her."

He handed her the box, as if he'd just remembered he had it. She carried it to the kitchen, got her purse, and paid him.

"We're all hoping Julie is okay." He folded the bills and stuffed them in a pant pocket. "Everybody really likes Julie."

"Do you know anyone who could have done something like this? You must know most of the local young people. Is there someone capable of robbing a convenience store . . . and killing the owner?"

"I guess I know most of the local kids. And kids always need money, that's for sure. But I don't think any of them I know need it bad enough to pull a cold-blooded murder." His tone held a hint of hostility, as if she were out of line for even suggesting that a local kid, especially one of his customers, could be involved in such a crime. "This isn't some California gangland."

"So all your young customers help little old ladies across the street, go to Sunday school every week, always put their garbage in trash cans, and never use offensive language?"

Steve managed an uncomfortable smile. "A few of 'em aren't exactly Boy Scouts," he admitted. "And sometimes stuff may go on out in the parking lot that Pastor Gordon over at the church wouldn't approve of, but—"

"Liquor? Drugs?"

He shrugged narrow shoulders. "Maybe. But the kids around here don't get by with much, not with Randy Wilson on their tail. Him and me, we've had a couple go-rounds, in fact, about him harassing my customers and driving away business. He came close to shutting me down one time over some baloney about drugs in the parking lot and illegal beer sales to minors."

"Well, if you hear any rumors, anything at all that might help, would you let Randy Wilson or Ben Mosely know? I understand Ben was retired, but he's gone back on the police force temporarily." She considered what Steve Lomax had just said about Randy, and added, "Or, if you'd rather not get involved with the police, just tell me what you hear."

Steve Lomax nodded, although she was uncertain if the stiff jerk of the ponytail meant he'd tell someone or he'd rather not get involved. "I'm glad to hear about Ben being back on the force. He'll find Julie and get your guy."

He turned and started to leave, but she stopped him with another question.

"Is anyone missing?"

"Missing?"

"The gunman stole my SUV. It hasn't been seen since he took it. It could be anywhere by now. I'm just asking if, since Friday night, you haven't seen some young person who usually hangs out around your place."

Steve's dishwater eyelashes jerked to widen his pale green eyes. A strand of long hair that had fallen loose from the ponytail now hung like a comma around his jaw. His jumpy gaze dodged hers and flicked from the doorway to the window at the far end of the dim hallway.

"That'd be hard to say. I mean, I'm in and out, like tonight. And not every kid shows up every day. Even if one didn't come around for a while, it might be a long time before it occurred to me that I hadn't seen him lately. Or they could be there regularly, same as always, and I just might not happen to see them. I can't keep track of everyone." Finally he managed to bring his eyes back to hers. "But I'll give it some thought and keep my eyes open. I sure will."

His nod was too vigorous, his direct gaze too bright and forced. Sarah hesitated. Steve Lomax's wordy defense implied the opposite of what he had said. She wanted to pursue her suspicion that he knew something, but she figured that at this point all she'd get out of Steve Lomax was a stout denial.

"Is there any other place the kids hang out?"

"Used to be the Calico Pantry, before I opened my place. But Helen Maxwell was always grumping at the kids about something. Kind of behind the times too, and kids go for a place with a little more action, video games, and—" He broke off, as if embarrassed to realize he was taking potshots at a woman who'd just been murdered. "Awful thing to happen," he muttered.

"So there's no other place the kids hang out, other than yours, now?"

"Well, kids have always hung out at the city park, from way back when I was that age. Used to be a lot of teen partying there, but Randy put a stop to that. And then there's Ryker's Bog, where kids like four-wheelin' in the mud. Among their other activities out there. The Bog's harder to police than the park. Especially when the town council's too stingy to let Randy have enough money for a four-wheel-drive vehicle."

Steve Lomax's agitation was now under control. He glanced down the hallway again when Nick appeared on the landing, mail in hand.

"Well, enjoy your pizza." Steve waggled his fingers in a friendly gesture of farewell. "We run a good special on submarine sandwiches every Friday."

Once inside, Nick handed the mail to Sarah and started opening the pizza box. She flipped through the accumulated advertisements and bills. No ransom note. *So what did I think? That there'd be a black envelope with "Attention: Ransom Note Enclosed!" printed on the outside?*

She put the mail down and told Nick about the odd encounter with Steve Lomax. "I have the definite feeling he knows something he wasn't willing to say."

"About someone who hasn't been around the last few days?"

Sarah nodded. "Or maybe I'm just getting paranoid," she admitted with a sigh. "All this hasn't exactly encouraged me to feel trusting about people."

Nick let the lid fall back on the pizza box and wrapped his hands around her upper arms. "You can trust me, Sarah." His eyes caught and held hers. "And don't ever forget it, okay . . . Okay?" he repeated, his hands tightening on her arms until she nodded. "And even if it does turn out to be just your imagination, I think you should tell the police what you just told me about Steve Lomax."

"I wouldn't want to make unnecessary trouble for him—"

"Julie is our first concern, not Steve Lomax."

Right. "I'll tell Randy."

Nick went back to opening the pizza box. Sarah got soft drinks from the fridge.

"Did you just open the door when he knocked?" Nick asked.

"He said he was the pizza guy."

"Anyone can say he's the pizza guy."

"What do you mean?"

"Sarah, a gunman bursts into a convenience store, kills one woman, and makes off with another in a stolen vehicle. It's all over the news that you're the person who witnessed the crime, and even though he was disguised, the gunman may be worried that you can somehow identify him."

"But I can't! With that disguise, I couldn't tell anything except that I thought he was about medium height. And I'm not even positive about that."

"He can't be sure of that."

"But if he's here in Julesburg, that could mean Julie—" Sarah broke off, refusing to contemplate what this might suggest about Julie's fate. She crossed her arms over her chest. "No. I don't think the gunman is around here. He and the SUV and Julie are miles away by now. He's someone who's missing. Or more likely just a transient. Julie's probably . . . talking his head off."

Nick walked across the room and thumped the thin wood of the door with his knuckles. "This door isn't much protection, even if you don't open it to someone who knocks. I could ram my fist right through it and unfasten the chain."

At the moment, perhaps disturbed by both the door's weakness and her carelessness, he looked as if he could ram his fist through a concrete wall.

"But it wouldn't make sense for the gunman to hang around here," Sarah argued. "That's why he stole the car. To get away."

"I just don't think you should open the door without being sure who's out there. I can send one of my men over to install a new door with a peephole and a stronger lock."

Danger right here in the apartment? Perhaps Nick was the one being paranoid. "I'll think about it. Right now, let's eat, okay? And I wanted to ask you if you think I should contact Julie's mother and father."

"You mean they don't even know that she's missing?" His eyebrows lifted in surprise as he and Sarah settled around the open pizza box on the table. "Wait a minute. You said your parents were dead."

"Different parents."

Sarah realized that the crime had created a bond between her and Nick that made their relationship seem deeper and of much longer duration than it actually was. Nick didn't even know the basic facts about Sarah MacIntosh and Julie Armstrong.

12

"Our birth mother was unwed, only seventeen, when Julie and I were born." With her fingers, Sarah separated two sections of pizza as she sorted details of the past in her mind. "Although we didn't know that until just a few months ago. Just as neither of us knew we had a twin, because we were adopted by different couples."

"Did the parents who raised you know?"

"I don't think so. The adoptions were private, arranged through the delivering doctor. Julie says she's decided not to ask her parents if they knew, and mine aren't alive to ask. But, knowing my parents, I'm sure if they'd known there was a twin, they'd have moved heaven and earth to adopt her too. My mom and dad, and I'll never think of them as anything other than that, were wonderful people. I had the best, most loving upbringing any child could have."

"And then your mother became ill."

"I was going to UCLA at the time, planning to become a CPA. I dropped out to move back home and help care for her through the surgeries and radiation. I could have gone back to college after she died, but Dad was so lost that I didn't want to leave him. I also loved the job I had by then, teaching stained-glass techniques at a crafts store, plus doing the bookkeeping."

"How did you acquire the stained-glass expertise?"

"It started as a project when I was in high school, and then I kept studying and taking classes. Julie and I had—*have* plans," she corrected instantly, panicky at the slip. Julie wasn't in the past tense. She'd be home any day, any minute now. "We have plans to try combining oil painting and stained glass. Such as a painting of a figure surrounded by a background of stained glass, or maybe a painted figure holding a stained-glass flower."

"I'll be first in line to buy one for my mother. She'd love that."

"I miss Julie so much," Sarah whispered. She dipped her head, suddenly overcome by the fear she was trying hard to reject. "I'm so afraid for her. Afraid of what's happened to her. Afraid of what may be happening to her now."

Nick reached to comfort her, but Sarah moved away, picking up her can of 7 UP.

"Julie wasn't so fortunate with her adopted parents," Sarah continued. In the back of her mind, she realized she did not want Nick's comfort; comfort made the possibility of Julie not coming back much too real. "The couple who adopted her already had marriage problems. She figured out, much later of course, that they'd hoped a baby would glue the relationship together. It worked for a while, though Julie remembers her childhood as full of silence and tension. She was always afraid it was her fault her folks weren't speaking to each other. They split up when she was ten. They both remarried and went on to have children quickly with their new mates. Let medical science explain that one," she added wryly.

"And made Julie feel left out."

Sarah nodded. "She was never abused—she's adamant about that—but she was shuffled back and forth between the two families and very much aware that she was not truly a part of either one. Like a purchase that turned out to be unwanted but couldn't be returned."

"That's a big burden for a child to cope with. But she doesn't seem like a bitter person."

Sarah appreciated that he kept Julie in the present tense. "No, she's not bitter. But she's also not close to either parent, and it isn't as if they can do anything even if I call them. So I'm thinking maybe I'll just wait until we know something definite before I contact them."

"You think that's the right thing to do?" Nick's tone was neutral, his attention concentrated on piling slices of tomato on his next helping of pizza.

Sarah's chest heaved a sigh. "You know just the right question to push my guilt button, don't you?"

"Hey, I'm not trying to push any buttons," he protested. "I'm just asking—"

"But you know not calling them isn't right. And so do I. They shouldn't hear about it on TV or read it in the newspaper."

"I'll call them, if that would make it easier for you." And, as if the matter about the parents was settled, he asked, "So how did you and Julie get together?"

Sarah smiled. "Our great-grandmother. She didn't know about our births or the adoptions at the time they happened. But she found out later and hired a detective to hunt down our families, and then kept track of us over the years. She said she'd thought many times about putting us in touch with each other, feeling we should know. But she also didn't think she had a right to interfere with how our adoptive parents were raising us, so she kept out of it. Until earlier this year, when she reached her ninety-fourth birthday. Then, she said, she decided it was something she had to do before she died. And she did die, just a couple of months after bringing us together."

"You speak of her with such affection, even though you didn't know her long."

Oh yes. I still feel the void left by that sprightly, independent, determined woman. "She first told us about each other by letter, then invited us to her home so we could meet. She had this beautiful old home in San Francisco, and servants, and she looked like a . . ." Sarah squeezed her eyes shut. "A tiny, white-haired doll, very fragile and elegant in her jewels. But then Julie asked if she wanted to be called Mrs. Forrester or Great-grandmother or what, and she got this sweet little twinkle in her eye and said, 'No one has ever called me Granny, and I always wished they would.' And I think I adored her from that very moment." She paused reflectively. "She was a very strong Christian, very open about her faith. Much like you."

"Thank you. I'm proud of the comparison. And did you call her Granny?"

"It got shortened to Gran, after a bit. And meeting her, meeting Julie, was so . . . so incredibly fulfilling. I was no longer alone. I had family again. Julie's parents weren't dead, as mine were, but she was alone too, in her own way. Then Gran died, but Julie and I still had family, because we had each other. And Julie is so very, very special."

"Like her twin sister." Nick said the words so casually that he was into another question before she caught their full impact. "Did your great-grandmother tell you anything about your birth mother?"

"Only that her name was Amelia, and that she had been a sweet and lively little girl who went 'astray.' She'd been dead for sixteen years. And she never named the father of her twins. Perhaps I'm different than most adopted children, but I never had any real curiosity or desire to know my birth parents. Mom and Dad were always 'real' parents to me."

"There must be other family members?"

Sarah shook her head. "The family is a soap-opera tangle of marriages and divorces, feuds, family estrangements, half brothers and sisters and stepchildren in all generations. None were as welcoming as Gran. I think they all suspected we were after her money. 'The Gold-Digger Duo,' I overheard one cousin call us. I think some of them even suspected we were trying to pull some big scam, that maybe we weren't even really related to the family."

"Where money is involved, suspicion is inevitable, I suppose."

"But it was all so untrue and unfair! Although . . ."

Nick lifted an encouraging eyebrow.

"She gave us each a hundred thousand dollars."

He whistled. "It would be an understatement to say *that* was very generous."

Sarah nodded. "She wanted us to have something, but she didn't want to entangle it in her will and set off some big legal battle after her death. So she simply did it quietly, as a gift. Neither of us wanted to take the money. We didn't want her to see us as gold diggers! But she insisted. Which is why I said earlier that Julie also has money to invest in the Nevermore."

The pizza box was empty. Sarah pressed a forefinger to a crumb of sausage and absentmindedly put it in her mouth. Nick crumpled the box and stuffed it in the trash.

"Thanks for telling me all this."

Sarah swirled her 7 UP can in a circle of moisture on the table. "I suppose the time has come to make those calls."

"I'll make them," Nick offered again.

"My job."

She found the numbers scribbled in the back of Julie's telephone book, along with an assortment of unfamiliar names. She perched on the arm of the sofa, one hand on the phone, one finger lightly rubbing the "1" key that would make the long-distance connection.

"I said a prayer last night. At least I think I did. I don't know much about these things."

"If you think you did, then you did." Nick smiled. "We may be amateur broadcasters, but God is always tuned in. I think he's more interested in sincerity than eloquence."

"I guess I feel as if I haven't much right to be praying at all." She twisted the phone cord around a forefinger. "I've never read the Bible. Never been to church more than a few times in my life."

"Somewhere in the biblical Book of Daniel is a line that says, 'We do not make requests of you because we are righteous, but because of your great mercy.' "

"Maybe, when Julie gets home, we can . . . look into this more together." She stiffened her back and punched the numbers for Julie's mother into the keypad.

Julie's mother, Janine Lockland, answered, but her three children were squabbling so noisily in the background that Sarah had to repeat the information twice. Janine burst into sobs when Sarah finally got the facts through to her. "I meant to call her last week. But Lisa's been sick, and I've been so busy getting Kevin to soccer practice and Brandi to gymnastics. . . ."

Sarah heard guilt behind the defensiveness. *Too bad you didn't feel guilt about neglecting Julie a little earlier.* But all she said was, "I'll call as soon as there's any further news."

The call to the father went better in some ways, worse in others. There were no tears or guilt from Mr. Armstrong. But his control was oddly chilling, and she shivered at the thought of being raised by such a cold man, in contrast to her own warm, affectionate father. He was, he said, leaving the following morning on a two-week business trip to London and Berlin, but he would be in touch when he returned. The thought of postponing the trip out of concern for Julie apparently did not occur to him.

Nick stayed until almost 10:00. Sarah knew he'd have bedded down on the sofa, protectively barring the way between her and any strange knocks on the door, if she'd uttered so much as a whisper of apprehension about being alone. Which she did not do, of course. She felt no sense of danger here in the apartment, and she was still convinced that Julie and her abductor were by now somewhere on the far side of the country.

A conviction shattered after a knock on the door the following morning.

13

Randy Wilson took off his brown police officer's hat and held it at chest level. "I'm sorry to come so early, but I didn't want to call."

Sarah felt the blood drain from her face. She clutched the doorknob for support. "Julie?"

"No! I'm sorry— I should have made that plain right away. There's no news about Julie. But we have found your SUV."

Relief flared, then collapsed, leaving a heaviness in Sarah's chest that made her breathing strained and shallow. Finding the SUV meant that Julie—

No, it did not necessarily mean that! Julie, alive and well, could still be *somewhere.*

"Where was it found?"

"At the north end of town, where the old Cougar Creek plywood mill used to be, before it burned down."

"You mean it's been there all this time?" An explosion of anger ripped through Sarah. "Right here in town, and you didn't see it?"

If her suggestion of police ineptitude bothered him, Randy didn't let it show. "There's a pile of salvage metal at the burn site. The SUV was parked behind that. A woman walking her dog spotted it this morning. We think it was put there last night."

"I'm sorry. I know you're doing all you can." A cloud of bewilderment swallowed Sarah's anger. "But if the SUV hasn't been there all this time, where has it been?"

"Probably stuck out in the woods somewhere. It's covered with mud, and there are scratches on it. But it doesn't appear damaged otherwise."

"Do I need to identify it as mine to help the investigation?"

"No, the license plates are still intact, and your registration and insurance papers are in the glove compartment. Ben is going over it with a fine-tooth comb now, vacuuming and taking fingerprints. Something is sure to turn up. There's always evidence of some kind left behind."

"I want to see it."

"We'll have to hold the vehicle temporarily. You'll get it back eventually, but—"

"I just need to *see* it," she said as she shook her head impatiently at his misinterpretation. She doubted she could ever drive the SUV again.

"Sure, that'd be okay." Randy sounded cooperative but puzzled by her insistence on something that would probably be upsetting. "It'll be at the old plywood mill site for several more hours, then we'll get it hauled into the police garage. We aren't cleaning the mud off yet. We think it could lead us to a specific location."

"Mud is identifiable?"

"It looks like it came from that wetlands area on the west side of town. There's probably sixty acres in there within the city limits that state regulations say can't be built on, and it's really wild, for being right here in town."

"Ryker's Bog?"

"Right. Officially, it's the Julesburg Wetlands, though no one here ever calls it that. We're going to check it out."

The implication of Randy's words chilled Sarah to the core. "Check it out for what?"

Randy shuffled his booted feet. "Well, matching tire tracks . . ."

"And Julie's body."

Randy nodded in reluctant agreement. "I'm afraid so." He looked down at his feet. "This is difficult for me, Miss MacIntosh. All along I've figured the killer was an outsider, maybe a transient passing through. That he'd taken your SUV and run as far and fast as he could. I guess I just didn't want to believe—"

"That we have a killer right here in Julesburg."

Randy nodded again. "But with the vehicle found here, there's no avoiding the obvious. Some local punk killed old Mrs. Maxwell and took the SUV and Julie." He sounded both chagrined and saddened at not having realized this from the start, but anger hardened his voice when he added, "And I'm not going to let him get away with it."

Whether heroic dedication to justice or a less noble ego and ambition fueled his determination, Sarah didn't know or care. Just so he got the job done. "I think you should talk to Steve Lomax."

"Steve?" Randy's narrow eyebrows lifted. "What would Steve— oh, you mean because Julie worked for him occasionally?"

"I'm not suggesting that Steve himself is involved," Sarah said carefully. "But I think you should talk to him about whether some regular customer hasn't been seen around Website X the last few days. Although maybe that's irrelevant, since the SUV was found here in Julesburg."

"We'll talk to Steve anyway. Actually, we've had some problems around Website X before. I've had tips that drugs were being sold out in the parking lot. . . . Are you okay, Miss MacIntosh?"

Sarah steadied herself as a devastating truth grabbed hold of her. *The car is here in Julesburg. The killer is here in Julesburg.* He could be keeping up an appearance of everyday life. Smiling. Smoking. Seeing his girlfriend. Going to his school or job. Perhaps that demon ski mask concealed one of the fresh-faced trio of teenagers who walked by that day as she and Julie sat in the car outside the Nevermore. Maybe he was the grandson of some elderly woman Julie ran errands for, or the boy who sacked groceries at the market. He could even be some young guy among the teenagers at the prayer meeting.

"I want to help with the search," she stated firmly.

Randy's back straightened in alarm. "Oh, that isn't necessary." Sarah could almost read his mind: *What if she finds the body? What kind of shape will it be in?* "We'll have plenty of volunteers. There's no need for you to go slogging around out there in the Bog."

There is also no need for me to sit here waiting by the telephone for a call that is never going to come. Yet even as that thought rolled over her, she fiercely refused to abandon all hope for Julie. *Maybe, just maybe, somehow in God's mercy . . .*

"Just let me know when the search will start. I have a friend whom I'm sure will also want to help."

"Well . . . okay. It'll probably be tomorrow morning before we get things organized. As I said, Ben is collecting evidence from the SUV now. We want to get everything off to the lab as soon as possible."

"I'll be down to look at the SUV in a few minutes."

"Actually, if you're up to it, that's probably a good idea. Maybe you can tell us if anything's different or missing."

Sarah closed the door behind Randy and dialed Nick's cell phone number. He answered immediately, as if he were keeping the phone at his fingertips. She gave him the news about the SUV and the search of Ryker's Bog.

Without hesitation Nick said, "I'll be there within an hour."

"The search won't get under way until tomorrow." Sarah peered out the window. An earlier drizzle had let up, but the day was still leaden and dreary. "So there's no need to drive over today—"

"I want to be with you when you go over to the SUV."

"I didn't say I was going there!"

"But you are."

Sarah felt warmed by how well Nick knew her already. And she didn't have to explain or defend her need to look at the SUV. He knew and understood and wouldn't try to talk her out of it. She also didn't bother to protest that he needn't take time off from work for this; Nick Nordahl was the kind of guy who would simply do it.

When they arrived at the site of the burned plywood mill, little evidence remained of the fire that had destroyed what had been the town's largest employer. The area had been leveled and scraped clean by bulldozers, and only the stack of salvaged metal, looking like a junkman's sculpture, remained to be hauled off. Rainwater puddled the raw earth. A small crowd of curious onlookers circled the yellow crime-scene tape attached to stakes surrounding Sarah's SUV. A television crew had a camera set up, and Randy was giving an interview, gesturing toward the vehicle.

Heavy black mud on the lower half of the Expedition almost obscured the paint, the spray pattern suggesting the driver had churned through mudholes with reckless abandon. The driver's door stood open.

"Do you want to get out?" Nick asked as they sat in his truck, surveying the scene.

"In a minute." Now that she was here, Sarah felt an unexpected reluctance to approach the vehicle where Julie may have spent the last hours of her life.

She felt no bond of familiarity with the SUV. Where was the snug security she'd once felt in it? Where was the delight with the power to burn under her foot? Gone. It seemed a lifetime ago that she and Julie, full of plans and laughter, had lightheartedly driven to Eugene in the Expedition.

The TV crew packed up their equipment and headed their van toward the street. Sarah steeled herself, and she and Nick got out of the pickup, Nick grabbing her hand as they approached the muddy SUV. The whirring sound of a battery-operated vacuum came from the open door.

Randy Wilson waved. "Be with you in a minute."

He tapped the burly man half hidden by the vehicle's door. The vacuum went silent, and Sarah watched the big man carefully empty the contents into a Ziploc plastic bag, then label and tuck the bag into a larger container. Both men came out to the yellow tape, and Randy introduced Ben Mosely to Sarah.

Ben took off a latex glove to shake hands with her. "Your fingerprints and hair are undoubtedly going to turn up here, so we'll need to take samples for comparison."

Sarah nodded. "Julie's hair and fingerprints will be there too, of course."

"Anyone else you can identify been in the vehicle recently?"

"Possibly some friends down in California." She looked off into space as she tried to remember. "The man who cleaned the interior at the car wash last week. A couple of Julie's friends we gave rides to."

"I touched the window frame the other day," Nick added.

The expanding list sent Sarah's spirits plunging. How, out of all the fingerprints and hairs that might show up in the SUV, could they possibly isolate ones that might be incriminating?

"I know it's difficult to remember things exactly, but would you take a look at the interior and see if you can tell us anything?" Randy asked.

Sarah stepped over the yellow tape. Nick started to follow, but Randy frowned and motioned him back.

Sarah braced herself and peered inside the SUV. "All I see is that the blanket that was covering Julie while she slept is missing." The jacket she'd folded into a pillow for Julie's head was still there.

Randy had her describe the blanket, and he wrote the information down in a notebook.

"She had a purse. A burlap bag, actually, with yellow flowers."

"We found that." Randy motioned toward the box of evidence items.

"Did you find cigarette butts in the ashtray? The gunman stole cigarettes during the robbery."

After he put on another latex glove, Ben reached in and pulled the handle on the ashtray. The small compartment held only the small change Sarah occasionally dropped there.

Randy peered over her shoulder. "Probably just tossed the butts out the window. But we did find this under the seat."

He pulled a small plastic bag from the box holding the other bits of evidence. The brightly colored parrot looked incongruously playful dangling from its palm frond inside the bag.

"That's Julie's earring!" Sarah gasped. Instinctively, she reached for it, suddenly frantic to touch this small connection with her twin.

Randy hesitated, then let her have it. She fingered the bumpy earring through the plastic. In disappointment, she realized that, like the SUV, the earring sent her no message. It was just a . . . thing.

"Was she wearing the earrings, both of them, the night she was abducted?" he asked.

Sarah nodded.

Ben took the plastic package and balanced it in his palm, as if he too were seeking some message from it. But it was a cop's observations, not a secret message, that he offered.

"She could have lost the earring in a struggle. But I'm more inclined to think it simply fell off while she was sleeping back there. It's the kind with a hook that simply slips into a pierced earlobe, nothing to fasten it in place, and there are no other signs of struggle. No blood."

Sarah realized he was offering her what little consolation he could, telling her that Julie hadn't suffered a terrifying bloodbath. At least not in the car. "Maybe he's holding her prisoner, planning to ask for a ransom," she said hopefully.

Randy looked startled, as if the possibility hadn't occurred to him. "That sounds a little far-fetched." He glanced at Ben.

The creases on Ben's weathered face turned into a thoughtful frown. "Julie isn't the type of victim usually involved in a kidnap-for-ransom scheme. Usually those crimes involve more, uh, wealthy individuals. Also, it seems obvious that taking Julie was unplanned, something that happened accidentally in connection with the robbery."

"I guess I'm just hoping to find some reason to believe she's still alive," Sarah admitted. She also knew she'd clung to that hope to shield herself from thoughts of the unspeakable horrors Julie might have suffered. "We aren't wealthy, but I want to offer a reward."

"I'm sure the community would rally to donate to such a cause," Ben said. "Everyone wants Julie found and this killer captured."

"I don't need to wait for donations." She turned and raised her voice so the small crowd gathered outside the yellow tape could hear. "I'm offering a hundred thousand dollars if Julie is returned safe and sound. Fifty thousand for information leading to . . . her body."

A rolling murmur suggested that the figures impressed the crowd. Sarah turned back to the two police officers.

Both Ben and Randy looked astonished at the size of the offer.

"That may bring some action," Ben said.

"Should I contact the media about the reward?"

Ben took a moment to consider this. "We can set up a special phone line so information can be left anonymously, and the money then also paid out anonymously, if necessary. It'll take a little longer to arrange, but it might bring information from someone who'd be reluctant to call in without a guarantee of anonymity."

"I'll get on it right away. Our regular phone line is getting a lot of other action," Randy said. "We've called our part-time secretary in to work full-time to handle the calls."

"What kind of calls?" Sarah asked.

"Advice. Complaints that we should have caught the guy and hung him by now. Tips. Theories. Everything from that good old standby, abduction by aliens, to a woman claiming Julie ran off with her husband. On a sensational crime, everybody wants to put in their two cents worth."

A sensational crime. Sarah felt a slow churn roll up from her stomach. "Are any of the calls helpful?"

"Not so far, although we follow up on everything that doesn't sound too off-the-wall. Ben and I both think searching Ryker's Bog offers the best possibility of . . . finding something."

Sarah thanked them and started toward Nick, but she paused when a county sheriff's department car pulled around the stack of salvage metal. Sarah recognized one of the two officers as the detective who had questioned her so relentlessly. Close behind the official vehicle came the van from the TV station, which had apparently turned around when the reporter spotted the new officers headed this way.

"Miss MacIntosh," the detective said politely when he stepped inside the circle of yellow tape.

Sarah, curious, waited while the four officers greeted each other like circling tomcats sizing each other up. *No love lost here.* She suspected Randy even resented the interference from county authorities.

"Wouldn't this be more effective if you brought the vehicle into our facilities for processing?" the detective suggested.

"We're doing fine," Ben muttered. He motioned to the container of collected bags of evidence. Randy stood with fists clenched, silent but hostile. The detective ignored him and started circling the SUV.

"Looks like somebody's had this baby out playing in the mud."

Playing in the mud. Sarah resented the casual comment that almost made light of Julie's abduction.

"Or had it out somewhere hiding a body," Randy snapped, as if he too resented the detective's attitude. "We'll start searching Ryker's Bog tomorrow. We figure that's where the mud came from."

Hands behind him as if he didn't want to dirty them, the detective leaned over to peer at a rear fender. Faint steam rose from the damp mud clinging to the vehicle. "Looks to me like it could have come from anywhere back in the hills around here."

Randy unexpectedly laughed. "Spoken like a true city boy. L.A., wasn't it, before you hit our backwoods county? Maybe you'd better leave the mud investigation to those of us who grew up with it."

The detective shrugged. "We're shorthanded because of budget cuts, but I can send a man and dog over to help with the search."

"I can call on the men in our local volunteer fire department, plus a couple of other local organizations. And I'd put Wylie Cotter's hunting hounds up against one of those highbrow dogs of yours any day." To Sarah, Randy added, "We'll need something of Julie's to give them a good scent to follow."

"What's more important here, you grabbing publicity and glory with your Lone-Ranger-style investigation, or actually catching the perp?" the detective snapped.

Sarah could see Randy Wilson's temper rocketing to the edge of eruption, but he managed to grit his teeth and vent his anger by slamming a rear door of the SUV. "This is my town, and I care what happens here. And if you'd like to look at the gas gauge, you'll notice it shows right at the half-full mark. Which means, given the information Miss MacIntosh already gave us, that it hasn't been driven more than a few miles. Which again points to Ryker's Bog, right here in Julesburg."

"Maybe."

Sarah strongly suspected that the detective would prefer Julie's body to be found far out in the mountains just to prove Randy wrong about Ryker's Bog. She also suspected that Julie was just a body to the detective, but that she was more than that to Randy. His ego might be involved and he might have a tendency to use the media for his own ambitious agenda, but Julie was a real person to him.

"I'm offering a reward for my sister's return, or any information about her," Sarah said. She again named the figures, and even the detective looked reluctantly impressed.

The TV crew, now realizing who she was, immediately cornered her for an interview. And she gladly gave one, feeling a sense of hope. Maybe the money would do it. Of course, the need to bring money into the situation didn't raise her opinion of humanity in general, or Julesburg in particular. She felt as if it reduced the value of Julie's life to X number of dollars.

But whatever worked.

"Very nicely done," the detective murmured after the TV crew packed up once more. "Maybe you and Randy ought to take your show on the road. It's sure going to bring out every crackpot within hearing distance."

Sarah turned away, gritting her teeth in an effort to ignore him. Yet his cynical words bothered her.

"Is that true?" she asked Ben and Randy. "Offering money does seem so . . . commercial."

"A reward can also elicit false information," Randy said grudgingly, as if he didn't want to agree with the detective. "Sometimes people throw out wild guesses in hopes that one will just happen to hit the mark. It can make time-consuming extra investigative work without really accomplishing anything."

Ben shot Randy an odd glance. "Money talks," he muttered. "It has a powerful voice."

"Your wife believes in the power of prayer," Sarah said impulsively.

He whacked a glob of mud on the vehicle with his fist. "Ask her how effective it's been in healing our granddaughter."

14

They'd asked at Julesburg's only gas station how to get to Ryker's Bog. And now they were here.

A few houses rose out of unkempt yards and straggly fences along one side of the unpaved street. An old travel trailer stood window-deep in blackberry bushes and Scotch broom, a rust-blotched white van without tires stranded on wooden blocks beside it. Farther down the street, a gate on a bedraggled picket fence hung by one hinge, and smoke rose from a chimney on the shack behind the fence.

On the other side of the street, a dark tangle of trees rose over an impenetrable barrier of undergrowth. Blackberries and vines coiled and twisted beneath a canopy of drooping branches. Beyond the Bog came the faint boom of surf, but no invigorating scent of sea reached here. Here was ancient dampness and rotting wood and decaying leaves.

Oh, Julie . . . no . . . please, not here. . . .

Sarah clutched the door handle as Nick turned onto a rutted dirt road leading into the tangled growth. Green-gray strands of moss hung from the branches of thick, twisted trees. Rank grass brushed the underside of the pickup. A branch slapped the windshield, and instinctively they both ducked. Nick braked at a pile of trash blocking the ruts.

"Something tells me this isn't a part of town they advertise to tourists or exhibit to visiting dignitaries," he muttered.

A sick feeling roiled in Sarah's stomach. They were only a dozen blocks away from the main highway through town, only a half mile from Lighthouse Hill, where a Californian was building a million-dollar house. Yet this was a different world.

Bullet holes decorated an abandoned refrigerator lying on its side, and a mattress with ripped-out stuffing leaned over it. A hair-covered mound of what had once been a dog lay beside a rotting log. To the left, fleshy lily pads floated on a pool of stagnant water.

Sarah stared at the water. In her mind's eye she saw a wrapped body sliding silently beneath those fleshy lily pads, sinking deep into the black mud. . . .

No, no, no! Not here, not discarded like some bit of human garbage! Last week someone had told Julie about a batch of kittens dumped in Ryker's Bog. Julie had come to search for them. Now they would be searching here for Julie herself.

Nick looked over to her. "I don't think you should join in the search," he said gruffly, and as he spoke, something unseen splashed into the stagnant water, and ripples undulated beneath the lily pads. "I'll come, but—"

"No, I want to do it. If—if anyone can find Julie, I think I can. We have a . . . connection."

Nick hesitated, as if he wanted to protest, but he finally nodded. "Do you want to drive farther back in there now? This pickup has four-wheel drive. We can probably make it through the mud."

"No. I don't want to do anything to disturb possible evidence." *And why wasn't this area closed off so possible evidence couldn't be disturbed?*

Nick backed the pickup toward the potholed street, tires briefly spinning and throwing dark mud before they caught on more solid ground. Relief surged through Sarah as they headed away from the tangle of trees and vines and stagnant water.

In the parking lot at the apartment, Sarah thanked Nick for coming with her. "If you'd like, I can make lunch before you go back to Dutton Bay."

"Something tells me you don't really feel like lunch. Look, I'll come back this evening, and we'll go to dinner, okay? Something healthy. Broccoli and tofu and all that good stuff." He smiled, and she knew he was trying to be cheerful, to keep her mind off Ryker's Bog.

She matched the effort and returned the smile. "I don't think tofu is a big item in Julesburg, but I've been reading that chocolate has unexpected health benefits. The Julesburg Café serves some good chocolate-fudge pie."

"Sounds like health food to me. In the meantime, a nap might do you good. I don't think you slept much last night." He leaned over and kissed her cheek. The gesture surprised her, yet it also seemed natural, as if he'd always done it. "See you tonight. About six."

She reached up to touch the spot on her cheek, then stared at him as an unexpected truth hit her. *I could fall in love with you, Nick Nordahl.*

"Did I do something wrong?" he asked.

"No, I don't think so." Actually, he'd done something that felt so very right. She studied him, the concern in his blue eyes, the strength of his craggy face, the tenderness of the lips that had just touched her cheek. *I am falling in love with you.* "Why?"

"You just had such an odd, surprised look on your face for a moment there."

Impulsively, she leaned across the seat and planted a kiss directly on his lips. Then, in spite of the lingering unpleasantness of Ryker's Bog, she laughed lightly as she slid out of the pickup.

"Now who looks surprised?"

A glow of awakening possibilities even in the midst of apprehension about Julie accompanied her upstairs. She thought about Nick, strong and dependable and caring. Not the kind of guy to make touchy-feely statements about "being there" for her. But truly being there when she needed him.

Yet this wasn't the time to fall in love. Guilt whispered accusations in her ear for even considering it. Only Julie should matter.

She lay down in the bedroom to take the nap Nick had recommended, but Julie's empty bed on the other side of the room reproached her. It was too heavy a reminder, too deep a condemnation for leaving the keys and engine running in the SUV.

She gave up on the nap. She sat up, and her eyes caught on something sitting on the nightstand beside the other twin bed. Julie's journal. It was nothing more than a spiral notebook, lines filled with Julie's sprawling scribbles, as if her hand couldn't keep up with her thoughts. Sarah retrieved the notebook and balanced it across her fingers. It felt heavy. Heavy with Julie's words. She opened a page. The first word she saw was Donovan.

Should I be doing this? Julie didn't share everything; she had her fences, a big one around Donovan. Sarah could almost see Julie watching her now, hands on hips, blue eyes snapping. *Sarah, I can't believe you'd do this. How could you?*

Randy and Ben didn't think Julie was coming back. Nick had doubts too. Ryker's Bog hung like a nightmare trapped on the edge of her consciousness.

Sarah shoved the notebook into a nightstand drawer and slammed it shut. *If I do this, it means she will come home safely.*

Out in the living room, she grabbed a handful of magazines from beneath the end table by the sofa. She flipped through the pages, searching for something, anything, to shut out the horrifying images relentlessly stabbing her consciousness. "Is Lip Liner Obsolete?" "Lose Weight While Eating Anything!" "Streamline Your Thighs in Six Weeks!" Something thicker slid out from between two magazines. The small red book looked familiar; Sarah had one exactly like it. Their great-grandmother had given them each one. New Testament, Psalms, and Proverbs.

She riffled through the small-print pages that crackled with unused newness. Yet here and there, pen marks showed that the pages were not entirely untouched. Occasional words were underlined, but more often Julie had scribbled question marks. Sarah felt a pang in her heart when she saw Julie's familiar little trademark square dotting the bottom of each question mark.

On a sudden impulse, Sarah grabbed her jacket, stuffed the little book in her pocket, and headed outside. The wind had picked up, soggy leaves swirled across the parking lot. But the wind had also blown the clouds away, so the sun shone strongly now. She drove down to the jetty, filled the wooden trough and dishes with food for the eager cats, then found a rump-sized niche between the jumbled rocks for herself. The calico, Clarissa, immediately curled up on her lap, and a tiger-stripe snuggled beside her.

I feel closer to Julie here than in the apartment, she realized.

She looked first at the passages Julie had underlined. One in Psalms read: "It is better to take refuge in the LORD than to trust in man." In Mark: "What good is it for a man to gain the whole world, yet forfeit his soul?" And in Matthew: "So in everything, do to others what you would have them do to you, for this sums up the Law and the Prophets." She applauded that one.

But she frowned as she looked at the verse underlined in Proverbs: "No harm befalls the righteous, but the wicked have their fill of trouble."

No harm befalls the righteous? She rested the small book against her knee and gazed off toward the rugged coastline fading into the undulating silhouette of blue mountains. *I'd put a question mark beside that one. Maybe even cross it out. Because at this point, the wicked are doing just fine, and Julie is the one who's been harmed.*

A new cat climbed up on her lap, and she absentmindedly stroked it as she studied the verses Julie had singled out with question marks.

The one in John was printed in red, which she knew from Gran to mean that these were words Jesus had spoken. "I am the way and the truth and the life. No one comes to the Father except through me." That verse had earned three question marks from Julie.

One from a section called Romans said, "If you confess with your mouth, 'Jesus is Lord' and believe in your heart that God raised him from the dead, you will be saved." Two question marks here.

Another verse with a question mark by it sounded vaguely familiar to Sarah. "For God so loved the world that he gave his one and only Son, that whoever believes in him shall not perish but have eternal life." Was its familiarity because Gran had quoted it to them?

The enigmatic markings deepened Sarah's yearning for her twin. Had Julie found these verses on her own? Or were they suggestions from Twila Mosely or Stefanie Harrison? Given the preponderance of question marks, Julie was apparently more skeptical than believing. Yet the lines under some words were firm and unequivocal. *I want to talk with you about all this, Julie. If we can understand Gran's faith—*

"Hello."

Sarah jumped, bumping her elbow and scattering the cats.

"Sorry. I didn't mean to startle you. I saw Julie's car and figured it was you. Just thought I'd come over and see how things are going."

Sarah stood up and massaged her bumped elbow as she tried to place the man. He was short, with a barrel chest, stubby legs, and a tattoo of a blue ship on his forearm. Black grease streaked his dark work pants and once-white T-shirt. His reddish-brown hair was curly to the point of fuzzy, his clear blue eyes attractive. A closer glance told her he was younger than he looked at first glance, probably midthirties.

"Joe Argo," he said, helping her out with the identification. "That's my boat over there." He jerked a thumb toward a rickety commercial fishing boat with the unlikely name "Wildfire III" painted on the side. "Been working for two days on an engine overhaul. Dirty job." He spread his hands, grease embedded under the fingernails.

Sarah remembered him now as Julie's friend who had recommended Nordahl and Sons for the remodeling. They'd run into him at the Julesburg Café. He'd been clean-shaven then, but now he was either in the straggly stage of growing a beard or simply several days without a shave.

"I heard the SUV turned up. It . . . doesn't look good, does it?"

"No, it doesn't," she reluctantly agreed. "They're planning to search Ryker's Bog tomorrow. Randy Wilson thinks the mud on the SUV indicates it may have been in there."

"You figure it's just like they tell it on the news, a simple store robbery that escalated into killing Mrs. Maxwell and taking Julie?"

"That's what it looked like to me, and I was there." Sarah tilted her head, puzzled by what struck her as an odd question.

"Yeah. Right. Just the wrong place at the wrong time. It happens. Well, I'd better get back to work. I'm sure sorry about Julie. I hope they find her. Safe and sound, of course," he added hastily.

"Thank you. I hope so too. Hey, how do you and Julie know each other, by the way?"

"She's always down here feeding and petting those cats, just like you're doing." He eyed several cats as they peered out from the rocks, as if he found such concern for the homeless animals perplexing. "We talk now and then, and she went out on the boat with me a couple of times. But she didn't like fishing. Said she thought maybe she'd never eat fish again." He smiled wryly.

"That doesn't surprise me. Julie is very kindhearted."

"Was—is Julie still seeing that Moran guy in Gold Beach?"

The question surprised Sarah, and she hesitated in answering. *Are Julie's personal relationships any of this man's business?* Yet because she sensed Joe Argo had something on his mind, she threw out bait to see what she could catch. "She hasn't done it yet, but she's planning to break up with him."

"I'd say that'd be real smart. Maybe she finally wised up about him. Like she did with the playboy rich guy."

"Playboy rich guy?"

"Black sheep son of the Volkman Laser System people. You know the company? A bunch of snobs who don't hire many locals. The kid's a would-be actor who comes running home to Daddy whenever he runs out of money down in Tinsel Town. He and Julie were pretty tight for a while. Except Julie didn't exactly approve of Daddy's company. When some outsiders came in and staged a protest march, she marched with them."

"And the company makes . . . ?"

"Who knows? Apparently some of it is top-secret, cloak-and-dagger military stuff. Laser sights for weapons, that kind of thing. But I hear even the workers don't always know what they're making."

Sarah stooped to pick up the calico cat that had returned to her side. "I talked to Donovan on the phone once, but I've never met him. Do you know him?"

"I used his charter helicopter a couple of times before the business got shut down."

"Why did it get shut down?"

"Moran lost his pilot's license. The helicopter was in some minor mishap, and he failed a drug test when it happened. I don't know if it's routine to test or if the authorities had a tip, but I think the FAA takes a dim view of that sort of thing. There were rumors he was transporting drugs in the helicopter, but apparently there weren't any on board that time. Or Julie would've been visiting him in a jail cell."

Sarah wasn't surprised by this information about Donovan Moran. Had something involving drugs caused Julie to decide to break up with him? "He sounds somewhat . . . disreputable."

"Moran is no saint in shining armor, that's for sure. Well, I gotta get back to work. A fisherman doesn't make any bucks with a boat sitting here on the dock." He turned to leave, but Sarah's voice stopped him.

"I'm offering a reward. Fifty thousand dollars for information leading to recovery of Julie's body. Or a hundred thousand for her safe return."

Joe whistled. "That should stir up the natives." He paused. "What about reward for information leading to the capture of the killer?"

"We don't know that Julie is dead!"

Joe lifted his burly shoulders in a gesture that could've been taken as an apology. Sarah immediately felt suspicious.

Was his question about a reward for capture of the killer mere curiosity . . . or does he know something he figures might be worth a reward? She thought back to his odd question that suggested the convenience-store robbery could have been something other than what it appeared to be on the surface.

Joe shuffled his feet, looking back toward his boat.

"They're going to arrange for a special phone line so calls can be received anonymously," Sarah said.

"Good idea. If somebody important or powerful around this burg is involved, somebody else who knows something might be leery about being known as an informant."

"But why would someone important or powerful rob a convenience store?"

Joe suddenly grinned, an unexpectedly disarming smile in spite of the gleam of gold in several back teeth. "My ex-girlfriend told me I listen to way too many murder mysteries and spy-story tapes while I'm floating around out there on the ocean. My imagination 'runs amok,' as she put it. I'm not much on reading, but I always have one of those audio tapes going." He looked down and shuffled his feet. "Anyway, it's sure too bad about Julie," he added. "Mrs. Maxwell too, of course. Julie was . . . Julie is a real sweet girl."

His nervous shuffle turned into a speedy exit.

Sarah showered and did a load of wash in the laundry room at the apartment house. Randy Wilson called and said the volunteers were to meet in the parking lot at the police station at noon the next day. She passed that information along to Nick when he called at 5:00. He said he and several other men from his construction crew would be coming to join the search.

"Would it be okay if we have dinner a little late tonight?" he added. "We had a man hurt on the job—"

"Nothing serious, I hope?" Sarah interrupted with concern.

"Compound leg fracture. A big dog ran into the ladder and knocked it down, and our man took a bad fall. I want to run in to the Coos Bay Hospital and make sure he's taken care of."

Sarah wanted to discuss her odd conversation with Joe Argo, but she didn't want to delay Nick's trip to the hospital, so she didn't mention it. "Why don't we have dinner another time? I don't think the Julesburg Café will run out of chocolate health food in the near future."

"True. But I'd really like to see you tonight. Look, my cell phone is playing games with me, but I'll call you again from the motel phone if it isn't too late when I get back from the hospital, okay? Otherwise I'll give you a ring in the morning."

"I'll be waiting." She took a shot at lightness. "Breathlessly."

He laughed at the exaggeration. But was it an exaggeration? Nick was special, becoming more special by the minute.

She walked down to the market, not escaping a shudder as she passed the Calico Pantry. It already had a forlorn, abandoned look; blown-in trash had accumulated around the front door. She picked up cheese, eggs, salad makings, and oranges at the store. When she got home she ate a grilled cheese sandwich and a salad. The small apartment felt desolate in its silence, but she didn't want to turn on the TV and hear yet another account of the nonprogress in finding Julie. She busied herself scrubbing the bathroom.

Later, she did switch on the TV, but the soap operas and game shows struck her as both inane and vulgar. She clicked the remote and retrieved Julie's little New Testament from her jacket pocket.

This time her attention wandered beyond Julie's underlinings and question marks. She tried to recall what their great-grandmother had said about her faith. She'd almost glowed with it, Sarah remembered, her lined old face lighting up as she spoke of "my Jesus."

Sarah skipped here and there, reading mostly the words in red. She read interesting parables, one about building a house on solid rock rather than shifting sand, which reminded her that Nick had called Jesus "The Rock" that day at the Nevermore. And she read other parables, simple but powerful, about wine and wineskins, mustard seeds and yeast, seeds falling on good soil and bad. Jesus had also spoken strong words about sin and intriguing words about eternal life.

She cradled the small book in her lap as she paused to consider whether she believed in a life beyond death. *Yes, I do believe in it.* She'd thought about this subject before—who hadn't?—but always in an abstract sort of way. But now that she was faced with the possibility of Julie's death . . . yes, she did believe in an existence beyond this one. It was comforting to think of Gran secure with her Jesus, and Julie joining them. It was nice to envision her parents together again.

She wandered on, pausing here and there to study a verse. She liked Jesus' words quoted in Matthew, where he spoke about storing up treasures in heaven rather than here on earth, "where moth and rust destroy, and where thieves break in and steal." And the wonderful promise of 2 Corinthians 5:1! "Now we know that if the earthly tent we live in is destroyed, we have a building from God, an eternal house in heaven, not built by human hands."

I could be a believer. This realization came to her cloaked in the same aura of surprise and wonder she'd felt when she realized she could fall in love with Nick, and perhaps was already falling.

She went to bed early, concerned about what was keeping Nick so long at the hospital but too tired to stay up. She woke groggily sometime during the night, her mind fogged with a jumbled dream about a car wreck and horns honking. It took her a moment to realize that the honk of horns in the dream was actually the sound of the telephone ringing in the other room. She turned on the bedside lamp and stumbled toward the jangling phone. As the awake part of her mind gained the upper hand over the fog of sleep, she realized it was probably Nick calling. She eagerly reached for the phone.

"Hello?"

A voice said something, but it was such a whispery, muffled voice that she couldn't understand what it was saying. She almost put the phone down, thinking it was a crank call. She'd had a couple of them. But instead, with a sudden jolt of apprehension, she clutched the phone more tightly.

"I'm sorry. I can't understand you. What are you saying?"

"I'm asking, do you want to know where your sister is?"

The voice was louder but still indistinct, with that same muffled, whispery quality. Like something not quite human trying to sound human. She pinched the skin between her eyes sharply, willing herself not to give in to terror. Then, in spite of her confusion and apprehension, a wild hope surged through her. Was this someone calling in response to the reward?

"Yes, oh yes. Please! Where is she? The reward is a hundred thousand if she's returned alive and safe—"

"You're offering me a reward?"

The whispery quality fell away from the voice, but it was still muffled. And it also held a hint of amusement. The fine hair on her arms prickled, and cold sweat slickened her palm against the phone.

"Just tell me whatever you know, please!"

The voice changed once more, becoming guttural. "I don't have nothin' to do with this, see? I'm just tellin' you because I thought you'd want to know."

"Where is she?" Sarah begged again. "Please, just tell me where my sister is!"

A chuckle now. "Why, where else but that favorite haunt of our local evil spirits? The Nevermore, of course. Happy hunting."

15

"Wait, please, don't hang up!"

But the line was already dead. She stared at the phone in the dim light spilling from the bedroom, as if, by staring hard enough, she could make sense of what had just happened.

Julie at the Nevermore. Was the call for real? *Oh, please, Lord, please let her be there!*

Sarah raced to the bedroom in a frenzy, haphazardly discarding her pajamas and pulling on jeans and a sweatshirt. *Shoes, where are my shoes?*

Yet with one shoe on and the other still in her hand, she stopped, reason and logic making her feel cold. She sagged as she sat there on the edge of the bed, her shoulders slumped.

What real chance could there be that Julie was *alive* at the Nevermore? What chance that she had been dropped off at the old theater as if it were a bus stop in the Twilight Zone?

In her mind's eye she saw the theater, yellow light from the wall sconces dimly illuminating the sloping seats and faded carpet. And in one of those seats, stiff and lifeless—

No, no, no! Sarah shook her head, desperately trying to erase the vision, feeling a scream stuck in her throat. Desperately she cast around for an emotional anchor. *Nick! Nick will know what to do.*

She ran back to the living room, found his cell phone number on a slip of paper under the phone, and punched in the numbers with a shaky finger. Nothing. She dialed again and heard only more empty silence, and in frustration she remembered that Nick had said his cell phone was "playing games" with him.

She glanced at the glowing blue numbers on the microwave in the dark kitchen. Quarter to four. She could try to locate him, call every motel in Dutton Bay . . . and waste precious minutes dealing with answering machines or cranky motel clerks roused from sleep.

She grabbed the phone again. She had the nine and one dialed before she dropped the receiver back in the cradle. She knew from past experience how long it took a car from the county sheriff's department to arrive in Julesburg. It had taken them at least twenty or thirty minutes to arrive at the Calico Pantry.

Randy Wilson must have a home phone. Frantically she looked in the phone book, but his name wasn't listed. Ben Mosely? His number was listed, but an answering machine picked up on the fourth ring, and once more she slammed the phone down in frustration.

She sat there for a moment. Then she resolutely slid the other shoe on her foot and tied the laces firmly. She found Julie's heavy-duty flashlight in the kitchen, fished the key to the Nevermore out of her purse, and stuffed it in her pocket.

This is insane! You can't dash over there alone in the middle of the night. This could be a trap. With Julie as bait. What if the killer's in there waiting for you? Wait until morning . . . it's just a few hours. Wait until you can get hold of Nick. . . .

But what if Julie is there at the Nevermore, alive but ill or injured, perhaps unconscious, disoriented, or terrified, and desperately in need of help?

She remembered what she had said to Nick: "If anyone can find Julie, I can." Because there was a connection between her and Julie, a connection created in the womb, a connection linking them even before they knew of each other's existence.

A connection now drawing her to the Nevermore.

She parked the car in front of the theater, but she didn't instantly jump out. Something was rattling. After a moment she identified it as the wind banging one of the letters still clinging to the marquee. She pulled the car forward a few feet so she could see around the corner of the building to be certain no one lurked along the wall dimly lit by a streetlight.

She saw only the empty parking lot, weeds pushing up through the cracked asphalt, broken board on the back fence swinging in the wind.

She slid out of the car, her gaze swiveling up and down the street as she tried to take in everything. Not a vehicle moving on the street, not even a stray cat prowling the night. She left the car door unlocked so she could make a quick escape if necessary.

I should have brought a weapon, she thought as she moved into the shadows beneath the marquee. Then the ridiculousness of that thought occurred to her. *What weapon? Rolling pin? Potato peeler?* Instinctively, she sought a stronger weapon.

Be with me, Lord. Help me. Protect me! Show me what to do. Help me find Julie. Keep us both safe from evil.

She stopped at the door, key poised. It didn't look as if anyone had been inside the old theater for days. Trash had blown against the garish red doors. A faint current of air whistled through the small opening in the cashier's cage. The tattered curtains swayed.

The killer could be waiting inside to make sure I can never identify him . . .

She started to turn and run. She desperately wanted to run.

Yet the feeling that Julie was there was powerful, the nameless connection between them pulling Sarah like an invisible magnet. Her head spun and her stomach curled with the combination of fear and longing.

She nudged a crumpled candy wrapper with her toe. The way the wind was howling, all the trash could have blown in within the last few minutes. The accumulation didn't necessarily mean the doors hadn't been opened recently. Which meant Julie could be in there now.

Resolutely, she flicked on the big flashlight, stuck the key in the lock, and turned it. Once inside, she fumbled for the light switches. When the lobby light went on, a wild-eyed face stared at her from the dimness.

Me, she realized shakily. Her own reflection in the mirror behind the candy counter. She inspected the lobby, poking the beam of the flashlight into corners, peering over the counter into the concession area. She checked the rest rooms, determinedly trying to ignore a fear that someone was watching her.

She moved on to the main seating area, bracing herself when the glow from the tarnished gilt sconces made the sloping seats look exactly as they had in the horrifying vision she'd had of finding Julie's body here. She stepped cautiously down the center aisle, systematically swinging the flashlight beam to search the rows of seats on both sides of the aisle.

Afraid she would find Julie's body crumpled on the floor or a seat.

Afraid she wouldn't find her.

Afraid of the unknown.

She said another prayer before she climbed the three steps to the stage and circled behind the curtain and screen. If there were lights here, she didn't know how to turn them on, and she held the flashlight in front of her as if the roving beam were a weapon, occasionally whirling to flick it behind her. She heard rustles, creaks underfoot, a moan coming from empty space.

No. Not a moan. Merely the wind.

Then she headed upstairs, where two old projectors still stood among the ruins of the fire that had burned there at some time. She saw footprints in the dust on the floor. She studied the prints, her neck rigid with tension. *Mine or Julie's footprints? Or someone else's?*

A splintering crack underfoot sent her scrambling backward. She quickly headed downstairs, where she tried to consider the situation logically. She had not given the old theater a meticulous search; Julie's body could still be hidden somewhere. But she was grimly certain that an alive Julie was not in the Nevermore.

She turned off the lobby lights and used the flashlight as she opened and relocked the door.

She was surprised when she stepped outside to see that a faint hint of dawn had lightened the sky, although pale stars still glimmered among the scudding clouds. She'd been in the theater longer than she had realized. The wind had not let up, and it whipped with savage glee around the corner of the building and banged the dangling letters on the marquee overhead.

Sarah had the car door open before a thought occurred to her. The eyes and face in the Calico Pantry had seemed alien to her. The voice on the phone also had an unreal, not-quite-human quality. Yet no matter what her frightened imagination had conjured up, both face and voice were *human.* Whoever had called her couldn't have spirit-walked through the walls of the Nevermore. Like anyone else, he'd have needed a key to get inside. Which meant if there was anything to his claim that Julie was here, he had access to a key, which could be important. Or . . .

Tentatively, she flicked the flashlight beam along the north wall of the building, again searching the parking lot. She saw only cracked asphalt and weeds whipping and twisting in the wind. She turned and made the same inspection along the south wall, which bordered the side street. Nothing.

Uneasily, she remembered touring the theater with Nick and opening a door on a narrow, cluttered space between the rear of the theater and the weather-beaten fence behind it.

She stood beside the car for a moment, irresolute. *I can't go back there to that ugly, isolated space . . . I just can't!*

Yet her feet carried her that way, along the edge of the weathered asphalt, weeds catching on her pant legs. A dog started barking somewhere beyond the fence. The broken board banged.

She took a deep breath and aimed the beam of the flashlight into that narrow space behind the theater.

16

The blanket-wrapped object lay among the bits of trash trapped between the building and tall fence. Old plastic bags and soft-drink cartons, bent straws and beer cans. Sarah's heart froze when she recognized the plaid blanket.

And the pale hand thrust out from under the blanket. A hand with slender fingers ringed with bright costume jewelry flashing phony brilliance in the beam of the flashlight. Something silvery-gray, like wide tape, circled the fine-boned wrist.

Sarah didn't burst into tears. She didn't shriek or collapse. She didn't run in panic or throw herself on the body. She just stood there, stunned.

It can't be true.

It is true.

She turned the flashlight off. She couldn't bear seeing that pathetic little hand peeking out of the blanket, couldn't bear seeing the vulnerable slightness of the wrapped body. The wind howled over the fence, but here in the sheltered nook where death hid in shadows, it murmured and whispered.

Whispered of death and anguish and loss. Whispered of laughter silenced, dreams ended, joy crushed.

Oh, Julie, Julie, twin of my heart. . . .

A storm of tears gathered now, and a corkscrew of pain ripped through her, tearing and shattering as it churned into her heart and soul. *Dead. Julie is dead.*

She fought against the tears and the pain. *No, I will not break down now! I have to think what to do.*

She couldn't run to a neighbor or back to the apartment to call the county sheriff's office. She wouldn't leave Julie vulnerable and alone. But should she flag down a passing car? Or simply vent her anguish and helplessness in a howl of despair?

Lord, give me your strength and wisdom. Don't let me collapse. Help me through this! Show me what to do. She stood there then, face lifted, opening herself to all the Lord had to offer, letting him fill and strengthen her.

She strode back to the car, her indecision gone. She started the engine and pulled into the parking lot. Weeds scraped the underside of the car as she parked near the fence. Then, hands clasped so tightly her knuckles gleamed, she simply sat there. Waiting. Guarding.

At 7:45 she reluctantly retreated from her sentry post and drove to the Julesburg police station. The parking lot was empty, but a few minutes later Ben Mosely's old blue pickup pulled up beside her car. Sarah got out and went to meet him.

Nick had tried to call Sarah before he left the motel. The workman's surgery had run into complications, and he hadn't gotten away from the hospital until after 10:00 the night before. Too late to call her then. Now he tried calling her again, and there was no answer. But she could still be asleep. He hoped she was. Sleep would be the best thing for her.

Yet he couldn't quite picture Sarah peacefully slumbering with the search of Ryker's Bog looming ahead of them today.

The fact that she still didn't answer when he tried to call from the pay phone outside the restaurant was nothing to be alarmed about. Or at least that's what he told himself. *She could be in the shower. At the post office. Feeding cats. The search of Ryker's Bog isn't scheduled to start until noon.*

He picked up a couple of workmen and drove to the job site. He got the plasterers lined out on the interior work and talked to the plumbing inspector who showed up unexpectedly. He checked the chandelier the electrician had ready to install in the dining room. But at 8:50 when he borrowed a cell phone from one of the plasterers and still got no answer at Julie's apartment, he gave terse orders to the crew for the rest of the day and headed for Julesburg.

He saw the gathered crowd as soon as he rounded the bend of the highway in the center of town. A police car with an open door and flashing lights, more vehicles lined up on both sides of the street, milling people. The fact that this activity was centered around the Nevermore struck him as ominously significant, and fear for Sarah instantly hit him like a jackhammer to the chest. Had the killer returned and eliminated the one person who might witness against him?

He had to park on a side street and run to the scene. The harsh wind had dwindled to fitful gusts, but a light rain was falling now. Once he reached the Nevermore, he was surprised to see that all the attention was centered around the rear of the building.

Several more vehicles with flashing lights crowded the parking lot. One was an ambulance, but the medical personnel were just standing around, not rushing to anyone's aid. A van with a television station's call letters and channel number stood near the rear of the building, photographer standing on the hood with a video camera aimed down on the narrow space between the theater and the fence. A flashbulb flared within the space.

Then he saw her, standing back from the crowd. She was leaning against the fence, head bowed, hand sheltering her eyes. He shouldered his way toward her.

"Sarah," he said softly.

Her gaze took a moment to focus on him, but then she gave a small, wounded-animal cry and tilted into his arms. He didn't ask questions; he simply held her, offering wordless comfort. She shivered uncontrollably in his arms, but she wasn't crying. It was as if some reaction beyond tears had hold of her.

Over her shoulder he saw a break in the clump of people crowding the space at the back of the building. Randy Wilson stepped through the opening, flashbulb camera in hand. He beckoned to the paramedics, and they came forward with a stretcher.

"Little late for an ambulance," someone nearby said.

"Yeah. Looks like what they need is a coffin. And a rope to hang the dirty scum who done it. Who's the dude in the suit?"

"Medical examiner. Autopsy guy." Rough chortle. "How'd you like to have his job?"

Death humor. Nick wrapped one arm around Sarah's head, shielding her ears from it.

The paramedics briefly disappeared behind the building. When they reappeared, a covered form lay on the stretcher. Randy Wilson stepped back to document the scene with more photos of the space where the body had been. The stretcher disappeared into the double doors at the rear of the ambulance. Sarah looked up, and for a moment Nick thought she was going to break from his arms and run after it. But she only stared, her gaze a mixture of grief and bewilderment and pain.

Ben Mosely was now putting up the yellow crime-scene tape, his air authoritative even though he looked more lumberjack than police officer in heavy work pants and suspenders. He hadn't looked good the first time Nick had met him, and now his appearance was even worse, as if a physical weight had dragged his face into a mask of bags and sagging hollows.

Yet a moment later, when a television reporter started interviewing Randy, Ben's back straightened and his eyes blazed with fury.

Nick turned his attention back to Sarah. She looked up at him, her eyes dark pools of pain. "I found her," she whispered. "There. In that dirty little space behind the theater. Like some . . . discarded bundle of trash."

"But how? Why were you here?"

"I had a phone call. A little before 4:00 this morning. He told me she was here. I thought . . . I hoped she was alive, but . . ." Her voice sagged in despair.

You came here alone, in the dark? A killer is on the loose! A killer who's killed not once but twice now. You could be next on his list, and you're out here responding to some anonymous phone call?

Even as knowledge of what she'd done chilled him, he couldn't ignore her loyalty and courage. And this was no time for chastisement or warnings, so he merely gritted his teeth and tightened his arm around her shoulders.

"Let's get you back to the apartment."

She glanced around. "Isn't there something I should do?"

"I'll check with Ben. You wait here."

He leaned her against the wooden fence, her body as inflexible as a tin soldier's. Ben was still watching the television interview, his arms folded and legs spread. He jerked when Nick spoke to him, as if he were concentrating so intently that he hadn't even noticed Nick's approach. Was he offended by how the media panted after murder? Or did he resent all the attention Randy Wilson was getting?

"Is there any reason Sarah needs to stick around?" Nick motioned toward Sarah standing by the fence.

"No. Take her home. Terrible thing. Her finding the body like that."

"She came because she got a phone call."

"I know. We'll investigate that."

"Do you know anything about the death?"

"We'll have the medical examiner's report on the autopsy in a couple days." Reluctantly, Ben added, "We'll also need some further information from Sarah. But later. Maybe you ought to get a hold of Doc Halmoose and have him give her something now."

Nick nodded and went back to Sarah. At the apartment he settled her on the sofa and fixed her a cup of tea. She stirred it with concentration, as if making precise circles with the spoon was of monumental importance.

"Do you want to talk, Sarah?" Nick asked gently. "Or lie down? Ben suggested the local doctor could give you something."

"Talking or not talking won't change anything. Julie's *dead.* And I don't want my head full of drugs." Her voice began in dull despair but rose to a ring of anger. Her fists clenched, as if she wanted to strike out at something but didn't know what to strike. "I guess deep down I knew she had to be dead by now. But I kept hoping somehow . . ."

Nick sat beside her on the sofa and wrapped his arms around her.

"Julie's been in my life only a few months. I didn't know she existed before that. But now that she's gone, it feels as if half my heart has been torn out."

"Give your hurt to the Lord, Sarah," he said gently. "Lean on him. One of the promises he makes in his Word is 'Never will I leave you; never will I forsake you.' "

"I prayed while I was searching for Julie in the Nevermore. And when I found her body, I prayed God would give me strength and courage not to break down right there. And he did. I felt his strength just pouring into me. I felt his presence all the time I stayed there alone until I could get the police."

She sounded amazed and gratified by how God had strengthened and helped her. Nick brushed her cheek gently with his palm, pushing a dark strand of hair behind her ear.

"He wants to help you through this, Sarah. Our connection with the people we love is fragile. Life is . . . tenuous. All we can really count on is that God will never leave us. He's our one constant."

She was silent, tears sliding slowly down her cheeks. He brushed one away with his thumb.

"Did you know Sarah is a biblical name? And the Lord did something very special for that Sarah?"

"I've been reading in Julie's New Testament. But I don't remember reading about a Sarah." The distraction he offered her was small, even irrelevant, but she sounded grateful, as if she knew he was trying to comfort her.

"She was Abraham's wife, far back in the Old Testament. He was almost a hundred years old, and Sarah was ninety, when God told them he would give them a son."

"And did he?"

"Yes. Even though Sarah was doubtful and laughed at the idea. Actually, I suspect she snickered. Probably even thought, 'Ah, c'mon, God, you gotta be kiddin'.' But God gave them Isaac, who is listed in the lineage of Jesus. That biblical Sarah was also very beautiful. Like her modern namesake."

She looked up again and managed a tenuous smile. "I think I would like to have my children before I'm ninety."

And would you consider me for the position of husband and father of those children? It seemed impossible that they had known each other only a few days, impossible that his feelings for her had intensified into love. But it had happened. He was also reasonably certain she had feelings for him. He'd seen them in her eyes and felt them in her touch.

But there was no normalcy in their relationship. No time outside the pressure cooker of fear and anguish to be ordinary people getting to know each other.

So all he said was, "I have a Bible out in the pickup for you, with both the Old and New Testaments. You can read about Sarah and Abraham for yourself."

"But God gave that Sarah something," Sarah pointed out. She straightened her back, and her voice hardened. "From me he has only taken."

"Are you angry with God? Resentful?" He remembered feeling that way when his father hadn't survived the heart attack. He'd briefly shaken his fist at God.

"Don't I have a right to be?" she challenged. "Julie thought it was God who arranged for us to find each other. Don't I have a right to be angry that he brought us together only to tear us apart? Maybe it would be better if we'd never found each other!"

"Do you really believe that?"

She slumped in her seat. "No. I'm grateful for the little time we had together. And I guess, down deep, I don't really blame God for what happened to her. There's evil in this world. Evil people doing evil things. But I desperately hoped God would answer our prayers and bring her home safely. I think now that it was too late even before our prayers began." She bowed her head, muffling her voice. "And in some ways I'm grateful for that. It meant she wasn't living in terror or suffering in the time before I found her body."

Nick was silent for a moment. He knew what she meant. He'd thought about that too, feared that Julie might be trapped in the hands of some sexual sadist.

"Sarah, do you have any idea who called you?"

"No. Except that it was the killer. He was disguising his voice. It sounded muffled. Whispery. And . . . evil.

He laughed when he told me 'happy hunting' at the Nevermore."

Nick puzzled over this. He didn't doubt Sarah's conviction that it was the killer who called her. But why would the killer want the body discovered? Why didn't he just dump it far out in the woods where it might be years before it was found? And why the Nevermore?

"Sarah, the first day I came to the Nevermore, what was all that Julie was saying about ghosts and evil forces and exorcism?"

"She'd just been telling me these creepy old stories about the Nevermore. About an unsolved murder and suicide there, and how terrible things happened to anyone who got involved with the theater. I thought it was all just exaggerated haunted-house nonsense."

"Julie thought differently?"

"I'm not sure how serious she was, but she decided we should have a ceremony to exorcise the evil spirits or whatever might be lurking in the Nevermore. I felt ridiculous when you walked in. But now . . ." Her throat moved in a convulsive swallow.

"Did she really believe in that New Age stuff, crystals and all that?"

"I'm not sure she believed. She was just so curious and open-minded about everything. Crystals and yoga and astrology, reincarnation and multiple personalities, even UFOs. But she read the New Testament Gran gave us too. I found places she'd marked."

"The advice in an astrology column is not exactly on a level with the words of Jesus."

"No, but she wasn't some weird cultist or Satan worshiper!" Sarah's voice flared in defense of her twin, and she moved a few inches away from him.

Troubled, he asked, "How do you feel about all the things Julie dabbled in?"

"Not for me. Though I want to be tolerant of other people's beliefs."

"I believe in tolerance too. I'm certainly not advocating intolerance. But tolerance and truth are two separate things."

She waved one hand in weary dismissal, then straightened as if an electric jolt had hit her. "I have to call Julie's mother."

"I'll do it for you—"

"No. I have to do it myself." Again he saw the loyalty and courage and determination that were so much a part of her character. Calling Julie's mother was her responsibility; she wouldn't back away from it to make things easier for herself.

He could hear only one side of the phone conversation, but he could tell that Julie's mother was falling to pieces on the other end of the line. Sarah, even in her own despair, was doing her best to comfort and soothe the woman. She leaned back against the sofa after she put the phone down. Her closed eyelids looked blue and fragile against her pale skin.

"At least I don't have to call her father. He's still out of the country. Her mother wants Julie's body brought down to California for burial."

"I don't suppose Julie left instructions or said anything?"

Her mouth twisted in a bleak smile. "Who does, at twenty-five?"

She closed her eyes again. The phone rang. Nick, after a quick glance at Sarah, reached for it himself.

The woman identified herself as Marianne Peabody from the Julesburg Café. He listened with a growing burn of outrage and anger. He glanced again at Sarah, hating to pass this on to her, but it couldn't be ignored. He put a hand over the phone.

17

"This is a Mrs. Peabody from the Julesburg Café," Nick said. "She says they have several of Julie's paintings hanging there."

"They've sold a couple of her seascapes. But it's mostly locals who go there, and they aren't much into art."

"She says they sold two of the paintings yesterday, two more today, and they're getting inquiries from out of town. She's uneasy about selling any more."

Sarah looked puzzled as to why the café no longer wanted Julie's paintings. Then as realization dawned, she surged to her feet in outrage. "People are buying her paintings now just so they can say they have something done by that woman who was murdered?"

Nick remembered reading about a serial killer whose paintings had sold for thousands. "I think that's what Mrs. Peabody is thinking."

"It's ghoulish!" Sarah gasped. "Tell her the paintings are no longer for sale, and we're coming to take them off the walls."

Mrs. Peabody was a middle-aged woman with blond hair and a round face that Nick suspected usually wore a cheerful smile. Now she looked as if she'd like to set a firecracker under someone.

"I just can't believe it," she said when she thrust checks for the sold paintings at Sarah. "People coming in and gawking like a flock of vultures."

Nick could see Sarah's reluctance to take the checks. She jerked back as if the money might explode in her hand.

"I think Julie would want you to have it," he offered in a low voice.

Sarah hesitated, then nodded and jammed the money into her pocket. Nick grabbed a chair to stand on and lifted the first painting off the wall.

Mrs. Peabody gave her ruffled apron an indignant flutter. "Some of those paintings have been hanging here for weeks. People always saying how good they are. But not putting out a cent to buy one until now."

Nick handed the other framed paintings down to Sarah while Mrs. Peabody rattled on. Sarah leaned them against the wall near the door. Few people were in the café, which Nick thought was fortunate. He suspected Sarah might give anyone who asked about the paintings a piece of her mind.

When they returned to the apartment, they set several of the paintings on Julie's bed and leaned the others against the bedroom wall. Sarah stood with hands clasped as she studied the paintings. Julie had captured the varying moods of the sea with sensitive skill. The fury of a storm, the sparkling calm of a sunlit day, the playfulness of small waves lapping glossy pebbles and seaweed.

"This has, at least, helped me make up my mind," Sarah said.

"About the paintings?"

"About Julie. I was doubtful when her mother said she wanted Julie buried down there. Julie chose Julesburg as her home, and I thought perhaps she should be buried here. But not now."

"Don't be too hard on the town just because a few people are being insensitive about the paintings—"

"Someone in Julesburg killed Julie. Others are grabbing her paintings because of the notoriety of her death. I do not want Julie in Julesburg."

"And what about you, Sarah? Afterward?"

She looked at him. "I guess I haven't thought that far ahead. I still have my parents' house in California."

He planted his hands on her shoulders. "I don't want to lose you, Sarah. I know we haven't known each other long, but you're already a big part of my life."

Sarah blinked, as if she only now realized that leaving Julesburg behind also meant leaving him behind. "I don't want to lose you, either."

But Nick knew it was not yet time for promises and commitments, much as he was tempted to press for one. Julie was dead. Julie's murderer was out there somewhere. And Sarah was still too lacerated, too fragile, too tightly wound to think of anything else.

Nick called to check on the injured workman and found he'd be hospitalized for at least two more days. Then he and Sarah retrieved the Honda from the parking lot at the police department and went to feed the jetty cats. Twila Mosely was there again, looking almost as bad as Ben, as if she'd shriveled in the last few days. Lines bit deep around her eyes and mouth as she rubbed her cheek against the white fur of a blue-eyed cat.

"How is your granddaughter doing?" Sarah asked.

"Deteriorating."

"I'm so sorry." Sarah squeezed Twila's hand. "They haven't scheduled a transplant yet?"

Money? Nick wondered, troubled. Such a medical procedure must be incredibly expensive. How sad if the granddaughter's life came down to a matter of dollars and cents.

"It takes just the right donor. I feel bad, hoping one will turn up. Because that means grief for some other family when they lose a loved one. But everything's ready with the doctors and hospital as soon as one does turn up." Twila managed a watery smile. "It's in God's hands."

"I guess we all are," Sarah agreed.

"And I'm so very sorry about Julie," Twila added. "It shook Ben, you know, you being the one to find her there behind the Nevermore. There are all those old tales about evil spirits and curses lurking around the old theater. But I don't believe—"

"What I believe," Sarah cut in flatly, "is that there's a killer right here in Julesburg. He's not some evil spirit. He's one of us."

On the way home, Sarah brought up something she said she'd forgotten to mention earlier.

"This guy came over to talk to me yesterday when I was feeding the cats. Joe Argo. He's a commercial fisherman, Julie's friend who gave us the name of Nordahl and Sons to contact about remodeling the Nevermore."

"Must be a great guy then."

Sarah bypassed the light comment. "He asked this odd question about whether I thought what happened at the Calico Pantry was just what it looked like on the surface, a robbery that escalated into something much worse."

"What else could it be?"

"My thought exactly. And then he made an even stranger comment, that someone 'important or powerful' here in town could be involved."

The fisherman's questions and comments puzzled Nick as much as they obviously did Sarah. Not a killing done in momentary panic, but premeditated murder? Why would anyone want to kill the elderly owner of a shabby, small-town convenience store? And who in tiny Julesburg could even be considered "important and powerful?" Although he'd heard the owner of Volkman Laser Systems kept a Lear jet at the Coos Bay airport.

"Did he mean someone important could be behind the crime?"

"Now that you mention it, I'm sure that is what he meant." Sarah sat up straighter in the seat. "I've been trying to place someone 'important and powerful' behind that ski mask, and it isn't working. But money can buy a killer."

"Joe didn't drop any names, I take it."

"No. But he did make some uncomplimentary remarks about the guy Julie was seeing, Donovan Moran. He suggested Donovan had been involved with drugs and the law. Which could be true. Julie was really upset that last night she saw him."

"Maybe Joe is just a disgruntled admirer taking digs at the competition?"

"Could be. He also took a dig at a 'playboy' Julie had dated earlier."

"A playboy? In Julesburg?"

"Sounds about as likely as a diamond in a box of Cracker Jacks, doesn't it? But sometimes I get the feeling a good many secrets may be hidden in little Julesburg."

Nick was still walking these thoughts around in his mind when they pulled into the parking lot at the apartment building. *A deliberate murder disguised to look like a simple convenience store robbery gone haywire. Is it possible? With Julie killed afterward because she was an unplanned inconvenience?*

Or because she recognized the killer?

"Have you told Randy Wilson or Ben Mosely about this?"

"No. With all that's happened, it didn't occur to me. It also seems a little . . . far out."

Maybe.

Sarah didn't want to eat out that evening, so Nick went to the store and picked up ingredients for a Chinese-style chicken-and-vegetables dish he hoped she'd like. The dish required a lot of chopping of meat and vegetables, sautéeing and shaking and stirring, separate cooking of a sauce and delicate rice noodles. Nick would gladly have done it all for Sarah, but she seemed to appreciate keeping busy and concentrating on the various steps of the recipe with him.

After they finally sat down to eat and after he offered the blessing, Sarah ate with unexpected enthusiasm.

"This is really good." She waved a forkful of noodles. "What's it called?"

"I'm not sure I should tell you. It's kind of gross."

She lifted her eyebrows with interest.

"Mom invented the recipe when Jason and I were just little kids. She said it was kind of a combination of chow mein and chop suey, but when I went running to tell Dad we'd helped Mom cook dinner, I got things mixed up and called it slop chewy. And the name stuck."

She laughed, and the sound was clear and honest, as if for a few moments she could set aside the heartbreak of the day. "You must have been keeping this marvelous slop chewy talent to yourself, or you'd have eager females flinging themselves at you en masse. More than there probably already are."

"Actually, I was hoping just one female would be impressed enough to fling herself at me." He waggled his eyebrows in an exaggerated leer and then smiled and softened the slightly suggestive statement by adding, "Figuratively speaking, of course."

She smiled back and blew him a kiss across the table. "Okay, consider yourself figuratively flung at."

While they cleared the dishes Sarah turned on the TV to catch the local news. The interview with Randy Wilson behind the Nevermore was the lead story.

"Impressive," Nick commented as they watched Randy, who came across as tough and determined, with a hint of TV charisma.

"Yes, indeed. Impressive," Sarah agreed. She tilted her head. "But he impressed me in a different way when I was being interviewed. He was the only one who really seemed to care about how devastated I felt. But I suppose he has to be more high-powered and aggressive when he's on TV. Twila Mosely says he has big-time ambitions in law enforcement."

The reporter then asked about leads in the case, and Randy said that they had certain information they were not releasing to the public at this point.

"I wonder what he means by that?" Sarah asked.

"I've heard that police sometimes hold back details of a crime so that if a suspect reveals such a detail, it's a pretty good indication he's involved."

"Then I should think it would be better not to announce that, because now the killer knows he has to be on guard not to reveal something incriminating."

Good point. But what do I know about police procedure? Perhaps this bit of information was designed to worry the killer, to make him wonder if he'd slipped up somewhere. Randy Wilson's confidence and determination might well be unnerving for a killer.

When asked if there were suspects or if an arrest was pending, Randy answered smoothly, "We're developing several promising leads. We anticipate an early resolution of this case."

Again, he sounded as if he knew more than he was sharing, but Sarah was skeptical. "And what does that police double-talk mean in plain English? 'We're completely in the dark, but we're hoping we get lucky and something turns up'?"

"Hard to tell."

"I feel so . . . helpless!" Sarah burst out as the weatherman came on the screen. She clicked the remote control to shut him off. "So useless. So guilty for not being able to give them better information. If I'd been more perceptive or observant, maybe they'd have the killer in custody right now."

An uneasy possibility occurred to Nick. "Promise me something?"

"What?"

"Promise me you won't do again what you did this morning."

"I found Julie's body this morning. I can never do that again!"

"I know. I'm sorry. I mean, promise me you won't go out alone again into what could be a dangerous situation. It's the authorities' job to figure out who did this, not yours."

"If there's any chance I could help, I want to do it. Any way I can."

"At least promise you'll get hold of me before you get involved in anything."

"I tried to get hold of you at 4:00 this morning and couldn't."

Nick groaned inwardly. *My cell phone.* It was gratifying to know that she'd turned to him in a crisis, but then for him not to be there for her . . .

"New cell phone coming up immediately," he promised. "And you will get hold of me before you do anything?"

"I'm going to the police station tomorrow to give Ben or Randy my fingerprints and hair sample. Services for Mrs. Maxwell are also tomorrow, and then I'll leave for California as soon as Julie's body is released after the autopsy."

She'd evaded the promise Nick wanted, and he realized he'd have to settle for plans that didn't appear to hold any specific dangers.

After kitchen cleanup, they wrapped themselves in warm clothes and headed for the beach in Nick's pickup. A lopsided moon played tag with scudding clouds. Once there, he held her hand as they descended the rough steps from the parking lot to the sand at the south end of town.

That night the beach was an obstacle course, a shadowy dreamscape of debris tossed up by the recent storm. Stumps with roots like grasping tentacles, piles of kelp in tangles, clumps of dark mussels torn loose from their rock moorings.

Sarah apparently did not feel like talking, and Nick didn't press her. They walked rapidly until a creek that flowed beneath a bridge on the highway and across the beach blocked their way. Outgoing creek and incoming tide met in a ragged tangle of jumping waves.

"Julie said it's called Wandering Creek," Sarah said. "It moves up and down the beach, depending on how much sand the ocean piles up."

"An appropriate name, then."

The moon slid out from behind a cloud, its radiance undimmed by city lights. Nick handed Sarah a sand dollar lying near his feet. It was whole and unbroken, a rare find on Oregon's wave-battered beaches.

She held up the round shell, and the powerful moonlight illuminated the graceful, flowerlike etching on the top side. She looked up at him. "I'm sorry I'm not very good company tonight."

"You're the company I want, in any form." He brought her hand to his lips.

She seemed startled but not displeased. "I just have so many things on my mind," she said awkwardly.

"About?" he inquired. They turned and started back the way they had come, walking more slowly now. Another cloud slid across the moon.

"Oh, big, deep thoughts about life and death and God and the universe. Sad thoughts about Julie. Angry thoughts about her killer. I feel murderous toward him. And yet . . . bewildered too, about how someone could actually do what this person did to Julie and Mrs. Maxwell."

"One person killing another is as old as Cain and Abel. As you said earlier, there's evil in this world."

"God could change that if he wanted! All he'd have to do is zap wrongdoers with instant punishment, and people would catch on pretty fast."

"That isn't God's way."

She stumbled over a twisted strand of kelp. "Aren't you sometimes bewildered or frustrated by God's ways?" Her fingers clenched his. "Doesn't it seem as if so many things in this world just don't make sense? That justice gets cheated? Don't doubts sometimes get in the way of your faith?"

"I sometimes have doubts," Nick admitted. "A few passages in the Bible confuse more than enlighten me. I don't understand why a lot of things happen in my own or other people's lives."

"Then if I become a Christian, I'm not suddenly going to become all-wise and all-knowing?" He caught an unexpected hint of humor in the question. "I won't instantly know what became of the dinosaurs or if there's life on other planets or why God made cockroaches?"

"Nope. You'll just be forgiven and saved."

"Saved." She said the word as if it were an unfamiliar flavor on her tongue. "What does that really mean?"

"Saved from condemnation, saved to spend an eternal life with the Lord after life on this earth. Where, we're told, 'he will wipe every tear from their eyes. There will be no more death or mourning or crying or pain.' "

"No crying or pain," she repeated, her tone rough with yearning to escape the pain surrounding her. "Who is he, Nick?" she demanded in sudden anguish. "Who did this to my Julie?"

Nick wanted to tell her that the police would soon pinpoint and apprehend the killer. But would they? The long-ago murder in the Nevermore had never been solved. He'd read not long ago that all across the country more crimes went unsolved than solved.

"It's getting late. I think I should get you back to the apartment."

She didn't move. "Is it okay to pray that the killer gets what he deserves?" she demanded. "That he doesn't get away with what he did?"

Nick hesitated. "The Lord can forgive even a killer."

"Forgive Julie's killer?" Her head jerked in shock as she looked up at him.

"Even Julie's killer, if he comes in honest repentance, can find forgiveness. Although that doesn't mean an escape from earthly punishment for crimes."

She started walking again, shoulders slumped. "It gets complicated, doesn't it?"

"It does. And I don't think full understanding of many things will come until we're beyond this life. But the Lord is always here to help us through doubts and problems."

"But I feel so ignorant! I'd never heard of that Sarah in the Bible. And the Cain and Abel you mentioned—I've heard of them, but I have no idea who they really are."

"God wants us to study his Word, all of it. But the basic truths it offers are simple. Salvation comes only through Jesus. He died on the cross for us, and everyone who believes that and accepts the salvation he offers will be with him after this life is over. It's a free gift, Sarah. All you have to do is accept it."

"I want to. . . ." The moon came out from behind the cloud, and he saw yearning on her uplifted face. Then a shadow crossed over her delicate features.

"But what about Julie?"

18

Julie.

The name hung in the damp night air. Nick hesitated uneasily before repeating what he'd said a moment earlier. "Salvation and the eternal life that comes after this one are a free gift from God. All we have to do is accept that gift."

"But we have to accept it in this lifetime?"

He felt a chill inch up his spine at the implication of her words. "Yes, that's true."

"No second chances?"

"God does offer second chances! Over and over. He doesn't give up on us—"

"But only in this lifetime." She pulled out of his arms and stared up at him. "And you're saying that because Julie didn't grab this gift before she was killed, that she's lost and condemned forever?"

"We have only this life in which to make our choices—" He broke off, uneasy with the holier-than-thou sound of his words.

"But Julie was *murdered!* That wasn't her choice! If God had protected her and given her more time, maybe she'd have made the choice he demands. She was a good person, Nick! Sunny and sweet and caring, always doing things for people." A blaze suddenly flared in her eyes. "And what about my parents? They didn't go to church, but they were the best, most wonderful and generous people I've ever known! And they're condemned too?"

"We can't save ourselves by being . . . nice guys and doing good deeds." He said the words with a troubled reluctance, knowing that this truth could be a fatal stumbling block for someone outside the faith. "As Christians we should do all the good deeds we can. We honor God by doing them. Our faith is expressed through them. But—"

"So you're telling me that Julie's killer still has a chance to believe and be forgiven. But Julie and my folks are lost forever. The pearly gates—" she edged the phrase with sarcastic scorn, "are forever closed to them. But the killer still has a chance to walk right through."

Nick flexed his fingers. This was not an easy tenet of Christian truth.

"Don't bother dredging up pious verses for me," she threw into his moment of silence. "Because at this point I don't care what your Jesus and your Bible say."

"Sarah—"

"I was willing to accept that Julie's death wasn't necessarily God's fault. I wasn't blaming him. But not preventing her death and then ruthlessly shutting her out forever after she was murdered . . . that isn't fair, Nick. Why should I even want to spend an eternity with a God like that?" She raised a palm, cutting off his interruption. "You tell me God wants to comfort me. But what comfort is there knowing he's shut out the people I love?"

Her words and tone held a finality that ended the discussion, and he knew that both her tentative relationship with the Lord and with him stood on the brink of collapse.

Her good-bye at the apartment was stiff. And she did not invite him in.

Sarah spent a difficult, restless night, thinking how she had briefly taken refuge with the Lord. She'd hovered on the edge of committing herself to him.

Now she felt only betrayal. And she was not going to desert and betray Julie and her beloved parents by turning to the one who was condemning them!

Nick's mother called the following morning to offer her sympathies. Sarah appreciated that, but at the same time she felt a reserve toward the woman whose relationship with God undoubtedly paralleled Nick's.

She went to the police station immediately after the call. Randy wasn't there, but Ben snipped a small hair sample and took her fingerprints. He kept up a low-key chatter about how doing it with ink was old-fashioned now, that the modern method was computerized.

"Randy gets frustrated by not having the latest equipment, but old guys like me, we don't mind doing things the old-fashioned way."

Gradually he worked into questions about the call that had drawn her to the Nevermore. It wasn't a formal questioning, and she knew he was trying to be gentle and tactful, but each question felt like the jab of a flaming torch.

"I'm sorry we have to ask all this," he apologized as a phone rang. The secretary, sitting in a cubbyhole off to the side, answered it. Randy came in through a rear door and went to the fax machine.

"And I'm sorry I can't give you information that would be more helpful," Sarah said.

"You don't think you'd know the voice if you heard it again?"

Sarah shook her head. "It kept changing. First a whispery, unreal voice, then guttural and slangy. And then

. . . sly and evil. As if he were running through some repertoire."

Randy gave a scornful snort. "Sounds like some punk kid who plays too many video games and watches too much television."

"I can't understand why he put the body at the Nevermore. Or why he wanted me to find it."

Randy looked at a fax, then crumpled it and tossed it at a wastebasket. "Running out of thrills, maybe. Looking for a new high by actually talking to you and sending you to the local spookhouse. Maybe hoping you'd freak out or something."

Freak out. Yes, I'm on the edge of that. But she managed to stumble away from the edge and say, "Is that everything?"

"I need to ask you a couple of questions relating to the autopsy," Ben said. "The medical examiner will be doing it this afternoon."

Sarah clenched her hands on the counter. "When will her body be released?"

"Tomorrow, I think. Unless something unusual turns up at the autopsy. Have you given them the name of the funeral home you want?"

"I'm not familiar with funeral homes here. Julie will be buried down in California."

"Gasgow's Chapel of the Hills can make the arrangements for the funeral."

"I'd appreciate it if you'd give them that name for me then. Now, you said you had other questions?"

"We need to know when and what Julie last ate. Whether she was on any medication. If she'd used any illegal drugs recently."

Sarah stared at Ben. "What does any of that matter?"

"It may help to determine how long she was alive after she was abducted. Whether she had anything to eat before her death. If she did eat, what it was could be significant. And if any chemical substances show up in her system, we need to know if they were something she'd taken herself earlier or if they were administered to her. I'm sorry." Ben turned up his palms in apology as Randy disappeared into a back room.

"We'd gone to a food court in Corvallis with a friend." Sarah swallowed the queasiness rising from her stomach. "It was between 6:00 and 7:00 when we ate. We sampled a little of everything. Sushi, Greek salad with feta cheese, some curried vegetables, an egg roll, noodles . . ." Tears tangled with dizziness as she remembered how carefree they'd been. She clutched the counter for support.

Ben patted her shoulder. She found a tissue and dabbed at her eyes, then steeled herself and went on.

"She wasn't on any medication, and she never used drugs of any kind. Never," she repeated emphatically. "She hated them."

"I figured that. But I had to ask."

Desperately needing to bring this discussion to an end, Sarah jumped to another subject. "Are you going to Mrs. Maxwell's services today?"

"Helen made all the arrangements a couple years ago and asked me to be one of her pallbearers. But given the situation here . . ." Ben lifted a beefy hand. The fax was spewing papers, the phone ringing again.

"The tipsters are still at it," he muttered. "I asked Wally Greer from the bank to take my place as pallbearer. I imagine the senior center will be crowded."

"The services aren't at the church?"

"Helen said she never got to church more than once or twice a year when she was alive, so there wasn't much point trying to sneak into heaven under false pretenses when she was dead. But you aren't going, are you?"

"Yes, I plan to."

"Nobody expects that of you."

"I want to do it."

To pay her respects, of course. But also for another reason, a reason no one would suspect.

He glanced at his watch as he crossed the parking lot to his car after eating a sausage and jalapeño pizza at Website X. *No nervous stomach for me.* He could eat anything, anytime. Even with the services scheduled only a half hour from now. Not that he had any intention of attending that maudlin sideshow.

Not because the funeral would be some uncomfortable emotional workout. Guilt wasn't eating at him. The treacherous old bat had gotten what she deserved. She wouldn't be dead if she'd just let things hum along.

No, he wasn't going because it would be a hypocritical waste of time. Everyone knew what an ill-tempered old crank she had been, but someone would eulogize her into an angel on earth. People would drag up how she used to give credit when the mill was shut down or slip a piece of candy to some grubby-fingered kid because his poor mama had barely enough money for a quart of milk.

If they only knew what sweet ol' Mrs. Maxwell's own grubby fingers had been into!

He wondered about all the dough the old biddy had raked in. She must have kept some of it hidden there at the apartment over the store. Too bad he hadn't had time to search. But that hadn't been part of the plan.

Something else had not been part of the plan.

Julie and her sister.

It was beginning to look as if he should have offed the twin sister right there along with the old lady. A witness was part of the plan, but it was supposed to be an outsider, not someone emotionally involved. If he'd gone ahead and killed the sister, it still could have looked like nothing more than a small-time crime gone bad. But for just a minute there, mistakenly thinking she was Julie, he'd let surprise and an unfortunate squeamishness overrule cool thinking.

And then to have Julie herself pop up in the backseat . . .

He had nothing concrete telling him that leaving Sarah MacIntosh alive had been a mistake. Nothing except a gut feeling that she was a loose cannon.

Although, with just a little luck, she'd soon be fed up with Julesburg and pack up and leave. Would a nudge help get her going? A threat, maybe something even stronger?

He frowned. No, probably not a good idea. Julie had shown a surprising amount of fight when he was trussing her wrists and ankles with duct tape. Her twin sister might be enough like her that a threat would only arouse her stubbornness. But if she didn't pack up and leave . . .

That possibility suddenly changed his thinking about today. If Sarah MacIntosh was anything like her sister, she'd be right there at Helen Maxwell's services. Keeping an eye on Sarah, seeing how she reacted there, what she was up to, could be important.

He could pull it off. Easy. He'd handled that dramatic skit at the Calico Pantry like a pro. Pulled off a great audio script on the phone. Kept up the daily activities of being himself, looking normal. He grinned. Who said he couldn't act?

And if she did hang around, got nosy and started making trouble . . .

He had two deaths to his credit now. One more wouldn't be any big deal.

19

The parking lot at the senior center was full when Sarah arrived. She squeezed the Honda into a small space between a Volkswagen bug and a van on the grassy shoulder of a side street. She intended to slip into a back-row seat, but all the folding chairs were already taken. Even the standing-room area at the rear of the room was full. She finally squeezed into a space alongside the rows, up near the front. Much closer to the casket than she wanted to be.

The casket was closed. Bouquets and wreaths from mourners angled in flowery wings around, but no blanket of flowers adorned the plain pine box. Sarah remembered Ben saying that Mrs. Maxwell had made the funeral arrangements herself, which probably meant she'd also paid for them. And money could not have been plentiful in her life.

Once seated, Sarah scanned the rows of people. *Actually this is an excellent location after all. I can see almost everyone in the room, and that's the reason I'm here.*

Because *he'd* be here. She was certain of it. And maybe something about him would trigger her memory and recognition. Maybe some flicker of guilt would give him away. Maybe, as Julie would probably have suggested, he'd simply give off vibes.

She jumped when a hand squeezed her arm.

"Sorry. I didn't mean to startle you," Twila Mosely whispered. "Nice to see such a big turnout, don't you think? That's Helen's nephew and family from Portland there in the front row."

Sarah's first reaction to Twila slipping in beside her was a silent groan. She wanted to be alone to concentrate on the crowd. But then she realized that Twila knew and could identify practically everyone.

"Her only family?" Sarah asked.

"She had a son, but he's dead now." Twila hesitated momentarily, and Sarah had the feeling there was something more the elderly woman wasn't saying.

"The nephew will inherit the Calico Pantry?"

Another hesitation. "I suppose so."

Sarah's thoughts momentarily focused on the nephew. Was ownership of the Calico Pantry enough to motivate murder? Given the rundown state of the store, unlikely. But murder had been done for less.

"That boy in the third row," Sarah whispered, "the one with the shaved head and the metal spike in his ear. Who's he?"

"The youngest Thuringer boy. He looks like he belongs in some awful rock group, but he's headed for Bible college in Missouri next year. Wonderful young man."

Wonderful young men sometimes turned out to be killers.

"How about the nice-looking boy in the dark suit, fourth row?"

"New family on Lighthouse Hill. Californians. I don't know their name."

"Why would they come?"

"Some new people make a real effort to fit into the community. And some don't."

"Do you know a guy from Gold Beach named Donovan Moran? Julie was dating him."

Twila nodded. "She introduced him one time when they came down to the jetty on his motorcycle. Big, good-looking guy. The kind who makes parents wish they could lock their daughters away for a few years. He used to live in Julesburg. Collected traffic violations like he was papering his walls with them."

A strong chord from the piano opened the service, cutting off further conversation. The ensuing selection of music struck Sarah as odd, but since Helen Maxwell herself had chosen the program, the songs must have had special meaning for her. "Red Sails in the Sunset." "Tennessee Waltz." "Oh, What a Beautiful Morning." The nephew read a few stilted words and then helped an older woman come forward. In an unexpectedly strong voice, she identified herself as Myrna Bettenworth.

"Isn't she the one you said Julie used to read to?" Sarah whispered. Twila nodded.

The tribute Myrna gave to her old friend Helen was tender enough to bring tears to Sarah's eyes. It also made her feel guilty that she'd called Mrs. Maxwell the Pink Grinch and hadn't made more of an effort to be friendly to her. But by the time Myrna was done speaking, Sarah's mind, along with her gaze, was beginning to wander, and she realized that she was not only an observer. She was under observation as well.

One woman nudged another, and the second woman peeked sideways at Sarah. Other eyes met hers for a split second, then quickly looked away. She was surprised to see the fisherman, Joe Argo, standing in back. Why would he come? She wiggled her toes. She couldn't shake the unpleasant feeling that she wasn't simply being curiously observed. She was being *watched.*

Sarah's uneasiness grew as the service plodded on. Her gaze darted from face to face, trying to trap those watching eyes. The killer could be *anyone.* A distinguished looking gentleman sitting on the far side of the room. She caught his surreptitious glance on her. Would he hire a killer? That blond, good-looking guy standing at the rear. Had he been behind that ski mask? The young father with the children in the third row. Could he have needed money desperately enough to rob and kill for it? The skinny guy with the baseball cap perched on his unruly hair. Had he called and sent her to the Nevermore?

Maybe coming here wasn't such a good idea. The killer knew who she was. Was he studying her, calculating her weaknesses, planning his next move? Her palms leaked perspiration, and she rubbed them on her thighs. She desperately wanted out.

Finally the pallbearers picked up the casket and carried it toward the rear door. As everyone stood, a glance hit hers. She snatched Twila by the shoulder.

"The guy just reaching the aisle over there, the one patting his pocket, looking for a cigarette. Who's he?"

He was in his midtwenties, with a sleek, athletic build and dark hair, good-looking in a sulky, bad-boy sort of way. He wore an expensively cut charcoal suit. *He may as well have worn a label: Not Homegrown Julesburg.*

"That's Travis Volkman, son of the Volkman Laser Systems people," Twila whispered back. "I've never met him personally, but someone pointed him out to me. He was on one of those beach-cop TV shows where the girls don't seem to own any clothes except bikinis. But he got in drug trouble down in Hollywood, and Daddy stopped financing his acting career and made him go to work for the company."

"Is he a good actor?"

"I think he figures he's so gorgeous he doesn't need to act." Twila gave a derogatory sniff as they moved with the crowd. "Maybe Volkman senior made him attend the funeral to try to make people think the company cares about the town. Their local image isn't all that great, you know. Mr. Volkman and his wife are too snooty to mix around here. Although . . ." Twila's head tilted, and her eyes narrowed.

Sarah's gaze followed Twila's to the man behind Travis Volkman. He was the same height and coloring but of heavier build, his neck thicker and face coarser. He looked like a boxer past his prime but still dangerous.

"That could be Volkman senior himself," Twila speculated. "I've never met him either."

Sarah felt a peculiar shiver. "A playboy rich guy," Joe Argo had called Travis Volkman. Would he go for easy money in a convenience store holdup if his father cut off the funds? Would the rich father protect him? If the elder Volkman cared about community relations, he wasn't showing it now as he bulled his way through the crowd. Was he attending this funeral more for reconnoitering purposes than community relations?

Sarah stopped short with another new thought. It hadn't occurred to her before, but had there been recognition behind the killer's alien eyes there in the Calico Pantry? Perhaps mistaken recognition of her as Julie? Travis Volkman had known Julie.

Sarah became separated from Twila in the crowd. She acknowledged murmured condolences about Julie from several people as she threaded her way to the door. A sign said sandwiches were being served downstairs, but Sarah headed directly for her car.

A lanky figure leaning against it straightened as she approached. She didn't bother with a polite hello.

"What are you doing here?"

"I thought maybe you could use some company or support," Nick said. "But I was late getting here, so I couldn't sit by you. I stood in back, on the far side of the room from you and Twila."

"I didn't see you."

And that fact rattled her nerves. If she hadn't seen Nick standing across the room from her, maybe she'd missed seeing the killer too.

"How about a cup of coffee? You look as if you could use one."

"I have some phone calls to make." She fished the keys from her purse and gave him a pointed look to tell him he was standing between her and the car door.

Before Nick moved, Sarah had to step aside to make way for several people walking by on the street, two older women and a balding man. The trio paused to let several cars pass in the street narrowed by vehicles parked on both sides.

"I feel bad that I haven't been in the Calico Pantry much lately," one woman said, sounding guilty. But a certain self-righteousness tinged her tone when she added, "But you know how it is, it's just more convenient to pick up everything over at the big market."

"Poor Helen. She had so many bad things happen in her life. Losing her husband, then her son too. Not that either of them deserved any gold stars." The stouter woman rolled her eyes. "And then to be murdered. For a few dollars and a carton of cigarettes."

"Well, she's in a better place now," the first woman declared.

Sarah looked at Nick after the trio passed. "Is she? Is Helen Maxwell in 'a better place' now? Ben said she didn't want her final services in a church."

"Sarah, it isn't for me to pass judgment and say this person is with the Lord and that one isn't. No one but the Lord knows what someone's real relationship with him is."

"You're dodging the issue. But you know what? I'd rather spend eternity with Julie and my folks, wherever they are, than with your God. Maybe that's what Mrs. Maxwell figured too, that she'd rather be with her son and husband somewhere."

"Sarah, this isn't a choice between God and Julie—"

"Isn't it?"

Nick looked troubled. "Lots of people have the warm, fuzzy view that going to heaven is some inalienable right. There'll be a big, happy reunion with friends and loved ones for almost everyone. And if you don't get to heaven, that's okay too, because most of your buddies will be in the other place anyway, and it'll still be a great reunion."

"And you're saying people are deceiving themselves, that unless you go with Jesus in this life, the bad is waiting out there to swallow you in the next life." Sarah didn't wait for a response. She jammed the key in the keyhole and yanked the car door open. "Well, you know what, Nick? I don't want any part of your hard-hearted, narrow-minded, vengeful God! Not in this life, not in the next. I don't want anything to do with a God who shuts out the people I love."

She slammed the door, but rolled down the window, not yet finished. "How can you expect me to even want to be 'saved'? You tell me the afterlife with Jesus will be this glorious place of no more tears or pain. But how can that be, if I'm there but I know that Julie and my folks are forever banished and condemned, even suffering somewhere? Will I forget them, if I'm there in heaven? Will I forget they're lost and shut out forever?"

"I don't think we forget those we've loved—"

"Then I don't see any eternity of peace and serenity with God. All I see is an eternity of loss. Eternal sadness. Eternal pain. Eternal tears."

She slammed the car into gear, raising a blast of grass and dirt as the tires grabbed hold in the soft shoulder. She didn't look back to see if the storm of debris caught Nick in its dark spray.

20

Nick jumped back as flying chunks of mud and grass punctuated Sarah's departure. He, along with several other people, watched the old Honda swerve down the street and barely miss a parked car.

He slid behind the wheel of his pickup. Sarah's bitter rejection of the Lord he loved frustrated and saddened him. Yet he understood it. He pounded the steering wheel with his fist. Sarah loved her twin sister and her parents with the fierce loyalty and devotion that were the foundation of her character. She had given up college because of that love and loyalty for her parents. She had braved the dark terrors of the Nevermore for Julie. It was no surprise that she felt accepting the Lord and the eternal salvation he offered would be turning her back on those she loved.

And she had raised a question that, oddly, he had never asked himself. How can there be peace in the life beyond this one if those you'd loved on earth were shut out, trapped in hell?

The question troubled him, but it did not shake his belief in the Lord's justice and eternal love. He was not swept into some turbulent storm of doubt. His love for the Lord could not be undercut by unknowns. Yet it was different for Sarah, who was in shock and despair about her sister, and whose faith had never moved into the full glow of the Lord's light.

He slammed the pickup in gear and crowded into the line of traffic creeping away from the senior center. He couldn't let this be a fatal blow to her relationship with the Lord. Or to the personal relationship between the two of them. *Lord, show me how to help her see beyond the hurt and bewilderment, and work through her angry rejection of you.*

A few minutes later he realized he would've made better time on foot. A fender bender at an intersection had brought traffic to a halt. A good half hour passed before he covered the few blocks to the parking lot and ran up the apartment stairs. He punched the doorbell.

Silence. Pretending she wasn't home? He tested the door lightly, tempted as he recognized again how flimsy it was.

Perhaps she too remembered that flimsiness, because the door suddenly flew open. She faced him with her chin high and her lips compressed.

"Sarah, I think we should talk—"

"Talk won't change anything." Her hostility suddenly collapsed, and a weary resignation slid across her face. She waved a hand and abandoned the door, as if whether he came or went was irrelevant.

"Are you okay?" he asked.

"I've been on the phone with Julie's mother and the funeral home. I'm leaving in the morning."

"Will you be back?"

She glanced toward the window looking out on Julesburg, her jaw clenched. She didn't want to return, that was obvious. Yet as he looked around the small apartment, Nick could see that it overflowed with remnants of Julie's life. No way could Sarah load all this into the Honda. She'd have to return. Which meant they might still have a chance to work things out.

She shook her head as if reading his mind. "No, it won't work, Nick. I do not want anything to do with your God. I don't want to hear about him or talk about him or read the Bible. I can't say it any more plainly than that, and I know what an uncrossable gap that puts between us." She regarded him thoughtfully. "In fact, I'm surprised you're here now."

"Surprised? Sarah, I love you! How could I not be here?"

She caught her breath as if a sharp pain had stabbed between her ribs. A shadow of uncertainty momentarily darkened her eyes. But she did not retreat or run into his arms.

"It won't work," she repeated softly. "The faith that means everything to you is a . . . poison to me. There's even a Bible verse about a relationship with someone who feels as I do, isn't there? I remember it from when Gran took us to church, something about not being yoked with an unbeliever." She laughed suddenly, but the sound was as brittle as shattering ice. "Now that's something, isn't it, me reminding you of a Bible verse."

Nick slumped to the arm of the sofa. He had never made some impassioned vow that he wouldn't fall in love with an unbeliever. He'd simply assumed it couldn't happen. But it had happened. He was in love with Sarah. And she'd made her rejection of the Lord as plain as words written in blood. She was not just a casual doubter; she'd looked and listened and felt the first stirrings of faith. And then she'd turned her back on God.

Yet now, as if she again read his mind, she came to him with unexpected compassion on her face. "You see?" She leaned over and kissed him on the forehead. Something swung out from her throat and brushed his cheek. "Thanks, Nick. Thanks for being here when I needed you. Thanks for everything. And I apologize for my rudeness earlier. That was uncalled for. You're a great guy, and you and some Christian girl will be happy together someday. But . . ."

She didn't finish the sentence, but simply backed away when her voice cracked. And then he saw what had touched his cheek.

"You're wearing Julie's crystal."

"Yes."

"Why?"

"Because it was Julie's."

But they both knew that wasn't the whole truth. The crystal was the defiant symbol of Sarah's rejection of God.

She cleared her throat, and her tone turned brisk and impersonal. "Now I do have more phone calls to make."

It was a pointed invitation for Nick to leave, and so he left.

But he sat in his pickup in the parking lot for a while, feeling lost and bewildered. He truly believed marriage between a believer and an unbeliever was outside God's will. He couldn't and wouldn't abandon his faith for her, and her rejection of that faith held no opening for compromise between them.

But that didn't make him love her any less.

Sarah blanket-wrapped two of the framed paintings to take to Julie's mother. They filled most of the backseat of the Honda. She kept her mind on details and resolutely locked her emotions in neutral. Nick's declaration of love had shaken her, but it didn't change anything.

Yes, I might have fallen in love with him too if things had been different. But things aren't different.

She started cleaning out a chest of drawers where Julie had kept various papers, making piles around her. This pile to throw away. That pile to be packed. Another pile of questionables. Old bills and receipts. Julie's tax return from last year. Cancelled checks. She rubbed the back of her hand across her forehead. So much *stuff.*

Suddenly, feeling overwhelmed, she picked up everything and haphazardly jammed the piles back into the drawers. *I'm not coming back. I'll just hire someone to come in and ship everything down to the California house and cope with it later. And never see Nick again . . .*

It's for the best.

The doorbell rang again just after 8:00. She hesitated, mindful of Nick's warning not to open the door to just anyone. A warning that now, after feeling the killer's eyes on her at Helen Maxwell's services, seemed even more potent.

She paused before touching the doorknob. "Who is it?"

"Ben Mosely."

She recognized the gruff voice. But she was momentarily appalled at how haggard he looked when she opened the door. His belt bunched his pants at the waist, as if he'd lost weight, and loose skin sagged under his jaws. Was the granddaughter's condition worsening? She stepped back, but he made only a single step into the room, just far enough so she could close the door.

"I talked to the medical examiner. He hasn't made his official report yet, but he did give me some preliminary information I thought you might want to know."

"Thank you." Sarah mentally braced herself. "I appreciate that."

"Julie was killed by a single bullet. It entered the back of the head and exited at the base of the throat. Death was instantaneous. The estimated time of death is approximately twenty-four to forty-eight hours after she was abducted. She had eaten pizza during that time. There were no drugs in her system, and no evidence of sexual molestation."

She heard compassion in Ben's voice, but his words painted agonizing visions in her mind. *Bullet to the back of the head. . . .* She swayed, and he reached out to steady her.

"But there's more to it than the bare-bones facts." He spoke hurriedly. "With the killer behind her, she didn't know the bullet was coming, so she didn't have some last minutes of terror. And she didn't suffer afterward. Giving her something to eat suggests the killer treated her . . . kindly before the fatal shot. And if she were my daughter, I'd be relieved to know this wasn't a sexual crime," he added gruffly.

Sarah would never have thought anything about Julie's death could be a relief, but Ben's interpretation did offer a certain comfort. Yet a moment later an unexpected resentment blazed at how Ben, in trying to soften the blow for her, almost made this cold-blooded killer sound decent.

"A real nice guy, huh?" she challenged bitterly. "A heart-of-gold murderer."

Ben's jaw clenched. "No. No heart of gold. A ruthless, calculating killer. She was bound with duct tape when she died. The killer cut the tape later, probably to make carrying her body easier." *The gray tape on Julie's wrist,* Sarah thought with dull horror. "But it could have been worse for her, much worse."

She heard the pain in his voice, and she was suddenly ashamed of herself. "I'm sorry. I appreciate your coming. I talked to the funeral home. They'll pick up Julie's body for transport to California. I'm leaving tomorrow."

"I can talk to Randy about releasing your SUV."

Sarah shuddered at the thought of ever driving that vehicle again. "No, that isn't necessary. I'll arrange to have it disposed of later."

"You'll be coming back?"

She hesitated. "No, I won't be back."

"That's good." He nodded approval. "Put Julesburg and everything that's happened here behind you."

Put it behind me? Does he really think that's possible? Because it wasn't. Not now, not later. Not here or anywhere else. Julie's death was a weight anchored to her heart.

"The killer was at Helen Maxwell's services today."

Ben jerked as if an electric shock had jolted him. "You recognized someone?"

"No. But I felt him. He was there. I was sure he would be. He was watching me."

"A lot of people took a look at you."

She didn't try to explain or convince him; she knew what she knew. "You were there after all?"

"Randy and I figured the same as you. That the killer might be there. We sat in the little upstairs room with a window overlooking the main room. We wanted to see if we could spot anything suspicious."

"And did you?"

"No."

"Has Travis Volkman's name ever come up in the investigation?"

"The Volkman kid?" To Ben, Sarah realized wryly, anyone under forty was a "kid." "Randy's nabbed him on DUI—driving under the influence—a couple times, and I think he outran me one time last year before I retired. But we haven't had any reason to think . . ." He paused, frowning as if reconsidering. "But anything's possible, and at this point we aren't ruling out anyone. The company brought a good payroll to town, but some people wish they'd just pick up and leave. They say, if you know what you're doing with that laser stuff, you can do anything from eye surgery to making counterfeit money."

"I still want to offer a reward. The hundred thousand is now for information leading to the capture and conviction of the killer." She gave him the phone number of her California house, plus Julie's mother's number.

"We'll spread the word." He hesitated. "But sometimes things just don't . . . come together."

That's quite a different attitude than Randy Wilson's. But unfortunately, probably more realistic.

Sarah loaded the last of what she could get into the Honda early the following morning. Heavy fog dampened her hair and swallowed the tops of the trees around the parking lot. She called Twila about feeding the cats, and Twila assured her she'd take care of them from now on. Sarah asked about her granddaughter, and the answer was bad, confirming what she'd seen in Ben's haggard face. Sharilyn's lungs couldn't hold out much longer, and no donor was yet available.

"I'm so sorry. . . . Is your granddaughter a Christian?"

"Oh yes!" Twila's despondent voice lit up. "That's one of the comforts and joys of my life. Sharilyn came to the Lord several years ago. I believe that came through prayer. And I believe prayer can heal her too."

Not a belief Ben shares, I think. "Yes, I hope so."

After the phone call, Sarah stopped at the post office for a final check of the mailbox. The post office window wasn't open yet; she'd have to mail a change of address. She passed the Nevermore on the way out of town. It stood in the thick drift of fog that held the town in a dreary embrace.

She still didn't believe in an invisible evil connected to a place or structure. The Nevermore was just what it looked like, a run-down old theater.

Yet just for a moment, as if mocking her, the red doors stood out like a lurid smear of lipstick on a corpse. And in that moment she knew that if it were possible, she'd fling a stick of dynamite at the old building and blast it into oblivion.

21

The four days in a Sacramento suburb with Julie's adopted mother stretched out like a suffocating dream from which Sarah couldn't escape.

Janine Lockland floundered under an incapacitating burden of grief and guilt. Her teenage son slouched around, sullen and resentful that Julie's death had interfered with a soccer match; the younger daughter was cranky with a cold. The stepfather's pointed questions suggested that Julie and Sarah must have been mixed up in something unsavory, that Julie's murder was somehow their own fault. Julie's adopted father was still in Europe and did not respond to the message Sarah had asked his office to pass on to him.

The graveside service the Locklands had arranged was officiated by a reserved, aloof man the funeral home had provided. Sarah sat in the front section of the two short rows of metal chairs facing the casket, which lay under a green canopy. The service was generic and impersonal, as if the man had taken a form and filled in the blanks. He surreptitiously checked his watch when he turned a page; once he mistakenly used the name Julia. Sarah listened with impotent frustration building toward fury. The teenage son's restless foot banged the back of her chair. The stepfather's chair squeaked as he shifted his weight. *Oh, Julie, what have I done, bringing you here?*

The people in Julesburg had flaws and shortcomings. But they'd have turned out in force to honor and mourn Julie.

After good-byes to the Locklands, Sarah drove aimlessly for half an hour, until she was certain everyone had left the cemetery. Then she returned and made her way across the damp grass to where the pristine white casket still lay beneath the green canopy. The chairs had been removed, but the workmen were taking a lunch break before lowering the casket into the ground. A warm California breeze fluttered the fringe on the canopy with incongruous gaiety. Everyday sounds of traffic drifted up from the street below. A power mower roared somewhere. Life went on.

Sarah stood beside the casket with her hands threaded together and head bowed. She felt cold, but it was a chill that came from deep within, far removed from the balmy temperature of the day.

I'm sorry, Julie. Sorry I didn't have a chance to know you longer. Sorry our big plans didn't work out. Sorry I failed you that last night. Sorry I brought you here! She choked on a swallowed sob and touched the crystal hanging at her throat. *Oh, Julie, I miss you so much! I miss your giggle and your caring and your sweetness. How could this happen? How could it end like this? Why?*

She stroked the smooth surface of the casket, then brushed her fingertips over the words written in gold script on a pink ribbon tucked into the floral spray she'd had delivered. *Beloved sister.* Tender words, loving words, but they couldn't begin to express the depth of her feelings for Julie.

"I love you, twin of my heart," she whispered now. She'd called Julie that so many times, but the words once spoken with lighthearted tease now came from the depths of her heart. *You were, you are, you will always be, twin of my heart.*

She fled then, sobs blocking the final words of good-bye she'd intended to offer.

Nick didn't expect to hear from Sarah, and he didn't.

He told himself he was relieved. Looking into a future without her hurt, hurt more than the saw blade he'd once accidentally ripped deep into the flesh of his leg. But she was right. It wouldn't work. He had to accept that and get on with his life. Yes, he should be relieved that she hadn't called.

He was not relieved with what he read and heard on the news, however. The police investigation was apparently stalled. And as he flipped channels one evening, he realized that the murders were slipping out of the news as well. Which meant that somewhere in Julesburg, a killer was breathing more easily. Nick slammed the remote control across the motel room.

By Thursday, when Sarah had been gone a full week, simple worry about her overrode all other thoughts. Shouldn't she be back by now? He'd been dialing the apartment in Julesburg at least twice a day and getting no answer. Could something have happened to her on the trip?

I'll drive down to Julesburg after work today. To . . . what? Check on the apartment. Or, if she's come back and just isn't answering the phone, maybe help with packing or cleaning.

He left work early and arrived in Julesburg just before 4:00. It was a beautiful day, with an out-of-season feel of spring in the air, the sparkling, jewel-among-stones kind of day the coast could produce at unexpected times.

The old Honda wasn't in the parking lot, but he went upstairs anyway. He had his finger poised to ring the doorbell when he heard muffled noises inside the apartment. Could she be here, perhaps with a car he didn't recognize? Or could the apartment already have been rented to someone else?

He rang the doorbell anyway. The muffled sounds ceased. He rang it again. Five times he pushed the button, the last time leaning on it so long that a door down the hall opened and an older woman yelled, "There's no one home! Can't you tell?"

Odd. Noises, but no one home.

He retreated to the stairwell, taking a position just around the corner where he couldn't be seen. Time dragged like a plugged hourglass, but his watch said that no more than five minutes had passed when he heard the soft closing of a door and a tread of footsteps. He took two steps up the stairs, blocking them with his body.

A man he'd never seen before was walking toward him down the hallway. He wasn't sneaking, but he walked lightly even in heavy boots. He was big, filling out the shoulders of a denim jacket, good-looking, with a lot of curly dark hair and one small gold earring. Nick remembered seeing a flashy Harley down in the parking lot; instinctively he knew he was facing its owner. The man didn't intimidate him, but Nick braced his muscles when he bypassed small talk and jumped directly to challenge.

"What were you doing in Julie and Sarah's apartment?"

The man's gaze raked Nick appraisingly. "What's it to you?"

"Family friend. And you are?"

"Friend of Julie's."

"Donovan Moran?" It was pure guess on Nick's part, but a small flicker in the man's eyes told him it was the right guess. "I repeat, what were you doing in their apartment?"

Donovan's big shoulders moved the denim jacket in a shrug. "I'd made a silver ring for Julie. I wanted it back, to remember her by. When I couldn't raise anyone with the doorbell, I went in to look for it."

You've been looking for something, all right. But Donovan Moran didn't strike Nick as the type of guy given to saving sentimental mementos.

"Did you find the ring?"

"No. She probably tossed it. She was . . . a little unhappy with me."

"Unhappy about what?"

Nick expected Moran to object to the question, but all he did was shrug again and say, "You know how women get worked up about trivialities."

Sarah had thought Julie's decision to dump Donovan Moran had to do with a possible involvement with drugs. Now it occurred to Nick that the reason could have been more elemental. Another woman. Moran's rough good looks probably drew considerable female attention. And maybe he wasn't too conscientious about resisting.

"How'd you get in?"

"You got some authority to ask all these questions?"

"As much authority as you have to search the apartment."

Moran's dark eyes narrowed, but he declined to answer.

"Maybe the police would be interested in knowing you're nosing around here. I understand you've already had a brush or two with the law."

"The cops questioned me about where I was and what I was doing on the night the old lady was killed." The answer was belligerent, but Nick caught an undertone of defensiveness.

"Because you knew Julie?"

"Maybe. Or maybe they were just checking out all the local bad guys. Anybody with a record. Julesburg's police chief is hot to nail someone so he can shine on TV again. Doesn't want any unsolved crimes messing up *his* record."

"But you had an alibi for the night Helen Maxwell was killed?"

"I was doing a custom paint job on a buddy's motorcycle. He vouched for me."

Buddies had been known to lie. Yet Nick didn't see that making such an observation would get him anywhere at the moment. He hesitated and then stepped aside.

"I'll tell Sarah that if she finds the ring, you want it."

Moran's dark eyes held a momentary blankness, but he recovered quickly. "Yeah. Do that. I'd appreciate it. She's coming back?"

"I'm not certain."

"Might be smarter if she stayed away."

"You think she's in danger?"

"Julesburg is beginning to look like a dangerous place."

Moran descended the stairs with a loose-jointed gait. Nick stood at the streaked window at the stairway landing and watched him put on a psychedelic-colored helmet and throw a leg over the Harley. Gravel spit from the rear tire as he roared out of the parking lot. Nick walked down the hallway and tried the apartment door. Locked.

Moran must've had a key to get in, one Julie had given him. Or he knew some shady secrets about opening locked doors without a key.

Nick tentatively put his shoulder against the door. He wanted in. Wanted to touch something Sarah had touched. Wanted . . . Sarah.

He backed off before he did something he shouldn't and returned to the window. Clouds had moved in, dulling the jeweled day like a shiny wet stone dimming to an ordinary dry pebble. He dipped his head.

Moran was not the only problem here.

Lord, I don't know what to do with my love for Sarah. I know I should have been more cautious. I should have heeded your Word more closely. But now I'm in love with her.

He'd spent a lot of time arguing with himself about his relationship with Sarah. What he should have been doing, he knew, was taking it to the Lord.

I give that love to you, Lord. I put it in your hands. Do with it what you will.

Sarah walked into the apartment shortly before 11:00 Friday night. The air felt cold, heavy and damp and unused. She turned up the heat, closed the drapes, and made a cup of orange-spice tea.

She carried the steaming cup to the sofa, slipped out of her shoes, and sat with her feet curled under her for warmth.

She'd driven south after leaving the cemetery. A few hours later she'd reached the house in Bakersfield where she'd grown up. She had logical plans. Call Twila Mosely and get the name of someone reliable to clean out the Julesburg apartment and ship everything to Bakersfield. Buy a new car. See about getting her old job back. Or a new one. Or perhaps not get a job and go back to college instead. Get on with her life.

Nice, logical, sensible plans.

Yet here she was. After two days at home she'd haphazardly thrown a few things in a suitcase and headed north to Oregon.

Why?

She looked around at the clutter that was exactly as she'd left it. *Because I can't bear to have some stranger poking around in Julie's things.*

Her mind felt dulled by the long drive, but she forced it into assessing the situation logically. *What has to be done here?* Get the paintings packaged and shipped. Finish the sorting and packing of Julie's personal belongings. Donate the furniture. Talk with Ben or Randy about final disposition of the SUV. See a lawyer about the legal process concerning Julie's financial assets, because she hadn't left a will.

Sarah determinedly walled off thoughts of Nick, as she had been doing all week. Yet when she spotted the sand dollar on the coffee table, the shell he'd given her that night they walked on the beach, the reminder threatened to shatter her carefully constructed wall. She grabbed the remote control and flicked on the TV.

In surprise, she saw Randy Wilson standing beside a ramshackle house near a densely wooded area that looked like Ryker's Bog. In the background Ben Mosely was loading a skinny, bearded guy in handcuffs into the police car. An arrest? Her heart thudded and an electric excitement charged through her body. She clicked the remote to turn up the volume.

"... biggest methamphetamine bust ever made in the county," an unseen reporter was saying.

Sarah's excitement sank into disappointment. No capture of Julie's killer, just a drug bust. She listened as Randy told the reporter that he had kept the house under surveillance for weeks, until he was sure enough to move in for the bust.

Sarah felt a flare of resentment that Randy had been pursuing this instead of chasing down Julie's killer, and she felt anger at his smile of pride. Wasn't Julie's murder more important?

But then she felt ashamed of the angry resentment. Randy and Ben had uncovered a big meth lab set up in a dugout room beneath an old house, and three suspects were under arrest. Crime went on, and Randy and Ben couldn't be expected to spend 100 percent of their time on Julie and Helen Maxwell's murders.

She knew the arrest should also give her assurance that Randy and Ben would eventually get Julie's killer. Weeks of surveillance on the meth lab had proved their determination. The criminals probably had thought they were too clever to get caught by a couple of small-town cops.

But they were wrong. They were caught. Just as Randy and Ben would catch Julie's killer.

Near the end of the interview, the reporter asked a question that hadn't occurred to Sarah. "Is there any possibility this big drug operation could be connected with the two murders in Julesburg that are as yet unsolved?"

"We'll investigate that possibility, of course," Randy said. The comment was smooth, but Sarah sensed a certain annoyance beneath it, as if he didn't like the reminder that the murders in his town were still unsolved. "Actually, we anticipate an arrest in the murder cases in the very near future."

The statement should have reassured her. She wanted to believe it. It confirmed what she'd just been telling herself. And yet . . . she didn't believe. Why?

Because she suspected that Randy Wilson's ego wouldn't let him admit if they were no further along in solving the case than they had been the day it happened.

She slept restlessly that night, dreaming disjointed dreams of wandering helplessly in Ryker's Bog, searching for Julie. And more dreams of a graveside service that went on and on, endlessly repeating itself. She got up in the morning with a grim determination to get out of Julesburg as fast as possible.

She opened the drapes to let in morning light before fixing breakfast. And the first thing she saw there by the window was Julie's unfinished painting of the homeless jetty kittens.

It was so . . . Julie. She'd captured the sweet playfulness of the kittens and the harshness of their rocky home. The painting held so much promise and talent. Like Julie's life—so full of sweetness and caring and hope.

Yet, like Julie's life, the painting was cut off, incomplete and unfinished.

Sarah studied the painting. Unfinished. Yes, just as her own life was on hold and unfinished.

She wasn't here in Julesburg because of a duty to *things*. She wasn't here just to see that the apartment was neatly closed up and bills paid. She was here because Julie's killer had not yet been brought to justice. And her life would be on hold until he was.

22

Sarah drove to the police station immediately after a breakfast of Cheerios, canned peaches, and canned milk; supplies remaining in the cupboard were minimal. The day was gloriously blue-skied and sunshiny, but she barely noticed. The Nevermore looked unchanged, forlorn and abandoned. Weeds already sprouted in cracks in the Calico Pantry's unused parking lot.

Randy wasn't behind the counter at the station, but Ben was. His face still sagged in haggard lines, but his bushy eyebrows rose in surprise. "I thought you weren't coming back to Julesburg."

"I realized there are some things I need to take care of here. I saw Randy on TV last night—"

"The big meth bust. It took a long time, but we got 'em."

"Randy indicated an arrest in Julie and Helen Maxwell's murders is imminent. Is that true?"

Ben's momentary lift of satisfaction and pride retreated. He shuffled a handful of papers on the counter. "We have some promising leads."

"That sounds like cop double-talk," she said bluntly.

"We're doing our best." He sounded neither defensive nor angry, simply old and weary.

Sarah picked up fresh groceries and a sack of cat food at the market. Down at the jetty, Clarissa ran to meet her, purr so loud it could register on the Richter scale. Sarah took a few minutes to snuggle the affectionate calico and fill the food dishes. Twila had been on the job. A few pellets remained in the wooden trough.

Sarah walked over to the dock. The Wildfire III was there, but Joe Argo wasn't around. She inquired about him at the office near the crane that hoisted boats into the water. The man behind the scarred counter told her that regulations had temporarily shut down commercial fishing. "Got more regulations than fleas on a hound," he grumbled. He said Joe had said something about repairing crab pots down at Gold Beach with a friend who sometimes crewed for him. And no, he didn't know the name of the friend.

"Joe's getting to be a popular guy," he added. "Someone else was here looking for him a few minutes ago."

Sarah was not interested in Joe's popularity, only in talking to him about the odd questions he had raised . . . and from which he had quickly retreated. She decided to drive down to Gold Beach. Joe might be at the dock, or someone there would know where to find him.

Wisps of mist started drifting across the highway just a few miles south of Julesburg's blue skies. The wisps had thickened to a murky blanket by the time she reached Gold Beach. Visibility was so limited that from the bridge the river looked as if it flowed into a foggy end of the world.

When she reached the dock, the fog was so thick that the boats appeared to float in it. Ghost boats. And for all the evidence she found of human activity, perhaps crewed by ghosts as well.

Now what? Apparently she wasn't going to accomplish anything here. Then it occurred to her that Julie's boyfriend lived in Gold Beach. It also occurred to her that, except for the one phone call shortly after Julie was abducted, Donovan Moran had been noticeably scarce.

He did not turn out to be difficult to locate, however. She inquired at a gas station about motorcycle repair and was directed to an unpaved side street. The weedy lane was vacant except for a rust-stained metal building at the far end.

A low-slung motorcycle leaned on its kickstand beside the building. A sign over the door read "Donovan's Cycle Shop," the words burned into a flat slab of driftwood. Inside, under a glare of fluorescent lights, motorcycles in various stages of dismemberment littered the concrete floor. A sharp odor of paint hung in the air.

"Anyone here?" she called tentatively.

"Yo," a male voice answered.

She followed the voice to a dark-haired guy kneeling beside a motorcycle. He was decorating it with a freehand painting of jagged lightning bolts and did not look up. She watched, unexpectedly impressed, as he worked with delicate precision. His hand was as steady with the fine lines as if he were writing on a Post-It note. When he finally glanced at her, she saw a jolt of shocked recognition on his face.

"You must be Julie's twin sister."

"I've just come back from her funeral in California."

He wiped the brush on a rag, dipped it in a can of liquid, and wiped it again. He didn't ask for details about the funeral, and she couldn't tell if he was concealing grief or if he just wasn't interested. She felt a flare of anger. *Julie had been in love with him. Surely her death deserves more reaction than this!*

He stood and leaned against the motorcycle's saddlebags, booted feet crossed. She remembered something

Twila had said about him, and she agreed. Not the kind of guy most girls' parents would be overjoyed to meet. She was also struck by a certain resemblance to Travis Volkman. Had Julie had a weakness for the intense, dark, and dangerous type?

He noted her appraisal and laughed. "You're wondering how a sweet, innocent girl like Julie could have been interested in a guy like me?"

The question momentarily threw Sarah off balance, but she tossed back a counterattack. "She'd decided to break up with you. She was upset after seeing you the night before she was abducted."

"Did she tell you why?"

"No."

Was there a slacking of tension in his manner? Sarah couldn't be certain. The outside door opened, and a guy wearing black leather motorcycle chaps took a final drag on a cigarette before tossing it aside and stepping inside. He asked about having some custom paintwork done. Donovan Moran lifted his dark eyebrows questioningly at Sarah, and she waved a hand to tell him not to delay a business deal on her account.

The two men went back to a small office. Sarah could see a single cot covered with a khaki blanket back there, as if this was where Donovan crashed as well as worked. Not a three-bedroom/two-bath, mow-the-grass-on-weekends kind of guy. Sarah wandered around, arms folded over her chest so she wouldn't touch anything.

The shop wasn't trash-can dirty, but like any repair shop, neither would it win any awards for spotlessness. Oil stains in abstract shapes darkened the concrete floor. Spiderwebs tangled in bare rafters overhead. A can of black grease stood open on the long counter that ran the length of one side of the building. Shelves on the opposite side held various motorcycle parts, as unidentifiable to her as fossil bones. She walked along the counter, peering at tools and supplies. Paints, thinners, paint sprayers, brushes, tape, cans of various kinds of oil, stack of repair manuals, girlie calendar on the wall.

When the customer left, Donovan returned to her. "So why are you here?" he asked.

"I've decided I can't leave Julesburg until Julie's killer is found. I think you might know people who could have been involved. I got the impression you are not unfamiliar with the . . . underside of Julesburg. Maybe you've heard something."

"The last I heard, the going rate for rumors was a dime a dozen. And probably overpriced at that."

"Rumors about what?"

He shrugged. "Some rumors suggest it was kids who planned a small crime to grab a few bucks, wound up in a big crime, and now are scared spitless. Other rumors say maybe it was something way bigger than kids. Maybe something to do with boat traffic in illegal aliens. Maybe counterfeit money passing through town. Maybe Volkman Laser Systems running a shady deal with some foreign outfit, sneaking classified technology out of the country. Maybe fishing boats that aren't all that involved with fishing."

The scope of his statements astonished Sarah. Was any of that possible in little Julesburg? Or did its small-town sleepiness make it the perfect place for such unlikely activities?

"It's hard to see how an elderly lady and a convenience store could be connected with any of that."

"Rumors, like government regulations, do not require logic."

"But if there was connection to something bigger, the convenience store robbery could have been a cover-up. Perhaps murder, not robbery, was the real intention all along. And Julie was just caught in the wrong place at the wrong time."

"It's a mystery." He lifted one shoulder in a not-my-problem shrug. "Now if you'll excuse me, I have to get this done by 1:00." He turned, pried open a small can of paint, and dipped the paintbrush.

"Don't you care about catching Julie's killer?"

"I'm a lot of things, but ace detective isn't one of them." He gave her a sideways glance. "You drive all the way down here just to find me?"

"Actually, I came looking for Joe Argo—" She broke off, sorry she'd mentioned the fisherman's name. Thinking back, she was almost certain Joe had been wary of Julie's intimidating boyfriend.

Donovan unexpectedly smiled, and Sarah could see what Julie had seen in him, even if it didn't appeal to her. The rugged good looks. The air of recklessness. Definitely some rough edges, but a certain dangerous charm, when he wanted to turn it on. "Oh yeah. Good ol' Joe. But I wouldn't take anything ol' Joe says too seriously. He spends too much time out to sea, in more ways than one, if you know what I mean. He never had a chance with Julie, but he was still teed off when she preferred me."

Sarah could think of no appropriate response to any of that, so she murmured a thanks and turned to the door.

"I've also heard ol' Joe isn't above squealing to the police to pick up a few extra bucks."

Did Donovan think Joe had provided the tip that cost him his pilot's license? "Somehow I doubt the Julesburg budget includes a line item for police informants."

"Then maybe Joe's just playing good citizen, doing his duty out of a noble concern for law and order." Donovan's mocking tone dismissed that possibility, and Sarah had the peculiar feeling he was playing with her, leading her in circles. "Although ol' Joe sometimes has a problem distinguishing fact from fiction."

What was he getting at? A possibility occurred to her. Donovan no doubt knew about the one hundred thousand dollar reward. Was he suggesting she shouldn't believe everything Joe Argo said if he tried to collect that reward?

"Oh, by the way, up at Julie's apartment yesterday, I ran into a guy who said he was a friend of the family. You might want to check him out."

"Oh?" she said warily. Was it Nick? Or the killer snooping around?

"I didn't get his name. Tall guy, reddish-blond hair. Friendly as a cruising shark."

Nick. Definitely. She felt a whoosh of relief.

Donovan circled a skeleton of a motorcycle on a stand. He still held the paintbrush in one hand, his other hand cupped below the tip now glistening with bloodred paint. "You know, if I were you, I don't think I'd go around poking my nose too deep in this stuff. Might not be healthy. You might tell your 'family friend' that too."

His smile had vanished, and Sarah just stared at him. Was he warning her? Or threatening her? Her skin prickled, and her throat closed. She was suddenly aware of the shed's isolation; she could scream and no one would hear.

Julie could have screamed, with no one to hear . . .

Sarah was suddenly frantic to get away. She muttered another hasty thanks and fled.

She was five miles up the highway toward Julesburg before she realized she hadn't even demanded to know what Donovan had been doing at the apartment. She hesitated—he probably wouldn't tell her if she did ask. She was also wary of confronting him again. Being there in Donovan's shop had directed her suspicions not just at what or who he might know, but at *him*.

Why had he gone to the apartment?

She U-turned at a pullout along the highway. She wasn't going to find Julie's killer if she ran for cover every time her nerves kicked up a storm.

A handpainted "Closed" sign hung on the doorknob. Either Donovan had been lightning-bolt fast in finishing up the motorcycle job, or he'd suddenly decided he had something more important to do.

She started north out of Gold Beach, then again changed her mind and returned to the dock. She walked the full length of it in spite of feeling as if the wooden planks might be some pathway into the Twilight Zone. The fog magnified sounds. Water sloshing against the pilings. Creak of wood. A foghorn booming in the distance. Cries of unseen gulls, the shrieks unnervingly sounding like the screams of a woman in terror. Scents of fish and sea, damp rope and oil. And a figure rising ghostlike out of the fog . . .

In alarm she realized he was between her and the walkway to shore. And unless she wanted to plunge into the oil-sheened water, there was no way around him.

Get a grip. This is a public dock. He's probably just a fisherman checking on his boat.

Then she recognized the reddish-blond hair. "Nick!"

"Sarah?" He peered at her, obviously as surprised as she was. "When did you get back? What're you doing here?"

"I got in last night. What're you doing here?"

"Look, can I buy you a cup of coffee? You're shivering," he said with concern.

"I thought you'd be home in Eugene over the weekend."

"You didn't answer my question."

"Thanks, no, I don't think so." She made a point of checking her watch, as if she were on a tight time schedule.

"Then how about you buying me a cup of coffee? *I'm* shivering."

Maybe it was his quick, cajoling flip of the invitation that got to her. Or his appealing smile. Or maybe it was because she'd felt so desperately alone this past week.

"I suppose I can't turn down a plea from a shivering, caffeine-deficient man lost in the fog."

She followed his pickup to a homey little café called the Sea Nest. It smelled of coffee and fresh doughnuts, with a faint scent of damp wool from a foursome of fishermen types crowded around a table. Nick nodded toward a booth in the rear of the restaurant. The window probably had a pleasant view of the ocean on a clear day, but today a wall of white fog pressed against the glass. Trickles of moisture ran down the inside.

The waitress brought their coffee in heavy blue mugs. Sarah gave Nick a brief report on the funeral and didn't exclude her regret that she'd taken Julie to her mother's for burial.

"Can I help with anything while you're here?" Nick asked.

No involvement, his light tone assured her. *No obligation.*

"Actually . . ." She twisted the heavy mug in circles on the table. "I've decided I can't leave for a while yet."

"Problems?"

She lifted her gaze to his. "I can't leave until Julie's killer is found."

"So you're planning to hang around and play amateur detective?" He sounded either exasperated or dismayed. Or maybe both. "Let the authorities handle this, Sarah. It isn't your responsibility."

"Isn't it?"

He didn't respond to the challenge in her words. "You were looking for someone down at the dock?"

"Joe Argo, the fisherman." She suddenly remembered what the man at the Julesburg dock had said about someone else looking for Joe Argo. Nick? She didn't have to ask the question. Nick's next statement answered it.

"I thought it might not hurt to talk to Joe myself."

"Why?"

"The police investigation seems to be . . . stalled. Sometimes the ideas you said Joe mentioned don't sound all that far out."

"Last night on TV Randy implied that they'll be making an arrest in the near future. He and Ben just busted a big methamphetamine lab right there in Julesburg."

"Without calling in help from the big boys outside," Nick said. "I suspect Randy Wilson isn't one to share the glory, if he can help it. Which isn't necessarily the most efficient way to track down a murderer."

"So *you* have decided to take a stab at playing amateur detective?"

Nick concentrated on his coffee mug. "I still feel some personal responsibility for what happened to Julie. And I'm not convinced Randy's ego isn't getting in the way of finding the killer."

"I don't think Ben's ego is getting in the way of anything. He just wants to get the job done." She felt defensive about the big officer who tried so hard to be kind to her. He was strained with worry about his granddaughter, to the point of physical illness, but she didn't doubt he was still doing his very best to find Julie's killer. "Someone just told me I shouldn't go poking my nose around in the murders. I don't know if it was a warning . . . or a threat."

Nick leaned forward, his blue eyes intense. "Joe Argo? You found him?"

"No. Julie's boyfriend, Donovan Moran. He lives here in Gold Beach. I don't think he appreciated my visit."

"You talked to Moran? Alone?"

"Actually, he included you in his warning. Or threat."

"Well, did he tell you I caught him snooping around your apartment?"

"He told me he ran into *you* snooping around the apartment."

"I wasn't inside it. He was."

That information brought Sarah's coffee cup to the table with a crash. She hadn't noticed anything missing or disturbed, but the very fact that someone had gotten inside . . .

"How did he get in?"

"Good question."

"What was he doing?"

"Supposedly looking for a ring he'd made and given to Julie. He said he wanted it back, to remember her by. Personally, I thought it was a flimsy story."

Sarah thought back to Donovan's mention of seeing someone at the apartment. At the time, it had seemed reasonable for him to bring it up. Now it occurred to her that he may have had a different motive. Maybe he'd figured she might hear something about his being at the apartment, so he brought up the information himself to defuse any surprise. But he'd also avoided the full truth, that he'd actually been *in* the apartment.

"Did you get anything out of him?" Nick asked, and she repeated Donovan's "dime a dozen" rumors. Nick tapped the side of his mug with a forefinger. "Interesting that he didn't mention drug rumors. Because there are some. I talked with some kids at Website X after Moran and I parted company at the apartment."

"Maybe the kids were talking about the meth lab Randy and Ben just shut down."

"Maybe." Thoughtfully, he added, "Has it ever seemed strange to you that the killer, once he realized Julie was in the car, didn't just dump her out? Get rid of her? She was surely an unnecessary complication."

"Ben came to see me the night before I left for the funeral. He said he'd talked to the medical examiner. Julie had been given pizza to eat before she was killed. And she wasn't sexually molested."

"Which suggests this could be someone who didn't really want to kill her. But figured he had to."

Their eyes met, and the silent question raced between them. Had Julie known her killer?

"Julie knew lots of people—" Sarah said, but broke off as a vision vaulted into her mind. Julie's hand peeking out of a plaid blanket. A band of silvery-gray around the wrist. Duct tape, Ben had said.

Then she saw another vision. The countertop in Donovan's shop. One full roll of wide, silvery-gray tape. Beside it, another roll, used almost down to the thick paper core.

Duct tape.

23

Nick saw the horror flash across Sarah's face. He leaned forward, alarmed. "What is it?"

Sarah told him. Duct tape. Donovan.

Nick cradled the coffee cup between his hands, elbows on the table. He'd been skeptical and uneasy about Donovan Moran ever since the run-in at the apartment. The shop Sarah now described made a credible site for holding a captive. Julie would certainly have recognized Moran, perhaps even in his disguise, which was a strong motive for killing her rather than simply dumping her out.

But the duct tape didn't hit him as hot evidence against the guy. "Moran probably has any number of legitimate uses for duct tape at his shop. It's handy stuff."

Their eyes met over the table, and he knew what she was thinking. *The killer had found it handy stuff with which to tape Julie's wrists and ankles.* Sarah swallowed, as if she were trying to erase the brutal pictures in her mind.

He reached for her hand. "I know this might look suspicious. But we use duct tape all the time on the job. It's kind of a joke, in fact, about duct tape being the 'handyman's secret weapon.' An all-purpose solution to everything from patching a rip in a car seat to holding a cracked shovel handle together."

Sarah frowned, but after a minute she leaned back and nodded. "I guess I'd rather not have to think someone Julie loved could have killed her."

"What was your impression of Moran?"

"Rough-edged lady-killer," she said promptly. Then her face paled. "I don't mean it that way! I mean, Donovan didn't strike me as some all-around good guy. He's had connection with drugs and run-ins with the law. I was uneasy with him there at the shop. But Julie was in love with him."

She made the statement as if it proved something, that Julie couldn't have been in love with a killer. Nick didn't point out that Julie had also been planning to dump Moran. He didn't want Sarah charging around like some amateur detective. Her next words relieved him.

"I don't think it was Donovan in the Calico Pantry that night. I couldn't tell much about the guy, but I'm certain . . . almost certain he wasn't as big as Donovan."

"The police are going to get him, Sarah. Whoever he is."

Are they? her blue eyes, dark with emotion, asked. But after draining her coffee cup and looking at her watch, all she said was, "I should be getting back to Julesburg."

"Youaren't planning to—"

"I'm planning to do whatever it takes to find Julie's killer."

"Look, Sarah, I know how much you want this guy caught. But going after a killer isn't the fun and games some mystery novels make it appear."

Sarah lifted her chin in a gesture of stubbornness he already recognized. The movement exposed the crystal hanging at her throat.

"Fun and games, Nick? No," she said. Her tone was dangerously soft. "I see it as a debt I owe my sister. Julie is dead, and the killer is getting away with it. He's the one enjoying fun and games. I'm not going to just sit around and twiddle my thumbs. And pray."

He knew she was trying to provoke him, but he didn't let her sidetrack him. "The rumors Moran mentioned sound far out. But they should also warn you that if big-time criminal activities are involved, this could be as dangerous as grabbing a high-voltage wire. It may be your life that's on the line if they find you prowling around in their affairs." He grabbed her hand again before she could snatch it away. "Sarah, I'm just concerned about you."

He almost added "I love you!" but he thought better of it. He'd given this love to the Lord, and he still didn't know what the Lord intended with it.

"I appreciate your concern," she conceded. "But you've been prowling around and asking questions yourself."

But the situation is different for me. I'm a man. I can take care of myself. After threats about a controversial building project a couple of years ago, he'd even gotten a permit to carry a concealed weapon, although he'd never actually done so.

"We could—" He stopped, reluctant to go on. He preferred for Sarah to stay away from any investigation. But he also knew nothing he said was going to deflect her from trying to find out who killed Julie. If they were in it together, he could at least keep an eye on her. "We could join forces."

"You sound as enthusiastic as if you were proposing a mutual brain transplant."

"I'm offering. I don't have to be enthusiastic."

She regarded him warily, but she didn't cover her cup when the waitress came with a refill. "No God talk," she said abruptly.

"Okay."

"No Jesus or Bible talk either," she added, as if she suspected she may have left a loophole.

He felt a twinge of misgiving. Was he stepping into the unequal yoking the Lord warned against? He couldn't let her plunge alone into this dangerous chase, but was that just the rationalization of a man in love?

So he inserted his own qualification in the bargaining process. "But no censoring of private thoughts or prayers."

She frowned at him, then dropped the subject. "Okay, then," she said briskly. "Let's figure out what we know, what we have to work with, and where we go from here."

They sat there in the maroon booth for almost an hour and a half, eating cheeseburgers and fries and downing more coffee.

At the end of that time, what they *knew* didn't add up to much. Julie's murder could not have been planned beforehand, because it was only a last-minute decision that had taken Julie and Sarah to the Calico Pantry that night. Julie had been alive for twenty-four to forty-eight hours after the abduction. That meant she was held somewhere during that time and, according to the medical examiner, given pizza to eat. Her body had also been kept somewhere after she was killed, and she was transported to the Nevermore in some unknown vehicle, because by that time Sarah's SUV had already been recovered at the old mill site. They could reasonably assume the killer hadn't run because he had strong ties to the Julesburg area and figured he could continue a normal life there without arousing suspicion. There was a strong possibility, even a probability if both their instincts were correct, that Julie'd known and recognized her killer.

Their questions far outnumbered their answers. Was the crime in the Calico Pantry a simple robbery that had escalated? Or was killing Helen Maxwell the underlying goal? And if her death was the goal, why?

Nick tossed out a possibility. "Could Mrs. Maxwell have known something incriminating about someone in Julesburg, and she was being paid off to keep quiet?"

"Blackmail?" Excitement lit up Sarah's eyes. "Yes, that could be it! And someone got tired of paying off and decided to end it."

"But what she knew doesn't have to be something criminal. She may simply have known about an illicit affair, and a husband was paying for her silence."

"Or a wife was paying." Sarah swiped a napkin across the window, wiping away a layer of steamy moisture. "A wife who hired a killer to get her out from under the danger of exposure and the financial drain."

"Which means we may be dealing with two suspects. The person being blackmailed and a killer that person hired."

"But for suspects," Sarah said, slumping against the vinyl seat, "we're right back where we've always been. The killer and the person who hired him could be anyone."

Nick nodded. The motive was tweaked, but no one was targeted or eliminated.

"And while we're considering possibilities," Sarah added thoughtfully, "I don't think we should leave out Joe Argo. I don't see any reason to include him, but—"

"At this point we can't exclude anyone."

Sarah nodded. "I think we should discuss your idea about blackmail with Randy and Ben. If you have time, we can go see them when we get back to Julesburg."

"I have time." No shortage of time for Sarah. "And I think I'll contact a lawyer friend over in Eugene and see what he can find out about Volkman Laser Systems." He was also thinking about suggesting a walk on the beach, then dinner and a drive up to Dutton Bay for a movie. They could use some diversion from the intensity of this brainstorming.

"Sounds good."

For a moment he thought he'd actually made the invitation, and Sarah had accepted. Then he realized she was simply approving his plan to contact the lawyer.

Saved by the bell. He was in this to help and protect Sarah, not circumvent the Lord's will regarding their personal relationship.

Sarah drove directly to the police station when they reached Julesburg. Nick was right behind her. They found the shades rolled down and the door locked. A sign gave the county sheriff's number for emergencies.

She'd forgotten this troublesome aspect of small town life. Obviously, two officers couldn't be on duty twenty-four hours a day, seven days a week, but she had to control an irrational urge to vent her frustration in reckless hammering on the door.

She halfway—more than halfway, if she was honest with herself—wanted to ask Nick to come over for dinner later. But she knew that would be going beyond their investigative agreement, so all she said was, "If you'll give me a number where I can reach you, I'll let you know what Randy and Ben say on Monday."

He gave her the name of the motel where he was staying, plus the number of his new cell phone. After he drove away, Sarah was reluctant to return to the silent apartment. She drove down to the jetty and lifted the sack of cat food out of the trunk of the Honda. Clarissa, always the enthusiastic, one-cat welcoming committee, rushed out to meet her. Sarah hoped she'd run into Twila Mosely. Twila knew everyone, and she might, if Sarah suggested the possibility of blackmail in connection with the murders, come up with information about an illicit relationship that could be helpful.

After a half hour of petting and snuggling the cats with no sign of Twila, she walked down to the beach, but the surf was big and rough in spite of the sunny day. Breakers rolled in almost to the tree line above the sand. She went to the apartment and started to fix a grilled cheese sandwich for supper but impulsively changed her mind. She had a better idea.

And if she was lucky, maybe she could pick up something more important than food.

She wasn't certain she was ready for Saturday night at Website X, however, when she pulled into the crowded parking lot beside the building. For a town the size of Julesburg, the number of teenagers it could gather into one place on a Saturday night was astonishing.

A sound system blasted hard rock, and Sarah felt very old and out of it as she ventured toward the front door. Inside, the squeal and screech of video games joined the din.

Practice clever detective work here? Fat chance. Nick had said he'd talked to some teenagers about local drugs at the pizza place. He must have chosen a less chaotic time or have been better able than she to operate in chaos. Still, the smells of pepperoni and hot cheese and onions were tempting, and she headed for the "Order Here" window.

Organization was a low priority around the window, but eventually she was pushed to the front. She ordered a small mushroom and olive pizza and a 7 UP from a girl in a red beret and skimpy black skirt. Most of the hired help were teenagers, but she spotted Steve Lomax working at one of the ovens. *How dumb of me to ask Steve if any of his customers were missing. Who would know in this feeding frenzy?*

Seating was communal and casual. She found an empty space on a bench at the end of a long table of teenagers where, with noisy encouragement from friends, one girl was trying to stuff a full slice of pizza into her boyfriend's mouth. Sarah was surprised that a couple of the teenagers noticed her when she sat down. One girl reached over and squeezed her hand. "We're really sorry about Julie. She was a neat person." It was her resemblance to Julie they'd noticed, she realized. Julie had apparently had a real connection with some of these kids.

Sarah edged her way through the crowd to the pickup counter when her number was called. The kid who handed her the pizza said, "I saw you at the funeral. I thought you must be Julie's sister." He spoke haltingly, with an uncertain uplift at the end of each sentence. Even though he was a year or two beyond being a teenager, the blush of a shy, probably not-too-popular guy crept up through the pitted acne scars on his face. Even his big ears reddened.

Sarah nodded. "I am."

"Julie was always really nice to me. She even gave me a cat. I call him Tiger. I wish nothing had happened to Julie."

The awkward but sweet words sounded sincere even though both he and she were yelling to be heard over the noise. His eyes watered when he talked about Julie. Sarah looked at the name scrolled in white on his red shirt.

"Thanks, Howard. I appreciate hearing that."

She headed back to the bench, where she'd staked a claim with her jacket. Along the way she spotted a familiar face. She'd spent the day looking for him, and now here he was.

"Joe, you're a hard guy to find." She spotted a sliver of unoccupied bench across from him. "Okay if I sit here?"

Joe Argo made a motion with his fingers to indicate that his mouth was full. *I'll take that as a yes.* She planted her pizza on the table, retrieved her jacket, and slid into the space.

"The kids kind of take over here on weekends, but the pizza's still the best. And I'm a real pizza connoisseur." Joe smiled as if it were an accomplishment he was proud of.

Sarah wanted to talk to him about his ideas on the murders, but it wasn't a discussion that was possible at a yell. So she just nodded to his bellowed comments comparing the Website Special to the Julesburg Jumble. That segued into a comparison of the various brands of frozen pizza he took out to sea with him. He downed slice after slice of sausage and onion pizza even as he kept up the constant dialogue. Sarah suspected he preferred pizza to murder as a subject of discussion. But even enthusiastic pizza-eater Joe couldn't get around all of the Giant he'd ordered.

"I'm going to get a take-out box for my leftovers."

"Would you pick up one for me too, please?"

They boxed their slices and walked outside together. After the noise inside the building, the blare of rock music now seemed relatively muted.

Sarah slowed as they neared the Honda. "If you have a minute, I'd like to talk to you—"

"Look, if you've been thinking about that stuff I said the other day, just forget it. Like I said, my imagination kind of cranks into overdrive listening to all those murder-mystery audiotapes. Although I listen to some educational stuff too. I went up to Dutton Bay today and rented a whole set of tapes. I'm figuring on learning to speak French."

"French," Sarah echoed, a bit nonplussed. Joe was edging away now, inching toward a nondescript pickup with a big winch on the front end.

"Don't you want to talk to me, Joe?"

He stopped inching away. "If I thought it would help Julie, I would, I really would. No way did she deserve what she got. But . . ." He frowned as if stuck on a "but" to justify his reluctance to talk.

She tried a different angle. "I was surprised to see you at Mrs. Maxwell's funeral."

"Yeah. Curiosity, I guess. And we all know what happened to the curious cat, right?" He tried a smile, but it turned into a rough swallow. He cleared his throat. "It might be better if you weren't too curious yourself."

"That's what Donovan Moran told me today."

Joe glanced at his watch. "Well, if I'm gonna start learning French, I'd better get at it."

"Au revoir," Sarah murmured, stifling her frustration and disappointment.

Joe looked puzzled, then nodded, his expression pleased. "Hey, I get it! That's French for good-bye. Au revoir to you too."

Back at the apartment, she put the pizza leftovers in the refrigerator. She felt tired yet restless. She flicked the

TV on, then off. She glanced at the stack of magazines on the end table. She'd already read everything of interest there, and she wasn't about to delve into Julie's little red New Testament again.

But there was one thing in the apartment that she hadn't read yet.

She considered the prospect uneasily, jumping back and forth over the fence dividing her arguments. On the one side, she felt like she would be invading Julie's privacy. On the other side, if the killer was someone Julie had known and there was even a slight possibility of finding something in the journal that might help bring him to justice . . .

She opened the drawer of the nightstand next to Julie's bed. This was where Julie had stashed her "treasures," an assortment that brought a pang to Sarah's heart. Rocks and shells from the beach. A photo of Julie and Sarah and Gran, arms draped around each other. A silly, cross-eyed creature made of bits of driftwood and beach stones. Several loose crystals. The first letter Sarah had written to her, another letter from Gran, an old "Still mad?" card from Donovan. A handmade silver ring.

Sarah carefully looped the ring over her finger so she could study it. The workmanship was rough, but the sentiment of entwined hearts was tender. So Donovan hadn't been lying about the ring. Although, obviously, he hadn't found it when he was in the apartment.

But . . .

Sarah frowned and shuffled the shells and letters aside. Hadn't Julie's journal been in there? Sarah remembered putting it in the drawer that night when she'd almost started to read it. A plain spiral notebook right here on top everything else in the drawer.

It was not here now.

And suddenly she knew what Donovan Moran had really been searching for in the apartment.

24

Sarah fished Nick's number out of her purse and dialed.

The cell phone rang but no one answered. She tried every fifteen minutes for an hour but never connected with him.

She stayed up late, distracting her thoughts with a movie about Jodie Foster contacting beings from outer space, then spent a restless night and wound up oversleeping. She guiltily jumped out of bed at 10:30 and ran to the phone to call Nick. Too late. At this time on a Sunday morning, he was probably already on his way to church.

She lifted a drape and peered out of the living room window. A dreary day, definitely not one of Julesburg's jewels. She showered and ate the last of the Cheerios and canned fruit cocktail for breakfast. It was not an appealing combination, but using up stuff from the cupboard at least made her feel as if she was accomplishing something. She realized she hadn't yet picked up the mail, so she walked down to the post office. When she returned, she wrote checks to pay bills, stamped the envelopes, and made another trip to the post office.

Now what?

Travis Volkman. The name popped into her head as if it had been poised for the chance to burst out of her subconscious. One of the rumors Donovan had mentioned involved Volkman Laser Systems. And Julie'd had some sort of relationship with Travis. Sarah looked in the phone book and found only the company listed; the Volkman home phone apparently had an unlisted number. With sudden inspiration, she looked in the back of the phone book, where Julie kept a list of personal numbers.

No Travis Volkman listed there. But the relationship with him was older, pre-Donovan. She dug around in the small cavern under the end table and found an old phone book. And in the back of it . . . success!

Sarah picked up the phone and dialed. She was so surprised when the call was picked up on the second ring that she stumbled awkwardly. "Is this . . . uh . . . Travis?"

"In person." He sounded flirty, amused, as if he was not displeased by a call from an unknown female on a Sunday morning. "What can I do for you?"

"You don't know me—"

"I think I'd like to. Especially since you already have my private phone number." The husky voice still held a flirty intimacy, now with an added touch of curiosity. He laughed. "If you found it scrawled on a wall somewhere, I hope the comments were complimentary."

"I'm Julie Armstrong's sister. Your number was in the back of her phone book."

"Oh?" he said, an edge of wariness replacing the flirty amusement.

"Someone pointed you out at Mrs. Maxwell's funeral," Sarah said.

"Yes, I saw you there," he acknowledged. "Julie had never mentioned a twin sister. I didn't know until after . . . after the crime that one existed. The resemblance is so striking that seeing you was something of a shock.

Although nothing to compare with the shock of Julie's death, especially under such despicable circumstances."

"I know you and Julie were friends at one time . . ."

"We dated for a while, but my acting career has necessitated several trips to L.A. since then. I'll be going back down shortly. I'm up for a lead role in a new Vietnam-era epic that's expected to be a blockbuster."

I'm calling about a murder. He's hustling a movie.

But she could play to his ego, if that's what it took. "I'm glad to hear you'll be showing up on the big screen as well as TV now. I'll watch for the new movie."

"You can see me before that." He laughed. "Lots of me. I'm August in next year's 'Hollywood's Hottest Hunks' calendar."

"How exciting," Sarah murmured.

"Julie had talked about our relationship, I suppose?"

If his ego was any bigger, he'd have to hire a truck to haul it around. "I know you must be very busy, but I was hoping we could get together so you could tell me a little about Julie. It's a long story, but we were separated at birth, and I didn't get to know her very well in the short time we had together."

"I didn't really know her all that well myself."

The unexpectedly stiff reluctance in his voice pumped Sarah's interest. Did he simply not want to bother with a discussion that wasn't all about him? Or did he or his family's company have something to hide?

"However . . ." he wavered, apparently debating with himself. "Sure, let's get together for dinner."

Wait a minute. Why the quick change of mind? He was up to something, she was sure of it. Had he decided dinner might be a good time to pick her brain? To find out . . . what? Her suspicions or theories about the murders? Because he or the company was connected to them in some way? A gust of excitement swept through her.

"I was thinking of lunch today, if it isn't too late. I may not be in Julesburg much longer," Sarah said.

"I'm tied up at the office for the rest of today."

"On Sunday?"

He laughed again, this time without the flirty intimacy. "The salt mines at Volkman Laser Systems do not grind to a halt just because it's Sunday."

Sarah cleared her throat. "This is a little awkward, but I understand Julie was not exactly a big fan of the company?"

Another laugh. "And my father was not delighted when he realized my girlfriend was out there picketing with the other protesters objecting to the company's involvement in producing some military laser systems."

Donovan Moran had suggested Volkman Laser Systems might be sneaking classified technology out of the country. Joe Argo had also mentioned "cloak-and-dagger military stuff." Was the company into international trade in restricted items? A scenario that, unlikely as it seemed on the surface, somehow involved the elderly Mrs. Maxwell? Could this somehow be the blackmail about which she and Nick had speculated?

"If you can't make lunch, then I'd really like to have dinner sometime soon."

"I think I'll be free tomorrow night, but I'll have to call you."

"Great! I'm looking forward to it. I'm staying at Julie's apartment. Her number's in the book."

When she hung up, she felt like the call had lifted the day out of the total-loss category. She filled out the afternoon with a hike on a Lighthouse Hill trail, moldering leaves soggy underfoot, air fresh and exhilarating. She returned to the apartment feeling invigorated, only to stop short as she slid out of the Honda.

The sun had come out. A bluejay squawked cheerfully in a nearby tree. A football game on TV blared from an open window. All so normal. Yet the skin at her nape prickled. Her palms inside her gloves became sweaty. She turned slowly, her gaze scanning the parking lot, then the windows of the apartment building.

Nothing.

Yet she felt like she had at the funeral. Like she had a couple of days ago when she was standing at the apartment window.

Someone was watching her. Studying. Calculating.

Cold sweat trickled down her ribs.

Then a crow swooped down to within a few feet of her and captured a discarded potato chip. It watched her with beady, wary eyes as it pecked at the chip. She shook her head ruefully. *This is my evil watcher? Get a grip.*

She heated leftover pizza in the microwave for supper. She was just scrunching the box into the garbage when the doorbell rang.

"Who is it?" she asked through the closed door.

"Police Chief Randy Wilson."

She opened the door. Randy didn't look jubilant. Police decorum wouldn't let him, she suspected. But tightly controlled energy gleamed in his eyes.

"I have something important I think you'll be happy to hear. May I come in?"

"Yes, of course."

Randy stepped inside, and she closed the door.

"I wanted you to be the first to know. We've arrested a suspect in your sister's murder. And Helen Maxwell's murder too, of course. This is our guy. Not a doubt in my mind or Ben's about him."

"That's wonderful! I'm so relieved to hear it. *Who?*"

"You probably don't know him. Punk kid name of Howard Mason. It's a situation just like we figured. He intended to rob the Calico Pantry for easy money, panicked, and shot Helen Maxwell. I doubt if he really wanted to kill Julie, but he didn't know what else to do with her.

He probably figured she could identify him. Anyway, we got him."

"He confessed?"

"No. He's swearing he's innocent. Don't they all? But you remember the earrings Julie was wearing the night she was abducted? We found one of them when we were going through your SUV."

Sarah nodded. "The parrot earrings."

"Right. Ben found the matching earring under a floor mat in Howard Mason's car. It must have come off when he transported her body to the Nevermore that night."

Julie's earring. Sarah remembered it dangling from her sister's earlobe. She swallowed and pushed away the shattering image of that same earring falling from Julie's dead body. She searched for something pleasant to say.

"That wraps things up, then, doesn't it? Congratulations on a job well done."

"Thank you. It's a big relief. We've been afraid the killer might figure he had to eliminate you too. Howard Mason's on the wimpy side, which is probably why he picked on poor old Mrs. Maxwell to begin with. But he might have gotten panicky enough to come after you."

"What made you go after him?"

"We got a phone tip."

"Someone looking for the reward?"

"It was an anonymous call, and he didn't mention the reward. Although we may hear from him again on that point. But all he said this time was that this guy worked at Website X, and we should check him out. Then I got to thinking that you'd said we should talk to Steve Lomax at Website X about someone missing around his place. We did that at the time. I thought then that Steve acted a little edgy, but he insisted he didn't know anything."

"I can understand that. I was in there last night. It's a madhouse."

"Anyway, we went back and talked to Steve again this morning. This time, after a lot of hemming and hawing, he finally admitted there was someone who hadn't been around Website X for three days right after Mrs. Maxwell's murder." Randy nodded. "This guy. Howard Mason. Howard is also Steve's nephew. Which probably explains why Steve didn't tell us anything about Howard the first time around."

Sarah remembered how strange Steve Lomax had acted that night he'd delivered the pizza, his too-talkative reaction when she'd mentioned a missing customer. A nephew. It fit.

"Anyway, we brought Howard Mason in, and he gave us permission to search his car. He'd cleaned it up pretty good and no doubt figured he was safe, and letting us search it would make him look innocent. But he'd missed this earring Ben found down in a crack. Not much gets by Ben. I'm proud to say that I learned from the best when I worked with him before I became police chief."

"I'm so very grateful for all your hard work and persistence. It's good to know there will be justice for Julie."

She shook his hand in thanks, yet the familiarity of the name niggled at her. Howard. "What does this Howard look like?"

"He's twenty-two, skinny, awkward kid. Face pockmarked with scars from old pimples." Randy spoke with contempt, as if the pimples were a blight on Howard Mason's character as well as his face. "He's been in trouble before. Marijuana and vandalism charges back in high school. Driving under the influence. Stealing tools from a local mechanic."

Sarah saw a young guy handing her a pizza. The name Howard embroidered on his red shirt. Big ears. "He works at the pickup counter at Website X?"

"Sometimes. The kids shift positions there."

She felt a surge of dismay. That awkward, unsure-of-himself kid was the killer? That sad face was behind the mask and the alien eyes at the Calico Pantry? That voice, which had sounded so sincere when he talked about how nice Julie had been to him, was also the whispery voice that had sent Sarah to the Nevermore to find Julie's body? This was the person who put a gun to the back of Julie's head—

"This fits with the autopsy showing Julie had eaten pizza," Randy added. "It's exactly what this punk would give her."

"But you said Howard hadn't been seen around Website X for three days, so he must not have been in there getting pizza for Julie."

Randy frowned. "True, but it may have been frozen or something. I doubt if they can tell details like that on analysis of stomach contents."

"Were his fingerprints in the SUV?"

"They haven't been compared yet. Although most likely he was still wearing the gloves you said he had on in the Calico Pantry."

"Does he have any explanation for the earring? Or where he was those three days?"

"No explanation at all about the earring. Which isn't surprising, since there's only one possible explanation. The earring was our ace in the hole, you know. Information we didn't release to the media. And now the earring's nailed him," Randy continued with satisfaction. "About those three days—Howard says he wasn't feeling good and was just home in bed. Not much of an alibi, right? He lives alone in a little shack over near Ryker's Bog. Which fits in with the mud that was on your SUV."

"Did you find the gun?"

"Not yet. Howard probably deep-sixed it in the ocean, so then we'll never find it. But we'll search the house as soon as we can get a judge to sign a search warrant."

My reason to stay in Julesburg is gone now, Sarah thought. *The killer is captured. I'm free.* Yet somehow the elation that should've accompanied that freedom wasn't surfacing. "Will I need to testify at the trial?"

"Yes, I'm sure you'll be important to the prosecution. But there's no telling how long before the case goes to trial. These things drag on."

"I'm not planning to stay in Julesburg, but I'll keep in touch and be available whenever I'm needed. And thanks again."

She closed the apartment door behind Randy. So it really was over. No need for her and Nick to work together to find the killer. The killer was in custody. No need ever to see Nick again, actually. Although she should tell him what had happened.

She dialed his cell phone number, and this time he picked up immediately. She relayed what Randy had just told her.

"That's great, Sarah. Criminals usually make mistakes, and it sounds as if this guy made a big one with the earring. It's a real relief to know they got him."

"Yes, it is."

"How does this affect your future plans?"

"I'll leave as soon as I can. But, I was wondering if I could have the name of your lawyer friend in Eugene. I need someone to handle the settlement of Julie's estate."

"Jefferson Schermerhand, Sherm to his friends. I've got his number right here because I talked to him last night."

Nick produced the number, and she scribbled it on a scratch pad.

"Thanks."

"No problem. Sherm said last night that he'd see what he could dig up on Volkman Laser Systems. But I'll call and tell him to cancel."

"Thanks. That won't be necessary now."

Small silence. "Sarah, is something wrong? You don't sound all that elated about the killer being caught."

She didn't want to say it. She didn't even want to think it. She wanted this to be over.

But she wasn't as sure as Randy Wilson that it was over.

25

"I want to be elated," Sarah said slowly. She touched the crystal at her throat. "I want to be relieved. But I'm not."

"Because?"

"Because I just don't think Howard Mason did it."

"You don't?" Nick sounded startled. "For what reason?"

"Nothing very logical," Sarah admitted. "I met Howard at Website X last night. He mentioned Julie, how nice she'd been to him. He seemed so shy and sincere and sweet. Okay, I know. The most innocent-looking guy can be a serial killer. But . . . but Julie gave him a cat! Julie'd never have trusted him with one of her jetty cats unless she was sure he was a good guy."

"Anyone can make a mistake about someone's character."

True. Julie had been in love with Donovan Moran, whose character was as questionable as a product on an infomercial.

"How about if I drive down and we kick this around a while?" Nick asked.

Sarah suddenly wanted out of the apartment. It felt claustrophobic, like a trap tightening around her. "I'll come up there this time."

Nick drove over to the coffee shop where they'd agreed to meet. He needed some caffeine-fueled thinking time before Sarah arrived. The small coffee shop wouldn't win any awards for ambiance, but it was conveniently located, clean, and lit with a blaze of fluorescent lights. The utilitarian setting would help keep their relationship on a businesslike level, a constraint Nick knew he needed. He didn't want to encourage her doubts about Howard Mason simply because he wished she'd stay in Julesburg.

Yet he trusted her instincts. Sarah desperately wanted her sister's killer found; the comfortable route would be to accept that the police had done that. Because she didn't accept that solution, he had to consider her misgivings.

He waved to her from the booth when she stepped through the main door. The wind, moving in ahead of a coming storm, had raked her hair into dark spikes. She hadn't dressed up, but she looked good, fresh-scrubbed and vital, in faded jeans and light blue windbreaker. She slid into the seat across from him.

"Okay, I'm an idiot," she muttered. "They find the killer, and I immediately think they've made a mistake."

He motioned for the waitress to bring more coffee. "Gut feelings shouldn't be ignored."

She managed a wry smile. "I appreciate your putting it in such basic terms. Because it is a gut feeling. And not much more."

"I appreciate your calling me."

She folded her arms on the table between them. "Okay, it's flimsy. But I can't imagine the Howard I met in Website X getting up nerve enough to rob anyone. I also doubt he has enough imagination to use a demon ski mask and space-alien contacts for a disguise. He calls his cat Tiger. How's that for originality?"

The waitress arrived with a steaming coffee mug for Sarah. Nick motioned to her to refill his cup also.

"I also have another concern," Sarah added. "I don't know that it's strong enough to qualify as a gut feeling, but it's a definite uneasiness."

"About?"

"I don't like to think it because I know how hard Randy and Ben have worked on tracking down the killer, and how conscientious they are. But I can't help worrying that in Randy's eagerness to solve this case—"

"And make a name for himself in law enforcement—"

"That he may have jumped too soon. And in the wrong direction."

"If they're convinced they have the killer, this also means the investigation basically stops at this point," Nick said.

"Exactly."

"But finding the earring in Howard Mason's car is powerful evidence. If he isn't the killer, how did it get there?"

"I've come up with a couple of possibilities. One is that Howard's car was actually used to move Julie's body to the Nevermore that night. Someone borrowed and returned it without Howard ever knowing. It would be easy enough to do on that run-down street across from Ryker's Bog where he lives. This person didn't intend to involve Howard and didn't even realize the earring had fallen off and was in the car."

"That doesn't explain the tip the police received."

"Right. My other theory is that the earring was deliberately planted by the killer to frame Howard. And then the killer made his phone call to the police."

"The theories could be linked," Nick suggested thoughtfully. "The killer 'borrows' the car to transport the body. He purposely plants the earring to incriminate Howard, then calls the police. Maybe someone with a grudge against

Howard? Why don't we talk to Steve Lomax ourselves and see what he has to say about his nephew?"

"Good idea. I'll do it first thing in the morning."

Nick tapped her hand. "May I remind you that we agreed to be in this together? I don't think you should go digging in dangerous territory alone."

"Danger from Steve Lomax?"

"Possibly. He's certainly in a position to plant something in Howard's car. Or to know how to borrow it without getting caught. And if he thinks your coming to talk to him means you're suspicious of him . . ."

"But to incriminate his own nephew?" she said.

"A guy who's willing to kill two people wouldn't have any qualms about that."

"But why would Steve have robbed the Calico Pantry to begin with? The money surely couldn't have been enough motive." She hesitated. "Although Randy mentioned something once . . ."

"About?"

"He got a tip about illegal liquor or drugs at Website X and came close to shutting it down. If Steve thought Mrs. Maxwell had made that tip or was planning to make some other trouble—"

"Maybe she actually did make the tip."

"That's possible. But is it reason enough for Steve to kill her?"

"If he's involved in something big and she was on to it, maybe he figured he had to kill her to protect his activities."

Sarah looked at the clock over the brightly lit counter. "It's too late for both of us to drive over and talk to Steve tonight."

True. And in the morning he had an appointment with the roofer about leakage problems, and another appointment in the afternoon with the electrical contractor. "Maybe we should just tell Randy or Ben our thoughts about Steve and let them handle it."

"Randy and Ben are convinced Howard Mason is guilty. And I'm not convinced they'll pay any attention to other suggestions." She touched his hand. "I'll be safe talking to Steve in public."

"I still don't like it. I can come down the next day—"

"No. I don't want to delay." She hesitated, as if she were groping her way through a fog. "I can't explain it, but I think time is . . . running out."

"It could be months before Howard Mason comes to trial," Nick argued. Yet even as he said the words he didn't disagree with her. "I think I'll just let Sherm go ahead and see what he can find out about Volkman Laser Systems."

"Yes. Good idea. I didn't have a chance to tell you yet, but I talked with Travis Volkman." She summarized their conversation. "He's supposed to call me about having dinner together tomorrow night. I think there may be an interesting friction between Travis and his father."

Nick took a gulp of hot coffee to keep from yelping an objection to Sarah having dinner with this playboy, and nearly scalded himself. "Even if there's friction, you can't expect the owner's son to suddenly confide that the company is involved in something shady. Or that Mrs. Maxwell was blackmailing them."

"Maybe neither the company nor blackmail is involved. Maybe Travis simply tried to pull off a robbery to get money for drugs. Drugs are why Daddy cut off his funds in Hollywood, so we've heard, but that doesn't necessarily cut off Travis's need for them."

"And you're *going out* with this guy?"

"We can't catch a murderer by playing safe and hiding under the covers." She impatiently waved her fingers. "Something else I haven't had a chance to tell you. I think

I know now what Donovan Moran was really looking for in the apartment."

"Not the ring?"

"I found the ring, so it does exist. But I think he'd have found it if he'd really been looking for it. Julie's journal is missing. It was in her nightstand a few days ago. It isn't there now."

"Did you ever . . ." He felt awkward asking this. He rephrased the question. "Do you have any idea what was in the journal?"

"No. Now I wish I hadn't been so conscientious about not reading it. She was writing up a storm after she came in from seeing Donovan that last night. I think Donovan is worried there could be something bad about him in the journal."

"Who besides Donovan may have a key and could have gotten into the apartment?"

"The manager has master keys, I'm sure. There isn't a full-time maintenance man, but various cleaning and plumbing and electrical people are around occasionally." Sarah hesitated before adding reluctantly, "It's possible Travis Volkman has one, left over from when he and Julie were in a relationship."

It was beginning to look as if their list of suspects was widening. Yet in a way it was also shrinking, cutting down to people Julie had known.

But not necessarily. "We can't be certain Julie knew her killer. He may have killed her simply because she was in the way, not because he and Julie knew each other. We shouldn't focus only on people she knew."

Sarah nodded, but their eyes met and she said quietly, "But we both think she did know him, don't we?"

Yes.

And what will a killer do if he realizes Sarah hasn't accepted Howard Mason's guilt, that she's still out there asking questions?

News about the arrest of a suspect in the murders was all over the late local news. The TV cameras had video footage of Randy and Ben delivering Howard Mason to the county jail. Howard's head was down, shoulders slumped and acne-scarred face hidden. In an interview, Randy did not specifically mention the earring but indicated that there was "strong physical evidence" linking the suspect to the crimes.

Sarah watched the handcuffed man being hurried into the building. *Maybe he is guilty.* Police evidence was surely stronger and more reliable than her gut feeling. The fact that Julie had once given Howard a cat was a flimsy defense against the incriminating evidence of the earring in his car.

Yet the feeling that a mistake had been made still churned deep in her gut.

Sarah was at Website X when it opened at 11:00 the next morning. She hoped to talk to Steve Lomax before he became too busy with lunchtime customers. Yet when she walked in she suddenly suspected Steve would have made time for her even if customers had stood a dozen deep around the counter. He slammed down the stack of metal pizza pans he was carrying and stormed toward her.

Taken aback by his anger, she stumbled over what she had planned to say. "I—I was hoping to talk—"

"You've talked enough already," he snapped. "You sicced the cops on me. You got 'em coming in here questioning everybody, making people nervous, runnin' off customers. Now they've got Howard in jail, accused of murder. Arrested him right there behind the counter! And that poor dumb kid wouldn't harm a petunia."

Sarah wasn't certain if Steve Lomax was more disturbed about his nephew's arrest or his own damaged business. But there was no uncertainty about his fury. She'd intended to approach him from a perspective of mutual belief in Howard's innocence, but his hostile accusations made her feel defensive.

"They found my sister's earring in Howard's car! And someone else, not me, tipped them to go after him."

"Yeah?" Anger mottled Steve's face. "You're the one sent 'em snooping around here to begin with. And how do I know you didn't get some guy to call in with the tip? Why don't you just mind your own business and go back where you came from?"

"This is my business! And my sister was murdered *here*."

"Yeah? Well, my nephew is facing a couple of murder charges here because of your nosy interference. So get out, go away. You've done enough damage." He lunged forward, stopping only inches short of shoving her.

"Just because he's your nephew doesn't make him innocent!"

"Just because Julie was your sister doesn't give you the right to sic the cops on me and some harmless kid."

Steve Lomax turned and stalked off. Everything had come to a pin-dropping silence during the exchange, but workers behind the counter now became very busy. Voices chattered and pans clanged.

Out in the car, angry and shaken, a different thought suddenly occurred to Sarah. Could Steve's anger and accusations be merely a pretense, a cover-up? If he had framed his nephew, how better to protect himself than by making a public show of fury over the nephew's arrest?

She thought back to that night he'd delivered pizza to the apartment, before Julie's body had been found, and how he'd looked as if he were seeing a ghost when she opened the door. He'd said he was startled by Sarah's resemblance to Julie. But was his shock actually because he'd momentarily thought she *was* Julie . . . and he knew Julie was already dead? Did the temper he exhibited today also show a frightening capacity for violence?

Distracted and upset, she drove down to the jetty and put out food for the cats. A predicted storm was still offshore, but the wind howled over the dock. Pounding waves blasted the rock jetty, and globs of sea foam whipped over Sarah's head. Clarissa meowed in plaintive protest.

Sarah spotted a figure moving around on the Wildfire III and made her way across the dock to the boat. Surging water visible far below the cracks between the wooden planks gave a dizzying feel of movement to the dock. She called Joe's name, and a windblown head of reddish-brown frizz appeared over the railing.

"Have you heard that they have a suspect for the murders in custody?" she yelled over the wind.

"Yeah, caught it on the news last night."

"I heard they got him because someone called in a tip."

"That right? I don't think that was on the news."

"Randy Wilson told me. Do you know this guy, Howard Mason?"

"I've probably seen him at Website X, but I don't know him."

The boat sat high on the wheeled trailer, though it listed a bit to one side from an old flat tire on the trailer. Sarah's neck muscles were cramping from looking up at Joe peering over the rail. She clasped her hands behind her head to brace her neck and capture her blowing hair. "Can I come up and talk to you?"

He disappeared, and she massaged her neck. She thought he intended to help her into the boat, but when he appeared beside her, he demanded bluntly, "What do you want?"

Sarah was also blunt. "I don't think Howard Mason did it. I think the authorities are so eager to solve the crime that they made a mistake. I think it may have been exactly what you once suggested, something bigger than a simple robbery gone bad. With someone important and powerful involved."

"If it wasn't just a robbery gone bad, then you and I had better stay out of it and watch our backs. Someone who was willing to kill two people is going to be just as willing to kill two more." He glanced around the deserted dock. "Nosy busybodies wind up like curious cats."

She pulled a strand of windblown hair out of her mouth. "I heard you sometimes give tips to the police. Did you give this one about Howard?"

A flicker of alarm in Joe's eyes told her he did not like his activities as an informant being public knowledge. "I pass along a couple of tips about stolen stuff showing up for sale. Maybe a pot deal or two. And that makes me kingpin of the informants?" he scoffed.

"Did any of these tips involve Donovan Moran?"

Joe's answer was no more than a shrug, but the nervous shifting of his eyes told her she was on target.

"What do you know about Steve Lomax? And Travis Volkman?"

"Look, from this point on, I don't care about anything or anybody in this little burg."

"How about an earring? Do you know anything about that?"

"All I know is, as soon as I can get this engine running, it's au revoir. I'm moving my boat north. Or maybe I'll just sell out and find another line of work."

"Have you been threatened?"

"Look, I don't know anything about the murders. Nada. Zip. Whatever I speculated was just my imagination working overtime."

"Well, do you think Mrs. Maxwell could have been blackmailing someone?"

"I'm not doing any speculating about anything or anyone." He sounded like a man with his back against a wall.

"But I figure if someone *thinks* I know something, and that same someone *thinks* I might squeal, then it might be a real good idea for me to chug on outta here. And if you're smart, you'll just hustle yourself on back to California."

"So you do think someone other than Howard Mason killed Julie and Mrs. Maxwell."

"Don't put words in my mouth. I'm not saying that. No way!"

"But if Howard's in custody and you think there's still danger—" She broke off, sensing from the tight crimp of Joe's mouth that he was going into clam mode.

She gave up and went back to the car. The cats had gobbled the food, then tucked back into their holes to escape the wind. Even Clarissa was out of sight.

Sarah decided to drive around by the street that ran alongside Ryker's Bog. Once on the potholed road, she had no trouble spotting Howard Mason's little house. It was surrounded by yellow crime tape. She parked across the street, heavy branches of the jungled growth in the bog reaching out to scrape the car.

Howard's house wasn't quite the "shack" Randy had described it as, but it wasn't much more. A cottage of weathered yellow shakes sat between two weedy vacant lots, with a fireplace chimney at one end, a patched roof, and a picket fence in need of paint. It looked as if he'd tried to brighten the place with plastic tulips on the windowsills and a welcome mat imprinted with daisies. A metal wind chime tinkled in the wind. The yard was mostly weeds, but it was mowed.

A queasiness worked out from her stomach and crawled on her skin as she studied the house. She could be wrong about Howard Mason, totally wrong. Perhaps right here was where her sister had been kept prisoner, bound with duct tape, fed a last meal of pizza.

Shot in the back of the head.

She swallowed convulsively. But she also noted that there was no garage. Howard Mason's car easily could have been "borrowed" from the driveway in the middle of the night. The car was nowhere to be seen now, undoubtedly impounded for evidence.

A big orange cat, meowing plaintively, wandered around the picket fence. Sarah got out and dumped several handfuls of cat food under the yellow tape. The cat, tail like an upright flag, scurried over to eat. An elderly woman was sweeping the porch of the house on the far side of one of the vacant lots. Sarah waved and went over to talk to her. The wind, slowed by the Bog, was almost benign here.

"I was concerned about Howard's cat," Sarah offered by way of explanation for her presence.

"Cat better find himself a new home. I don't think Howard's gonna be around for a good long spell. You a friend of his?"

"More like an acquaintance."

"Real shocking it is, what he done. Sickening."

"He's just a suspect," Sarah protested. "They don't know for sure that he did anything."

"I don't figure Ben and that new policeman would be arresting somebody just for the fun of it." The woman whacked the broom against the porch railing. "But these shyster lawyers, they're always gettin' guilty people off."

"Have you known Howard long?"

"I've lived here going on thirty-six years. When I think now how I let my grandkids come and play and him just a few feet away over there." She rolled her eyes.

"Does Howard own the house?"

"Nah. Guys like him don't own anything. Some investment outfit bought up a bunch of cheap places for rentals."

"Did he ever act strange or do anything suspicious?"

"Well, he played that screamin' music loud enough to wake the dead. But I don't guess I ever saw him do anything illegal," the woman conceded. "Borrowed my lawnmower a few times. But mostly kept to himself."

Kept to himself. Wasn't that what was always said of a person who did something so gruesome no one could quite comprehend?

"Did you hear anything like a gunshot at Howard's house?"

"They make those silencer things, you know."

The neighbor was obviously convinced of Howard's guilt, but Sarah thought of what Nick had said about someone having a grudge against Howard. "Do you know his family?"

"His mother died, oh, years ago. His father took up with that Erickson woman, but he still had a roaming eye, and she managed to get the house when they split. Though I don't think she was so lily-pure herself." The woman nodded meaningfully. "I heard she moved back East, and he's dead, of course."

Plenty of hostility in that family. But with the main players long gone, probably irrelevant. "Howard lives here alone then?"

"Mostly. Though another guy comes and stays once in a while. A cousin, maybe. I don't know his name."

A cousin who came and went. And could sneak out and use Howard's car. Or, conversely, could perhaps provide Howard with an alibi and help prove his innocence. "I wonder where I could find him?"

The woman's shrug offered no help and even less interest.

Sarah returned to the apartment, and Travis Volkman called a few minutes later. He said he'd pick her up at 7:00 for dinner at the Singing Whale. She countered with a suggestion that they meet at the restaurant. She wasn't about to get in a vehicle with him.

After the call she decided there was one more thing she could accomplish that day. She went down to the main floor and tapped on the apartment manager's door. A female voice called to her to come in.

They were a middle-aged couple, the woman confined to a wheelchair. They both offered sympathies about Julie, but Sarah suspected they were relieved that the crimes hadn't happened there in the apartment building.

"You're welcome to continue renting the apartment," Mr. Legerman said. "We'll need to make out a new rental agreement, but the security deposit can just carry over."

Sarah decided against announcing her plans. "Thank you. That's very nice. What I was wondering at the moment . . . Could you tell me who has keys to the apartment?"

Mrs. Legerman instantly prickled even though Sarah had tried to make the question innocuous. "Has there been unauthorized entry into the apartment?"

"It's just that I can't find some of Julie's papers."

"We have keys, of course, but I haven't been in the apartment in months," Mr. Legerman said. "Not since Julie had a problem with the refrigerator. Repair people aren't given keys. We let them in when necessary."

"Of course, someone young and popular like Julie . . ." Mrs. Legerman's tone held disapproval of Julie's "popularity," but she broke off, apparently reluctant to impugn a dead girl's character. But her implication was clear: Julie gave her young men keys.

"Are the locks changed when a tenant leaves and someone new moves in?"

"We used to do that, but the owner of the building recently informed us that expenses had to be cut."

That information was not reassuring, although it probably didn't affect Julie's apartment because she'd lived there almost two years. "And you don't know of anyone else who might have a key?"

"We weren't privy to details of the transaction when the new owner bought the building, but I assume the former owner passed on his set of master keys. Actually, we've never met the current owner." Mr. Legerman scowled, as if he took this as a personal slight.

"And the current owner is . . . ?"

Sarah expected an absentee landlord, probably someone from out of state. But the familiar name hit her like a wave sweeping over the jetty.

26

Nick spread the papers on the table in the motel room, page after page outlining planning commission regulations about a zone change for some property on which a client wanted to construct a commercial building.

After ten minutes, he hadn't gotten beyond page one. Paragraph (1) and Subsection (A) kept losing out to images of Sarah with Travis Volkman. Sarah had told him that she was having dinner with Volkman at the Singing Whale this evening. If Volkman was somehow involved in the murders, and he decided Sarah was a threat . . .

After another ten minutes Nick gave up, threw on his jacket, and headed for his pickup. He'd just keep an eye on Sarah from a distance. She didn't have to know he was anywhere in the vicinity.

The Honda wasn't in the parking lot at the apartment when he pulled in at 7:15. *Good. Sarah must be meeting Volkman at the restaurant, certainly preferable to getting in a car with him.*

But there was no battered brown Honda at the Singing Whale either. He then checked the parking lot at the Julesburg Café. No Honda.

Surely Volkman wouldn't take her to dinner at Website X! Nick checked anyway. Nothing. The last place in town was more tavern than restaurant, but they did have a grill. Another negative. Had Sarah and Volkman decided to go up to Dutton Bay or down to Gold Beach? Or even worse, could Volkman have talked her into dinner at his place?

He drove around the elegant condominiums on Lighthouse Hill, then up to the ridge of expensive homes overlooking town from the east. After a half hour of fruitless prowling, he was fully aware of just how many dark side streets lurked on the lowlands and hillsides, how many houses were concealed behind thick coastal vegetation, how impossible it was even in a town as small as Julesburg to pinpoint someone's whereabouts.

He was braking at one of the town's three stoplights when his cell phone rang. On this tense night, the familiar sound startled him. He pulled to the curb. "Yes?"

"Hi, Nick. Sherm here."

Sharp disappointment that it wasn't Sarah hit him, but he hid the reaction under a jovial greeting. "Hey, Sherm, good to hear from you."

"You'd said you wanted whatever I could dig up on the Volkmans and their company. I haven't had time to do more than scratch the surface, but you do know intriguing people, my friend."

Intriguing indeed, Nick thought as he listened. *And more than a little ominous.* When he dropped the cell phone on the seat, he wanted to find Sarah *now.*

After another five minutes of searching, he was ready to head for the police station to see if Randy or Ben were working late. They'd undoubtedly label him either lovesick or paranoid, but at this point he didn't care.

Then he spotted a dark Honda. Only because he had turned a corner and his headlights arced across the narrow driveway flanked with rhododendron bushes did he happen to see it. He braked and checked the license plate he'd memorized. *Yes, that's it!*

The small house with a vine-draped porch didn't look appropriate for the son of the owner of Volkman Laser Systems. Yet it was isolated by a tree-covered hillside, and the closest house was almost a block away. *If Volkman is messing with Sarah . . .*

He cut the lights and pulled in behind the Honda. *Maybe it's time to start making use of that permit to carry a concealed weapon.* For now, making do with what he had, he grabbed a heavy pipe wrench from the toolbox in the back of the pickup.

He cautiously circled the house, but drawn shades hid the rooms inside. He hesitated only a moment, then hammered on the door. It opened a crack, then wider.

"Nick! What are you doing here?" Sarah stood in the doorway, her slim figure haloed by light from within. She stared at the wrench clenched in his hand.

Her own hand held a book. Behind her he could see the arm of a dark sofa and a white-haired lady wrapped in a purple afghan.

"At the moment, feeling foolish," he admitted. He shuffled the wrench out of sight behind his leg. "I thought you were out to dinner with Volkman. When I couldn't spot your car at any of the local restaurants, I . . . got worried."

"So you decided to do a search of the town and track me down?" She sounded half angry, half astonished.

"Something like that. I was worried," he repeated defensively.

"As you can see, there's nothing to worry about." She stepped aside, giving him a better view into a room cluttered with heavy, old-fashioned furniture. The light came from a floor lamp with a beaded shade, and crystal bowls gleamed behind the leaded glass doors of a mahogany cabinet. Crocheted doilies sprouted from every surface. A white cat filled the elderly lady's lap.

"Travis called at the last minute and said something had come up. We postponed dinner until tomorrow night. I was feeling at loose ends, so I called Myrna here—" Sarah motioned to the elderly woman on the sofa, "to ask if she'd like me to read to her, like Julie used to do."

"I apologize for my overzealousness," Nick muttered.

"I suppose I'm impressed that you found me. If I'd been in trouble, it's comforting to know you'd have charged in like gangbusters to the rescue."

"You're letting in a draft, dear," the elderly lady called.

Grudgingly, Sarah said, "Since you're here, you may as well come in." In a lowered voice, she added, "Actually, there are a couple of things I'd like to discuss with you."

"I have interesting information about your date for you too."

Nick stepped inside, and Sarah made introductions. Myrna Bettenworth peered at him with bright, shrewd eyes.

"Are you Sarah's young man?" she inquired.

"Just a friend," Sarah cut in before Nick could answer. She motioned him to a chair. "We're reading some verses in Ephesians."

He noticed that the book in Sarah's hand was a Bible, its pages edged in shabby gilt.

"Myrna requested them," Sarah added, as if she wanted to make certain he understood that reading Bible verses was not her idea. She pointedly fingered the crystal still hanging at her throat.

"I like to hear about putting on the armor of God," Myrna agreed. She closed her eyes, and Sarah began reading about buckling on the belt of truth and taking up the shield of faith. Myrna stroked the purring cat and nodded occasionally.

Sarah briskly closed the book when she came to the end of the passage, but Myrna stretched out a veined hand. "Just a little more," she wheedled. "The fourteenth chapter of John would be nice."

"'In my Father's house are many rooms; if it were not so, I would have told you. I am going there to prepare a place for you,'" Nick quoted from the chapter.

Myrna straightened in surprise, bringing a meow of protest from the cat. She beamed at Nick. "My, my, you know your Bible, don't you? I find that verse very comforting. At my age, it's nice to know there's a place prepared for me. I may be claiming it very soon."

"I'm wondering, since your reading is limited now, if you've thought about getting an audio version of the Bible so you could listen to it whenever you wanted?"

"I'm not into all that complicated technical stuff."

"This isn't complicated. You just slip a cassette into the little player. Actually, I have an old one out in the glove compartment. I keep it there so I can listen while I'm driving sometimes. I'll go get it. I think the cassette I have in it now starts with Ruth."

"Oh, I love the Book of Ruth!"

The entire conversation about chapters in John and a book called Ruth may as well have been spoken in Hebrew, for all the sense it made to Sarah. Yet as Nick showed Myrna the workings of the cassette player and as they listened to various sections of the tape, she found herself reluctantly interested.

"Maybe if Helen had had one of these to listen to, the Bible would have come to mean as much to her as it does to me." Myrna sighed. She leaned her head back against the sofa, light shining through the wisps of white hair to her pink scalp. "Back when I could drive I tried to get her to come to church with me, but she couldn't afford to hire help at the store and wouldn't close on Sunday mornings. And what do all those extra hours she worked matter now?"

"You're talking about Helen Maxwell?" Nick asked.

"I miss her so much. We've been friends since both our sons were catching frogs and building treehouses. I know most people thought she was grouchy and bad tempered, but she was so good-hearted and kind to me. I knew I could always count on her."

"Julie said much the same thing about her," Sarah murmured. She did not mention the "Pink Grinch" name that had been her own reaction to Mrs. Maxwell.

"Julie always saw the best in everyone, didn't she? Helen and I used to talk on the phone almost every day. Twila Mosely phones or comes by more often now that Helen is gone, and I'm so glad she does, but she isn't as . . ." Myrna hesitated, as if searching for an appropriate word.

With a sudden twinkle in his eye, Nick said, "Gossipy?"

A pink blush tinted Myrna's wrinkled cheeks. "Yes, gossipy," she admitted. "Because that's what we did. We gossiped. Do you suppose the Lord holds that against me? I didn't have much gossip to tell, stuck here in the house like this, but Helen picked up lots of tidbits at the store."

Including a tidbit she was using to blackmail someone?

"I don't know how anyone could have killed Helen." Myrna shook her head. "Especially Howard. Although Twila said Randy Wilson found Julie's earring right there in his car."

"Do you know Howard Mason?" Nick asked.

"His mother was a second cousin of my husband's, and Howard used to come over and play with my grandson when I took care of him. Howard was a sweet boy then, though Helen said he's been in trouble." Myrna's bright eyes narrowed. "But if he did anything bad, I'd bet my socks it was that cousin of his leading the way."

Sarah's throat tightened with a jolt of excitement. "The cousin who lived with him part of the time?"

"That sounds like Van. Always mooching off someone. Van Daggert. Vandervort Daggert, actually. His mother gave all her children those strange, uppity names. His sister is Anastasia, can you imagine that? Van was always so smart. He could do math just like he had one of those computer chips in his head. But he'd rather cheat someone out of a dollar than earn five dollars honestly."

"Do you know where I might find Van Daggert?"

"Probably sponging off his mother. She lives down on Eleventh Street, the old house with all the ceramic deer and squirrels out front."

"Did anything seem different about Helen in the past few months?" Nick asked. "Did she seem afraid or nervous or upset?"

"Well, she was all of that, of course. So worried about her granddaughter."

With sudden intuition, Sarah knew. "Sharilyn?"

"You know about Sharilyn being Helen's granddaughter?" Myrna looked surprised. "Not many people do. Having a baby out of wedlock wasn't as acceptable back then as it seems to be now, and Helen and Ben and Twila kind of kept the details about Sharilyn's father to themselves."

The story, as Myrna told it in rambling detail, was that Helen Maxwell's son, Mike, and Ben and Twila's daughter, Emily, had both fled the limited opportunities in Julesburg the minute they finished high school. Mike was older and left first, but a few years later they met in Southern California. They'd both made bad choices and were into drugs and doing petty crime to support their habits. They didn't marry, but they had a baby, Sharilyn. Mike was knifed in a brawl a few months later. Emily several times lost her daughter to foster homes, but she'd eventually straightened out. Then several years ago she was killed in a car accident.

"And now Sharilyn has that terrible cystic fibrosis disease. She's always had it, I guess, but it just keeps getting worse. And now she needs a big transplant and—Oh, I don't know how it works, but I guess there just isn't one to give her! We pray for Sharilyn all the time, but Twila is just about going out of her mind with worry. So was Helen.

"Twila and Ben are going down there in a few days," Myrna added. "Ben just went back to the police force temporarily, you know, until they found who killed Helen and Julie. And now they've done that." She was silent a moment. "It just seems so . . . unreal that two people I was so close to were both murdered."

Then her veined hand reached out and squeezed Sarah's. "But for you, losing your very own twin sister that way . . ." She shook her head, as if she couldn't find words to express that loss. "Julie gave me Clementine here, did you know?" She stroked the white cat as tears trickled down her lined cheeks.

"Myrna, I'm sorry to ask you this, but do you have any idea, if it wasn't Howard, who might have killed Helen?" Nick asked.

"Just anyone who was willing to rob an old lady for a few dollars, I suppose."

"But what if the gunman really wanted Helen dead and just made it look like a robbery?" Nick suggested.

Myrna's droopy-lidded eyes opened wide. "Wanted Helen dead? And went in there intending to kill her? Oh no, I can't imagine why." She frowned. "Although . . ."

"Yes?" Nick prodded gently.

"Well, now that we're talking about all this, Helen did seem different the last year or so. I thought it was because of worry for Sharilyn, but maybe there was something more. She said, oh, odd things sometimes. She was angry about that new pizza place stealing so much of her business. She'd mortgaged the Calico Pantry to get money to help Sharilyn with some experimental medical treatments several years ago, and I know she'd had trouble keeping up the payments so she wouldn't lose the store. Although she hadn't mentioned any money problems recently."

Sarah and Nick exchanged glances. Had Helen Maxwell figured out a blackmail scheme to solve her financial problems?

"But she wasn't eating well at all. One time she came here for dinner and hardly picked at the nice tuna casserole I fixed. And she was . . ." Myrna frowned and tilted her head thoughtfully. "More secretive than she used to be. Sometimes I thought maybe she had a boyfriend she didn't want me to know about. One time a neighbor took me downtown to get groceries, and I saw a bakery truck at the Calico Pantry, and I was suddenly really hungry for some nice bearclaws. But when I went in, Helen was all cranky and out of sorts, and she said their pastries weren't on the shelves yet, so she couldn't sell me any. And I could kind of see then why everybody thought she was such a grouch. But then she made a special trip up here to bring me some bearclaws the next morning, so I guess maybe she was just having a bad day."

Sarah and Nick exchanged another glance. Myrna was rambling now, no doubt getting tired. Sarah picked up her jacket. "Maybe I can come read to you again?"

"Oh yes, I'd like that. Don't forget your little machine," Myrna added to Nick.

"It's yours," he said. "I'll bring the other cassettes by in a few days so you'll have the complete Bible to listen to."

"Oh, I couldn't accept that." Myrna pressed her hands together under her chin, like a small child wistfully contemplating a toy in a store window.

"Yes, you can." Nick smiled and patted her shoulder. "Save me a nice room next to the one the Lord has reserved for you, if you get there before I do."

Sarah momentarily had an odd feeling of being on the outside looking in. *I'm being ridiculous. Rooms reserved in heaven are just some . . . fantasy.*

"You come back now, anytime. Both of you. Either of you," Myrna waggled a finger at them, then spoke to Sarah. "This one's a keeper. Don't let him get away," she advised sternly. "Not like that young man who came here looking for Julie one time. Big, good-looking guy, rode in on a motorcycle that sounded like a jet engine."

Donovan Moran.

"He was up to no good," Myrna said. A frown curved her mouth downward. "Even if he did go to some fancy college back East, you can count on it, he was up to no good."

27

The predicted storm was moving in by the time Nick followed Sarah to her apartment. Wind bounced an aluminum can across the graveled parking lot, and rain spattered the windshield of the pickup like opening shots in a battle. Low branches of the dark firs along one side of the parking lot dipped and swooped against the ground below.

Nick started to open the door of the Honda for Sarah, but she motioned him to the passenger's side. He slid inside and peered at her in the shadowy light from the parking lot. "Is something wrong?"

"I think we need to talk about some things I found out today, but . . ." She glanced upward, where the light she'd left on in the apartment shone dimly through the closed drapes.

"Look, I've already promised no God talk," he muttered. "And I'm not going to make a pass at you if we're alone in the apartment for a few minutes."

Her quick smile told him he was coming at her out of left field. "I found out today who owns this building. And probably has a set of master keys to the apartments."

"And that is . . . ?"

"A corporation called Volkman Investments." She paused as another thought occurred to her. "From what a neighbor told me, I'm pretty sure they also own Howard Mason's rental house."

Volkman. Nick felt as if he'd just rounded a corner and found his fears staring him in the face. It hardly seemed coincidence that this name kept turning up.

"I can't imagine the elder Volkman sneaking in and stealing Julie's journal," Sarah said. "I can't imagine the journal could contain anything remotely relevant to him. I'm certain Donovan Moran took it. But . . ."

At this point Nick wouldn't rule out anything about the Volkmans. "Could Julie have had a personal relationship with the elder Volkman himself at some time?"

Nick could see the shock on Sarah's face, but she didn't lash out at him. "I don't think so," she said after a minute of thought. "But Julie was . . . unpredictable."

"Sarah, I'm sorry. I shouldn't have even mentioned that."

"It's okay. We have to consider all the possibilities." She glanced up at the window again. "But I don't want to talk about any of this in the apartment. I've been thinking that if someone has access to it, perhaps it's been . . . bugged. And a couple of times I've had the feeling that I'm being watched."

"Watched? In the apartment?"

"Once I felt it when I was standing by the window. Another time when I was getting out of the car." Embarrassment flared in a fleeting smile, and she threw up her hands. "I know. It's ridiculous. Eyes don't send out rays you can feel. And the idea that my apartment has been bugged is probably preposterous. Just call me Ms. Paranoid."

Yes, perhaps she was paranoid. But Nick didn't discount the idea that you could feel hidden eyes watching you. After all, one of his fears had been that the killer could be monitoring her activities. Bugging the apartment seemed a far-out possibility, though. But what was that old saying? Just because you're paranoid doesn't mean they aren't out to get you. He suspected both the elder Volkman and Donavan would know where to obtain the necessary electronics and how to install them.

"I don't even know how such things work," Sarah said, sounding frustrated. "Does someone have to be stationed nearby to listen? Or does the bug record what's said, and later someone retrieves the device?"

"I have no idea. I wouldn't recognize a 'bug' if it bit me on the ankle," Nick admitted. "But I think exchanging our information somewhere other than in your apartment is a sensible safety precaution. There's a wide overlook a few miles north of town. Let's drive out there instead of sitting here in the parking lot."

They went in Nick's pickup. He suggested stopping at Website X for take-out cups of coffee, but Sarah said she'd rather not. While wind battered the pickup and sheets of rain veiled the windows, Sarah told him about her encounter with an angry Steve Lomax that morning.

"Of course, it may have been a righteous anger. Steve may honestly think it's my fault his nephew is in jail."

She went on to tell him about talking with Joe Argo again. "And now I'm wondering if he, rather than Helen Maxwell, gave the authorities the tip on possible drug activities at Website X."

"Steve could still have thought it was Mrs. Maxwell."

"Right. And maybe Joe's afraid that if Steve figures out it really was Joe supplying information, that the same thing will happen to him that happened to her. In any case, he's scared and is figuring on getting out of Julesburg. He thinks I should too."

They had reached the overlook. There were no lights, only the occasional rain-blurred arc of headlights passing on the highway. Below, the roar of the sea was lost in the fury of the storm exploding around them. Nick remembered hearing about a freak storm blowing a vehicle off an Oregon cliff, and it was not uncommon for a rain-driven landslide to block a stretch of the coastal highway. Yet it was the possibility of dangers lying in wait for Sarah that rattled Nick more than the fury of the storm surging around them.

"I think Joe could be right. I don't want to see you go, but I'd rather see you leave Julesburg than stay and have some disaster happen."

"No. I'm not leaving until the real killer is found. Or until I'm convinced Howard Mason actually is the killer."

Her stubbornness didn't surprise him; he didn't argue the point. "Who is this cousin of Howard's that you and Myrna were talking about?"

Sarah explained about the conversation with Howard's neighbor. "I have two thoughts about the cousin. One, especially given Myrna's low opinion of him, is that he could easily have used Howard's car to move Julie's body. The other is that he may have absolutely nothing to do with the murders and could possibly provide an alibi for Howard." A passing car briefly lit her wry smile. "Never let it be said I can't straddle both sides of an argument."

"You were a very busy lady today." A fact that made him uneasy. "Did Travis Volkman say why he had to postpone dinner?"

"He said something had come up and he had to go back to the office. I don't think he was too happy about it."

"Sherm called me tonight. After what he told me, I suspect the midnight oil may burn often at Volkman Laser Systems these days."

"They're involved in something?"

"Both the company and Willard Volkman personally are in big trouble with the IRS. When he moved the company over here from Eugene—a move that in itself struck some people as odd—they had a couple of big, profitable government contracts. For a while Volkman had money to throw around—"

"Like buying up rental houses and investing in the apartment building where I live."

"Right. But now the company is in deep trouble financially, right on the edge of bankruptcy. They're also under investigation by the FBI and probably the CIA as well. It's all hush-hush, but Sherm got a hint that the investigation may concern sale of sensitive technical information to some unauthorized foreign country."

"Donovan mentioned something like that. Who'd suspect it, a little company right here in Julesburg?"

"There's more. A former business partner of Willard Volkman was killed during a terrorist ambush when the two of them were on a business trip in the Middle East. But there's some suspicion that Volkman may have eliminated a troublesome business partner by arranging for a murder that looked like an ambush."

Sarah's momentary silence showed she was as stunned as he had been by all that information. "But what could Mrs. Maxwell have had to do with any of that? Why would she need to be 'eliminated'?"

"Good question."

"Did your lawyer friend come up with anything about Travis?"

"Not much more than we've already heard. Some small-time drug involvement in the L.A. area. But it's still possible he could have pulled the robbery at the Calico Pantry to get drug money, then panicked and killed Mrs. Maxwell. In some ways, it does look like an amateurish crime. Even dumb, robbing the store with another customer present rather than waiting until Mrs. Maxwell was alone."

"And Julie could have recognized him, which would make it necessary to get rid of her." Sarah leaned her head against the seat. She sounded emotionally drained. "So where do we go from here? Sometimes it feels as if we're just floundering in some giant web."

"You're still planning to go to dinner with Travis Volkman?"

"If he calls, yes."

"Then you call me about when and where, okay? I want to keep an eye on you. And it'll be easier if I don't have to chase all over town looking for you."

"You'll bring your wrench?" she teased.

"I may bring more than that."

They started back toward town. Nick drove slowly because the highway was barely visible as pounding rain collided with drops bouncing upward from the asphalt. The wipers waged a losing battle trying to keep up with the waterfall flooding the windshield. On a curve, another vehicle skidded on the water-coated pavement and fishtailed toward them. Sarah screamed and threw up her hands. Nick twisted the wheel and braked. The two vehicles missed by mere inches.

"Enough of that." He swiped at the beads of sweat on his forehead. "We'll wait until this lets up."

He stopped the pickup at a paved pullout where a hillside rose between the highway and ocean and provided a bit of shelter from the wind. A high, chain-link fence bordered the pullout, its industrial metal links clashing with the untamed tangle of trees crowded behind it. The pickup headlights shone on an array of signs.

One was like the many rustic signs that marked points of interest along the coastal highway. But the words "Riptide Viewpoint Trail" on this sign were partially obscured by a "Closed" sign nailed at an angle across it. A red-lettered sign on the locked gate warned of extreme danger and stated even more emphatically that the trail was now closed to all public usage. One more sign added an additional warning: "Keep Out! Trespassers Will Be Prosecuted."

"If the 'danger,' whatever it is, doesn't get you, apparently the authorities will," Nick said.

Back at the apartment, despite her protest that it wasn't necessary, Nick walked Sarah to the apartment door. "Brace the back of a chair under the doorknob," he told her. "Even someone with a key can't get past that."

He waited until he heard the scraping sound of a chair against the door before heading down the stairs.

After bracing the chair under the doorknob, Sarah draped her coat over another chair to dry; it had gotten soaked in the brief dash across the parking lot. Then a thought occurred to her. Had she locked her car before they drove out to the overlook?

She dismissed the question. What did it matter, especially on a night such as this? She heated water in the microwave and made a cup of vanilla chai. With curiosity overcoming her reluctance, she picked up the Bible Nick had given her and looked up the Book of Ruth.

It was a short book, and a warm feeling seeped through her as she read the four chapters. These weren't stern men making grandiose pronouncements about God and eternity; there were no grand visions or harsh laws or confusing revelations. These were just two simple, likable women sharing heartbreak and loss, the widow Ruth devotedly following her mother-in-law to a new land and taking on her mother-in-law's faith. It proclaimed God's love and caring without ever saying an actual word about such matters.

As she finished the last chapter of Ruth, Sarah felt a lonely yearning. *I wish—*

She snapped the Bible shut. The only yearning she should have at the moment was a powerful hunger to find her sister's killer.

She went to the bathroom, intending to take a long, soothing bath before slipping into her pajamas, but whether or not she'd locked the car niggled at her. Chastising herself for being a fussbudget, she nevertheless slipped on a hooded raincoat and went down to the parking lot.

She felt a certain satisfaction when she found that the car door was indeed unlocked. Although the unlocked door meant she'd been careless, it also meant this jaunt in the rain was not unwarranted. She opened the door and pressed the lock button down.

And spotted a folded piece of paper lying on the seat.

28

Sarah didn't even notice the rain hammering her back as she read and reread the message composed of printed words cut from magazines and newspapers and sloppily glued to the sheet.

Californian go home we don't need your kind here if you stay you'll be sorry

Shock rocketed through her. Threat? Warning? Sick joke? She glanced around. *Is someone watching to see my reaction? Willing to carry out the threat now?*

Her glance skittered around the parking lot, but she saw only the usual hodgepodge of cars and pickups, all unnaturally shiny in the rain. The only movement was tree branches whipping in the wind.

She ran up to the apartment and jammed the chair under the doorknob. She read the note once more.

She tried to think logically. She knew there was some local resentment about the influx of Californians. Some longtime residents simply objected to change. Other hostility, she'd heard, came from recent transplants who wanted to close the gate behind them and not let any more "outsiders" in. But she couldn't believe that sour attitude could have prompted this note, delivered in the middle of a storm.

What about Steve Lomax? He'd actually yelled almost the same words to her. *Why don't you just mind your own business and go back where you came from?* Or maybe Joe Argo was adding emphasis to his advice that she get out of town. Donovan Moran had also warned her not to get involved. Were any of them worried she'd implicate them in the murders? And, of course, there were the Volkmans, both Travis and his father.

Or maybe a killer whose name she didn't even know.

She struggled against a rising tide of panic. *I'll call Nick.* She ran to the phone, but she halted before she punched the first number. *Could Nick have put the note in my car?* It seemed unlikely, but she knew he was afraid for her. Would he do this as a form of protection, to scare her into leaving before she stumbled into danger? He'd had the opportunity to do it.

She put the phone down. If Nick had done it, she needed time to collect her thoughts before talking to him. If he hadn't done it, hearing about the note would simply disturb him.

And it could be nothing. Maybe there really was some disgruntled kook running around trying to scare Californians into going back where they came from.

That was how she put it to Randy Wilson when she showed him the note the following morning. "I know some people resent outsiders, but I didn't realize there was an organized Unwelcoming Committee." A nervous titter escaped her before she could squelch it.

Randy didn't smile at her weak attempt at humor. "You say you found this in your car? He carefully took the sheet by the edges, and Sarah guiltily realized she'd already spread her own fingerprints all over it.

"Yes. Last night. A friend and I went for a drive. Later I got to wondering if I'd locked my car. When I went down to check, the note was there on the front seat."

"This may sound, uh, impertinent, but have you stepped on any toes around here? Had any unpleasant run-ins?"

"I went to see Steve Lomax yesterday. He was quite . . . emotional about blaming me for his nephew's arrest."

"Oh?" Randy looked up from the letter. "Steve can be hotheaded, all right. I don't think he'd pull a malicious stunt like this, though, but I'll check it out." He located a clear plastic folder in a drawer and slid the sheet inside, careful not to snag the glued-on words.

"I'm wondering if it has something to do with the murders."

"In what way?"

"I've discussed them with several people. Maybe someone doesn't like what I said or the questions I asked."

"What did you say?"

"I . . ." She hesitated, reluctant to suggest Randy had made a mistake and arrested the wrong man. She carefully chose softer words. "I have some doubts about whether Howard Mason is really the killer. I talked to several people about that. Maybe . . . maybe I made the real killer uneasy, and he wants to get rid of me."

"I see." Randy sounded more taken aback than angered by her doubt. "Do you have some reason to think Howard may not be the killer?"

A gut feeling. The fact that Julie had given Howard a cat. The way Howard, at Webside X that night, had seemed so truly distressed about Julie's death. *I may as well claim Julie's crystal spoke to me.*

She swallowed. "I feel awkward saying this, because I know how conscientiously you and Ben have worked to find the killer. But sometimes I wonder if maybe . . . possibly . . . in your eagerness to solve the crime . . ."

"You've heard I'm considering running for county sheriff next year. That I'd like to move beyond Julesburg's one-man, one-car, one-fax police department." Randy smiled wryly and waved a hand toward that one fax machine.

Sarah nodded.

"You think maybe I wanted to polish up my image by solving the case, so I jumped the gun and grabbed the wrong man."

"I'm sorry—"

"Well, it's true that I'm ambitious," Randy said. "I'm not ashamed of it. When I was a kid I had this big dream of becoming a lawyer. I suppose I saw myself as some brilliant Perry Mason, cleverly outwitting criminals with my superior brain power." Another wry smile. "But it was a dream that never got off the ground, because I didn't have the money to go to college, much less law school. I was born in a little lumbermill town on the other side of the mountains. In my family, finishing high school was considered a waste of time." His short laugh came out as a bark.

"I'm sorry," Sarah said again, not knowing whether she was apologizing for her insinuations or his lost dreams.

Randy didn't acknowledge her apology. "So I worked in the mill for a few years, and got even more frustrated and unhappy and bitter. One year I came over here to the coast to spend the skimpy vacation time the mill employees got. I heard about Julesburg deciding to hire a second police officer to help Ben. I . . . adjusted my resume and got the job." His dark eyes glared defiance as he made the admission. "But in spite of whatever shortcomings I had in training and experience, I've been good for this town." His voice was low and almost fierce. "It isn't any high-profile Perry Mason role, that's for sure. But I keep law and order and bring in the people who break it. I have the satisfaction of knowing I'm making a difference here."

"With much gratitude from the townspeople, from what I've heard."

"I work hard. I used my vacation last year to take an intensive training course in law enforcement in Portland. I've taken several night classes at Coos Bay. I try to keep up on new techniques and skills. After county sheriff, I'd like to move into FBI or CIA work, maybe even get that law degree someday."

"That's wonderful," Sarah said and meant it. "I hope you make it. In fact, I'm sure you will."

"In any case, I'm not about to mess up by sending the wrong guy to prison and having the mistake come back to haunt me. I know it takes a trial to prove legal guilt, but I haven't a doubt about Howard Mason."

"I don't have any real reason to believe Howard didn't do it," Sarah admitted.

"Maybe, if you're like Ben and me, the thought occurred to you that the earring could have been planted in Howard's car."

Relief that Randy had been the one to bring up this possibility whooshed through her. "Yes! Exactly."

"And it worried us, because, at the time of the arrest, the earring was the best evidence we had. But since then we've searched Howard's house. We didn't find Julie's fingerprints. In fact, we found practically no fingerprints, not even Howard's, which in itself is suspicious. It looked as if the place had been wiped clean with Armor All and Pledge. But we did find several medium-length brown hairs under a sofa cushion, and the lab says they match Julie's. There was also a half-used roll of duct tape on Howard's back porch."

Sarah felt sick. *So Julie* had *been held prisoner there in Howard's shabby little house, lived out the last terror-filled hours of her life there, helplessly bound with duct tape.*

But after a few aching moments, a semblance of relief flowed through her. She could lay her doubts about Howard's guilt to rest. She swallowed and touched a corner of the plastic folder holding the letter.

"I can just ignore this, then? Figure it's the work of some crackpot with a grudge against Californians?"

Randy scowled and stroked thumb and forefinger along his angular jaw. "I don't know that you should ignore it. Crackpots can be unpredictable and dangerous. But since you said you were planning to go back to California anyway, it might not be a bad idea to do it as quickly as possible." Randy shook his head. "I've heard how the full moon or a heat wave increases crime in some areas. I sometimes think that here our storms rile up the crazies."

"I still have my home down in California. I'd planned to sell it when I came here to be with Julie, but I'll probably go back there."

"That would be for the best, then. Although I'm sorry you'll be leaving. Perhaps we could have gotten to know each other better."

There was nothing flirty about the statement or the sideways glance. Just a subtle acknowledgment that he found her attractive and a small hint of regret. She was trying to decide how to respond when the door behind her opened. Ben Mosely stepped inside, his big shoulders hunched against the continuing rain.

He exchanged hellos with Sarah. "I just have a few things to pick up in the back room," he said to Randy. To Sarah he added, "I suppose you know that now that we have the killer in custody, I'm going back into retirement where I belong."

"Well, before you retire, maybe you could take a look at the note I received?" Sarah asked impulsively.

Randy turned the plastic-enclosed sheet so Ben could read it. Ben pulled his glasses out of his shirt pocket almost reluctantly, as if he'd rather not become involved.

"Not much originality," Ben muttered. "Every nut who wants to send an anonymous letter does it by cutting the words out of a newspaper."

"I suppose I can just ignore it."

"No. I wouldn't do that." The unexpected vehemence in Ben's voice surprised Sarah. "I'd say it's a definite threat, and you should take it seriously."

"But it can't be the killer, because he's in jail—"

"Maybe somebody else has it in for you, then. Unpaid bill? Scrape your fender on somebody's car? Dump a boyfriend?" He sounded as if he were annoyed with her about something. He dropped the plastic-covered sheet with a twist that sent it spinning down the counter. Only Randy's quick grab kept it from sailing to the floor.

"I had a dinner date with Travis Volkman, but he broke it." Sarah felt her face reddening. She usually wouldn't tell such an irrelevant bit of personal information, but the change from Ben's usual friendly, fatherly attitude rattled her. He hadn't shaved, and the gray stubble made him look older and more haggard than ever.

Ben planted a beefy fist on the counter. "Look, it's none of our business who you date." Ben sounded more like himself, gruff and concerned. "Let's just say the Volkman name doesn't earn a strong recommendation from the Julesburg police department."

"Could they have something to do with the murders?"

"We've got the killer," Randy said. "With more evidence piling up all the time."

"But with some weirdo sending notes, it'd still be a good idea to put Julesburg in your rearview mirror as quick as you can," Ben said.

"Okay, thanks." In a quick rush she added, "I don't know your granddaughter, but I understand you're going down to see her soon, so give her a hug for me, okay? And tell her I'm—tell her I'm hoping the best for her."

When she returned to the apartment, Sarah loaded boxes in the Honda and ferried them to the senior center.

Twila had said they would be glad to accept donations for their rummage sale. It wasn't until noon that Sarah realized she'd forgotten about Van Daggert and his mother.

Contacting them was not necessary now, of course. Howard Mason, unlikely as he seemed as a killer, apparently *was* a killer. Ben had been as convinced as Randy that Howard was the man. So she could stop wondering about Donovan Moran, Joe Argo, Steve Lomax, Howard's cousin, the Volkmans, and any other suspects.

From the way Ben and Randy had reacted to mention of the Volkman name, Sarah suspected that they already knew the information Nick had acquired from his lawyer friend. However, even if the company was involved in something shady, something the local authorities were keeping tabs on, it had nothing to do with the murders or with her.

Although . . . could her phone call to Travis and her interest in talking to him have triggered enough concern on the part of the elder Volkman to warrant the threatening note?

While she was mulling that thought, Travis Volkman called. On impulse she accepted his dinner invitation for that evening. She then decided not to stop there. Immediately after a canned-soup lunch, she drove over to Eleventh Street. She had no difficulty spotting the house Myrna had described; several of the cheap lawn ornaments looked a little worse for wear. A squirrel's head was missing and a spotted fawn had a shattered leg. A middle-aged woman with dyed auburn hair and red polyester slacks answered the knock. Her expression was more disinterested than unfriendly, but she held the door as if poised to slam it.

"Yes?"

"I'm an acquaintance of Howard Mason's, and I understand you're his cousin Van's mother?"

"Stepmother, actually."

"I was wondering if I might speak with Van?"

"I suppose you might." Her tone was tart. "But you'll have to do it at the county jail. He's been in there a month for stealing a car."

A month in jail. No involvement in the crimes himself. No alibi for Howard.

"Maybe it'll teach him a lesson. What's all this to you?"

"I'm the sister of the woman who was abducted from the Calico Pantry and murdered. I'm just . . . uh . . ." Sarah was uncertain how to explain what she was doing. *What am I doing?*

The woman stepped forward, releasing her hold on the door. Sarah felt an instant change in her attitude. "That was an awful thing. Terrible. Somebody said you and her were planning to buy the old Nevermore, but you'd gone back to California after she got killed."

"I went down just temporarily, for Julie's funeral. Although somebody wants me to leave Julesburg permanently. I received an anonymous note telling me I'd better, or I'd be sorry."

"No kiddin'? That's awful." The woman's black-lined eyes widened.

"Did Randy or Ben talk to you about the murders?"

"Me? No. Why would they? Van was in jail when everything happened. But I'm going into the police station to file a complaint today. See what happened to my sculptures last night?" She waved toward the broken statues. "Kids like to use 'em for rock-throwing target practice."

"Did Van actually steal the car?"

"At first he claimed he didn't, but he finally admitted he had done it. I was pretty sure right from the beginning that Randy Wilson wouldn't have nabbed him if he hadn't."

Another gold star on Randy's impeccable record. Yet, stubbornly, the thought resurfaced that he could have made a mistake about Howard. Julie's hair was on Howard's sofa, but Julie had given Howard a cat. Maybe she'd gone inside his house.

"I've heard people say that Howard doesn't really seem like a killer," Sarah offered tentatively.

The woman frowned. "That's true. He's not the brightest bulb on the block, but I never figured he'd hurt anyone. He was hoping to get on with Van at Volkman Laser Systems, but then Van got fired there, and I guess Howard gave up that idea."

Volkman. The name seemed to show up behind every door she opened.

And tonight she'd have the chance to meet a Volkman for herself.

29

Sarah called Nick on his cell phone and told him dinner with Travis was on. She decided to postpone mention of the note until later. She didn't think he'd done it. But neither was she entirely convinced he hadn't.

She walked into the Singing Whale promptly at 7:00. No Travis Volkman, no reservation in his name. She had no problem getting a booth, however; the dimly lit room was almost empty. Tourists were not flocking to Julesburg in this weather.

Nick entered just behind her, and the hostess gave him a table in a corner. Sarah hadn't realized he intended to keep such an up close eye on her. *Are we making a melodrama out of a simple dinner?* She ordered coffee so she wouldn't be sitting there rearranging the salt and pepper shakers.

Finally, almost twenty minutes later, Travis Volkman stalked in. He muttered only a minimal apology. His expensively cut dark suit, carefully protected by a full-length raincoat, emphasized his dark eyes. He was wearing a musky aftershave or cologne, not an objectionable scent but a bit sophisticated for Julesburg.

He immediately demanded a wine called Valpolicella. He rolled his eyes when the waitress said they didn't have it, but Sarah sensed a certain satisfaction, as if he'd just been proven right about something. He let Sarah order ling cod for herself. "The New York steak for me. And I want it rare." He slapped the menu shut. "Not cooked to leather like it was the last time I was in here."

Oh, this is going to be a really fun evening.

Then, as if abruptly deciding to take on the Compassionate Ex-Boyfriend role, Travis threaded his perfectly groomed fingers together and smiled benignly. "Now, you wanted to talk about Julie?"

"Yes. As I said, due to the circumstances of our birth, we didn't meet until recently. I'd just like to know what you remember of her."

Apparently devoid of curiosity, he didn't inquire about those circumstances. "She was a sweet girl. Lots of bubbly energy and fun, always thinking up wild things to do even in a boring little place like Julesburg. I appreciated the diversion. It's not been easy, balancing my acting career with responsibilities in the company."

"I understand lasers have all kinds of uses that most of us know nothing about," she offered brightly. "It must be exciting being a part of that."

"Yes, very exciting," Travis agreed, no excitement discernible. "Although I'll probably return to L.A. in the spring if the part I'm expecting comes through."

"Your father won't object if you leave the company?"

"Reorganization plans are in the works."

Their salads arrived, and Travis jumped the conversation back to Julie. Perhaps he preferred not to discuss the company, and if he couldn't talk about himself he'd settle for talking about Julie.

"Your twin was an odd mixture of fun and seriousness. She and my father argued about everything from wearing fur to high-tech military weapons to companies exploiting third-world labor." From an unexpected glee in his voice, Sarah suspected he'd egged Julie on in those arguments.

"She nearly had a fit when I wore a belt made of alligator leather, and she was a fanatic about those scroungy cats down at the jetty. She'd be strictly vegetarian for days, but then she'd get hungry for a burger, and we'd tear up to Dutton Bay to gulp down a Whopper." He laughed, as if the memory was a fond one. The genuineness of the laugh took away some of the phoniness that clung to him like his cologne.

"Julie was also totally against drug usage of any kind," Sarah tossed out.

"Yeah, I remember that."

Sarah hesitated, squeamish about what she was about to say. She hated giving a false impression that her own attitude toward drugs was anything other than condemning. "I'm not that opposed to recreational drugs myself."

"Oh?" Travis's dark eyebrows lifted. But if she thought he would somehow reveal Julesburg's secret underworld, she was mistaken. "I think you're out of luck in Julesburg. A little pot and meth used to float around Website X, but now our local cop pounces on a pinch of marijuana as if it were a threat to world peace. Did you see him on TV after he made that big meth bust? I thought he was going to break into a Tarzan yell and pound on his chest any minute."

"I've heard Julesburg has a few secrets even Randy Wilson doesn't know." That didn't even rate a lift of eyebrows. "Have you heard of a guy named Donovan Moran?"

"Sounds vaguely familiar."

"Julie was dating him. I got the impression he could be into drugs in some way."

Travis shook his head. "One hint of drugs and Julie would have tossed him like a rotten tomato. And Julesburg's gung-ho cop would have lit into him like a movie critic with a grudge. Although . . ." Travis tilted his head speculatively. "One time down in L.A., I did hear something odd. A guy was really interested when I told him I was coming up here temporarily. He said he'd heard from a confidential source that some little town here on the coast, and he thought it was Julesburg, was the hub of some drug distribution network. He was . . . I think this guy was into a little drug dealing himself and he wanted to get in on it, if something was going on here. I told him to forget it, that Julesburg might be the coastal capital of boredom, but it sure wasn't the hub of anything else."

"That is strange," Sarah murmured.

Travis scooted away from the subject of drugs. "Julie was sweet, but she did have some nutty ideas. All that weird New Age stuff about crystals and shamans and reincarnation. Although I guess you believe in that stuff too?"

Sarah wondered why he'd think that, then realized he was eyeing the crystal hanging at her throat. She fingered the sharp edges of the stone.

"Do you really think they have some magical power?" he asked.

"Maybe," Sarah hedged.

"Julie dangled one of those crystals over my head one time and said it told her that in a former life I'd been a fierce warrior in Atlantis."

"That sounds like Julie."

Travis smiled, and it was a fabulous smile, even though Sarah suspected he practiced in front of a mirror to give it that high-voltage dazzle. "I told her no way. I'm a lover, not a fighter. In this or any other life, no one is going to catch me brandishing a sharp instrument and endangering essential portions of my anatomy."

In spite of his shallowness, Sarah liked him a little better for being able to laugh at himself.

"Then Julie went to church a couple times and got all worked up about some idea that Jesus was coming any day now." This time he rolled his eyes. "I was never sure if this was more reincarnation stuff or if she thought he might zoom in by UFO. But next I heard, Jesus was out and chakras, whatever they are, were in. Anyway, it's hard to believe she's dead. I'm glad they got the guy who did it."

"If he is the guy who did it."

Travis's fork paused halfway to his mouth. "You don't think this guy's the killer?"

"I have some doubts." She watched his face carefully as she added, "I think it's possible the robbery of the convenience store may have been a cover-up for something bigger."

"Interesting," he murmured, although she heard no real interest in his voice. *But he's an actor. Maybe a much better actor than Twila gave him credit for being.*

Their meals arrived. Travis cut a couple of bloodred bites of his steak, then put his fork down as if he'd come to a decision. "Look, this is awkward, but early on, I wasn't happy coming up here to work in the company. I confided some things in Julie. I know she kept a diary—"

"And you think she may have written something incriminating about you or the company in it?"

"Incriminating?" The fork clattered to the table. "No, of course not. Just little things that could be . . . embarrassing."

"She did keep a journal. But it's disappeared." Sarah expected this to further alarm Travis, but instead he appeared relieved.

"She probably got bored and tossed it. That's what I did after keeping one for a while. Too much contemplation of the navel gets tedious."

Now he dug into the steak with considerable gusto.

"Does your father know you're having dinner with me tonight?"

"He thought I should go back to the office to prepare for an important meeting we have scheduled in a few days.

But I told him I didn't want to cancel on you. With your sister being dead and all."

You're all heart, Travis Volkman. "Did he comment on your meeting me?"

"Only that I couldn't let social life take precedence over company responsibilities." Travis sounded resentful, yet Sarah suspected the elder Volkman hadn't put his foot down, or Travis wouldn't be here. Would he quiz Travis about tonight?

"I understand a company called Volkman Investments owns the apartment building where I live. Plus various other rentals around town."

"Oh? Could be. I've tried to interest my father in some good movie production investments but never got anywhere. This one I'm up for now would make a terrific investment. Although I suppose . . ."

Sarah wondered if he'd started to say, *Although I suppose there isn't any money to invest now.* She waited, but he seemed absorbed in adding a blob of sour cream to his baked potato.

"Did your father know about Julie's journal?" Sarah asked.

"I have no idea." He was getting bored now, perhaps even a bit offended by her persistence in discussing Julie. Travis Volkman had a short attention span except when it came to discussing Travis Volkman. She obliged.

"I'm so eager to hear more about your movie."

That seemed to liven Travis up. He covered, in excruciating detail, everything from possible director and costars to plot twists, special effects, and location. She tried to maintain an appearance of breathless fascination, even though her thoughts, and a careful peek, strayed to Nick.

After chocolate mousse, Travis paid with a credit card and they walked to the door. "Can you believe this storm? Why my old man chose to move the company to this forsaken place is beyond me," Travis grumbled as he pulled on his gloves. Wind-driven rain still hammered like lead pellets against the glass. "I was going to suggest we get together and take in a movie at Dutton Bay Saturday evening, but I think I'll spend the weekend at my mother's apartment over in Eugene."

Sarah's attention perked. "She stays there part of the time?"

"Actually, she's never lived here full time. Not that I blame her. You'll be leaving Julesburg soon, I suppose?" He spoke as if any thinking person would.

"My plans are still indefinite. I imagine Eugene is more lively than Julesburg for your mother?"

"Definitely. She has lots of friends and club activities. She loves golf." He laughed. "That'll be the day, won't it, when Julesburg gets a golf course? I believe the local concept of a hole-in-one is killing some varmint in its burrow with the first blast of the shotgun."

"Does your father also like golf?"

"Hates it. Although he gets bored in Julesburg too, and takes a jaunt down to Reno or Las Vegas now and then."

The possibilities for blackmail flashed in neon. Willard Volkman alone here in Julesburg, taking "jaunts" to the bright lights. Mrs. Volkman alone over in Eugene, living a busy social life. It was unlikely Helen Maxwell had known secrets of the company, but she might have gotten wind of personal indiscretions. Had one of the Volkmans been paying her off to keep her quiet? And ended the payoff with murder?

30

Nick leaned across the pickup seat and opened the door for Sarah. He'd pulled into the apartment parking lot right behind her. She hopped inside, bringing a flurry of raindrops and a hint of flower-scented shampoo.

"You appeared to be having a fine time this evening," he grumbled. "I take it Volkman is a fascinating conversationalist?"

"He had some interesting things to say."

"Do you want to go inside or somewhere else to talk?"

"I guess I'm still paranoid the apartment could be bugged." She glanced up at the light coming from the building. "But first . . . last night, not long after you left, I found a note in my car. It told me to go back to California, that I'd be sorry if I didn't. Did you put it there?"

"Of course not!" His astonishment bordered on outrage. "How could you think I'd do something like that?"

"You think I should leave Julesburg because I may be in danger—"

"I think that, all right," he agreed. "But I'll come right out and say it, not hide behind some anonymous note."

"Are you angry? I'm sorry, but I had to ask."

She scooted across the seat and gave him a quick kiss on the cheek. Without thinking, his arms went around her and his head dipped toward hers, hungry for more than a quick peck.

He felt her tense, but she didn't pull away. But as quickly as he'd grabbed her, he released her and pulled back. *No. Not on the agenda.* He'd given this love to the Lord, and he didn't have the Lord's word on it yet. She scooted back across the seat, and after an awkward moment he said, "May I see the note?"

"Randy has it. Both he and Ben think some crackpot sent it, nothing to do with the murders, but a crackpot could still be dangerous."

"I wouldn't rule out the killer's authorship."

She nodded, then frowned. "But with a suspect in custody, it seems unlikely a real killer would make a threat. Because that could make the authorities suspect they didn't have the right man."

"Unless the killer figures we're getting close enough to something so important that he has to take the risk and act." Of course, it seemed to him that they were doing little more than floundering. But maybe they were on to something and didn't realize it yet. "Did you find out anything from Volkman?"

She reported what she'd learned about Travis Volkman's parents. "Somehow it seems unlikely that Willard Volkman jaunted to Reno and Las Vegas solo."

Nick agreed. A definite potential for blackmail. Travis's concern about the journal was also interesting, but they agreed his mention of it probably eliminated the possibility he'd stolen it. Sarah then repeated a rumor Travis said he'd heard down in L.A., that Julesburg could be the hub of some big drug operation.

"Travis seemed to think the whole idea was preposterous. Actually, he spent most of the time telling me about this new movie he hopes to get the lead in." She rolled her eyes. "That wasn't fascination you saw at the restaurant. It was my eyes glazing over."

"So what's your opinion of Travis then?"

"Self-centered. Egotistical. Easily bored. Not a heavy drug user but definitely a dabbler. Fantastic build and gorgeous looks but emotionally immature."

Nick blinked. "Remind me not to ask your candid opinion of me."

She glanced at him as if she indeed had a list of his qualities, but she just smiled and didn't itemize. "I could be wrong, of course, but I don't think Travis had anything to do with the murders. But the elder Volkman strikes me as a definite possibility. Probably blackmail about his personal activities, although it's remotely possible Mrs. Maxwell got hold of something about the company. But if he wanted to get rid of someone, I suspect he'd hire a killer rather than do it himself."

"And that person would have to be identified before Volkman himself could be cornered. Which puts us right back to the problem that the man who pulled the trigger could be anyone."

"Anyone," she echoed.

"Okay, let's let it rest for tonight." Nick tilted his wrist so the parking lot lights shone on his watch. "Is it too late to run over to Myrna's? I made a quick trip to Eugene this morning on business and picked up the other Bible cassettes to give her."

"She's probably up. She said she wasn't going to become one of those little old ladies who conk out right after *Wheel of Fortune*."

The lights were indeed on at Myrna's house, although it took some heavy knocking to bring her to the door. Her rumpled hair and blurry eyes suggested she'd been dozing, but she became wide awake when she saw Sarah and Nick.

"Come in, come in! I was just going to make some chamomile tea. Isn't this weather terrible? If it keeps up we'll all be building arks. The TV said there's been a big mud slide on the highway south of town."

Nick gave her the cassette tapes, and while they drank the tea, Myrna reported that she'd talked to Twila that day. "Sharilyn is going downhill every day. If she doesn't get that transplant soon . . ."

"Ben's face shows it," Sarah said. "I saw him at the police station this morning. It's such a sad situation."

"But a wonderful relief and blessing for Twila that Sharilyn knows the Lord. Although I don't suppose that means anything to Ben." Myrna's expression was momentarily pensive, but then she gave herself a little shake. "Did you talk to Van Daggert?"

"I went to his stepmother's house, but I didn't get to see Van. He's been in jail for a month. He stole a car."

"I wonder if he and Howard see each other? I hope not. Howard would be better off staying away from Van and his no-good friends." Myrna hesitated, frowning. "Though I guess you can't do anything worse than what Howard already did."

Sarah took a deep breath. "Myrna, do you think Mrs. Maxwell could have been blackmailing someone?"

"Blackmail? *Blackmail?* Helen wouldn't do that!" She paused, her brow furrowing. "But then, she did start keeping a gun at the store . . ."

As Nick drove back to the apartment, Sarah toyed with the radio, then the heater control, then the radio again.

"I wish I could talk to Van Daggert." She restlessly changed the radio station again. "He sounds like a person who just might know someone who could be hired to do some dirty work. He also got fired from a job at Volkman Laser Systems, which I find interesting."

Yes, interesting indeed.

"But since he's a cousin of the accused killer and I'm the sister of the victim, my visiting him in the jail probably wouldn't be appropriate." Frustration crept into her voice.

"Probably not," Nick agreed, relieved. But Sarah's next words evaporated the brief relief.

"So I think what I need to do next is confront Donovan Moran about Julie's journal."

"I'll do it," Nick said instantly. "No need for you to get further involved with Moran."

"No. I want to talk to him. But I will," she added as a reluctant-sounding compromise, "wait until tomorrow evening so we can do it together."

The following morning Sarah went to talk to Howard Mason's neighbor again. It was not a fruitful discussion, although the woman conceded that someone could have borrowed Howard's car in the night without anyone knowing. Sarah next visited the neighbor on the other side of Howard's house, where Tiger, curled on a rag rug by the woodstove, appeared to have found a new home. That elderly gentleman seemed less convinced of Howard's guilt, but with his hand cupped around his ear and his dialogue frequently punctuated with "Eh?" and "What's that?" she suspected an explosion could have happened next door and he wouldn't have heard. The house beyond, the scene of the meth lab, was vacant, and the next one was occupied by a couple of scruffy-looking characters who seemed a little overeager to invite her inside. She quickly backed off.

Instead, she went down to the jetty to feed the cats, where Clarissa was, as always, the first to greet her. The calico cat wound around her ankles, purring wildly. "Okay, when I leave Julesburg, I'm taking you with me," Sarah promised with a hug.

Joe Argo's boat trailer was still in its usual place, although the boat was not on it. She checked with the crane operator, who said Joe had gone out to sea that morning, not saying when he planned to return.

She drove around by Volkman Laser Systems, the first time she'd viewed the company's site up close. It was the only building in what an oversized redwood sign optimistically called "Julesburg Industrial Park." The sleek building, all concrete and blue-tinted glass, with an outdoor fountain gushing water into an oval pool, proclaimed high-tech prosperity. The employees' half-empty parking lot hinted the façade of prosperity was deceptive.

She had a midafternoon lunch at the Julesburg Café, where the walls were now bare. Marianne Peabody, the talkative woman who had earlier called about Julie's paintings, served Sarah's salad and tea. She was horrified that a local boy had done the killings, but her confidence in Ben Mosely was unwavering. "If Ben says Howard Mason did it, then he did," she declared stoutly.

"Mrs. Peabody, do you know Donovan Moran?"

"Yes. He and Julie used to come in once in a while."

"He hasn't been in since then?"

"No, but I saw him drive by when I went to the post office the other afternoon. At least I think it was him. He usually drives that hopped-up motorcycle, wearing that helmet that looks like somebody's nightmare on LSD. But this was just a plain old brown van. My son says he can get three or four hundred for those fancy paint jobs on motorcycle helmets. Can you imagine? It'd give me a headache wearing that many colors on my head."

Odd, Sarah thought as she walked back to the Honda. *Why would Donovan be in Julesburg? And why in a van?*

She offered to fix dinner when Nick arrived a little after 5:00, but he suggested they drive down to Gold Beach first. While waiting in line for a one-lane detour around the mud slide, Nick told her about visiting Van Daggert at the jail that afternoon.

He smiled at Sarah's surprise. "I didn't see anything inappropriate about my going," he said.

"What did he have to say?"

"He admitted he knows some guys who'll steal a pickup or fence a stolen stereo system for you. Someone who can get you a gun without going through the state's background check system. But he was adamant about not knowing any killers for hire. He said it was hard to believe his cousin had killed two people, but he guessed Howard must have done it. There've been some threats against Howard, so they keep him off by himself."

"What about Van's job at Volkman Laser Systems?"

"He said that workers like him, the 'peon class,' as he put it, rarely even knew what they were working on."

"And he got fired for being nosy and wanting to know?"

"He *said* that was the reason." Nick smiled wryly. "Although there was the little matter of the foreman catching him with several of the company's combination pen and laser lights that happened to slip into his pocket."

"Well, no help from Van Daggert, then," Sarah said regretfully.

Winter darkness had turned on the streetlights by the time they reached Gold Beach. Nick was unfamiliar with the town, but Sarah directed him to the gravel lane leading to Donovan's motorcycle shop. A yard light shone from the peak of the metal building, carving surrealistic shadows around the man standing beside a motorcycle in front of the building. Nick recognized the psychedelic swirls on the helmet.

Nick pulled in beside the motorcycle, surreptitiously patted his jacket pocket, and rolled down the pickup window.

"I just closed up," Donovan said. He slipped off the helmet and set it on the seat of the motorcycle. The leather of his black jacket rippled with a silvery gleam. "But if it can't wait until morning . . ."

In contrast to his tough appearance, his attitude was accommodating about reopening the shop for a customer. Then he peered within the shadowy cab, and Nick could see the click of recognition.

Sarah leaned across him and thrust her closed hand out the window. "Here's the ring you made for Julie. Nick said you were looking for it."

After a moment's hesitation, Donovan held out his hand. Sarah dropped the ring in his palm, and he stuffed it in the pocket of his jeans with a mutter of thanks.

"I think you found something else while you were in the apartment," Sarah said.

"Oh?"

"Julie's journal."

"It's missing?" Donovan asked.

"Yes, it's missing."

"And you think I took it?"

"You're the only one who's been in the apartment and had the opportunity to take it."

Unexpectedly, Donovan laughed. "You think so? Julie kept a spare key on the ledge up over the apartment door. That's how I got in. So who knows who else was in there?"

Nick looked over at Sarah and could see the shock on her face. He chastised himself for not getting that flimsy door and lock changed. *First thing tomorrow.*

"Perhaps someone else could have gotten in," Sarah conceded tightly. "But *you* took the journal. I want it back.

It was Julie's, and it's precious to me. The same as the ring is a precious memento to you."

Nick doubted Donovan was sentimental enough to value the ring, but the man was in no position to deny the comparison. He also was no dummy. He knew Sarah wanted the journal for more than sentimental reasons.

"You want the journal because you figure it may say something that would point to Julie's killer. To be specific, something that would incriminate *me*."

"That would seem a good motive for stealing it," Sarah agreed.

"Okay, I figured Julie had written something in her journal about me. I've been involved in a few little . . . deals she didn't approve of. Nothing big, just small-change stuff to get over some financial humps—"

"Drug deals?" Nick interjected.

Donovan shrugged, as if details were unimportant. "I figured if Julesburg's hotshot police chief got hold of the journal and saw something, he'd use it against me."

"How?" Nick asked.

"At the very least, use it to get my probation revoked. Maybe even try to link me to the murders."

"Okay, tear out anything in the journal that refers to you, and then give it back," Sarah offered. "There may be something else that will be helpful. We think Julie recognized her killer."

"That, obviously, isn't going to be in the journal," Donovan pointed out.

"I want it back anyway."

"I burned it."

"Burned it!"

Donovan slid the helmet onto his head and yanked the strap tight. "Look, I'm sorry about what happened to Julie. I cared a lot about her."

Nick touched the cold metal in his pocket. Yes, perhaps Donovan was sorry about what had happened to Julie.

But that didn't prove he hadn't had something to do with it. Didn't prove he wasn't a hired killer.

"If you really cared for her, don't you want her killer caught?" Sarah challenged. "If you know something—"

"Just back off!" Donovan threw a leg over the motorcycle, and his voice turned to a snarl. "I'm not going to admit to anyone else I took the journal, and you can't prove anything. Just leave me out of this."

Donovan cranked the starter on the motorcycle, revved the engine, and squirted gravel as the big bike roared around the pickup. An oversized blaze of lights across the back of the motorcycle gleamed as it rocketed up the dark road.

Sarah stared after him. "Is that the action of an innocent man? One who doesn't know anything?"

Innocent? Questionable. A man who didn't know anything? Also questionable. A man who was scared? Yes.

The question was, was Donovan Moran scared of the killer? Or scared of being exposed as the killer?

31

The apartment building was easily visible from this vantage point. The storm had finally passed over. Sunlight glinted on the ocean, and a puddle on the unpaved street below mirrored blue sky and fluffy clouds. The wet hillside squished under his feet, but the sun warmed his back. *Even Julesburg isn't too bad on a day like this.*

He braced his back against the tree and swung the binoculars to his eyes. Now he could pick out her windows in the apartment and identify individual vehicles in the adjoining parking lot. He'd watched her come and go several times. Once he even saw her clearly as she stood at the window, looking out. The old Honda wasn't in the lot this morning.

Which meant what? That she was out playing amateur detective and shooting off her big mouth again? He'd made a mistake not getting rid of her that night in the Calico Pantry. He knew it now. Big mistake. Now it looked as if a witness hadn't been such a hot idea. He pulled the binoculars down and turned his head back and forth to loosen the taut muscles. Sometimes it felt as if a noose was slowly tightening around his neck.

The feeling infuriated him. He should be home free. The old biddy was out of the way. Julie was dead, unable to identify him. The "killer" was in custody.

But he wasn't home free, and it was all because of her. She was everywhere, digging and snooping and prying. Planting wild ideas, stirring up questions.

He clenched his fists. He'd tossed the gun at Riptide, but that didn't matter. He could get another easy enough. It would be better if the bullet came from a different gun than the one used in the first killings anyway. Keep 'em guessing.

I'll call her. Suggest I have valuable information for her, arrange a meeting somewhere isolated—

No. He dumped the tempting idea before it sucked him into a trap. He shouldn't let jitters make him reckless. If he stepped back and thought about the situation rationally, there was no reason to panic. Sure, her snooping was troublesome, but it was no big deal. She wasn't going to find anything. He'd covered his tracks every step of the way. *Unless . . .*

He frowned as he dangled the binoculars against his thigh. Yes, he'd covered his tracks. But what about old lady Maxwell? Could she have let something slip before he shut her up? She was the town crank, sure, definitely no nomination for Miss Congeniality. But she was buddy-buddy with a few other gossipy old biddies around town. Now there was also the guy hanging around Julie's twin. He could be trouble. Especially if something happened to the twin.

One more try at scaring her out, then. One that made it plain what was in store for her if she didn't get out. And the guy, if he got in the way? Expendable. At this point, one more killing didn't really matter.

Puddles still dotted the parking lot, but the day was glorious enough to decorate a come-enjoy-the-coast poster. The sun shone brilliantly in a cloudless sky, as if nature was trying to atone for its fit of bad temper. Sarah felt relaxed and refreshed as she locked the car. Nick had been right. Staying at the motel in Dutton Bay last night had been a good idea.

Nick had spent the night before that in her apartment. He'd checked the ledge over the door when they returned from seeing Donovan in Gold Beach. No key. Which raised the question, Who now had the key Julie had kept there? Nick had then planted himself on the sofa and said he wasn't moving.

The next morning, after Nick left for Dutton Bay, she'd tried to contact the apartment manager to get authorization from him to install a stronger door and lock. But the Legermans were gone for the day, so she'd had to call and tell Nick to postpone the work. That was when he'd insisted she come to Dutton Bay and get a room at the motel where he was staying.

They'd enjoyed a pleasant evening. Dinner at a Chinese restaurant, a Tom Hanks movie, and then a good night's sleep in the quiet motel.

Today, I'll tackle the boxes Julie had stored on the top shelf of the bedroom closet, Sarah decided as she unlocked the apartment door. Later, she'd get the okay from Mr. Legerman about the new door, notify Nick, and he'd send a workman down to do it.

She'd left the thermostat turned down, and the apartment was chilly when she stepped inside. She dropped her overnight bag on the arm of the sofa. *Brrr. Gotta get the heat turned up.*

And then she saw the colorful splotch on the sofa.

Sarah recognized the furry ball of black and orange and white instantly. Clarissa! Sleeping on her sofa? But what was she doing here?

She stepped closer and reached out to the cat, puzzled. Her hand recoiled before she touched the familiar fur. She slapped the hand to her mouth to stifle a scream. Clarissa's glassy eyes stared at her from a head grotesquely twisted backwards on her body.

No, no, no!

She forced herself to look closer. Maybe her imagination was playing sadistic tricks on her. No. The horror was there, the body curled in a parody of innocent sleep, the neck contorted in a twist of death.

One part of her wanted to run from the apartment and never return. Another part ached to take Clarissa in her arms and comfort her. Sweet, loving Clarissa. It wouldn't have been difficult for someone to do this to her. She was always the first out of the holes in the rocks, eager and trusting and purring.

But who? Why?

The killer. Because I didn't heed the warning to get out of Julesburg. His newest threat screamed at her as it raced along her nerves and exploded in her brain. *Stop prying and digging and asking questions. Get out now. Or wind up like the cat. With a broken neck.*

She thought of Joe Argo with his warning hints about how curiosity killed the cat. Travis Volkman speaking disdainfully of scroungy cats down at the jetty. Hard-eyed Willard Volkman at the funeral. Donovan Moran roaring into the night on his motorcycle. Steve Lomax . . .

Her head pounded with the possibilities.

With shaking hands and with eyes averted from the pitiful body on the sofa, she punched in Nick's cell phone number. He answered immediately. She could hear busy noises in the background. A power saw. Hammering. The thud of a board dropping.

She stammered out a disjoined version of what had just happened. "I guess I should call Randy—"

"Look, this is nothing against the Julesburg police force, but I think they're amateurs compared to what we're up against here," Nick said roughly. "Right now I just want you out of that apartment."

"Leave Julesburg?"

"Whatever it takes. Just load up and go." His voice was steady but urgent. "Finding Julie's killer is important, but it doesn't warrant something also happening to you."

Sarah eyed the furry body on the sofa. Something about the viciously twisted neck only strengthened her resolve. "I'm not going, Nick. I'm not leaving until Julie's killer is caught."

"Then come back up here to the motel. This killer sees you as a threat, and he's getting desperate to get you out of the way."

Sarah couldn't disagree. Yet she had things to do. She swallowed the nausea that rose in her throat as she looked at the furry ball on the sofa. "I'll be there later."

She hesitated briefly, her finger poised to dial Randy's number at the police station, in spite of Nick's advice. But things were rather casually run there. If someone happened to be in the station when the call came, Randy might make some comment, and soon the whole town would know about Clarissa. And Sarah was suddenly wary about this getting out. Perhaps it was information best held back, the way the police themselves held back on releasing information.

She had picked up boxes of various sizes at the grocery store to use in packing up Julie's belongings. She retrieved one of them from the bedroom, plus a fluffy bath towel from the bathroom closet. With loving care she wrapped Clarissa in the towel and tucked her in the box. As she carried the box out to the car, her legs felt wooden, her joints jerky and uncoordinated.

She hesitated after slamming the trunk shut. *Is the killer watching me even now?* She circled several blocks after leaving the parking lot, checking her rearview mirror. When she had decided no one was following her, she drove along a road that appeared to lead back into the hills.

She stopped in a grassy clearing near a big pine. A stream trickled nearby, and the sea glittered in the distance. With the shovel that Julie, like all prepared Oregonians, carried in her trunk, she dug a hole. The soil smelled of old pine needles and damp earth. She carried the closed box to the hole and set it inside, then carefully shoveled dirt to cover it. She worked methodically even as the anger and despair ached within her, and tears streamed down her cheeks.

Sacrificing an innocent animal just to intimidate me.

When she was done, she decorated the little mound with a circle of pebbles and a bit of ribbon she'd brought from Julie's treasure drawer. "I'm sorry, Clarissa," she whispered. She scrubbed the back of her hand across the rivulets slipping down her cheek. "So very sorry. You deserved so much better."

When she went back to the apartment building, she stopped by the manager's apartment to talk to Mr. Legerman about installing a new door and lock. He was pleasant but insisted that he'd have to get the owner's okay before authorizing such a major project. Since letting the elder Volkman know about this was the last thing she wanted, she told Mr. Legerman to let it go.

Once in the apartment, she cautiously checked the rooms, including the closets, to make certain no one had entered and hidden there while she was gone. When nothing appeared suspicious, she wedged a chair under the knob and used another chair to reach boxes on the closet shelf.

The first box was filled with various craft projects Julie had started and abandoned. Sarah set it by the door to take to the senior center. The next box held miscellaneous sketches Julie had done. The jetty cats, Myrna, starfish. One of Donovan, curly hair tousled, smile rakish, male charisma powerful. A caricature of Julie herself that turned her into a mischievous elf.

Sarah wasn't hungry at lunchtime, but she made tea and carried it back to the bedroom to sip while she dug into another box. This time she caught her breath when she saw what was there. Spiral notebooks, a half dozen of them, all similar to the one that had disappeared from the nightstand. *These must go back months, maybe even years.*

She opened the first one, no longer uncomfortable about infringing on Julie's privacy. She felt as if she were opening a door into her twin's heart. The first thing she noted was that the pages were not dated. *Oh, Julie, how typical of you!* Days of the week were the only identification. On a Monday, Julie had painted a border of dancing elephants and bears in Joanna M.'s nursery for her new baby. On a Thursday, she'd watched a gorgeous sunset from the jetty. *Ed says spectacular sunsets are just caused by dust and stuff in the atmosphere, but I think God paints them for us,* Julie had written.

Ed? Sarah had never heard of an Ed before. Another possible suspect?

A knock at the door interrupted her thoughts. She scrambled to her feet. She didn't touch the door before asking, "Who is it?"

Nick heard the scrape of a chair being pulled away from under the doorknob after he identified himself. Then the phone started ringing, and Sarah called, "C'mon in. I unlocked it." He stepped inside, and she gave him a fingertip wave as she spoke into the phone. "Hello?"

He saw her lips part and her hand go to her throat. "Wait!" she cried. She grabbed hold of the phone with both hands. "Who are you? What do you—"

She pulled the phone away from her ear and stared at it, as if the instrument itself held secrets.

"What is it? What happened?"

She set the phone down, her face pale. "It was a man. He said—" She squeezed her eyes shut so she could remember the message word for word. "He said, 'You want to know who killed your sister? Find out what's going on out at Riptide.' And then he hung up. He never asked my name or anything."

"Was it the same voice that told you to go to the Nevermore to find Julie?"

"I don't think so. That one was muffled and whispery, and this one was gruff. Kind of . . . growly. In fact, I almost feel as if I know it. . . ." She shook her head. "But not quite."

"Maybe it will come to you later."

"Maybe." Sarah paused. "What are you doing here?"

"I went back to the motel," Nick said. "They said you hadn't been there. I got worried."

"I was coming up later."

Yeah, but I'm worried now. He crossed the room to the window and stared out without really seeing the parking lot below. "Riptide. That's where we parked that night during the storm, after the car almost hit us. Where the signs said the trail to a viewpoint was closed."

"What could possibly go on there?"

"It could be the killer baiting a trap. Figuring you'll go there to investigate and then be waiting for you."

"But not a very efficient trap. How could he know when I might go there? Or if I'd bring the authorities along?"

True. Nick rapped the windowsill with his knuckles. So if not the killer, who? Someone who knew or guessed something, but was too scared to get involved?

"The first thing we need to do, I think, is to find out about Riptide. What it is and why it's closed."

"We can ask the old guy at the service station," Sarah suggested. "Marvin, I think his name is. He knows a lot about the area."

"I don't think we should let any locals know we're interested in Riptide. Maybe I'm getting paranoid too, but . . ." He glanced around, suddenly remembering Sarah's earlier fears about the apartment being bugged. He touched a finger to his lips, and her eyes widened as she realized what he meant. He pointed to her overnight case on the arm of the sofa. Without frown or argument, she disappeared into the bedroom and returned a few minutes later with the overnight case freshly packed. He reached to carry it for her and found it much heavier than before.

"What's in here?" he whispered.

She just smiled and touched a finger to her own lips.

Sarah slowed the Honda as she passed the chain-link fence with its cluster of warning signs. Behind her, Nick's pickup also slowed. From the highway on this sunny day, the heavily forested hillside appeared green and beautiful, certainly not menacing or dangerous. The ocean could not be seen from the highway here.

At the motel Sarah got a room across the parking lot from Nick's. She dropped her overnight case on the bed, then went over to tap on his door. He was on the phone when he let her in.

His end of the conversation consisted mostly of "Uh-huh" and "I see," and ended with, "Thanks, I appreciate the information. Sounds like a dangerous place."

"Who was that?"

"I called the state police. I thought they'd know something since the signs indicate the Riptide area is state property."

"And?"

"The trail has been closed off for several years. I'd assumed it climbed that hill, but he said the viewpoint was a rocky ledge down close to the ocean. But the El Niño current changed the shoreline there, as it did in various places along the Oregon coast. It undercut the ledge, which collapsed and took a section of the trail with it. The conclusion was that the area was too hazardous for repair, so it was just fenced off. Although it's always been a dangerous place."

"So what does the Riptide name mean?"

"As he explained it to me, a riptide is an exceptionally powerful current, kind of an aberrant current running out from shore, much stronger than a simple outgoing tide. In some areas they're seasonal or perhaps affected by a storm, but out there at Riptide it's a constant current. A riptide is usually relatively narrow, but it's practically impossible to swim against. Even in shallow water it can sweep anyone unfortunate enough to get caught in it out to sea. The officer I spoke to knew of at least two drownings there when the trail was still open. But one time a girl fell in and her father jumped in to save her, and they both washed in alive in a cove to the north. Apparently they somehow worked their way across the riptide current and got out of it."

"So no one goes there now?"

"He said the state checks the area occasionally, and Randy keeps an eye on it because there was some teen partying going on there. But it isn't a high priority. Which doesn't mean no one ever goes in there, of course. Some people regard fences more as challenges than barriers."

Sarah's head tilted quizzically. "Are we some of those people?"

Nick hesitated. "I'd rather you weren't—"

"If you are, so am I."

He glanced at his watch, then peered out the window. "Whatever goes on there, if anything actually does, it probably happens at night. But I think we'd better have a first look in daylight."

Nick parked the pickup at the spot where the highway widened to make an ocean viewpoint, about a quarter mile north of the chain-link fence. A metal guardrail bordered the pavement with a slope of jumbled rocks, apparently hauled in to stabilize the highway, making a breathtaking drop to a cove below. A sign read, "DANGER! UNSTABLE ROCK AREA. DO NOT VENTURE OVERGUARDRAIL." To the south, the hill within the fence dropped in a series of jagged cliffs to the sea and cut off further view of the shoreline.

They walked back along the edge of the highway to the chain-link fence. Up close, it was intimidating. Strong metal posts, some of them braced, chain links twisted to points at the top, well above Sarah's head.

"If someone is getting inside, I don't think they're crawling over the fence," Nick observed. He checked the padlock on the gate. Heavy steel. The state didn't mess around with cheap stuff.

He led the way along the fence. Here the road curved inland, but the fence plunged straight ahead, down a slope. A strip had no doubt been cleared when the fence was built, but heavy underbrush had taken over now. Most of it was thorny or viney or both. Branches slapped Sarah's face. The storm had passed by, but the brush was still wet, regularly spattering and drenching them. The barrier of forest muted the sounds of vehicles on the highway, and it felt as if they had plunged into a more primitive world, the fence a remnant of some long-vanished civilization. At the thick corner post, they paused in battling the brush to catch their breath.

"If anything is going on here, I don't think they're using this route to get in," Sarah gasped. She raked fingers through her hair to dislodge twigs and a spiderweb. "I doubt anyone has been along here since the fence was built."

That observation did not deter Nick. He kept going, and Sarah followed. After turning the corner, they headed down another slope, this time toward the sea. The sea's dull roar deepened to a steady thunder, and patches of rough water and offshore rocks appeared through gaps between the trees. Then, abruptly, the fence dangled in empty space over a broken sprawl of dirt and rocks and downed trees. Tangled roots rose like the tentacles of underground monsters. The fence that had looked so strong and impenetrable at the road was here only a mangled monument to the stronger forces of nature. A trickle of muddy water ran along one edge of the slide, and the raw scent of wet earth hung in the air.

"Did this just happen?" Sarah asked. She warily stamped the ground at the edge of the slide. A trickle of dirt gave way beneath her, answering her question about ground stability. She grabbed the cold metal fence for support.

"Within the last couple days, I'd say. All the rain that caused the slides on the highway must have done this too."

"Which means this isn't the way someone has been getting in."

"But it is a way we can get in."

He slid down the loose slope, digging his heels into the fresh dirt and gripping the bottom of the fence for support as he ducked under it. Sarah followed his lead and wound up sliding on her pants and filling her shoes with dirt. On the far side of the fence, Nick stretched out a hand to help her scramble up to solid ground.

She froze when something crashed above them. Nick shoved her into a bank of brush. Then they both saw what had caused the noise, and Sarah gave a shaky laugh.

The doe paused on the slope above, peering down on them with liquid eyes both fearful and curious. When the doe bounded away through the brush, Sarah saw what was in Nick's hand.

"A gun?"

"I thought it was time I started carrying it." He studied the weapon, as if he wasn't certain how it had jumped from his pocket to his hand.

Sarah didn't like guns; the deadly explosion in the Calico Pantry would forever roar in her ears. But she had to admit to a certain relief knowing Nick had a weapon.

They struggled through wild rhododendrons growing higher than their heads. Burrows made by digger squirrels booby-trapped the ground underneath. Beyond the rhododendrons, blackberry vines webbed a patch of Scotch broom. The old trail to the viewpoint was still visible when they finally reached it, but ankle-high fir seedlings encroached the path.

Nick stooped beside the overgrown trail to study the dirt. Recent rivulets had washed shallow gashes and piled up pine needles and other bits of debris. If there had been tracks, they'd been washed away by the recent storm.

"Look," Sarah said, pointing.

The overgrown bushes met to form a canopy over the trail in places, but some small branches had been broken to make the passage easier. The breaks were fresh.

They followed the trail toward the sea, stopping often to look and listen both ahead of and behind them. The trail ended abruptly at an older slide. Peering over the broken edge, they could see the rocky ledge that had once been the viewpoint. It had slid downward and now rested just below water level, the dark surface washed by waves. Beyond, jumbled rocks broke the surface of the sea like jagged monsters struggling to freedom. A few were large enough to support sparse vegetation near the top, but most were bare and inhospitable. Waves crashed, climbed the rocks hungrily, fell and plunged into surges flung back from other rocks. It was beautiful and savage, wild and dangerous. And the biggest danger, the riptide, wasn't even visible.

"I don't see how anything could be going on here," Sarah said. "Maybe the caller just wanted to send us on a wild goose chase."

Nick was studying the fallen, flat ledge barely visible in the waves below. "Where's the tide now?"

Sarah peered at the rocky shoreline in both directions. "Near high tide, I'd guess, though I don't know if it's coming in or going out. The high-tide line on shore is only a foot or so above where the water is now. Although a storm tide has apparently been much higher at some time." She pointed to a scattering of driftwood flung considerably higher on the hillside.

"Which means that rock ledge will be out of the water at normal low tide. A small boat could come into shore here."

"Through all those rocks?"

"If someone knew what he was doing. Which could make it the perfect place for doing . . . something."

The shoreline curved here, not enough to make a cove but enough to give some shelter. Steep headlands isolated the area and shielded it from visibility both north and south. While Sarah was studying the shoreline, Nick ducked into the brush and disappeared. A moment later he yelled at her from below.

She peered down and saw him standing with his feet sloshed by the waves on the rock ledge. Following his shouted directions and arm motions, she scrambled down to join him. The route wasn't worn enough to be called a trail, but it had definitely seen some foot usage. Nick's footprints stood out clearly in the soft dirt, and their visibility made her uneasy. If the killer came, he'd know someone had been here. Would he guess who it was?

They stood at the sea's edge for several minutes, until deepening shadows warned of coming darkness. Back at the gate, Nick inspected the gate's chain, padlock, and hinges thoroughly.

"If someone is getting in here, he's using a key," he said.

Sarah knew that any number of employees with the highway department or the state police or some other government agency might have a key. But keys got misplaced or stolen or copied. It was hard to say who might have one.

"Now what?" she asked.

"Now we come back when the tide is out. And we hide and watch to see what happens."

32

They returned just before midnight. Both wore jeans and dark jackets, a tide pamphlet tucked in Sarah's pocket. Nick had changed pickups, and this one bore no identifying company name. He first drove slowly past the gate, scanning to see if anyone was around. They returned from the opposite direction and hastily dropped off and hid the equipment Nick had borrowed from the job site. He again parked at the overlook farther up the road. They hiked back, hands linked. Sarah didn't examine the why of that; it simply seemed the natural thing to do.

Back in the brush, well beyond sight of the highway or gate, Nick placed one stepladder beside the fence. With minimal use of a small flashlight, he dumped the other ladder inside the enclosure, gingerly crawled over the rigid fence, and dropped down inside. Sarah had the easier task of climbing up one stepladder, stepping over the sharp, upright ends of the links, and climbing down the other stepladder Nick had placed on the far side.

"Almost as easy as taking an elevator," she whispered as Nick guided her into the pit of darkness below the inside ladder.

They didn't use a flashlight, and there was no moon, but once their eyes became accustomed to the night it was surprising how much they could see by starshine. Sarah marveled at their sparkle undimmed by the intrusion of man-made lights. She remembered what Gran had said her mother had called stars when she was a child: God-lights.

They hiked silently to the edge of the old slide; having seen the trail in daylight helped. Nick often paused to listen for sounds ahead or behind them on the trail. And there were sounds that Sarah hadn't noticed in daylight. Whispers. Rustles. Creaks. Chirps. Nick squeezed her hand reassuringly.

"Night sounds," he whispered. "Nothing to worry about."

The fallen ledge was already out of the water when they peered down at it. The surface shone slick and treacherous in the starlight, but it extended from the shore almost like a dock and could definitely provide a landing place for a boat.

Nick picked a spot sheltered by brush from which they could look directly down on the ledge. They settled in to wait. With the retreat of the tide and the uncharacteristically calm wind, the waves were not as wild now. But more rocks cut the surface of the sea at low tide, their jagged shapes somehow even more menacing in stark silhouette. A muffled roar came from farther out, where the waves rolling across unbroken miles of open ocean endlessly hammered the outer rocks.

Sarah's bottom grew damp from the wet ground. Occasional specks of light flickered far out at sea. Passing ships? Fishing boats? The someone or something for which they waited? She tried to discern if any of the lights were coming closer, but they were too elusive to pin down.

The relentless roar of the waves eventually faded into the background of her consciousness, and a deeper sound rose to the surface. Sullen, sucking, menacing. The ocean working beneath the ledge. And someday the ledge would be gone, claimed by the sea.

She felt a moment of emptiness, of cosmic aloneness, as if she were lost in time. As if she'd always been a watcher here at the cold edge of the sea. And always would be . . .

Instinctively she pushed closer to Nick, and he gave her knee a reassuring squeeze.

What is he thinking? she wondered as she glanced sideways at his profile. *Is he feeling that gut-deep emptiness too? No. Nick is never alone. He has his God.*

"How long do we wait here?" she whispered.

"At least an hour after low tide."

A small eternity. She shifted position, and the gun in Nick's pocket bumped her hip. Her thoughts sloshed like some bit of driftwood caught in the surf. What were they waiting for? Someone or something to arrive by boat? Or something or someone to be taken away? Didn't the Coast Guard patrol the waters for suspicious activity? Had Mrs. Maxwell known about something going on here? Whose voice telling her about this place was it on the phone? Sometimes she almost thought she had it, but then it would slip away again.

She thought of Julie. Julie bubbling and laughing, curious and caring. Gran, her parents, how blessed she'd been by all of them. If only she could know they were all together somewhere, safe and laughing and happy . . .

But God had shut Julie and her parents out.

God. The centerpiece of Nick's life, as he was of her great-grandmother's. God. Who kept slipping into her thoughts even as she tried to shut him out.

Eventually the tide started back in. A triangular rock, almost like the fin of a shark, disappeared first beneath the surging waters. A flat-topped slab a hundred feet from shore slipped out of sight next. The waves, as if injected with new life, lapped with fresh vigor at the shoreline and gurgled deep below the rocky ledge.

The never-ending cycle went on.

Back in his motel room, Nick restlessly flicked on the TV and watched the end of a nature program about wolves. He'd wanted to kiss Sarah good night. He was almost certain she'd wanted to be kissed good night. Yet they'd both refrained from any move in that dead-end direction.

He woke sometime in the night, his mind murky. *How long have I been asleep?* An hour and a half, according to his bedside clock. He jumped out of bed, went to the window, and shoved the drape aside. He felt an irrational terror that Sarah had been abducted in the night and that was what had wakened him.

No. No abduction. But the light was still on in her room. Was she nervous or frightened, unable to sleep?

He slid into pants and a shirt and slipped shoes over his bare feet. He tapped on her door a minute later. The drape beside the door moved as she peeked outside.

"Did you know you have your shirt on inside out?" she inquired when she opened the door. She was in a blue velvet robe, hair freshly shampooed, feet bare.

"I wasn't trying to make a fashion statement," he muttered. "I was worried. I woke up and saw your light." He felt a little grumpy now. She looked crisp and perky. Spiral notebooks dotted the bed. "What's this?"

She motioned him inside. "These are what made my overnight case so heavy. I just found them today; well, yesterday, I guess it is now. They're Julie's old journals."

"Are you finding anything helpful?"

"No . . . and yes."

She'd been reading on the bed, a pillow propped behind her. Her dark hair shone with dampness in the lamplight. *The kind of hair a man could run his fingers through.* Nick detoured that tempting thought. "In the middle of the night, lady, you don't make a whole lot of sense," he grumbled. He took off his shirt and turned it right side out.

"I could make coffee." She waved toward the Pyrex carafe and packets of instant coffee on a shelf.

"Sounds good."

"You'd wondered if Julie could possibly have had a relationship with the elder Volkman," Sarah said as she put the carafe of water on the burner. "The answer is no. She speaks of him strictly as Travis's father. She found him totally materialistic, totally infuriating."

"What about Mrs. Volkman?"

"She never mentions her."

"Does she say anything about the company?"

"Only one remark." Sarah picked up one of the journals and opened it to a page marked with a folded corner. "'It's really weird what Travis says is going on at his father's company,'" she quoted. "But she doesn't say what kind of 'weird.' She also says Travis offered her a joint. That's when she told him good-bye. A detail Travis failed to mention when we had dinner." Sarah smiled wryly.

"What about Donovan Moran?"

"Lots about Donovan. She hints about his involvement in some drug deals. But she was in love with him, so he got second chances. She argued with him instead of dumping him, like she did to Travis. But if she wrote anything truly incriminating, it must have been in that journal he burned. I didn't find anything in these."

"So basically the journals aren't any help." *Okay, so tact isn't my strong point in the middle of the night.*

Sarah scooped the scattered notebooks into a pile. "No, they aren't. Which is disappointing. But they offer wonderful clues to Julie herself. I feel I know her much better now." The radiance of Sarah's smile suddenly made up for the late hour.

The water was bubbling by then, so she dumped instant coffee into Styrofoam cups, stirred, and handed him one. She sat on the foot of the bed. He took the room's one upholstered chair.

"And something jumped into my mind while I was reading the journals. You know how you aren't thinking about something, and then it's suddenly there?"

He nodded.

"I think I know who that was on the phone. I'm almost sure it was Joe Argo."

"Argo the fisherman?" Nick leaned forward.

"It didn't sound exactly like him. But kind of like Joe trying to come off tough and macho. There's something else. I hadn't thought about it before, but I remember now something Julie said about Donovan. He has a boat he uses for diving for sea urchins. There's a special season when commercial divers go down to harvest them."

Had Donovan found other, less legal but perhaps more profitable, uses for the boat? And Joe Argo knew that?

At breakfast Sarah told Nick that she was going back to Julesburg for the day. "I want to maintain the illusion that I'm living a normal life there," she explained. "We don't want the killer knowing about our nighttime jaunts to Riptide, right?"

Nick agreed, although Sarah could see it was definitely a reluctant agreement. "Keep a chair wedged under the knob all the time. No exceptions, okay?"

The first thing she did in Julesburg was buy a timer so she could set lights to go on and off in the apartment, thinking maybe this would convince someone watching that she was there at night. Although the absence of the Honda was a giveaway, of course. But perhaps the killer was watching the lights, not the car.

A curtain fluttered at a ground-floor window as she crossed the parking lot at the apartment house. The manager's apartment. *What if the watcher is within the building? Could the Legermans have reported to Willard Volkman my wish to change the door and lock? And had he asked them to keep an eye on my activities?*

Or am I getting even more paranoid?

The day moved slowly. She took more boxes to the senior center. She called Myrna and offered to bring pizza for lunch. She made up for lost sleep with an afternoon nap. Afterward she drove down to the jetty to feed the cats, fresh hurt clogging her throat when there was no sweet Clarissa to meet her.

She then decided to see if Joe was on his boat. She knew he wouldn't admit to making the call; she wouldn't even ask him about it. But she did hope that hearing his voice again would help her decide for certain that he was indeed the caller.

Sarah walked past the space the boat usually occupied. She backtracked and stared at the oil-stained planks. No boat. No trailer. Just one rusty old bolt. She didn't have to be told that the Wildfire III would not be returning.

Joe Argo had chugged on outta there.

Nick and Sarah sat concealed on the hillside for almost three hours that night. They followed the same pattern for the next three nights, adjusting their time of arrival to match the changing hours of the tide. By now Sarah felt a certain familiarity with the Riptide trail. How to climb over the fence quickly without getting impaled by the points. Where to dodge the bush that snagged her hair. Where to step carefully to miss the tree root that tried to trip her. Two does lived here in the forest, she knew now. An owl sometimes hunted, graceful and silent.

She was also getting discouraged by now. Perhaps the killer had ceased his activities at Riptide, either temporarily or permanently. Perhaps whatever happened here happened only once a month. Or once every three months. Perhaps only on moonlit nights. Perhaps only on stormy nights.

Nick never complained, but Sarah knew the nighttime surveillance was hard on him. She could catch up on sleep with a nap in the afternoon, but he put in a full day on the job, snatching only a little extra sleep after dinner. They couldn't keep up this schedule indefinitely.

The next day at breakfast, over Sarah's bagel and Nick's ham and eggs, Nick made a suggestion.

"I figured if anything was going on at Riptide that it had to be at night. But maybe not. Let's try a daylight watch. Maybe someone figures daylight activity would look normal and draw less attention than nighttime lights."

The first day-watch produced nothing but the activities with which they were already familiar: gulls wheeling and squawking, waves crashing, wind blowing.

Sarah was tempted to skip the following day of watching when she peered out the motel window. Clouds hung low, spitting rain. Wind grabbed the door when she opened it. It was a good day to spend in Julesburg, holed up in the apartment. Maybe it was even time to call this a wild-goose chase and give up.

Nick seemed to have no such thoughts. At breakfast he suggested they try the late afternoon low tide.

So once more they parked at the viewpoint north of Riptide and hiked to the gate. The clouds hung low, a fog bank blending with the sea to the west. The wind flung occasional raindrops. Nick checked for footprints or scrapes on the ground to indicate the gate had been opened. Nothing. They started down the fence line toward the hidden stepladders.

A car pulled in behind them, and they turned to look. In surprise, Sarah saw Julesburg's police car. Randy got out of one side, Ben the other.

"Looking for something?" Randy called. "This area is closed." He stopped short, apparently only then recognizing them. Sarah had the hood of her vinyl raincoat fastened tightly around her face. Nick's stocking cap was pulled down to his eyebrows.

"What're you doing here?" Randy demanded as they walked back toward the police car, away from the hidden stepladders.

"Just stopped to take a look around," Nick said in a mild tone. "We wondered why the area is all fenced off."

Sightseeing on a day like this? Randy won't fall for that. "I had a phone call," she blurted. "Someone told me that if I wanted to find out who killed my sister, I should find out what was going on at Riptide. But then we found it like this." She waved a hand toward the locked gate.

"Who called you?"

Sarah hesitated, reluctant to drag Joe Argo's name into this. "I don't think it was same person who called and told me Julie was at the Nevermore."

Randy's hand rested on his holster. He wore a heavy brown jacket with a police patch on the upper arm over his regular uniform. Ben, in jeans and denim jacket, just stood there, feet spread, arms folded. *Why is he here? He's resigned his temporary spot on the police force.*

"We had the same phone call," Randy said. "That's why we're here. We figure it was just a crackpot call. Somebody with nothing better to do on a lousy day. But we'll check it out."

From under the jacket, he produced a ring of keys attached to a chain on his belt. "I cooperate with the state police in keeping an eye on things out here. Some of our teens thought they were going to move their partying out here after I clamped down on them in town."

Randy put a key in the padlock, and Ben spoke for the first time. "You'd better move on now. We don't expect to run into trouble here, but you never know."

Sarah and Nick exchanged glances. Sarah started to say that they'd been watching for almost a week and hadn't seen trouble or anything else, but the tightening of Nick's arm on her shoulder stopped her. She hadn't realized until then that his arm was around her.

"I'm glad we ran into you," she said instead. "It's good to know you're . . . uh . . . on the job."

They started up the side of the highway toward the pickup. *I feel eyes watching me,* Sarah thought. It was an unpleasantly familiar feeling. When they climbed into the pickup, Sarah sat silently, her clasped hands tucked between her knees.

"Does this strike you as . . . peculiar?" Nick said after a moment of silence.

A little odd, perhaps. But the state police had said Randy kept an eye on Riptide for them. Checking out an ambiguous phone call about Riptide wouldn't be an unusual thing for him to do. It could, in fact, be encouraging proof that his mind wasn't closed to the possibility of a killer other than Howard Mason. *I should be reassured that Randy and Ben are investigating this.*

Yet Randy had said his phone call had come on a "lousy day," which must mean today. Her call from Joe had come a week ago. And Joe was long gone now. Could someone else have made both calls?

"Look, I'll just go back down there and sneak a peek at what's going on. You can wait here in the pickup," Nick said.

Sarah shot him a glance across the seat. "You're kidding, right?"

33

They didn't take their usual route on the old trail down to the ledge. After climbing over the stepladders, Nick led the way along the inside of the south fence until they could crawl through the brush into their usual spot. It was not a particularly secure hiding place in daylight. Even in the spitting rain and drifting fog, the screen of twigs and leaves felt much too flimsy, her raincoat much too visible.

But they had a good view of the two men below. Randy paced back and forth at the outer edge of the exposed ledge, hands jammed in his jacket pockets. He kept looking out to sea, although the world was lost in fog just beyond the outer rocks. Waves occasionally rose over the end of the ledge and slopped around his feet. He didn't seem to notice. Ben sat on an exposed boulder, shoulders slumped.

Nick's knee nudged her leg. A fractional tilt of his head motioned her to look out to sea. For a few moments she glimpsed a boat beyond the outer rocks before fog enveloped it again. Not a commercial fishing boat like Joe Argo's. Something smaller. Nick's binoculars were in her pocket, but she didn't dare risk the exposure of a glint of glass.

Randy had seen the boat too. He turned and yelled something to Ben. Sarah heard the sound, but wind and waves swept the words away. Ben lumbered to his feet. Sarah's heartbeat quickened. *Something's happening—*

A swish of brush. An explosion of thuds and crashes as one of the does spooked behind them. Sarah's muscles froze. How could one animal make so much noise?

Randy wheeled and looked toward the hillside. Surely he'd know it was just a deer! Ben waved a dismissive hand. *Yes, Randy, forget it. Just a deer.*

Randy looked toward the outer rocks again. No sign of the boat. Then he did another inspection of the hillside. A trick of the wind brought his words clearly this time. "I'm going to take a look." He unholstered his gun and climbed around the slide cautiously, gun hand outstretched, eyes working both sides of the trail.

We should probably just stand up and tell him we're here. People accidentally got shot in situations like this. Even if Randy's actions did look odd, he was probably just jittery while trying to figure out if anything was going on.

He was within a dozen feet of them now. The gun swiveled in their direction and stopped. She could see his finger curl around the trigger. Her lips felt glued together. A wind-driven branch whipped across her eyes. She didn't move.

People got shot not *accidentally.*

Sarah's breathing stopped; she could swear Randy was looking right into her eyes. Nick's hand inched toward his pocket. Then the gun moved on, and Randy disappeared up the trail.

Sarah's frozen muscles melted. Randy wouldn't find anything now, not even if he went all the way to the highway. They'd moved the pickup to an overgrown road south of the fence, and recent rain had washed out any tracks they may have left on the trail over the past few days.

They waited. A dozen questions jammed Sarah's mind. Questions about the boat loitering out in the sea. Questions about Ben and Randy's presence. Questions about murder.

And under these questions lurked a terrifying possibility: Randy and Ben were involved in this. Involved not as investigators but as participants.

A chill beyond cold wind and damp ground seeped through Sarah's muscles and bones and soul. *The man in the Calico Pantry.*

No, please no . . .

She felt the familiar bore of watching eyes on her back. *Nerves. Imagination.* But she turned to look anyway.

The barrel of a gun poked through the brush less than six feet away. Sarah looked at the deadly hole with a sick familiarity. She'd seen this end of a gun before.

"Stand up." Randy pushed through the brush. "Hands on top of your heads."

He herded them to the open trail. Sarah clutched her hair to keep the dead weight of her arms from collapsing. She dared a sideways glance at Nick. He'd had no chance to go for the gun, but the faint sag of his pocket said it was still there.

We'll just apologize for returning here. Randy will be angry, but we'll convince him that we were just overly curious.

Ben had climbed up to stand beside Randy. "I'll take them back to the gate." To Nick and Sarah he said roughly, "This is police business. This area is closed. We told you to move on—"

"I want to know why they came back to spy on us." Randy targeted the gun on Nick's chest. Sarah stared at Randy's eyes, digging deep into her memories of the Calico Pantry. His were not alien eyes, but dark ice lurked in their depths. "How'd you get in?"

"Climbed the fence. Too curious for our own good, I guess," Nick said, managing to sound cheerfully rueful.

"I'll take them back to the gate," Ben repeated.

A faint sound filtered over the slap of waves on the ledge and rocks. The chug of a boat motor. They all looked seaward. The boat was smaller than a commercial fishing boat, closer to pleasure craft size, with an enclosed cabin. No people were visible.

"It's too late. The boat's here," Randy said. Sarah heard finality in the words. His quick smile was suddenly feral. "You should have paid more attention to the messages you received."

The note. Clarissa.

"Hey, c'mon, Randy. It's just some sports fishermen," Ben protested. He cut a sideways glance at the incoming boat. The rain was coming down heavier now, the waves churning harder among the rocks, and the boat bounced and rolled, one side coming close to slamming into a rock. "They aren't up to anything. Probably just looking for shelter from the storm in here."

Sarah knew that Ben was trying to play down the presence of the boat for her and Nick's benefit. Just fishermen. Harmless. No one they knew. He put a hand on Nick's shoulder, as if to shove him up the trail toward the gate. But the truth sledgehammered Sarah's chest. There hadn't been a second phone call to the police department. Randy and Ben were here to meet the boat.

"No. I've had it with these two. They've been all over town, even up to the jail and the FBI. Blabbing and asking questions. They're trouble." Randy motioned with the gun to move Nick and Sarah down the trail toward the ledge. "Don't chicken out on me now, Ben."

Randy sounded reproachful, but Sarah heard something else beneath the words. Warning? Ben wasn't wearing a gun.

"But you can't just . . ." Ben's glance flicked from Randy's gun to the water.

"Don't worry about bodies washing up," Randy said. "At least not along here." He glanced out toward the rocks. The boat was out of sight again. Whoever was on board was playing it cool, making a good show of fishing among the rocks in case interested eyes were watching.

"You're going too far," Ben muttered.

Sarah's hopes leaped upward. Whatever was going on, Ben didn't like this part of it. He stood with fists clenched, seeming to be unaware of the rain falling on his face. If Ben was with them, they could be three against one. Randy had a gun, but Nick had one too.

As if he'd heard Sarah's thought, Randy jerked his head toward Nick. "Search 'em."

Ben turned Nick around and patted him down. His hand stopped on the pocket with the gun. *Leave it. You don't want Randy to kill us. Pretend you don't feel the gun. Give us a chance.*

Ben pulled the gun out of Nick's pocket. Randy jerked his thumb. After a moment's hesitation, Ben heaved the gun over the ledge. Their ace in the hole, gone.

Ben gave Sarah a minimal patting down while Randy laughed at her. He leaned back against a boulder. "Did you think Ben was going to save your hides? Think again. Ol' Ben was elbow-deep in this long before I was."

The boat was unmoving again, engine idling just enough to keep the boat away from the jumbled rocks. Two men were outside the cabin, and for all appearances were checking their fishing poles.

"You killed Clarissa and put her in my apartment. You put the note in my car." Sarah took in a ragged breath. She felt Nick nudge her with his hip, warning her to shut up. But what did it matter now? "You killed my sister. Why? *Why?*"

"I had no choice. She recognized me. I made it as easy as I could for her."

Easy? Sarah felt fury like a fever burning its way from the core of her body to the surface. Yet she couldn't let it explode. Not yet. "You gave her pizza. Where did you keep her?"

"At my house. She just about drove me crazy. Talk, talk, talk."

"Talk about what?"

"Everything. You. Some grandmother. Jesus. Oh, she was really big on Jesus and God. She said she was praying for me. I finally had to gag her."

Julie gagged, bound and helpless . . . Okay, Sarah, stay calm. Keep Randy talking. Maybe Ben will have a change of heart and help us.

"But why kill Mrs. Maxwell to begin with?" she asked.

Randy laughed. "If you think I'm going to tie it all up with a neat little bow for you, think again. Julie was just in the wrong place at the wrong time. So are you and lover boy here. Too bad, but that's the way it is. You should have just buried your sister down in California and stayed there."

Sarah's hands were still on top of her head. Her fingers felt numb; her forearms and shoulders ached. "Can I put my hands down?"

Randy nodded indifferently. But when Nick also started to lower his hands, Randy swiveled the gun. Raindrops bounced off the polished metal. "Not you."

Nick kept his hands on his head, but he shifted position fractionally, turning a shoulder to Randy. He had something in mind. Sarah took a step away from Nick. *I've got to keep Randy's attention targeted on me.*

"Did you bug my apartment?"

"Bug your apartment?" His eyes flickered surprise, then amusement. "You overestimate the resources of the Julesburg police department. Though I did watch you through binoculars a few times."

"Why did you put Julie at the Nevermore?" Sarah said, fighting tears as she saw again that ugly, trash-filled space behind the old theater and the wrapped bundle that was Julie.

"It was vital to keep the investigation in Julesburg. Under my jurisdiction."

Yes, to keep the county sheriff's office and especially the FBI out of it. Randy had planted the SUV within his own jurisdiction too. And she could now see how he'd carefully played down the information about her reward money.

"Actually, Julie messed up everything," Randy said, sounding resentful. "It was a perfect plan. Clean and simple. And then there she was."

"Sarah shouldn't have had to be the one to find the body," Ben muttered. "That wasn't necessary."

"You planted the evidence in Howard Mason's car and house," Sarah said. Randy didn't respond—he didn't need to. She knew he'd deliberately saved one of Julie's earrings for further use. "Are the Volkmans involved?"

"Volkman Laser Systems is up to something all right. Half the secret agencies in the government are interested. But it's nothing to do with us. And I'll help nail them any way I can."

Dedicated law-officer Randy. Polishing up his image.

Out of the corner of her eye, Sarah saw Nick flex his fingers to keep circulation going. *I've got to keep Randy's attention diverted.*

"What's coming in on the boat? Marijuana?"

Randy laughed again. "Pot? That's a laugh. You have to handle marijuana by the bale—by the *ton*—to make a buck. Can you see Ben and me hauling bales of it up to the highway and hanging them out the trunk of the police car? But heroin, now, that's different—"

Nick launched the attack shoulder first. Randy went down. The gun fired. The bullet ricocheted off a rock at Sarah's feet, and chips sprayed her leg. Nick and Randy rolled on the ground as fists and legs flailed. Nick was taller and heavier, but Randy coiled up and kicked. Nick grunted, but he was on top, his hands pinning Randy's shoulders.

Sarah never saw the blow coming. Neither did Nick. For a big man, Ben moved like a snake. His heel hit Nick on the side of the head. Nick sagged, and Randy scrambled out from under him. Sarah jumped for the fallen gun, but Randy beat her to it.

She turned and ran to Nick. She knelt beside him as he sat up groggily. She twisted to face the two men, tears and rain blurring her eyes. "Randy I can almost see doing all this. But not you, Ben. Not you!"

Ben didn't meet her eyes. "Sharilyn needed money for the transplant. *A lot* of money. This was the only way Helen and I could figure out to get it for her. I told Twila it was from good investments I'd made. Then Randy found out what we were doing and wanted in." The glance he shot Randy was close to venomous. "I never figured on anybody getting killed."

If Randy saw Ben's resentment, he ignored it. "But dear old Helen got an attack of conscience. 'Here we are, wrecking all these innocent young lives with these nasty ol' drugs. Oh dear, oh dear,' " he mimicked in falsetto. "She decided she was going to spill her guts. I couldn't let that happen."

So the elderly owner of the Calico Pantry wasn't blackmailing anyone. She was in on it. "What was Mrs. Maxwell doing?"

"We took the stuff to her. She passed it along to a guy driving a bakery truck."

I'm sealing our fate asking all these questions. But she knew it didn't matter. Their fate was already sealed.

"Of course, there's a change in operations now," Randy added.

The boat was moving again, heading straight for the ledge. Ben grabbed the rope when one of the men on board tossed it toward the ledge. Randy kept the gun trained on Sarah and Nick.

"Getting rough out there," he called to the men in the boat.

"What's with the woman?" the man demanded. He spotted Nick still on the ground. "And him."

"Just a couple of passengers for you," Randy said. "They know too much. But I can't take care of them here. Bullet holes in washed-up bodies stir up messy investigations."

"Do 'em in town. You're the law there."

"I can't risk more dead bodies in Julesburg. The county sheriff is breathing down my neck as it is. Take them out to the ship and give 'em a swim. Skip the lifejackets."

The man scowled, as if Randy's order annoyed him. Then he shrugged.

Both men were dressed in typical fisherman gear—old work clothes, rubber boots, floppy yellow rainhats. The shorter, barrel-chested one even had a smear of fish blood on his jacket. The fishing poles set in holders along the sides of the boat looked old and well used, and the blue-and-white boat was so ordinary that it would never draw attention.

The men started unloading cardboard boxes. Ben helped. The work was tricky, with rough waves bouncing the boat and occasionally slamming it against the ledge. One box was labeled pork and beans. Another said soup, chicken noodle. The men handled them as if they were heavy for their size.

"Don't have to bring this stuff in by the bale," Randy said with pride and a satisfied glance in Sarah's direction. With less satisfaction he added, "Not that we get more than a pittance of what it's worth on the street."

They're doing all this in open daylight, Sarah thought with amazement. The main coastal highway was less than a quarter mile away, but what danger was there? With a police car parked right up front, no trespasser was going to wander in. And to any Coast Guard patrol, these two could surely pass as just a couple of good ol' boy fishermen. Everybody knew rabid fishermen would fish in any kind of weather. And Sarah figured the boat was properly registered, the "fishermen" properly licensed, in case they were ever stopped.

Ben and one of the men made several trips up the hill with the boxes. It looked to Sarah like they had more than what would fit in the trunk of the police car, so they must be stashing part of it for later pickup. The storm was getting worse. Even though the tide had barely started back in, waves were already washing over the ledge. Farther out, waves climbed the rocks like hungry sea monsters, the spray of their cold breath shooting skyward.

Maybe they'll decide the storm is too rough to head back out to the ship immediately. Darkness isn't more than a half hour away—surely it's too dangerous to head out to sea. She glanced at Nick. His face was stony, his forehead creased, the mark of Ben's heel turning from smudge to lump on the side of his head. Was he praying?

If prayer can do anything, do it! Make it the most powerful prayer you've ever said.

But if Nick was praying that the small boat wouldn't launch in the storm, it didn't work. Randy got behind them with the gun and herded them into the boat. The two fishermen seemed disinterested. Cargo in, cargo out.

Randy tossed the rope in the boat. The engine growled, deep and guttural. Rain battered Sarah's face, blinding her as the boat surged away from the ledge.

But she could still see Ben standing there. His face held no expression. He didn't move. He only watched.

34

The shorter of the two men, the one with blood on his jacket, opened the door of the small cabin and shoved them inside. "Should we tie 'em up?"

His dark-bearded buddy was already behind the steering wheel. "They aren't goin' anywhere."

Shorty jerked his head toward a torn red-vinyl bench behind the man at the wheel. Dials and gauges filled a dashboard in front of the man. He had one hand on the steering wheel, the other on a control lever at his right side.

Sarah and Nick sat on the bench. The lump was ballooning on Nick's temple, and a bluish vein ran across it. She wanted to lean over and kiss it tenderly. But in the tossing boat, she'd only batter him with her head. *Oh, Nick, I got you into this. I'm sorry.*

The second man moved both hands to the wheel as they got under way. The wheel jerked and shivered, and once whipped a full half-spin before he got it under control. The front of the boat rose in the water when he moved the lever forward to increase their speed. The slam of the bow hitting the waves shook Sarah from her toes to her teeth. Wham. Wham. Wham.

This is idiocy. We can't possibly make it through these rocks! The spray-shrouded window beside her dipped so close to a black wall of rock that she instinctively ducked. But neither man seemed alarmed about the surges and plunges of the boat. *Maybe it isn't as bad as it feels to me.* The man at the wheel seemed to know what he was doing, although they didn't appear to be making much forward progress. The engine coughed several times, but he adjusted a knob and didn't seem concerned.

In the mist and dense sea spray, the shore loomed as an indistinct blur of dark hillside receding behind them. Randy and Ben would already be leaving, locking the gate neatly behind them. *How far out is the ship? How long will it take two bodies to wash to shore? If we wash in at all—*

No. Wrong thinking. She clenched her teeth against useless prophecies of doom and instead tried to think what to do. Nick's gaze was searching every cranny of the small cabin. A weapon? There was a fishing tackle box by the door. A glassy-eyed dead fish in a bucket. A toolchest under the opposite bench. A big toolchest. Big tools. But they'd never have a chance to get it open before Shorty was on them. She spotted a metal thermos among a tangle of yellow life jackets spilling out of a cubbyhole. *If one of us could grab it, swing it—*

Shorty, sitting half turned in the front passenger's seat so he could watch them, smiled at her as if he knew what she was thinking. He reached under the seat and pulled out a gun. After spinning the chamber so they could see it was loaded with bullets, he stuffed the gun in a jacket pocket for easy access. And smiled again.

Sarah slumped, a numbness creeping into her brain. She recognized it as hopelessness, but fighting it seemed to be slipping beyond her control. She glanced sideways at Nick. He was frowning slightly. Praying? Calculating? At this point, what hope was there?

God could send an angel to save us. Ten thousand angels, if you want to, Lord. Will you do it?

Sarah realized her fists were so tightly clenched that her hands were cramping. She spread her fingers on the sides of her thighs. The engine coughed again, and added a gasp this time. The sound didn't seem all that different to Sarah, but the guy at the wheel lunged to his feet.

"Hey, what the—" He yanked the lever at his side, clawed at some control on the dashboard, jerked the steering wheel frantically.

Nothing happened. Now Sarah felt the difference under her feet. No rumble. No steady wham against the bow. The engine had quit. In spite of wind and waves, the world felt dangerously silent.

Shorty grabbed the cabin door and flung it open. The other man was right behind him. They flipped a cover on the dirty deck, exposing the engine below. A mechanical maze, dark and greasy. A scent of oil and exhaust billowed up.

"We can't be out of gas!" Shorty sounded panicky.

"No, it's not gas. It's—" Wind and waves ripped the bearded man's words into meaningless sounds. "Get a wrench and I'll—"

Without the power of the engine, the boat twisted and flopped helplessly. Sarah's stomach flopped with it. A wave crashed over the side, drenched the men, filled the engine compartment, and swept the cover away. Some of the backwash sloshed into the cabin. Sarah felt Nick's arm tighten around her as water rose around their ankles. The bow humped, plunged, shuddered when it slammed sideways into the ragged face of a rock.

Sarah had never felt more helpless, not even when she stared into the dark barrel of a gun. *Lord, please—*

"Get on the radio!" the bearded man yelled.

Shorty scrambled toward the front of the cabin. He didn't make it. A wave lifted the bow and flung him backwards. He slid out the door, skidded across the engine compartment, and flew over the back railing. A cross wave flung the boat sideways. The boat hit a rock and climbed it like some waterborne bulldozer.

In horror Sarah saw the floor breaking up beneath them. Water fountained up from below.

"Get out!" Nick yelled. "Grab a life jacket!"

He tangled something around her neck and yanked a fastener. Seawater avalanched between them. His face sloshed dizzily as if trapped on the other side of a washing-machine window. She tumbled backwards, sideways, head over heels. The world splintered and disintegrated around her. *Am I in or out of the boat? Oh, Nick, Nick, Nick.*

Water. Above, below, all around her. In her mouth and nose and lungs. Flinging and tossing her. She choked, gasped, felt a limp darkness surround and fill her.

Floating. Ramming into something. Drifting back. Bumping again.

She weakly grabbed at it. Rock. She got a knee over something hard and slippery. Tried, with some gut instinct for survival, to pull herself up. Hadn't the strength. Felt her fingernails sliding and scraping, her knee slipping. *Please, Lord, help!*

She floundered and got the knee up again. A wave lifted and pushed her. She flopped on the slanted surface of the rock. *Thank you!* She drew in a waterlogged breath and struggled for a higher spot out of reach of the surging waves.

She leaned her head back against the hard rock rising behind her and tried to get a breath. Swallowed seawater rose in a sick billow from deep inside her. She released it in waves of retching. Something felt tight around her neck, choking her. She clawed at it weakly.

The life jacket. It was twisted and tangled, but somehow it had stayed with her. *Nick couldn't have had a chance to get one for himself. His only thought had been of saving me. Oh, Nick, no, no—*

Think. Think. She blinked against the burn of saltwater in her eyes. She wasn't as far from shore as she expected to be, perhaps two or three hundred feet. Her rock rose to a jagged peak, with a sloping outcropping where she had landed. The sea had calmed a little, as if crushing the boat had satisfied its primal urge to destroy. Debris from the boat littered the water around her.

She couldn't stay here long. Could she swim to shore, make it up to the highway, and get help for Nick? She shivered and another spasm of choking and coughing shook her. She felt as if she'd been in the water for hours, but she knew it couldn't have been more than a few brief minutes or she wouldn't be conscious. How much longer before hypothermia got her? Water lapped up to cover her outstretched foot. How much longer before the incoming tide covered her tiny sanctuary?

She picked a spot on shore. *I'll head for there.* She rearranged the life jacket so it was fully wrapped around her body and tugged the fasteners tight. It was a wonder the jacket hadn't come off long before. *Lord, did you do that?* She braced herself for a plunge into the water.

The debris from the shattered boat was moving, caught in the inexorable pull of the riptide. Just as she would be if she hadn't washed up on the rock. And once she was in the water, she'd be caught in the riptide again.

But she had to chance it. There was no hope on the wave-swept rock. *Is there hope out there, Lord? Do you care? I don't know why you should, but please, if you do . . .*

A larger chunk of the boat sloshed around her rock, a section of the bow keeled over on its side. Something was clinging to it.

A wave hid it, lifted it. A glimpse of tangled reddish hair, a dark jacket. Nick!

He was stomach down with his arms outstretched, his fingers clutching a piece of wooden framework, his legs trailing. He could slip off at any moment. Was he even conscious?

She slid into the water without thinking of the riptide or hypothermia or making it to shore. *Just get to Nick. Please, Lord, help me get to Nick.*

She floundered toward the shattered section of boat. The waves were less violent now, but they tossed her with disdain. As she kept losing sight of the severed section of boat, frantic bargains flooded her mind. *God, if you'll save him, I'll be a better person. I love him! I'll go to church. I'll pray. I'll give. I'll do anything you want if you'll only—*

Bargains she knew God didn't want.

Just give me your mercy, Lord. Please.

The section of bow suddenly loomed up in front of her, slamming into her shoulder. She gritted her teeth and fought her way around to the open end. She hooked her elbows over the jagged edge of splintered fiberglass and hauled her upper body up beside Nick.

"Nick! Nick!" She shook him with one hand and slapped his back. Maybe he was already dead. *No, please!*

He choked, roused groggily, looked at her as if she were a vision of an angel.

"I was on a rock," she said quickly. "Maybe we can get back to it."

Too late. The rock was already ten feet behind them. For a moment she felt as if she and Nick and the chunk of broken bow were standing still and the rock was drifting away.

But the rock wasn't moving. They were. The riptide was taking them out. Frantically, kicking and paddling with one hand, she tried to turn their awkward craft and head it toward shore. Nick lifted his head.

"No, don't fight it," he gasped hoarsely.

"We have to fight it! It'll take us out to sea!"

"We'll drown . . . from exhaustion . . . if we fight it." He retched. "We have to go across it, try to get out of it."

Darkness and fog were closing in on them now, but Nick, drawing on some strength beyond the physical, started kicking. Sarah hesitated, then slid farther back into the water and kicked with him. She closed her eyes and gritted her teeth and kicked. Kicked until the muscles in her legs burned like fire. Kicked until her lungs rejected a full breath. Kicked until she felt as if this was all that had ever been in her life.

"Don't give up," Nick muttered hoarsely. "Keep kicking."

When she paused to look at the shore, the mist-shrouded trees were farther away than ever. She and Nick were too weak, the riptide too strong. How long before they were swept beyond the outer rocks, lost forever in the open sea? Beside her, Nick put his head down and continued a robotlike kick.

Nick, it's useless.

But then she noticed they were north of where they had been. Farther out from shore, but no longer directly out from the old slide above the ledge.

She craned her neck around the side of the broken bow. Ahead, the shoreline looked closer. Was that possible? Yes! This was where the hillside plunged steeply to the sea, making the point that cut off view of the Riptide area from the north. *If we can angle shoreward just a little and make that point . . .*

She started kicking again with revived energy, urging Nick on. "Hang in there! I think we can make it. Think about good things . . . a hot cup of coffee . . . the Book of Ruth . . . I love you."

He kept kicking.

But they weren't making it. The point was no more than thirty feet off to their right, but it may as well have been a thousand. They couldn't kick hard enough against the riptide to get to it, and it wouldn't do any good even if they could reach the point. Sarah saw that the hillside ended in a ragged cliff at least ten feet high, a place only a seagull could land.

Her legs trailed wearily in the water. Nick too had stopped kicking.

Rub-a-dub-dub, three men in a tub. Sarah felt a touch of hysteria as the old nursery rhyme slogged around in her mind. They weren't even three men in a leaky tub. Just one exhausted man and woman.

She felt almost peaceful, bobbing in the sea, numbness seeping into her body, waves sloshing the broken bow gently.

Gently. They *were* simply bobbing, no longer moving out to sea. She hammered Nick's back. "Nick! Nick, I think we're out of the riptide!"

Here, past the point, the shore curved inland. Fog blocked the highway above, but she knew this must be the cove below the overlook where they'd parked so many times. Nick's body slid a few inches farther back on the edge of their makeshift vessel. She grabbed for him. *Lord, don't let me lose him now.*

With strength from somewhere beyond herself, she kept one hand tangled in his jacket while she squirmed and wriggled her body onto the chunk of bobbing fiberglass. Then she pulled him up beside her.

She could see he was shoeless now. So was she. And one pant leg flapped loosely around a long gash in his leg.

They were drifting into the cove—the shore wasn't more than a hundred feet away. Seventy-five. Fifty. But this side of the hill was all a jumble of cliffs, with only a few twisted trees clinging precariously to an occasional crevice. No place to land.

But somewhere in this cove was that slope of jumbled rocks they'd seen from above. Surely there'd be someplace they could land there.

She slid her legs back in the water and kicked again. Yes, there it was! A steep slope of tumbled gray rocks rose into the mist.

The slabs and chunks were larger and more irregular than they had appeared from up on the highway. Huge. One stuck out like a giant gravestone. Another looked like a precariously balanced Volkswagen. Surging water spewed out of a hole several feet above the waterline.

Not a hospitable place, but who cared? It was shore. They were safe!

The sloshing waves carried them into the rocks. Sarah lunged and scrambled to a flat surface. She hadn't the muscle power to pull Nick and the awkward chunk of fiberglass onto the rock, but she held it tightly so it couldn't drift away while she gathered her strength.

Again she felt as if she'd been in the water for hours, but again she knew it couldn't be true. Their physical exertion had helped to keep them from succumbing to hypothermia, but they probably wouldn't be alive if they'd been in the cold water much more than a half hour or so.

She tried to get Nick onto the rocks. He roused at her efforts and somehow managed to flop to the flat rock she was on.

Now what? *Rest, sleep . . .*

She rejected the tempting pull. *Climb! Climb to the highway somewhere up there.* She grabbed the sharp edge of a rock above her.

It was dark now—only a faintly luminous glow shone on the sloshing waves below. But it didn't matter; they wouldn't lose their way. Down was wrong. Up was right.

"Nick?"

A gasped breath. "Right behind you."

She scrambled over the rock above her and plunged into a hole that covered her to her shoulders. All that kept her from falling farther was her life jacket caught on a sharp edge of rock. Her feet dangled in emptiness. The slope of jumbled rocks loomed over her. *The rocks are moving! I'll be trapped, crushed!*

She wasn't aware that she was screaming until Nick grabbed her arm. "Don't panic!" he commanded roughly, and she realized the rocks weren't moving. For the moment. "I'll get you out."

He put his hands under her arms and pulled. She helped as much as she could, grabbing for handholds with both her feet and hands. Her heart thundered with the awareness that at any second she might dislodge some vital connection and start the jumble of rocks moving.

She finally collapsed on the slanting surface of rock next to the hole. Nick grasped her shoulder as if he too felt a looming danger in this spot. "C'mon. Over here."

Sarah lifted her head and looked upward. The rocks didn't slope upward at an even slant. El Niño had been at work here too, undercutting and loosening and shifting the rocks. A bulge protruded above where she lay. Off to the side, darker shadows hinted at more gaping holes among the rocks. An ominous gurgle of water came from far down in the hole that had almost trapped her.

"We can't climb up through these rocks in the dark," Nick said, his voice raspy. Sarah knew what he said was true. In the dark they could be trapped in some treacherous hole or bring the entire slope of rocks down on top of them. "We'll have to wait until daylight."

Daylight. Sarah slumped to the harsh surface of the rock. She didn't voice the obvious. They were cold, wet, weak, shivering. It was a miracle they hadn't already succumbed to hypothermia.

How much chance that they could survive the night?

35

I'm going down to get our piece of the boat. It'll be a little protection."

Sarah slumped into a niche between rocks. She simply wanted to sink into oblivion, but she managed to rouse herself and help Nick drag the chunk of fiberglass above the tide line. He broke off one section to make a backrest to separate them from the rock behind them, then arranged what was left as a makeshift shelter over and around them. Sarah removed the life jacket so they could sit on it and keep the cold of the rock beneath them from seeping deeper into their bones.

Think of warm things. Mind over matter. A steaming bubble bath. A roaring fireplace. A tropical beach.

"Hey, I just remembered something." She felt Nick digging around under his wet jacket. "I put it in my pocket before we left the motel. It's still here. I can't believe it."

He handed her something cold and clammy. In the darkness it took her a moment to realize what it was. At any other time this might have been just a treat. Now it felt as if Nick had just produced some fabulous treasure. Or a special gift from God. Her hands shook as she broke the Snickers bar in two and handed half back to him.

Her teeth felt odd as she bit into the bar. *Is this how false teeth feel?* The bar was a little worse for wear. Most of the chocolate was gone, and the peanuts had a seawater sogginess. But at the moment she reveled in taste more glorious than any feast set out by a five-star restaurant. As they munched in appreciative silence, she determinedly ignored a hackneyed old line that rose out of her subconscious. *The condemned ate their last meal.*

She tucked one foot under Nick's leg when they finished the meager snack. She could feel that his pants were torn. She wrapped a cold hand around his bare knee. He had big, bony, very appealing knees. She leaned over and rested her cheek against the cold knob of bone and wished she could have gotten to know those knees better.

"I love you, Nick," she said.

"I love you too." Their fingers wound together. She put her head on his shoulder.

They sat in oddly comfortable silence. The statements needed no explanation.

"Do you think we'll make it until morning?" she finally asked. She felt a lethargy creeping over her. She no longer felt so cold, and she knew that was bad.

"Maybe."

"Does all this make you angry or resentful toward God?"

"I wouldn't have picked this situation if I had a choice, that's for sure. But I figure he knows what he's doing even if I don't."

"I guess what makes me most angry is that they're going to get away with it." She pounded his bony knee with her fist. "Randy and Ben are going to get away with murdering Julie and Mrs. Maxwell." *And us.*

"God's justice goes beyond this life and this world."

"Sometimes it's difficult to think on such a grand scale. But I think . . ." Sarah hesitated, balancing the despair she'd felt after Julie's death with what Randy had said about the hours before he killed her. Those hours when she had talked to him about God and Jesus. Could she have spoken so passionately without believing the words herself? "I think maybe God gave Julie a second chance before she died."

Nick didn't immediately respond, and Sarah's throat spasmed in a painful swallow. "Or is that just wishful thinking?"

"Sometimes God has to bring us to the edge before our eyes are opened and we face the truth."

"Sometimes he lets us plunge over the edge."

"Yes."

They sat in silence again, both shivering. "I think he's given me a second chance too."

"Oh?"

"I kept praying out there in the water. God didn't have any reason to listen to me. Why should he? But he did listen, and he didn't say, 'You had your chance, but you rejected me. So, too bad. Life's tough.' Instead he answered. He answered my prayers for you. He answered my prayers for strength and help."

"He saved you so you could go out and change the world? Do all sorts of grand and noble deeds? We may not make it until morning, Sarah. Even if we do, we may not be able to climb out of here." She heard an unexpected harshness in Nick's raspy voice. "This may be all there is."

"I don't mean a second chance at this life. I know that may not happen. I mean a second chance at eternity. In spite of my anger, I think God cares whether I die without him. He didn't let me die out there. We're here." She ran her fingertips across the side of their flimsy shelter. "I know it's a little late to come to him. I feel . . . guilty about that."

"As if you're trying to make a last-minute sneak across the finish line?" She heard a smile in his voice. Then he wrapped her hand in his. "It's never too late, Sarah. Forgiveness and salvation happen when you ask Jesus to come into your heart, when you believe he went to the cross and died for you. It's a *now* thing, a gift. Not something you have to add to or earn after X number of years sitting in church."

One moment a person was lost; the next, safe for eternity. Had Julie accepted that gift in her final hours? *Oh, please, I hope so.*

With a burst of strength, Sarah fumbled at her throat, groping beneath the wet clothes. She pulled out the crystal. In the darkness she couldn't see it, but even with her fingers almost numb with cold she could feel the sharp edges, the point at the bottom. She yanked and the chain snapped. She pushed their makeshift shelter aside and rose to her feet. She lifted her arm and threw the crystal, threw it as hard and as far as she could.

Then she just stood there, face lifted, eyes closed. *Thank you for giving me this second chance, Lord. I don't know all the right words to say, but the belief is here in my heart. Belief that you love us, that you never abandon us, that you sent your Son to go to the cross and die for us. To die for me, for all the wrongs I've done. Take me, Lord. I want to be yours. In this life and the next.*

Nick stiffly struggled to his feet beside Sarah. The lump on his head throbbed, and only his clenched teeth kept his jaw from chattering. He put his arm around her, feeling more than seeing a new radiance surrounding her. Yet he *did* see something. He blinked, trying to clear both his clouded vision and soggy mind. A light. A strange light, like a beam—no, a cone. No, that couldn't be.

But it was. A moving cone of light.

Then he heard a sound as well. A whir and chatter. The fog had lifted or blown away, and now he saw dots of red light above the cone.

A helicopter!

Sarah saw it too. "Here! Here, over here!" she yelled. She waved her arms frantically.

The cone of light moved northward, toward the cove. *If only we had something to signal with, a flashlight, a mirror, anything.* He grabbed the only thing they had, the bright yellow life jacket, and waved it wildly overhead.

Sarah let her weakened arms drop for a moment. "Is it the Coast Guard? Are they looking for us?"

A sudden apprehension rammed Nick's chest. Maybe it wasn't the Coast Guard. Drug runners had deep pockets. Was this some private helicopter Randy and Ben had gotten ahold of, a way to make certain there were no survivors?

"Someone up on the highway must have seen the boat hit the rocks and called the authorities," Sarah said.

Maybe.

Sarah waved again, but the helicopter was moving south, farther out over the rocks this time. It appeared to be working a grid pattern.

Three times the light reversed directions. On the last trip it was at the outer edge of the rocks.

In spite of his apprehension, Nick knew that, friend or foe, this was their only chance. *Lord, make them turn! Come this way. We're over here!*

36

"It's coming this way!"

The moving cone of light teased them. It drifted slowly across the opening into the cove, surging water showcased in the circle of light.

"Here! Over here!" Sarah yelled. Her already weakened voice gave out, and the words ended in a garbled spasm of coughing.

But the light was coming. Nick almost forgot the helicopter above. The light itself seemed alive. It moved along the north curve of the cove, stopped on a bit of debris from the boat bobbing in the surf, and moved again.

Nick waited, gathering his strength for the crucial moment. Here it was, the light shining down on them. Now! He waved the yellow life jacket frantically.

The cone of light did not move on. It stayed above them, holding them in its mesmerizing circle. Nick let his tired arms fall. He almost expected two bullets to tell him this was not a rescue.

Instead he saw a basket lowering. It swayed, wavered, swung out over the water, and swung back again. The whir of the helicopter filled the atmosphere now, shuddering through Nick's bones.

Someone was in the basket. The man looked like some space alien in his survival gear, but what Nick saw that really mattered was the Coast Guard insignia on the man's arm.

The rescuer took Sarah up first, then Nick. The whirling vibration of the chopper was all around them now, as if they'd been absorbed and become a part of it. They were informed that an ambulance was waiting to take them to the Coos Bay hospital when they landed. Nick protested.

"I'm fine. I don't need . . ." But when he heard his own slurred words, he realized that he was not so fine and that he *did* need.

Nick was released from the hospital the following day, Sarah a day later, but not before both had been questioned by everybody from local law people to Coast Guard officials to the FBI. Sarah was told that Randy and Ben were in custody, but beyond that, all she got from the various authorities were questions, not answers. "We'll be in touch," they all said smoothly.

On the day she was released, a nurse ferried Sarah to the hospital entrance in a wheelchair. Sarah protested. Her face was a road map of scratches, her hands were ragged, her ribs were bruised, and deep breathing was still not an option. "But I can walk," she said with determination. The nurse then cheerfully informed her that this was standard hospital policy and that she may as well enjoy the ride.

Nick was waiting at the door. He swooped her out of the wheelchair and carried her to the pickup. She started to protest this also. *I'm fine, a little worse for wear maybe, but I can walk.* Then she changed her mind and applied the nurse's advice. *Enjoy!*

Nick set Sarah gently in the passenger's seat of the pickup, then kissed the lump on her cheekbone. She was wearing the jeans, blue sweatshirt, and socks he'd brought her. No shoes, because there hadn't been extra shoes among her clothes in the motel, and he hadn't had a chance to drive down to the apartment in Julesburg. He'd had a different errand to run this morning.

She fingered the bare spot on the side of her head, shaved so that stitches could repair a cut. "I feel like the poster girl for boat safety. 'Don't let this happen to you!' "

"You look beautiful." And he meant it.

Her eyes searched his face. She brushed the multicolored lump on his temple with a finger. "So do you."

They hadn't spoken about the personal words that had passed between them there on the rock, huddled under their makeshift shelter. He hadn't wanted to hold her to words spoken in crisis, words perhaps reconsidered when the crisis was over.

Yet he did not doubt the sincerity of her commitment to the Lord. They'd prayed together when he'd visited her in the hospital. She'd spoken again of Julie and how she hoped her twin had accepted the second chance the Lord had offered her. They'd talked about her great grandmother' s convictions too. He knew there were still unanswered questions in Sarah's mind—his too, for that matter—but now faith covered the gaps. She had a long journey ahead of her, but she'd taken the first step.

Now she looked at him as if waiting for him to say something. When he didn't, she spoke up, sounding mildly exasperated. "If you aren't going to say it, Nick Nordahl, I am. I love you. I wasn't just making polite conversation out there on the rocks."

"Neither was I. And I believe I've spoken the words a time or two before that."

"Women like to hear the words."

"I love you, Sarah." He leaned into the car and kissed her, long and thoroughly. "I'll put it on a billboard. Write it in the sky with an airplane. Take out a TV ad."

"Just saying it will be fine. Again?"

"I love you. But we have details to discuss."

She smiled. "I think the only important detail is settled."

They stopped for lunch in Dutton Bay. Nick brought hamburgers, fries, and shakes out to the pickup so Sarah wouldn't have to struggle in and out of the cab. The day was one of the coast's winter jewels. Puffy clouds decorated a blue sky. Sunshine warmed the cab of the pickup, and as Sarah opened the window a few inches, the fresh scent of sea flowed in. It smelled good, in spite of their too-close encounter with the sea itself.

"Did you ever find out who alerted the Coast Guard that we were out there?" she asked as they ate.

"Yes. It was Ben."

"Ben?"

"Ben," he repeated. "They're holding him in the county jail. I went to see him this morning. I wanted to thank him. There's a lot to blame him for, but in the end, we owe him our lives."

"What made him change his mind about us?"

"He and Randy saw the boat smash into the rocks and break up. Randy was pleased. He said something like, 'That takes care of our problems, doesn't it?' It wasn't the worst thing Randy had said or done, of course. Not by a long shot. But I guess everybody has his breaking point, and that was Ben's. He said it all just crashed down on him finally, the awfulness of everything he was entangled in. And that he just couldn't let it go on. He grabbed Randy's gun, locked him in the back of the patrol car, and radioed for help."

It had seemed hours before the helicopter came, but in truth, it was a miraculously short time. A lifesaving short time. God hadn't sent ten thousand angels to save them. But he had changed Ben's heart.

"I don't think Ben's an . . . evil person," Nick said slowly. He rescued a pickle fallen from the hamburger. "He got into the drug action shortly before he retired. He hated what he was doing, but he wanted to see his granddaughter live, and he didn't see any other way. A small town police chief doesn't accumulate much in the way of financial assets. I suppose all that was true for Helen Maxwell too, and she was also desperate to help Sharilyn.

"And who'd ever suspect them of anything?" Nick added. "The town's longtime, well-respected police chief. The cranky proprietor of the local convenience store."

"And the new law officer. So ambitious and dedicated."

"Ben said a police officer makes a lot of connections over the years. He learns about crime and how it's done. He used his knowledge and connections the wrong way."

"Where were the drugs coming from?"

"Somewhere in Mexico. It was a legitimate company running a regular shipping route and making legal imports to Seattle. Except they had this little sideline in black tar heroin going. Very pure, very dangerous. They carried the small boat right on the ship and used it to make one drop-off at Riptide, another on the Washington coast. Not a big operation, as drugs go. But comfortably profitable."

"Ben told you all this?"

"He said he was through sneaking around and covering up and trying to justify what he'd done. He's telling everything he knows."

"So all those times Ben had looked so haggard, so close to breakdown, he wasn't just worried about his granddaughter. He was feeling guilt," Sarah said. "What will happen to him? And Randy?"

"Randy's in it for two counts of murder in addition to the drugs. That's lifetime stuff. Ben will testify against Randy on the murders. He said he had no idea Randy was going to kill Helen Maxwell, that he was horrified when it happened, and I believe him."

A french fry stopped halfway to Sarah's mouth. "That doesn't make him innocent! He was an accomplice to covering up both murders."

"No, not innocent. And Ben isn't claiming he is. He says he's ready to spend the rest of his life in prison. He won't fight even the death penalty if it comes to that. He's haunted by the possibility that if he'd turned both himself and Randy in right when Randy shot Helen, then maybe Julie wouldn't have been murdered. He said he was stupid to think that Randy wasn't ruthless enough to kill Julie too, that they could work out something for her."

"And it all just kept escalating. Getting bigger and bigger. Deeper and deeper."

"Yes."

"What about Howard Mason?"

"He's already been released. Ben said Randy planted the earring in Howard's car and the hairs in his house."

"I want to tell Howard I never thought he killed Julie." Sarah was silent for a moment, then said, "I wonder how Twila is taking all this?"

"I saw her when I was leaving the jail. She looked . . . bad. She got a double blow in all this. Their granddaughter died last night."

"Oh no!" Sarah paused. "To think that all Ben's concentration on money, all his dealings in drugs, couldn't save his granddaughter. Will Twila stand by him, do you think?"

He hesitated, reflecting. "Yes, I think so."

Nick pulled the pickup into the parking lot at the apartment. Everything looked just the same. A Mountain Dew can sat atop the Honda, where someone had casually placed it. Shallow puddles, remnants of the storm, decorated the uneven gravel. The curtains were still drawn in the windows of Sarah's apartment, just as she'd left them.

"It seems like . . . some other lifetime when I was last here," Sarah said. She absentmindedly massaged the back of her hand where a blue bruise stretched from thumb to little finger. "It doesn't seem quite real sitting here now, that someone actually tried to kill us."

"A plan foiled by God. And gave you, as you put it, your 'second chance' with him."

"I think God gave *us* a second chance too."

Yes. He wrapped his arms around her. He'd given this love to the Lord. And the Lord had given it back to him.